Dear Dragon Goes to the Bank

by Margaret Hillert
Illustrated by David Schimmell

NORWOOD HOUSE PRESS

DEAR CAREGIVER,

The *Beginning-to-Read* series is a carefully written collection of classic readers you may remember from your own childhood. Each book features text comprised of common sight words to provide your child ample practice reading the words that appear most frequently in written text. The many additional details in the pictures enhance the story and offer the opportunity for you to help your child expand oral language and develop comprehension.

Begin by reading the story to your child, followed by letting him or her read familiar words and soon your child will be able to read the story independently. At each step of the way, be sure to praise your reader's efforts to build his or her confidence as an independent reader. Discuss the pictures and encourage your child to make connections between the story and his or her own life. At the end of the story, you will find reading activities and a word list that will help your child practice and strengthen beginning reading skills.

Above all, the most important part of the reading experience is to have fun and enjoy it!

Shannon Cannon

Shannon Cannon,
Literacy Consultant

Dedicated to Comerica Bank, Branch 49 in Birmingham, Michigan—M.H.

Norwood House Press • P.O. Box 316598 • Chicago, Illinois 60631
For more information about Norwood House Press please visit our website at
www.norwoodhousepress.com or call 866-565-2900.

LIBRARY OF CONGRESS CATALOGING-IN-PUBLICATION DATA
Hillert, Margaret.
  Dear dragon goes to the bank / by Margaret Hillert ; illustrated by David Schimmell.
    p. cm. -- (A beginning-to-read book)
  Summary: "A boy and his pet dragon open up a saving account and learn
about saving money and fiscal responsibility"--Provided by publisher.
    ISBN-13: 978-1-59953-502-9 (library edition : alk. paper)
    ISBN-10: 1-59953-502-5 (library edition : alk. paper)
    ISBN-13: 978-1-60357-382-5 (e-book)
    ISBN-10: 1-60357-382-8 (e-book)
  [1. Banks and banking--Fiction. 2. Dragons--Fiction.] I. Schimmell, David,
ill. II. Title.   PZ7.H558Deb 2012
  [E]--dc23
                          2011038941
Manufactured in the United States of America in North Mankato, Minnesota
                        295R—062016

Oh, oh, ooohhh!
Look at this.

Father. Father.
Look at this.
My pig. My pink pig.
What can I do now?

We can get all of the money into this bag.
Then there is something we can do.

The pig is a little bank.
We will go to a big bank.
Come on. Come on.

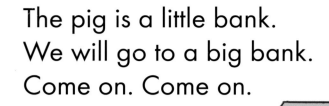

Here we are.
We will take the money in here.

Can I help you?
What do you have?
Oh, I see.
I can put it away for you.

Where will you put it?

This is a good spot.
I will put the money
in here.

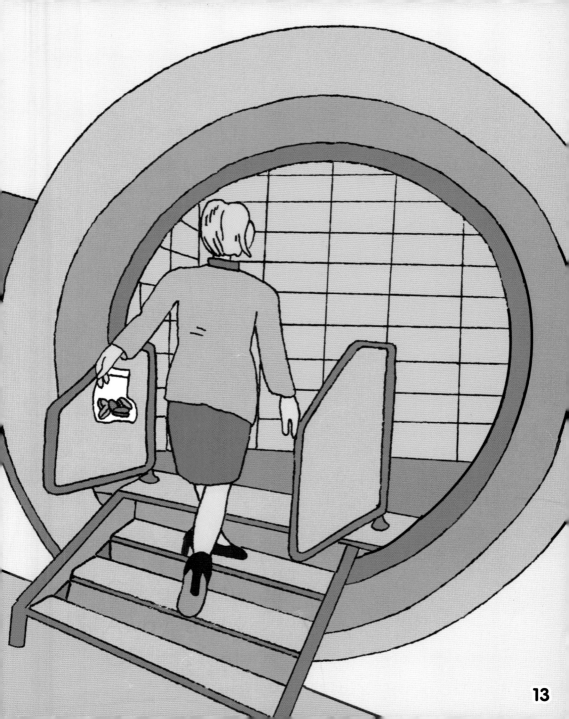

How will I get my money?
How much money is there?

Look here.
It is all in here.
The book shows you how much money
there is.

Now we have to go there.
We have to get you a new pig.

Here we are.
Look here.
What do you like?

Oh, I don't want a new pig bank.
I want that one—that green dragon bank.
It looks like you.

This was a good find!

What do you have there?

My pig bank money
is in a big bank now.
You can do it, too.

I have to go now.
I want to show my mother something.

Mother, mother.
Look here.
I have a dragon bank.

I see it. Now look here.
See what I have—
Cookies that look like a dragon!

I will put some money in this
little bank.
Then we will put it in the big bank.
That is how it works.

So here we are—
You are with me and I am with you.
What a good, good day, dear dragon.

READING REINFORCEMENT

The following activities support the findings of the National Reading Panel that determined the most effective components for reading instruction are: Phonemic Awareness, Phonics, Vocabulary, Fluency, and Text Comprehension.

Phonemic Awareness: The /b/ sound

Oddity Task: Say the /**b**/ sound for your child (be careful not to say buh). Say the following words aloud. Ask your child to say the words that do not end with the /**b**/ sound in the following word groups:

tab, tap, tub	ball, bat, cab	cub, job, bus	bean, crib, bib
sob, cub, big	crab, bad, grab	bump, sob, knob	scrub, bun, club

Phonics: The letter Bb

1. Demonstrate how to form the letters **B** and **b** for your child.
2. Have your child practice writing **B** and **b** at least three times each.
3. Ask your child to point to the words in the book that begin with the letter **b**.
4. Write down the following words and ask your child to circle the letter **b** in each word:

bark	boot	lab	cab	bubble	bed	bib
bag	nibble	bone	crumble	bean	dab	thimble

Vocabulary: Opposites

1. The story features the concepts of big and little. Discuss opposites and ask your child to name the opposites of the following:

hot (cold)	near (far)	short (tall)
soft (hard)	front (back)	happy (sad)

2. Write each of the words on separate pieces of paper. Mix the words up and ask your child to put the opposite pairs back together.

Fluency: Echo Reading

1. Reread the story to your child at least two more times while your child tracks the print by running a finger under the words as they are read. Ask your child to read the words he or she knows with you.

2. Reread the story, stopping after each sentence or page to allow your child to read (echo) what you have read. Repeat echo reading and let your child take the lead.

Text Comprehension: Discussion Time

1. Ask your child to retell the sequence of events in the story.

2. To check comprehension, ask your child the following questions:

   • What happened to the pig bank?

   • Where did the boy and the father take the money?

   • How will the boy get his money if he needs some of it?

   • Do you think it is a good idea to try and save money? Why?

WORD LIST

***Dear Dragon Goes to the Bank* uses the 75 words listed below.**
This list can be used to practice reading the words that appear in the text.
You may wish to write the words on index cards and use them to help your
child build automatic word recognition. Regular practice with these words
will enhance your child's fluency in reading connected text.

a	do	in	oh	there
all	don't	into	on	this
am	dragon	is	one	to
and		it		too
are	Father		pig	
at	find	like	pink	want
away	for	little	put	was
		look(s)		we
bag	get		see	what
bank	go	me	show(s)	where
big	good	money	so	will
book	green	Mother	some	with
		much	something	works
can	have	my	spot	
come	help			you
cookies	here	new	take	
	how	now	that	
day			the	
dear	I	of	then	

ABOUT THE AUTHOR Margaret Hillert has written over 80 books for
children who are just learning to read. Her books
have been translated into many different languages and over a million children
throughout the world have read her books. She first started writing poetry as
a child and has continued to write for children and adults throughout her life. A
first grade teacher for 34 years, Margaret is now retired from teaching and lives in
Michigan where she likes to write, take walks in the morning, and care for her three cats.

Photograph by Glenn Washburn

ABOUT THE ADVISER Shannon Cannon contributed the activities pages that appear in
this book. Shannon serves as a literacy consultant and provides
staff development to help improve reading instruction. She is a frequent presenter at educational
conferences and workshops. Prior to this she worked as an elementary school teacher and as
president of a curriculum publishing company.

Praise for the Work of Alexandria Bellefleur

"With perfectly woven vulnerability and playfulness, *Written in the Stars* is a riotous and heartfelt read. I was hooked from the very first page!"

—Christina Lauren, *New York Times*
bestselling author of *In a Holidaze*

"*Written in the Stars* is everything I want from a rom-com: fun, whimsical, sexy. This modern *Pride and Prejudice* glitters with romance."

—Talia Hibbert, *USA Today* bestselling
author of *Get a Life, Chloe Brown*

"Alexandria Bellefleur is an author to watch. Her writing is joyful and heartfelt, and her voice sparkles with a delightful mix of wit, humor, and good-natured sarcasm. I can't wait to see how she wows us next!"

—Mia Sosa, *USA Today* bestselling
author of *The Worst Best Man*

"*Written in the Stars* had me hooked from the first page. It's an adorable and heartfelt romance with everything I adore: a killer meet-cute, loads of cute banter, steamy love scenes, all the feels, and a happily ever after that left me in happy tears . . . Alexandria Bellefleur's debut will have readers seeing stars in the best way."

—Sarah Smith, author of *Faker* and *Simmer Down*

"A dazzling debut! The perfect combination of humor and heart really makes this book shine."

—Rachel Lacey, author of *Don't Cry for Me*

"*Written in the Stars* is what you might get if your favorite Instagram astrologer wrote you an adorable romance novel. Delightful, funny, and sweet, with just the right touch of woo-woo."

—Scarlett Peckham, *USA Today* bestselling author of *The Rakess*

"A disastrous blind date kicks off Bellefleur's excellent rom-com debut. . . . Readers will be rapt by the sensuous love scenes. . . . This is a delight."

—*Publishers Weekly* (starred review)

"Fans of pop culture–inspired astrology sites will love the effortless and entertaining way the author weaves zodiac memes throughout the text. The stars align in this charming queer rom-com."

—*Kirkus Reviews*

"Bellefleur has a droll, distinct voice, and her one-liners zing off the page, striking both the heart and funny bone. She has a gift for comedy, possessing more style and panache than a debut writer has any right to. . . . There's a sparkling quality here, one that mirrors the starry title. Bellefleur writes as if she's captured fairy lights in a mason jar, twinkly and lovely within something solid yet fragile."

—*Entertainment Weekly*

Hang
the
Moon

By Alexandria Bellefleur

Written in the Stars
Hang the Moon

Hang
the
Moon

A NOVEL

ALEXANDRIA BELLEFLEUR

AVON
An Imprint of HarperCollinsPublishers

HarperCollins books may be purchased for educational, business, or sales promotional use. For information, please email the Special Markets Department at SPsales@harpercollins.com.

FIRST EDITION

Designed by Diahann Sturge

Title page image © Khaneeros / Shutterstock, Inc.
Emojis throughout © FOS_ICON / Shutterstock, Inc.
Clown emoji on page 359 © Cosmic_Design / Shutterstock, Inc.

Library of Congress Cataloging-in-Publication Data has been applied for.

ISBN 978-0-06-300084-1

21 22 23 24 25 LSC 10 9 8 7 6 5 4 3 2 1

Hang
the
Moon

Chapter One

What Summer Song Are You Based on Your Zodiac Sign?

Aries—"Cruel Summer" by Taylor Swift
Taurus—"Summertime" by George Gershwin
Gemini—"Summer Lovin'" by John Travolta and Olivia Newton-John
Cancer—"Summertime Sadness" by Lana Del Rey
Leo—"Hot Girl Summer" by Megan Thee Stallion
Virgo—"Summer Games" by Drake
Libra—"Cool for the Summer" by Demi Lovato
Scorpio—"This Summer's Gonna Hurt Like a Motherfucker" by Maroon 5
Sagittarius—"Summer of '69" by Bryan Adams
Capricorn—"The Boys of Summer" by Don Henley
Aquarius—"Summer Girls" by LFO
Pisces—"Summer Love" by Justin Timberlake

Friday, May 28

*A*nnie nearly wept tears of joy. Starbucks, the holy grail of coffee, was within spitting distance of Gate D2. Something cold, creamy, and above all, caffeinated was exactly what she craved after a day of planes, trains, and automobiles.

Dragging her carry-on with its one busted wheel behind her, she joined the line, fishing around inside the chaos of her bag for her wallet. Her fingers brushed the creased edge of her boarding pass and the plastic wrapper of the protein cookie she'd purchased before sprinting to catch her connecting flight in Atlanta. It claimed to be birthday cake flavored but instead tasted like sawdust and sadness. What a waste of five bucks.

She found her wallet just in time to step up to the counter, where a pretty barista with lilac-colored hair and an ear full of silver jewelry smiled at her, Sharpie at the ready. "Hi. Can I get an iced quad grande cinnamon dolce latte?"

The barista grinned, revealing an intriguing glimpse of silver hardware in her tongue. "Can I get a name for your order?"

"Annie." She slid her credit card inside the reader and waited for it to chirp before tucking her card back inside her wallet.

"You in town for business or pleasure?" the barista asked, handing Annie her receipt. "Or are you from here?"

If Annie had a dollar for every time she'd been asked that question, she'd have been richer than sin. Thanks to her job at Brockman and Brady Inc., an independent human resource consulting firm that specialized in international mergers and acquisitions, she traveled thirty weeks out of the year. But that wasn't why she was in Seattle.

"I'm visiting my best friend."

If she didn't visit Darcy now, who knew when she'd have a chance? In little more than a month, she'd be moving to London, *permanently*, having accepted a promotion as the managing director of the new Brockman and Brady London branch. She didn't know when she'd be able to take off to visit her best friend again, with an ocean and the entire United States separating them.

"Well then, I hope you enjoy your stay." The barista winked and handed over her receipt.

Annie's face went pleasantly warm as she stuffed the receipt and her wallet back into the black abyss of her bag, before stepping over to the bar. She adjusted the French tuck of her button-down shirt, smoothing the wrinkles from eight hours of sitting in a crammed window seat, then snagged her phone from the back pocket of her jeans.

She hit *call* and cradled her phone between her shoulder and her ear, lips curving in a smile when Darcy picked up on the second ring.

"Annie?"

"*Guess where I am,*" Annie answered in singsong, sliding to the side to make room beside the coffee bar.

"Mmm . . . Istanbul?"

Her grip slipped and her hand lurched out to save her phone before it clattered to the tile floor. Her screen already had a decent-sized crack across it, a fine spiderwebbing that rendered the bottom left corner ineffective no matter how hard she pressed or swiped. "Why the hell would I be in Istanbul?"

Darcy huffed. "You told me to guess, I guessed."

Annie squawked sharply, doing her best impression of a buzzer. The man beside her looked at her funny. "Wrong! Try again."

Behind the counter, the barista with the lilac-colored lob passed Annie her latte with another wink. Annie mouthed, "*Thank you*," and snagged her drink, taking a sip while Darcy deliberated. The coffee hit the back of her tongue, sweet, but not quite sweet enough to combat the extra shot of espresso. Annie wrinkled her nose and popped the plastic lid with her thumb before snagging some sugar off the bar. She dumped the entire packet into her cup and gave the drink a quick stir with her straw so the granules would dissolve.

"Northern Hemisphere?"

"No cheating."

Darcy scoffed softly. "Come on. At least tell me if I'm on the right continent."

"Are you asking if I'm in Asia or Europe? It could be either, you know."

She was 99 percent certain Darcy called her a smart-ass through a poorly muffled cough. "*Annie.*"

"I'm not in Asia or Europe. There."

"Are you at home?"

Home. If Darcy meant Annie's apartment in Philadelphia, the one she was almost never at, the answer was a big fat no. Not that Philadelphia felt much like home these days.

"I'm not in Philadelphia. I'm in Starbucks."

"Oh gee, that really helps narrow it down."

And Darcy called *her* a smart-ass. Annie rolled her eyes. "I'd tell you which Starbucks, but I'm not sure that would help. I'm still in the airport."

With perfect timing, a voice announced over the loudspeaker, *"Flight two twenty-three departing from SeaTac for Portland."*

Annie grinned at the choked-off sound Darcy made.

"You're in *Seattle?*"

"Surprise!"

"I'm—I mean—you're here and—*why?*"

Annie cringed. "Yeesh, Darce. Do I need a reason beyond wanting to visit my best friend? My best friend whom I haven't seen in . . ." She quickly did the math and cringed harder. "Over a year?"

It was the longest they'd gone without seeing each other since they became best friends in fifth grade.

"No, no, of course not. I just wish you would've told me . . ."

Annie juggled her drink, carry-on, purse, and phone as she stepped aside, clearing room for the customers still awaiting their beverages. "That would defeat the whole point of it being a surprise."

Darcy exhaled loudly, her breath turning to static over the line. "Right, Annie . . ."

Darcy didn't sound nearly as excited to see her as she was to see Darcy.

She set the drink aside before adjusting her hold on her phone. "Yes?"

"I'm not in Seattle. I'm in Canada. On vacation."

Annie palmed her face with her now free hand. "You? Take a vacation?" She huffed out a laugh. "Wonders never cease."

Better Darcy discovered a work-life balance sooner rather than later, but did it have to happen *now?* Talk about terrible timing.

"Ha ha," Darcy deadpanned before clearing her throat. "I'm in Vancouver. *Elle* and I are in Vancouver."

Ah, *Elle*. Suddenly it made sense. Of course it would take Darcy's new—did it still count as new if they'd been dating over six months?—girlfriend to convince her to step away from her desk and take a much-needed vacation.

Annie smiled. After talking to her via numerous texts and phone calls, she was looking forward to finally meeting the girl who had her best friend totally smitten. Or she *had* been looking forward to it. Annie's smile wavered, but she mustered up some semi-genuine enthusiasm. "Sounds fun! About time you took a vacation."

Enthusiasm Darcy promptly saw through. "I wish I would've known you were flying into town, Annie. I'd have—"

"What, you'd have canceled your plans?" She scoffed. "Oh, please. It's fine." Totally fine. She'd figure it out. Find a hotel and explore Seattle on her own until Darcy returned. By this point, she was a pro at exploring cities solo.

"We got in last night, an extended weekend because of Memorial Day." Darcy paused. "But we can come back early if you—"

"Nope." Annie shook her head even though Darcy couldn't see. "Absolutely not."

"But, Annie—"

"Hush." She laughed. "I'll be fine. I'm a big girl; I can handle a few days in a city by myself."

"How long are you in town for?"

Annie picked at the cardboard sleeve of her cup. "A little over two weeks. I fly back to Philly early in the morning on the thirteenth. So really, a few missing days is nothing in the grand scheme of things."

"Two weeks? That's a long vacation."

Abort, abort.

"Some of us actually use our paid time off," she teased.

"Are you *sure* you don't want us to come back early?" Darcy asked, ignoring Annie's jibe entirely. "Because we can. Elle's nodding. Just say the word and we'll hit the road tomorrow morning, bright and early."

Yes. Annie shut her eyes. "No way. I'll be super pissed if you do that. I mean it. I'll passive-aggressively replace your toilet paper the wrong way the entire time I'm here if you do that. And I'll leave, like, an inch of juice in your carton and not tell you about it. I know you hate when I do that."

"*Annie.*"

"*Darcy,*" she said, mimicking Darcy's tone. "Go. Have fun with Elle in Vancouver. I'll see you on . . ."

"Monday evening."

"Monday evening," Annie agreed. "I've got to go. I bet my luggage hit the carousel by now."

"No, no, wait! Where are you staying?"

She'd been hoping to crash at Darcy's, but that was a bust. "I'll find somewhere. No worries."

Darcy made a soft sound of discontent. "No. *Yes, worries.* That's ridiculous. Just stay at my place. You have my address, right?"

"I do. But I don't have a key."

Darcy paused. "Don't worry. Just take a cab or an Uber over and I'll take care of the rest."

C

"Knock, knock!" The door to Brendon Lowell's office glided open silently. Katie, One True Pairing's head of public relations and communications, poked her head inside. "Got a minute?"

Brendon scrambled to exit out of "The Ten Most Romantic Proposals of All Time" on YouTube, sniffed hard, and waved Katie inside. "For you? Always."

"Are you all right? You're looking kind of"—she pointed at his face—"teary?"

Outside his window, a giant alder tree was dumping a load of pollen, dusting the sidewalk yellow. "Allergies. Pollen count's through the roof," he fibbed.

She wrinkled her nose. "You were watching mushy videos again, weren't you?"

For a split second he considered lying, then thought better of it. "Guilty."

"*Well.* I'm glad you're sitting down and hopefully circulating loads of happy-making dopamine." Clutched against her chest was her trusty tablet. His pulse leaped.

Katie stared at him, unblinking, for an unsettling beat. Then her eyes rolled skyward. "I'm kidding. Relax, before you burst something." She stepped inside his office, shutting the door behind her. "Chill out, okay? It's just the annual independent study on intimacy and relationships. The one you asked me to show you as soon as it was published?"

"Way to give me a heart attack." He pressed a hand to his chest. "I should have you written up for insubordination."

She cocked her head. "Insubordination? I don't think that's in the employee rulebook. I remember *You shall not yuck anyone's yum and slander ships you do not personally sail,* but insubordination? I think not."

Corporate culture at OTP was less *corporate* and more an amalgamation of all the truisms Brendon subscribed to—don't be a douche, listen to the dungeon master, and the only way to fail was to not try.

He eyed the tablet in Katie's hands, her bright orange nails clicking against the black protective sleeve. "Did you look at it already?"

Once a year, the Dew Research Center reported their findings regarding the public's perception of intimacy and dating in the digital age. No apps were named, but the trends were enlightening and helped OTP to better understand their target demographic, along with the overall pain and pressure points felt with online dating.

Katie passed him the tablet. "I did. Most of it's what we expected from the previous two years. The whole market is seeing a slowdown in growth of new users, not only us."

He cradled the tablet in his hands. "Overall outlook?"

She reached for the smiley-face stress ball on his desk, giving it a good squeeze. She made a serious of *hmm*s and *meh*s, sounding like an out-of-tune piano, and shrugged.

That didn't sound promising.

He skimmed the intro section on methodology and polling practices, scrolling with his index finger until he reached the section labeled "Outlooks and Experiences."

Roughly half of users who had used one or more dating

apps reported their experience left them feeling *more* frustrated, rather than hopeful. Forty percent of users reported their experience left them feeling *more* pessimistic than optimistic, while nearly 40 percent reported feeling neither.

A whopping 30 percent of users expressed that dating apps made courtships impersonal and devoid of romance.

Devoid of romance?

Meh was right.

Katie sighed and set his stress ball aside. "I know. Some of this is . . . less than ideal, but remember, none of this is app specific. According to our last in-house survey, over half of our users report high levels of satisfaction, and that was even *before* the updates we made last quarter. We *own* the market with Gen Z and younger millennial users, and users of other apps who switch are most likely to download OTP. Focus on *those* figures and be happy. This survey? Hardly relevant. Pretend it doesn't exist. You saw nothing."

Easier said than done when almost a third of people polled believed dating apps had killed romance when OTP was trying to *revive* it. Not that he'd believed it was dead to begin with.

The poll wasn't personal, it wasn't a jab at him or his company, but it was the principle of the matter. OTP's entire raison d'être, the canon he clung to without fail, was that everyone had a perfect person. Not a person who was perfect, but a person perfect for them. Puzzle pieces slotting together just so. OTP promised to help users find that person.

It was disheartening to see that so many people were jaded.

He smiled wanly, having gone from buoyant to bummed in under five minutes. "Mind emailing me this?"

"As if it's not already sitting in your inbox." Katie rolled her eyes and snagged her tablet, powering the screen down into sleep mode. "I figured you'd want to study the data."

Agonize over it, more like.

"You know me so well," he joked.

"It's almost like I've worked with you for the past five years," she teased, standing and adjusting the tuck of her Captain Marvel T-shirt into the band of her pencil skirt. "You're coming out with us tonight, right? Six-dollar rum slushies?"

He shook his head. "Can't. Rain check?"

Katie pouted. "I see how it is. Boss is too cool to hang out with the plebes."

"Oh please." He rolled his eyes. "You just want me to pay for the first round."

Her smile went sly as she inched toward the door. "Guilty as charged. See you on Monday?"

"Tuesday. Holiday, remember? Don't you and Jian have big plans?" Next week, Katie and Jian, OTP's senior VP of analytics, were getting married after two years of dating. The whole office was invited and it had been all everyone could talk about for weeks. Weddings and happy endings were a big deal at OTP. "Bachelor and bachelorette parties? Couple's shower?"

Katie scoffed. "If you mean will I be sleeping as much as humanly possible before my family comes into town and I forget the meaning of the word *rest*? Then, yeah. *Big* plans."

She smiled and stepped out of his office, shutting the door behind her.

Five minutes later, Margot, his friend and sort of business partner, texted him.

MARGOT (4:35 P.M.): Katie said you're bailing?! What the fuck?

MARGOT (4:36 P.M.): Did she mention $6 happy hour rum slushies?

Margot and his sister's girlfriend, Elle, were the voices behind Oh My Stars, a social media astrology account turned viral sensation. He'd brought them on to consult with OTP and incorporate astrological compatibility into the app's matching algorithm back in December. He'd also fixed Elle up with his sister, Darcy, and he and Margot had become good friends as a result.

BRENDON (4:37 P.M.): I've got a date tonight.

MARGOT (4:39 P.M.): Ofc you do. Remind me, what's this one's name? Tiffany? Diana? Susan? They're all starting to blur together.

Yeesh.

There was nothing wrong with any of the girls Margot had mentioned, but by the third date, he hadn't been able to picture his future with them. There was a . . . disconnect, something missing that was mission critical, no fault of theirs and hopefully not of his, either.

Fireworks.

Undeniable, irrefutable, heart-stopping chemistry. Not love at first sight—he wasn't naïve—and not just physical attraction, but a spark, a flame that could be fanned into a once-in-a-lifetime, roll-the-credits, *Thank you for writing the screenplay, Nora Ephron* kind of love. There were plenty of fish in the sea and he wasn't going to stop searching until he found *the one*, the

Sally to his Harry, because unlike the 30 percent of dating app users polled, he believed romance was alive and kicking.

BRENDON (4:41 P.M.): Her name is Danielle.

MARGOT (4:43 P.M.): Well, have fun with Danielle.

MARGOT (4:43 P.M.): Good luck?

MARGOT (4:44 P.M.): Break a leg?

MARGOT (4:44 P.M.): May the odds be ever in your favor? Not quite sure the proper sentiment here.

He rolled his eyes, powering down his monitor for the day. He was supposed to meet Danielle at six, but traffic at this time on a holiday weekend was guaranteed to be a pain.

The opening notes to the *Twilight Zone* intro song filled his office, his phone lighting up in his hand. "Hey, Darce. How's Vancouver?"

"You're on speaker," she answered, her voice ever so slightly muffled. "And it's nice. Like Seattle, but even cleaner."

Of course that was what Darcy cared about.

"Hey, Brendon!" Elle shouted.

He swapped his phone from his left hand to his right and tugged at his collar, loosening the top button. "Elle, how's it going?"

"You're not busy right now, are you?" Darcy asked.

He glanced at the clock and frowned. "What's up?"

"I need a favor."

He sat up straighter. "Is everything all right?"

"Technically. I need you to swing over to my place and drop off my keys."

"Drop them off with whom?" Darcy was with Elle and the only other person he could imagine needing to get inside her apartment on such short notice was him.

"Annie."

His arm slipped off the edge of the desk, elbow rolling over his ulnar nerve. A flash of pain rocketed up his arm as his chair slid backward on its wheels, knocking him into the wall behind his desk. There was nothing funny about the "funny bone."

"Annie? Annie Kyriakos is in town?" A vision of smooth, golden skin and eyes the color of the Aegean Sea flashed through his mind, the phantom scent of watermelon candy and sunscreen filling his nose. He hadn't seen Annie in . . . hell, eight years. Not since the summer after his freshman year of college. "I didn't know she was visiting."

"Neither did I," she said, sounding wry. "She decided to surprise me. Hence my asking you to bring her my key. She's downtown waiting. I gave her the code to my building, but she can't get inside my apartment."

He reached inside the front zippered pocket of his laptop bag and grabbed his keys, double-checking that Darcy's spare was still on the carabiner. He tossed the keys back inside, zipped the pocket, and stood, hauling the strap of the bag onto his shoulder. "On it. I'll be there ASAP."

Chapter Two

*E*ight. Six. Seven. Two. Six. One. Four.

The keypad to Darcy's apartment building flashed green and Annie made a break for it, grabbing the heavy brass handle and wrenching the door open. She waved at her Uber driver over her shoulder as she ducked for cover from the out-of-the-blue rain shower. The wobbly back wheel of her suitcase snagged on the threshold, causing her to stumble backward when she tugged harder, her black strappy kitten heels slipping on the slick marble floor.

Slightly out of breath, she dragged her suitcase out of the immediate path and posted up against the expansive wall of windows. Outside, the rain picked up, a gust of wind splattering the panes with droplets. Luckily she'd made it inside when she had, a little damp, but not soaked to the bone like she would've been had she still been on the street. She gathered her damp hair off the nape of her neck and twisted it into a messy bun, securing it with the band around her wrist, before getting her bearings.

Darcy's building was impressive, all black marble shot

through with gold veins, and immaculate—if impractical—white leather couches facing one another on either side of the lobby. Directly across from the door she'd stepped through was a gleaming silver elevator. She double-checked the text Darcy had sent her as soon as they'd gotten off the phone.

DARCY (4:44 P.M.): The code is 8672614.

DARCY (4:52 P.M.): Brendon's on his way with the key. He should be there in 20 minutes.

Brendon Lowell. Last time she'd seen him in person had been eight years ago, back when he was a gangly college freshman with an adorable penchant for talking with his hands when he got fired up about something. For a guy who'd created one of the most popular apps on the market, he was shockingly bad at keeping his personal social media up to date. It would be interesting to see how he'd changed. If he'd changed.

Ten minutes later, the rain had passed, the cloud cover overhead breaking. The sun hovered at the horizon, painting the sky fiery orange, fingers of pink and yellow bleeding up into the beginnings of purple evening. Twilight approached, daylight burning away. Golden hour, her favorite time of day, when the shadows weren't so dark and everything was bathed in shades of amber warmth. Leaving her suitcase inside, she stepped back out onto the sidewalk, breathing deep, inhaling the smell of rain-soaked pavement. The temperature was dropping and she crossed her arms against the breeze.

Darcy's apartment was located on a steep hill several blocks northwest of the internationally famous Pike Place Market, in what appeared to be a quiet, older neighborhood. Traffic was lighter than it had been in the thick of downtown, and Annie's vantage point afforded her an unencumbered view of the street. A silver Smart car shot down the hill like a bullet, cruising to a stop beside the curb.

It even had a giant windup key affixed to the trunk that was too cute not to document. She dug her phone out of her back pocket and snapped several pictures before flipping over to video and recording a brief clip of the key as it rotated.

The engine shut off and the driver's-side door opened and—Annie blinked twice. *Hello.* Her lips parted, her jaw falling open a smidge, just enough to let out a choked gasp of appreciation as the driver unfolded himself from the car, all six feet, *several* inches of him.

It was a clown-car situation—how the driver had managed to pack all of that inside such a small space eluded her, but she wasn't going to complain. No sir. She was going to thank the universe wholeheartedly for bringing her to this place, at this time, so she could appreciate the sight of this gorgeous guy shutting the door to his tiny car and lifting an arm—holy biceps, Batman—to . . . wave?

Heat crept up her neck, spreading like wildfire over her jaw. Oh God, he was looking right at her while she recorded him in all his long-legged, broad-shouldered, "*hello* forearms" glory. She fumbled her phone, tapping the button to stop recording, but her stupid cracked screen was having none of it. To save face, she pivoted hard to the right, pretending to record the sunset instead.

From the corner of her eye, she watched as the driver of the

Smart car hopped the curb and—Jesus, he and his snug shirt were coming her way.

"Annie Kyriakos."

That was her name. Smart car guy knew her name. He was standing a foot from her, smiling so broadly that the corners of his brown eyes crinkled and his dimples deepened and—

Holy shit.

Smart car guy was Brendon Lowell, Darcy's not-so-baby brother, and he and his biceps and dimples and bronze-haired beauty had rendered her mute. Mute and frozen, like someone had pressed the pause button on her body, her system coming back online only when he reached out, wrapping his arms around her, drawing her in for a hug that eked a squeak from her lips. *"Brendon?"*

Her face pressed against the solid muscle of his chest, her nose buried in the soft, warm cotton of his shirt, which smelled like laundry detergent and rain. After a moment, she stepped back, her knees missing the memo and nearly giving out beneath her. She scrambled for stability, hands wrapping around—*forearms.* Brendon's forearms.

Tearing her gaze from where her bright blue nails were biting into the pale, freckled skin of his forearms, leaving little crescent moons behind, her eyes made a slow, meandering path up his body.

By the time she'd made it back to his face, his grin had gone crooked. "It's been a while."

Understatement of the century. It had been long enough that he had gone from *cute*—all auburn hair and freckles, tall and lithe, his limbs a touch too long and his light brown eyes wide, doe-like—to *this*. She swallowed hard. Brendon had grown up *exceptionally* well. "Only eight years."

He laughed, the sound coming from somewhere deep inside his chest. "Only." Eyes still crinkled with laughter, he studied her. "You haven't been waiting out here this entire time, have you?"

"N—no." She jerked her thumb over her shoulder, her suitcase visible through the glass window of the lobby. "I was inside and then it stopped raining so I decided to come back out here because it wasn't . . . raining." *Wow*. Brilliant. She cleared her throat, suddenly jittery. Probably thanks to the quad grande latte she'd sucked down on an empty stomach. Yeah, that must've been it. "I, uh, really appreciate you coming all the way over here to drop off the key. I hope I didn't interrupt your evening."

He fished inside his front pocket, withdrawing the key to Darcy's apartment. One hand grazed the small of her back as he stepped around her. She stood up straighter. With a quick wave of the key fob, a sensor flashed green and he opened the door, moving aside to let her pass. "Nah, I'm happy to help."

She smiled sheepishly. "I guess this is what I get for flying into town without checking with Darcy first."

He followed her inside the lobby, trading the key for her suitcase. She smiled gratefully and shouldered her purse, following him to the elevator.

"How long are you in town for?"

"Two and a half weeks." She joined him inside the elevator. "Roughly. I fly back on the thirteenth."

He punched the button for the ninth floor and whistled. "I wish I got two and a half weeks off."

She tutted, starting to regain her bearings. No longer *quite* so topsy-turvy over the difference eight years made. "Ah, the plight of Mr. *Forbes* Thirty Under Thirty."

He grinned. "Been keeping tabs on me, have you?"

Heat crept up the front of her throat, a startled laugh spilling from her lips at Brendon's brazenness. "Darcy brags."

He hummed, rocking back on his heels. "Did she tell you I made the *Fortune* Forty Under Forty list, too?"

"She forgot to mention how humble you've become." She pressed her lips together, smothering a smile as she stepped out of the elevator and to the side, letting him lead the way. She didn't know which unit was Darcy's.

He stopped in front of the third door on the left, apartment 909. She unlocked the door and stepped inside, blinking at the sudden brightness when Brendon flipped the switch.

"Thanks." She took her suitcase from him, wheeling it over the threshold and inside Darcy's foyer, her blasted back wheel proving itself a bitch once again.

Darcy's apartment, while minimalist in design, was cozier than any hotel room Annie could've picked on the fly, and far more spacious. Annie spun in a quick circle, getting the lay of the land. "Nice place."

He lingered in the doorway, one hand tucked in his pocket. "Other than Darcy's allergy to color, yeah."

She swallowed a laugh. The place *was* monochromatic. "I'm guessing the guest room's—"

Brendon jerked his head to the left. "Down the hall, second room on the right. There's a Jack-and-Jill bathroom shared between the two bedrooms and a half bath across the hall. Linens are in the bathroom closet and spare toiletries are under the sink."

Darcy had already given her that spiel, but Annie appreciated the reminder. Not that Annie needed spare toiletries. Her collection of travel-sized shampoos was getting out of hand. "Thanks. Let me just put this in my room. I'll be right back."

She wheeled her suitcase down the hall, careful not to scuff the baseboards as she turned the corner. Like the rest of the apartment, the guest bedroom was simple and streamlined, with dark wood floors mostly covered with plush white rugs and white walls unadorned, save for the occasional piece of black and white art that probably cost a fortune.

Annie left her suitcase beside the queen-sized bed—she couldn't wait to faceplant onto it as soon as she showered off her travel grime—and returned to the foyer. Brendon tucked his phone back inside his pocket and smiled. "Anything you need before I let you get settled?"

Not that she could think of. "Nah. I'm just going to clean up and unpack." Her stomach gave a growl that made him laugh. She smiled wryly. "Okay. First I'm going to raid Darcy's fridge and *then* I'm going to clean up and unpack."

Brendon made a face, lips twisting and drawing to the side. "You can look, but knowing Darce, she probably cleaned out the fridge so nothing would spoil."

"I'm sure I can scrounge something up." Hopefully.

He scratched his jaw. "*Or* there's a place on Sixth Avenue that has great dim sum. If you're interested."

What else was she going to do? The protein cookie buried at the bottom of her bag wasn't going to cut it.

Her stomach gave another grumble, making the decision for her. "I'm in."

☾

"Two whole weeks in Seattle. What's on your agenda?"

"Aside from visiting Darcy, I don't really have one." She reached for her wine, swirling it thoughtfully. "I don't know. See the Space Needle maybe?"

When he nudged the last dumpling toward her, she waved him off, completely stuffed.

He plucked it from the basket with his chopsticks. "The Space Needle? Isn't that one of those places you visit once? One and done?"

She sipped and shrugged. "I guess I'll let you know once I see it if I feel compelled to go again."

His brows rocketed to his hairline. "You've never been?"

"First time in Seattle," she said, laughing when he stared. "What?"

"I just assumed you'd been." His lips twitched. "You've been everywhere else."

"I haven't been *everywhere*."

Technically she *had* been to Seattle, but until today, she'd never left the airport. Which didn't count.

He set his chopsticks aside. "Let's see. Berlin. Prague. Paris." He ticked each city off on his fingers. "New York. Singapore. Should I keep going?"

"Been keeping tabs on me, have you?" she teased, using his words from earlier against him.

"Darcy talks about you all the time."

She ducked her chin, burying her pleased smile in her glass of wine. It was nice knowing Darcy thought about her often.

Belatedly, it struck her that she'd only been in Prague for less than a day thanks to a long layover. "I don't think I ever told Darcy I was in Prague."

The tips of his ears turned pink. "All right. I might've seen that on Instagram."

She bit back a smile. "So you *have* been keeping tabs on me?"

"You make it sound creepy." He palmed his face, groaning softly into his hand. "Like I was Facebook-stalking you or something."

She snickered. "Were you?"

Humor danced in his whiskey-brown eyes as he rested his elbow on the table and ran his thumb over his bottom lip. "Now, why would I do something like that?"

Why indeed. She didn't know what to say that wouldn't turn her into a total hypocrite, seeing as she'd stalked his Instagram, too. First, because Darcy didn't have one and he was the best source of updates on her friend. Then, because his content was interesting and the handful of selfies he'd posted over the years were cute. Rather than speak, she smiled.

"Okay, there's a question I've been dying to ask." He leaned in, resting his forearms on the table. "Just how many languages do you speak?"

She laughed. "Fluently? Or 'I can fumble my way through a conversation but I might stick my foot in my mouth'?"

"Why do I feel like there's a story there?"

She pressed her hands to her fiery cheeks. "It's so embarrassing."

"You realize you're obligated to share now, don't you?"

It was a good story, only she wished it hadn't happened to *her*. "I was in Rome on business, but I decided to take a guided tour on my one day off. After it was over, I told the tour guide I was going to need a nap after the day spent trekking around the city on foot. Which would've been fine, except the word for nap is *pisolino*, which is staggeringly similar to the word *pisellino*"— she shut her eyes—"which means 'small penis.'"

He sputtered into his fist. "You told your tour guide you were going to need a—"

"Mm-hmm." She nodded miserably. "Awkward."

Brendon's broad shoulders shook with silent laughter. He wiped his eyes and grinned. "Okay. All languages, then."

She enumerated them on her fingers. "English, obviously."

"Obviously."

"Greek."

"You were born in Greece, right?"

She was surprised he remembered that. "Yeah. My dad is from Thessaloniki and was working at the consulate, and my mom was a translator for the US embassy in Greece. That's how they met." They hadn't moved to the States until she was seven, at which point she was fluent in both English and Greek.

"I'm fluent in French. I know enough Italian to embarrass myself, apparently; enough German to order food or get a cab that will take me to the right place eighty percent of the time;

and"—she smirked—"thanks to Duolingo, I can even say a few words in High Valyrian."

He grinned and lifted a hand to his chest. "Be still my heart."

"I figured you'd get a kick out of that."

His eyes narrowed playfully. "Are you calling me a nerd, Annie?"

She shut one eye. "If it walks like a duck . . ."

He barked out a surprised laugh and threw his napkin at her across the table. It missed her wineglass by a narrow margin and she had a startling flashback to Darcy's first disaster date with Elle, wherein Elle had toppled over two glasses of wine into Darcy's lap.

Brendon blanched, likely thinking the same thing. "That could've been bad."

She balled up the napkin and hurled it back at him, laughing when his eyes widened. "Lucky for you, I'm not attached to this blouse."

His eyes dipped before darting back to her face, the tips of his ears turning adorably pink once more. "It's a nice blouse."

His teeth sank into his bottom lip, a smile flirting at the edges of his mouth. On anyone else, that smile would've been dangerous. The sort of smile that got Annie to do ill-advised acts after a first date. But this wasn't a date and this was Brendon, her best friend's baby brother. He was harmless.

"Thanks."

His tongue slipped out, wetting the lip he'd trapped between his teeth, and a tiny flicker of heat flared to life in her stomach. She cleared her throat and took a sip of water. *Totally* harmless.

"Getting to travel for work, this must be your dream job."

She snorted into her glass. "Is HR *anyone's* dream job?"

It took his frowning for her to realize how awful that sounded.

"I'm really good at what I do, don't get me wrong. I like visiting new places and I love languages. But most of what I see is the inside of boardrooms and hotels, and even though they considered my being multilingual an asset, most business is conducted in English."

Reality had fallen short of her expectations. Story of her life. Sometimes her job was a bit of a soul-suck, but it paid her bills. She had no business complaining.

She gave a sharp shake of her head and pasted on a smile. "We've spent practically the whole time talking about me."

He leaned a little further over the edge of the table, his shoulders bunching. His smile was puzzled. "I'm not complaining."

Not yet, maybe. "Speaking of dream jobs." She stared pointedly at him.

"Me?" He laughed and slumped back in his chair. "Oh, no. This isn't my dream job."

Her brows rose. "It isn't?"

"No. I had much higher aspirations," he said, face solemn.

"Higher aspirations than creating a successful dating app? Owning a company?"

He looked over his shoulder, then leaned forward and dropped his voice to a conspiratorial whisper. "I wanted to be Hugh Grant."

She blinked. "Hugh—Hugh Grant."

He hummed and the corner of his mouth twitched.

"You're fucking with me." She laughed.

"Am not!" His grin stretched from ear to ear. "I wanted to be Hugh Grant. I was ten years old, granted." He tried to wink and failed miserably, both his eyes shutting in a stuttered blink that made her grin. "Pun unintended."

"Ten? That doesn't count."

His jaw dropped, his eyes sparkling beneath the dim lights of the restaurant. "It counts. Don't belittle my dreams, Annie."

She pinched her lips together. "My apologies. Please, tell me more about how you wanted to be"—she sputtered—"Hugh Grant."

"He was in all my favorite movies. *Notting Hill, Four Weddings and a Funeral, Two Weeks Notice.* He was charming in an accessible, awkward way I identified with on a soul-deep level." He dimpled at her. "And he always got the girl."

Her cheeks hurt from smiling. "So you wanted to be an actor?"

"No." He frowned thoughtfully. "Just Hugh Grant. Minus the arrest record, obviously."

"Obviously." She rested her chin on her palm, mirroring him. "You changed your mind?"

He heaved a dramatic sigh. "Alas, like Highlander, there can only be one Hugh Grant. So, I spent several years adrift. Unsure of my direction in life."

"And then you discovered your true calling, creating the greatest dating app known."

His cheeks colored. "That's kind. But no. Then I took a screenwriting class in college because I figured if I couldn't be Hugh Grant, I could be Nora Ephron."

"Makes *perfect* sense."

"I had a bit of a problem, though," he confessed. "I hated writing conflict between couples. Which, would you believe, is actually necessary."

"Stories need conflict?" She tutted. "Who'd have thunk it?"

He ducked his chin, chuckling quietly. "Unfortunately, not freshman me. My professor commended me on writing a spectacular script"—he winced—"if I was aiming for late-night soft-core porn."

She clapped a hand over her mouth. "Please tell me this script still exists."

And that she could get her eyeballs on it ASAP.

"Uh-uh." He crossed his arms. "No way."

"You can't tease me with soft-core porn and then not deliver. That's rude."

"It *wasn't* porn, that's the thing. There was—there was character development." He made what he probably thought was an innocent gesture with his hand, fingers pointed up and spreading. "*Growth.*"

She struggled to keep a straight face. "I'm sure there was lots and *lots* of growth."

"Quit." He groaned softly. "Needless to say, I decided to leave the writing hobby to my sister."

"And the rest is history."

He shrugged. "So if working in HR wasn't your childhood dream job"—she snorted—"what did you want to be when you grew up?"

She smirked. "Who says I wanted to grow up?"

He beamed at her.

"Don't laugh," she warned.

"You laughed at me."

Fair point. "Okay. Do you remember *Total Request Live*? Or was that before your time?"

"You are two years older than me," he deadpanned.

"Every day after I took the bus home from school, I'd plop down in front of the TV and watch MTV until my parents came home. I was kind of obsessed with *TRL*. I wanted to be a VJ when I grew up. Then *TRL* went defunct and my hopes and dreams were obliterated." She wiped an imaginary tear from the corner of her eye.

"And you were forced to settle for your second passion, business strategy implementation."

"I think you mean *corporate* strategy and strategic management, but it's easy to mix them up. I'm sure OTP has a whole human resources department that knows the difference for you," she teased.

"I can see why you have such a deep, abiding passion for what you do. It sounds riveting," he fired back.

Deep, abiding passion and human resources didn't exactly go together, at least not in her mind. It wasn't her calling in life or what got her out of bed in the morning. It was her job. Nothing more, nothing less.

His tongue poked at the inside of his cheek. "So, what you're telling me is you wanted to grow up to be Carson Daly?"

She buried her face in her hands and peeked through her fingers. "Oh God. I kind of did?"

His laughter trailed off until he was staring at her, a smile playing at the edges of his lips.

Either it was her, or the restaurant had gotten warm. She

worked the band around her wrist over her hand and threw her hair up in a quick bun. "Jokes aside, how are things with OTP?"

Suddenly sheepish, Brendon ran his hand over the top of his head. "Good, good. Mostly. We're contending with an overall slowdown in market growth, and the annual I-and-D survey results were . . . mixed, but good. We're seeing a bit of an increase in anti–dating app sentiment. Burnout, I guess." He shrugged. "Dating's fun, but it has its frustrations."

Fun was not a word she'd have used to describe dating.

Her brow knit. "I and D?"

"'Intimacy and dating.'" He tugged at his collar, undoing the top button, revealing the hollow of his throat and a strip of skin beneath. His Adam's apple bobbed and she swallowed, too. "Once a year, the Dew Research Center publishes their findings on the public's perception of dating in the digital age. It's in general, not about OTP, but it's important to keep abreast of the trends and impressions so we can get ahead of issues before they arise."

"And the results were mixed?"

He cracked his knuckles and shrugged. "Decent overall, but thirty percent of respondents reported feeling like apps have made dating impersonal and devoid of romance."

"On the bright side, that means seventy percent don't feel that way."

"This is true."

She reached for her wine and took a long, slow sip. "I feel like an all-or-nothing attribution isn't fair."

He cocked his head.

"I mean, I wouldn't say dating apps are solely to blame."

His brow furrowed. "Solely? As in you think—sorry, what are you saying?"

Uh-oh. She'd managed to insert her foot into her mouth in English just as well as she could in Italian.

"Nothing," she said, backpedaling.

"Come on." This time, he nudged her under the table. "You won't offend me. I want to hear what you have to say."

"I don't even use dating apps anymore. I'm not in your demographic."

She didn't use dating apps anymore because she didn't *date* anymore. Period.

"That isn't what I asked."

With a resigned sigh, she accepted there'd be no wiggling her way out of this. That would be too easy.

"I wouldn't say dating apps are responsible for the death of romance, but—"

"Whoa, *whoa*." His jaw hung open as he stared at her. "*Death* of romance?"

Who was to say what exactly had killed it, but she had a suspicion modern dating had delivered the final blow. With the advent of dating apps, people didn't have to *work* to get laid, which was all most people were after. The old, tried-and-true bare minimum of wining and dining someone wasn't even necessary anymore, not in this world of instant gratification. And those who claimed to be looking for more, for love? They might put in the effort at first, but it was only ever a matter of time before the mask slipped and people showed their true colors.

People stopped trying, then they stopped caring.

She'd watched it happen, experienced it firsthand, too many times, so many she'd lost count. Sparks that fizzled. Forgotten birthdays, breakups that happened via text if they even happened at all, with ghosting the new norm. Having expectations for more was exhausting. She would rather expect the worst than suffer constant disappointment, hoping one day someone might surprise her.

She took another fortifying sip and proceeded with caution. "You have to admit, people have ridiculously short attention spans."

"Most people," he agreed, causing her shoulders to slump in relief.

"*Most* people want a thirty-second sound bite, two hundred and eighty characters or less. Anything longer than that and they move on, because they don't really care. And no one remembers anything, because why should they? It's all online. When was the last time you remembered a friend's birthday without Facebook reminding you?"

He frowned. "It's convenient."

"Since when are friendships, let alone love, supposed to be convenient? Swiping through pictures—"

"We aren't swipe based. We have an algorithm that matches users based on several key compatibility variables determined via questionnaires and what we hope are fun personality quizzes. We evaluate shared interests and values, communication styles, senses of humor." Forearms once again resting on the edge of the table, Brendon spoke zealously, his eyes brightening. "Actually, one of the common complaints about OTP is that we *aren't* as convenient as other apps. No one wants to answer a fifty-question survey just so they can access their available matches in hopes of *maybe* finding someone to get laid. It's easier to download a different app. Which is fine. I'm not worried about being the most downloaded app, the one with the greatest number of users. That's not what we're about. It's not about ad revenue. It's not about the money from premium account upgrades. It's about making people happy by helping them find love. *That* is what I want OTP to be best at."

She smiled tightly, biting her tongue. She didn't want to burst his bubble by telling him she believed that he could try, but for every person who cared about finding love, there'd be a dozen more who didn't care at all. That they might say they did, might bemoan their singledom, might even start out with the best intentions, but when push came to shove, most people wanted easy. "That sounds . . . commendable."

He stared, gaze intensely locked on her face, while he chewed on his lip, the gears in his head all but visibly whirring. She crossed her ankles and braced herself for him to give her his best. Worst. *Whatever.*

"You know, Darcy sounded pretty jaded about dating before she met Elle."

She threw her napkin on the table beside her plate and shook her head, laughing under her breath.

"Oh my God. I cannot believe I walked into that." She should've seen this coming a mile away. She should've seen this coming *light-years* away. From outer space, a galaxy far, far away. "I don't even know where to start. You're so many shades of wrong, it's not even funny."

His lips twitched. "And yet you're laughing."

"Because I am *flummoxed* by how we went, in the span of five minutes, from discussing Carson Daly to *this*."

He laughed harder, which spurred her on, making her pinch her lips together to keep from chuckling.

"You're ridiculous and I shouldn't have expected anything less. Darcy told me you were like this."

"Like what?" A curious divot appeared between his brows.

Upon moving to Seattle, Darcy had suffered through countless blind dates set up by her brother, who refused to listen when she told him time and time again that she wasn't interested. Granted, Darcy's heart had been broken by her good-for-nothing ex, Natasha, so when she said she wasn't interested, it didn't exactly take a genius to understand she was scared of putting her heart on the line. Brendon had had good intentions in pushing her to put herself back out there, and he'd successfully found a match for Darcy in Elle, but none of that changed the fact that he didn't know when to pump the brakes when it came to his meddling.

She twirled the stem of her nearly empty wineglass between her fingers. "Stubborn, for starters."

"I prefer *tenacious*."

She sputtered, glad she had yet to take a sip. Brendon would've wound up wearing wine. "Pretty sure the exact word Darcy used was *pigheaded*."

He smiled roguishly. "You sure she didn't say *pleasantly persistent*?"

Her pulse pounded. Something about the flash of his white

teeth against the pink of his lips paired with their rapidly heating argument caused her heart to race.

"Pushy, more like. And she said you have a penchant for armchair psychology." She tucked a strand of hair she'd missed behind her ear. "I'm not your sister, Brendon."

Something she couldn't put a name to flickered in his brown eyes. "No. You're not."

She swallowed hard, her throat inexplicably dry. "And I'm not nursing a broken heart, either. Nor am I secretly waiting around for someone to sweep me off my feet."

"Sure." He nodded dismissively. "Whatever you say."

She pursed her lips. "I'm *not*."

The way he smiled and said nothing was infuriating.

She polished off her wine, setting the glass aside. "All right. You want to know what *I* think?"

"What's that?" He leaned in eagerly.

"I think it's interesting how you're *so* invested in what everyone around you, even strangers, thinks about love to the extent that you go the extra mile to try to fix their problems."

He held up his hands. "What can I say? I'm a selfless guy."

While she wouldn't argue against that, she had a sneaking suspicion there was a lot more to Brendon than that. "Maybe. But I wonder why it's so much easier for you to solve everyone else's issues with love than your own. Hmm. Avoidance, maybe? Repression? No, what do they call it . . . projection?"

He scoffed out a laugh, head shaking. "Tiny flaw in your logic. I don't *have* any issues with my love life."

"Repression it is." She nodded sagely.

A muscle in his jaw spasmed. "I *don't*."

"Are you still single?"

Thanks to Darcy, she already knew he was.

His eyes narrowed. "I am."

"Hm."

"*Hm.*" He mimicked her. "What's that supposed to mean?"

"Nothing. Just thinking about how on airplanes they advise you to put your oxygen mask on before you assist others."

His jaw slid forward, just a hair, so little that it might have been only a twitch to the unsuspecting eye. "I haven't found the right girl yet."

She traced the stem of her empty glass. "Ever wonder why that is?"

A muscle in his jaw jumped. "There's what, seven billion people on the planet? Lots of fish in the sea."

"Well, I'm sure with a few more swipes, you'll hook your dream girl."

The waiter swooped by, dropping off the check. Brendon reached for his wallet.

"I've got it," she said. "It's the least I can do to thank you for dropping off Darcy's key."

He snagged the check holder and shook his head. "I invited you to dinner. My treat." He tucked his credit card inside the leather holder and placed it on the edge of the table. "Back to our discussion."

"I don't want to argue with you, Brendon."

"You sure? It seemed like you were having a good time."

Strangely, she was. Brendon gave as good as he got, his verbal sparring witty without crossing a line into territory that would piss her off.

"I don't think there's anything left to discuss. I have my opinions—"

"And I'm going to change your mind. Romance isn't dead, and I'm going to prove it."

Laughter burst from between her lips. "You can try."

His mouth twitched. "Do or do not, Annie."

She'd walked right into that one. "How exactly do you plan on changing my mind?"

He scoffed, his smile belying the sound. "Reveal my methods? What do you take me for? An amateur?"

All those dates Brendon had set Darcy up on sprang to mind. "No blind dates. I don't live here, remember?"

"Wasn't planning on it."

"Then how—" She bit her tongue. It didn't matter because it wasn't going to work. "Fine. Good luck."

The left corner of his mouth curved in a smirk that brought out the dimple in his cheek. "I don't need luck, Annie."

Chapter Three

What Romantic Movie Gesture Are You Based on Your Zodiac Sign?

Aries—*Sweet Home Alabama*'s kiss in the rain
Taurus—*Pretty Woman*'s fire escape serenade
Gemini—*Never Been Kissed*'s first kiss on the baseball field
Cancer—*The Notebook*'s dream house
Leo—*10 Things I Hate About You*'s bleacher serenade
Virgo—*Love Actually*'s cue cards
Libra—*Notting Hill*'s Chagall painting
Scorpio—*The Breakfast Club*'s diamond earring gift
Sagittarius—*Beauty and the Beast*'s library access
Capricorn—*Pride and Prejudice*'s Darcy paying for Lydia's wedding
Aquarius—*Say Anything*'s boom box serenade
Pisces—*Bridget Jones's Diary*'s undie run + diary gift

Saturday, May 29

$\mathcal{B}$rendon's calves burned as he stretched up on his toes, his left arm extended above his head, reaching for the yellow hand-hold. His fingers skimmed the bottom; close, but no cigar. He gripped the dusty pink rock a little tighter and adjusted his footing, hiking his right leg up to his waist, bracing the ball of his foot against the green sliver of a hold at hip height. Bouncing on his toes, he used the momentum to heave himself up, his fingers pinching the higher handhold. Sweat trickled down his spine, soaking into his gym shorts. *Success.*

Several feet below, Margot grunted as she hefted herself up the rock wall. "You're awfully quiet this morning."

His right foot slipped and his stomach went into free fall. He caught himself, hugging the wall as his breathing evened out. "Sorry. Just have a lot on my mind."

Last night he'd lain in bed wondering how someone like Annie had become so jaded. Darcy, he'd understood. But what had pushed Annie to the point of swearing off love? It didn't seem like she had towering, fortress-style walls erected around her heart like Darcy, whose guardedness had been plain to see. Granted, he'd only spent a few hours talking to Annie, but she'd seemed more . . . apathetic about love than someone who'd been burned by it.

None of it sat right, her resignation nor her flippant attitude to his promise to prove her wrong. She'd seemed as sure of herself as he was, which only made him more determined to change her mind.

Problem was, he didn't know where to start.

"About?"

Knowing Margot, she'd give him shit for this, but maybe she could help him look at things from a different angle. Illuminate a blind spot. "Let's say I needed to prove to someone that romance isn't dead."

"*Someone.* Does this have something to do with OTP?"

In a sense. If he could figure out how to change Annie's mind about love, it might help him better understand the disconnect for that jaded 30 percent of dating app users.

"Kind of? This is more of a . . . personal project."

His fingers started to ache, the tendon crossing the meat of his thumb cramping.

"Personal—" Margot exhaled roughly and muttered something he couldn't quite make out under her breath. "Get down here."

He let his feet dangle and breathed through the burn in his shoulders before dropping to the ground, knees bent to cushion his landing. Margot wiped the back of her hand against her forehead, leaving a trail of chalk dust against her skin.

"Someone *who*?"

Brendon crouched down, digging his water bottle out of his gym bag. With his teeth, he tugged on the spout, tipping the bottle back and drinking deep, draining half in one swallow. He ran his hand against his mouth and sighed. "Darcy's friend Annie flew into town yesterday."

Margot's eyes widened gleefully. "*Annie?* As in the girl you had a total hard-on for as a kid? The girl you—"

He held up a hand, stopping her before she could mortify

him further. He was going to have a *long* talk with Darcy about what was and wasn't acceptable to share about his childhood. Telling her girlfriend was one thing, but sharing in the presence of her girlfriend's roommate? Who happened to be his friend? His friend who took great joy in giving him shit? Out of bounds.

"Yes, that Annie. She wanted to surprise Darcy by visiting. I had to drop off her spare key."

"Well, well, well. Suddenly your Saturday morning crisis makes all the sense."

"I'm not having a crisis. I just need to prove a point."

"About *love*." She drew the word out, giving it several extra syllables. "To the girl you used to *be* in love with. Interesting."

He was beginning to rethink asking Margot for help since it looked like all she was going to do was rag on him. "It's not interesting. At dinner, she said—"

"Dinner? What happened to you having a date with Diana?"

"*Danielle*," he said, correcting her. "And I canceled. Or, rescheduled."

Danielle was going out of town to visit family in Lake Chelan and they'd agreed to play their rain check by ear.

Margot smirked at him. "So that you could go on a date with Annie instead. I see how it is."

She really didn't. "That's—that's not how it was." He cupped the back of his neck, his skin burning beneath his palm. "It wasn't a date."

Margot lay down on the floor, staring up at the ceiling. She hugged her knee to her chest, stretching out her hamstrings. "Dinner is the quintessential first date."

"People have to eat, Margot." He sighed. "We're getting off topic. We had dinner. We talked. Annie told me, get this—she believes romance is dead. I told her I was going to prove her wrong, but honestly? I'm stumped. Setting her up with someone is off the table; she's only in town for a little over two weeks and I don't know her type well enough to know someone, off the top of my head, who'd mesh well with her."

And not that he'd admit it, but the thought of setting Annie up with someone put a terrible taste in his mouth.

"The app? Can't you just get her to download OTP and problem solved?"

That was a hard no; she'd made her thoughts on dating apps clear. "I think dating apps might be part of the problem."

He needed to think outside the box. Something he was usually stellar at.

Margot frowned. "It's times like these I truly pity your Venus-Mars placements."

What the fuck. "Margot."

"I'm just saying." She held up her hands. "You poor little Aries Venus, Cancer Mars. You are a funky cinnamon roll who knows what he wants but not how to get it."

She tutted, shaking her head. Her exaggerated pout gave away the fact she was fucking with him.

"Can you be serious for a second?" he begged. "I'm asking for your help."

"Why do you care whether Annie thinks romance is dead? It's no skin off your nose what your sister's best friend thinks."

He couldn't stand the thought of anyone thinking love was a lost cause, believing they needed to settle for less than fireworks because they hadn't found the right person yet. *Yet* being the operative word.

"It's the principle of the matter. It's *sad*. And, okay, from a professional standpoint I *do* have skin in the game. Annie's not the only person who thinks romance is dead. The annual intimacy-and-dating survey was pubbed yesterday. *Thirty percent* of people polled think dating apps have removed the romance from dating. I can't just ignore that." OTP couldn't ignore that, either. Maybe he couldn't convince everyone, but if he could convince Annie? It would be a start.

A line formed between her brows, and her lips twisted downward in a frown. "I say this with all the love in my heart, but you need to accept the fact that you can't single-handedly deliver happily-ever-afters for every person on the planet. Even you have limits, Brendon."

Limits, his ass. He shot her a grin. "Says who?"

She pressed a hand to her forehead. "Didn't you learn *anything* from what happened with your sister and Elle? Like, I don't know, *not* to meddle in other people's love lives?"

Sure, there'd been that hiccup where Darcy's fear of winding up with a broken heart had led to her pushing Elle away and ruing the day Brendon set them up, but she'd gotten over it, proving that love could, in fact, conquer everything, including your deepest, darkest fears. "Everyone keeps throwing that in my face, but I'm pretty sure my intervention paid off. Besides, this isn't meddling. I told Annie I'm going to change her mind. I just don't know *how*."

"And you thought, what? *Let me ask Margot. She's a fount of knowledge.* You're the expert on mushy shit, not me."

"Mushy shit?"

She rolled her eyes. "I said what I said. All that *you complete me* and *had me at hello* and *you've bewitched me* and *you make me a better man* and *you're perfect* and *you're a bird*—which, what the fuck does that even mean?" She stuck out her tongue. "Mushy."

"There were at least five butchered romance references in there, maybe more. You sound pretty knowledgeable to me," he teased.

"All movies *you* have forced me to watch. You live for sappy shit, is what I'm saying."

"They aren't sappy. And even if they were, there's nothing wrong with a little sap. They're hopeful. They show that love . . ." He trailed off. An idea formed, hazy and incomplete but more than anything he'd been working with so far.

Margot's brows rose. "Show that love . . . ?"

He riffed out loud, "What better way to prove to Annie that romance isn't dead than to show her?"

"Show her *what*? No offense, but I don't think forcing her to sit through a remedial rom-com marathon's really going to do the trick."

A lightbulb went off, puzzle pieces clicking into place. "You're a genius."

"Duh." Her expression faltered. "Mind filling me in on *why* I'm a genius?"

"Because you're right. Showing her a bunch of movies isn't going to cut it." He tossed his water bottle back into his bag with a grin. "Which is why I'm going to woo her."

"Woo her?" She shut her eyes and groaned. "You've got to be fucking kidding me."

"No, I'm serious. I'm going to woo Annie, and what better way to do it than by using my favorite movies as the blueprint?"

The greatest grand gestures and romantic moments? He was going to re-create them.

She stared at him blankly from behind her glasses.

"I'm serious, Mar. Do you know how many movies were either filmed or set in Seattle? *Say Anything, Sleepless in Seattle, 10 Things I Hate About You, Singles*—"

"I get the picture."

"This city's more romantic than anyone gives it credit for. We've got the greatest restaurants, the waterfront, a giant Ferris wheel—"

"What the fuck does a Ferris wheel have to do with romance?"

"Have you seen *The Notebook*? *Love, Simon*? *Never Been Kissed*?" Ferris wheels were a romance staple by this point. "You have no chance of being interrupted, you get a stellar view, it's private—"

"Ergo, romance." Margot rolled her eyes. "And your end goal with all of this is *what*? Make Annie fall in love with you?"

"All I'm looking to do is show her romance isn't a lost cause. That there's someone out there for everyone and the right person will be willing to sweep her off her feet. At the very least, we'll have fun."

If, on the off chance, something more came out of this plan? He wasn't going to complain. What was meant to be would be.

"And you don't think—" Margot pinched her lips together.

"You know what? Never mind. There's no point trying to reason with you when you get like this."

"What?" He grinned. "When I'm right?"

Margot shook her head. "One of these days, your hero complex is going to bite you in the ass. And *I* am going to have to bite my tongue to keep from saying I told you so."

Chapter Four

Thanks to bouncing from one time zone to another for work, Annie's internal clock was utterly botched. She had no problem falling asleep; the problem was staying asleep. Between overly firm hotel beds and early checkout times, seldom was she able to stay in bed past dawn.

To combat her insomnia, she'd taken up the highly masochistic hobby of early morning running.

Feeling thoroughly punished yet also a little loopy on endorphins, she used the bottom of her ratty old shirt to mop the sweat from her forehead and toed her way out of her running shoes, before padding into the kitchen with a single-minded purpose.

Coffee.

Her eyes swept the counter in search of Darcy's—*no*.

Eating up half the space beside the stove was a silver monstrosity with a wheel of buttons and more knobs and spouts than she could begin to guess what their function was.

This was not a coffeemaker, this was a contraption, one she was pretty sure she wasn't qualified to operate. There were too many buttons and no words, only symbols whose meaning was far more ambiguous than the manufacturer assumed. A coffee bean. A droplet of water. Two squiggly lines running parallel to one another, looking an awful lot like the zodiac symbol for Aquarius. A plus and minus sign beside one wheel, dots increasing from small to large beside another.

She squinted and scowled. Caffeine was not supposed to be a prerequisite to operate a coffeemaker . . . espresso machine . . . *whatever.*

Beside the professional-grade gadget were Darcy's mugs, bowl sized, white, and stacked upside down within their silver stand, no doubt to keep dust from gathering inside. She grabbed the top mug and clutched it in front of her chest, staring at the coffeemaker with disdainful eyes.

She could figure this out. She'd watched the baristas at Starbucks pull shots of espresso countless times. Worst-case scenario, she'd wind up with a too-strong brew she could doctor with cream and enough sugar to render the caffeine superfluous.

She set the mug beneath the spout to the right, her finger hovering in the air in front of the center wheel. She pressed the button with the cup-shaped symbol beside it and the whole machine came to life, the buttons on the front lighting up bright blue, the appliance whirring and churning as beans from the back cascaded down into the bowels of the machine and—

The nozzle at the front sputtered and a rich dark brew streamed down the front of the machine, down the cabinets, and onto the floor. *Fuck.* She fumbled for the mug and slid it beneath the proper spout before she made a bigger mess.

At least she'd figured the coffeemaker out. It hadn't been *that* difficult, just a little—

She had spoken too soon. Coffee reached the rim of the mug and sloshed over the sides, pooling on the counter and dripping onto the floor, the puddle growing. Hot espresso reached her toes, her feet slipping and sliding on the tile.

Fan-fucking-tastic.

She spun the knob in the center of the machine like she was on *Wheel of Fortune*, but the only change was that the coffee coming out of the spout was darker, blacker, *sludgy*.

Hands braced on the counter, her legs in a split around the puddle, she reached behind the coffeemaker, tugging the cord from the wall.

All at once, the machine cut off, not even powering down. Everything just stopped, the whirring and grinding and sloshing and sputtering giving way to blessed silence save for the thrum of her heartbeat inside her head.

The place was a wreck, a coffee-splattered war zone.

She sighed and grabbed a fistful of paper towels. Starbucks, it was.

One steamy shower later, she was dressed in a pleated maxi skirt in her favorite shade of blush, a white cropped T-shirt, and a sensible pair of gladiator sandals, her weather app promising sunshine and a high of seventy-four degrees. Flipping over to her web browser, she started to type.

Top ten things to do in Seattle—

Alone, autofill suggested.

"Thanks, Google," she muttered into the quiet of Darcy's living room.

Armed with an agenda of places to go and landmarks to see, a map of the downtown area bookmarked on her home screen, she shot one last glare at Darcy's coffeemaker. She snagged her keys from the entry table and opened the door.

Standing in the hall, fist poised to knock, was Brendon. Cradled in the nook of his right elbow was a white, nondescript box.

"Brendon. Hey." She stepped aside, waving him in. "What brings you by?"

"Believe it or not, I was in the neighborhood." He hefted the box a little higher. "On Saturday mornings, Margot—Elle's roommate, I'm sure you've heard of her—and I go rock climbing at a gym near the Seattle Center. Then we swing by this bakery on Roy Street and pick up pastries before heading over here for breakfast with Elle and Darce. It's turned into a tradition. Like game night, which I'm sure Darcy will tell you all about." He flipped the box around, opening the lid. Oh, sweet Jesus. Inside were at least a dozen flaky-looking pastries, all golden brown, the heavenly aroma of butter and fruit preserves wafting up to her nose, making her stomach grumble. His lips twitched. "I know Darcy's out of town, but it's hard to break a habit. I didn't think you'd mind."

Mind? She had to swallow so she wouldn't drool. "Yeah, I'm so offended right now. How dare you bring me something that looks this delicious. *Rude.*"

He laughed and stepped past her into the kitchen, setting the box on the counter. "The marzipan roll's my favorite, but I have it on good authority the white chocolate cherry Danish is damn good, too."

She plucked the cherry Danish out of the box, eager to dig

in. She moaned around her first bite, flushing when Brendon grinned. "'S good."

So good it almost rivaled the pastries she'd gorged herself on the last time she was in France.

"Told you." He snagged a marzipan roll and leaned his hip against the counter beside the evil espresso maker.

He was wearing a simple T-shirt with a giraffe on the front. The words above it proclaimed *Giraffes have ginormous hearts* and a speech bubble above the giraffe's mouth added, *I care a lot.* The cotton hugged his biceps, drawing her eyes to his arms. His pale skin was sprinkled with light brown hair and a smattering of freckles that crept up the side of his hand. His long fingers wrapped around his pastry, the tendon in his wrist flexing beneath the cross of dark blue veins.

She finished chewing and swallowed, tearing her eyes from his muscled forearms. "So. Rock climbing, huh?"

He dusted his hands off over the sink. "Margot got me into it."

Her eyes darted to the door. "Is Margot coming?"

He'd said this was their tradition, after all.

"Nah, she had other plans," he said, leaving it at that. He jerked his chin in the direction of Darcy's foyer. "Were you headed out?"

She nodded, eyeing the box of pastries, the almond croissant calling her name. Maybe he'd split it with her. "I was about to scout out the closest Starbucks."

Brendon made a choked sound and stood up straighter, shaking his head. "You're in Seattle. You can do better than the swill they call coffee."

Swill? She coughed. "Snob."

"They over-roast their beans!" His hand moved in front of his body as he gesticulated zealously. Powdered sugar dusted the room.

"Don't hurt yourself." She nodded at the espresso machine behind him. "I'm guessing I have you to thank for buying Darcy that infernal contraption?"

She certainly hadn't owned it when she'd roomed with Annie. Not to mention, Darcy didn't strike her as the type to own something so frivolous. As far as Annie knew, Darcy had been Team French Press. Maybe moving to Seattle had changed her, but Annie thought it was more likely someone else was responsible for the coffeemaker. Someone like Brendon.

He pressed his lips together, chin quivering. "Infernal contraption?"

She narrowed her eyes. "That is, by far, the nicest thing I've called it this morning. I spent ten minutes mopping espresso off the floor after it overflowed my mug. The buttons are incomprehensible. You shouldn't need a manual to make a cup of coffee."

"You push the button with the coffee cup on it and then set the dial to six, eight, or twelve ounces," he said, lips twitching.

Her face warmed. When he put it like that, it sounded straightforward.

"Or I could pay someone four dollars to do it for me. Plus, they have cinnamon dolce syrup. Darcy does not."

His face scrunched in obvious distaste. "Over-roasted *and* overpriced. You're killing me. You're going to pay four bucks for burned bean water?"

She smirked. "Burned bean water with milk and sugar."

Brendon shivered in mock horror. "No way. Absolutely not."

"Excuse me?" She was *going* to get her coffee come hell or high water.

"You heard me. I can't in good conscience let you settle for Starbucks while you're in Seattle. I'll show you good coffee."

She shifted awkwardly on her feet. While she wouldn't mind the company, she didn't want to impose. "You don't have to do that. I'm sure you have plans."

He rocked back on his heels. "Now I do." He grinned, dimples flashing. "Grab your keys. I'm going to introduce you to Seattle."

☾

Brendon did a shitty job of disguising his revulsion, his lips puckering as Annie slurped her extra-large caramel crunch frappe through her straw.

"Want a sip?" She held out her drink, laughing when he nearly tripped over the curb in his haste to back away.

"No, I do not. It's not even *coffee.*"

"The three shots of espresso in here beg to differ." She smiled around her straw.

"It's a glorified milkshake. A six-dollar glorified milkshake."

"And it's tasty." Between the sugar and caffeine, she was feeling much perkier. "Besides, what do you have against milkshakes?"

He grimaced. "You don't remember?"

She craned her neck to look up at him. "Remember what?"

The freckled bridge of his nose crinkled. "That time I bet you I could finish my milkshake first? Ring any bells?"

The memory hit her like a freight train. Immediately, her eyes scrunched shut, her lips rolling inward, the rest of her shuddering. "Don't. You're going to retraumatize me. You ruined me for French fries for over a year."

A serious feat seeing as French fries were one of her favorite foods.

"I ruined *you* on French fries?" His shoulders shook with laughter as they wiggled their way through the Saturday morning foot traffic near Pike Place Market. "I'm the one who had the fry lodged up his nose."

She gagged. "Don't talk about it!"

A simple bet on who could finish their milkshake first—Darcy had been unable to participate, what with being lactose intolerant—had resulted in Brendon, thirteen at the time, barfing in the parking lot of In-N-Out. She'd gotten the worst brain freeze of her life and somehow—she still wasn't entirely sure how it was physiologically possible—Brendon had wound up with a poorly chewed French fry lodged up his nose in the aftermath of puking his guts out. It was stuck inside his nasal cavity to the point where it had required a trip to the emergency room to dislodge it.

"Talk about it? I had to live it. I can't look at a milkshake without my sinuses stinging."

Her own nose burned sympathetically. "Fair. But the point stands—you don't have to like it, but this counts as coffee."

"I take you to the coffee shop that, arguably, has the best organic, ethically sourced coffee in the city and you order *that*." He clucked his tongue against his teeth. "Shame."

She slurped. "I feel *awful*."

Crossing the street, he guided her alongside the market, past stalls of handcrafted soaps, locally sourced honey, bright bouquets of flowers, fresh produce, jewelry, and mason jars full of pepper jelly. A few yards away, a crowd gathered around men in heavy-duty orange rubber overalls hurling huge salmon across a counter while shouting.

A gentle tug on her wrist stopped her from stepping inside the covered market for a closer look. Brendon jerked his chin to the left. "Come on. I want to show you something."

Without letting go of her hand, he led her around a corner, veering off down a shadowy tunnel that opened up into an alley, the brick walls covered in—

"Gum?" She laughed.

So much gum, more gum than brick. Pink and red, vibrant blues and dusty yellows, off-white, orange, green—wads and wads of gum were stuck to the walls of the alley, several inches thick. It was as disgusting as it was fascinating.

"The Gum Wall." He reached inside his pocket and withdrew two sticks of Juicy Fruit, offering her one. "I know it's touristy, but it's a Seattle landmark. You've got to go at least once."

She set her drink down on the cobblestones close to the wall and unwrapped the stick of gum, sliding it between her lips, biting it in half. A burst of watermelon hit her tongue, tart and sweet. She chewed until the stick lost its shape, fruity flavor flooding her mouth.

Brendon's lips rolled together and his tongue slipped out, covered in green gum. His cheeks puffed, his nostrils twitching, a ginormous bubble forming in front of him. It went from opaque to translucent, the gum growing thinner and thinner.

She wasn't entirely sure what possessed her to do it, but she reached out, popping Brendon's bubble. A thin sheen of pale green gum covered his lips, his cheeks, the tip of his nose, the little cleft in his chin.

He froze, eyes wide and lips parted, gum stringing between them. "I can't believe you just did that."

She snickered and grabbed her phone, snapping a quick shot of Brendon covered in gum. "Sorry?"

Chuckling, he began the arduous process of scraping bits of gum free from his stubble. Finally, he figured out that it was easier to roll it off, his fingers making little concentric circles until most of the gum was gone, save for the bit clinging to the side of his nose.

She stifled a laugh and pointed. "You've got some right there."

He rubbed at the wrong side. "Did I get it?"

"No, it's—" She stood on her toes, reaching up to do it for him, huffing when it wouldn't budge. "It's really sticky."

His breath tickled her hand. "That's what she said."

She snorted and smacked his arm. "Hold still. I can't get it if you keep wiggling your head."

His nose scrunched. "Sorry. It tickles."

Her calves were beginning to burn from standing on her tippy-toes. "You're too tall."

One of his hands dropped to her waist, holding her steady as he leaned closer. Close enough that she could count the freckles on the bridge of his nose. His tongue sneaked out, wetting his bottom lip. His breath smelled fruity sweet, wafting gently in her face. "Better?"

She nodded quietly, tongue-tied.

Ding! Ding!

She jerked forward, colliding into Brendon as a bicycle passed behind her, skirting the wall as it zipped down the alley and around the corner, disappearing from sight.

"You good?"

They were pressed tightly together from their chests to their knees. The hand he'd had resting on her hip had curved around her waist, holding her against him, keeping her steady.

Her tongue stuck to the roof of her mouth, her knees suddenly stupidly weak. "Mm-hmm."

She lifted her face from where it was buried against his firm chest. Sunlight caught on his pale, enviably long lashes when he blinked, bringing out the flecks of amber in his irises, his pupils appearing blacker by contrast.

He chuckled, the vibration of his laughter rumbling all the way down to her toes. *All* the way. "You sure?"

She stepped back, dropping her hands, flushing hotly as her fingers brushed the solid steel of his arms on the way down. "Yep."

Just peachy.

His gaze dropped to the ground. "Ah shit. Dropped my gum."

It was impossible to tell which piece was his, the cobblestones covered, nearly as much as the buildings to either side of them.

"Better the ground than stuck in my hair," she said, shaking off how being pressed up against him had bizarrely knocked her off-kilter.

He hummed his agreement. "True. Want to add yours to the wall?"

Heat crept up her jaw. "I, um. I swallowed it."

Between the cyclist and being pressed against Brendon, she'd gulped it down without thinking.

"You want a picture?"

"Sure." She smiled at his offer, passing him her phone.

He snapped several pictures in quick succession.

When she held her hand out for her phone, he lifted it out of reach. "Got to make sure they turned out."

He swiped, chuckling when his gum-covered face appeared. He swiped once more and the last picture she'd taken flashed across the screen, a shot of Trafalgar Square at dusk.

"London?" he asked, passing her the phone.

She nodded.

"What's your favorite place you've traveled?"

She slipped her phone inside her bag and grabbed her drink off the ground. "Are we talking for work or in general?"

"In general."

"Hmm. That's tough, but I'd have to probably go with France."

"Paris?"

She shook her head. "Paris is beautiful, but I was lucky enough to spend three weeks in Provence during lavender season. It was all rolling fields of purple flowers and the air smelled amazing. I slept with the windows open."

His eyes crinkled. "That sounds beautiful. And it makes me think of this little town, Sequim, that's not *too* far from here. It's known as the 'Lavender Capital of North America.' It's where most of the lavender at the market comes from."

That sounded—and, no doubt, smelled—amazing. "I wish I were here longer. I'd love to see it."

He smiled. "Well, you've been to Provence, so . . ."

She laughed. "It *was* pretty unparalleled. The views were breathtaking." She sidestepped what appeared to be a fresh wad of gum, not wanting to ruin her shoes, and her arm bumped his gently. "How about you? What's your favorite place you've ever been?"

With a chuckle, he ran a hand across his jaw. The way he glanced at her from the corner of his eye seemed almost bashful. "It's . . . well, it's not Provence."

She bumped him with her hip. "Come on. Tell me."

"It's . . . *gah.*" He covered his face. "You're going to laugh."

She did, but only because he was making a big deal out of it. "Does it have a funny name? Is it, like, Wank, Germany? Or Bendova, Czech Republic? Intercourse, Pennsylvania?"

He threw his head back and laughed loudly. "*No.*"

Then it couldn't be that bad.

"Okay." He calmed down, clearing his throat. "It's Tomorrowland."

Tomorrow . . . "Disney?"

A flush crept up the side of his jaw as he stared straight ahead. "Yup."

Her smile grew. "*Brendon.*"

"I know, I *know.* It's ridiculous that you've traveled to all these amazing places and my favorite place on the planet is Disneyland."

That wouldn't do. She poked him in his very solid arm. "I'll have you know, Space Mountain is my all-time favorite roller coaster. I used to think—well, I still do—the asteroids looked like giant chocolate chip cookies."

His eyes widened. "I love Space Mountain. As soon as I was

tall enough to ride, I made Darcy ride it with me over and over again. She got so sick of it."

"I could never get sick of Space Mountain. I love roller coasters."

"Yeah?" His smile grew and he nodded his head to the right. "I've got an idea. Let's go this way."

She followed him deeper down the alley and around the corner. He stopped in front of a long wooden pier and pointed up at a giant Ferris wheel. "It's no roller coaster, but it's close."

Hand cupped over her brow, she shielded her face from the glare of the sun and stared up at the wheel. "Let's do it."

Frappe empty, she ducked over to a trash can beside the public bathroom. She hesitated, eyeing the door to the restroom. In the last two hours, she'd consumed a whopping thirty-two ounces of iced coffee and her bladder had reached capacity.

"Annie." She turned. The line had moved and Brendon was at the front, standing near the attendant, waving her over. She glanced back at the restroom and frowned. It was a Ferris wheel; how long could it take to go in a circle? Fifteen minutes?

"Come on!" Brendon called again, the attendant tapping his foot behind him, beginning to look annoyed, as if she were holding things up.

She could wait fifteen minutes.

Having hit the sweet spot on timing, they were the only two people in their cabin. She settled in atop the leather bench seat, wiggling a little to get comfortable. The bench could've comfortably sat four grown adults and yet Brendon sat directly beside her, their knees knocking gently as he stretched his long legs out in front of him.

The wheel was relatively slow moving; it took five minutes for their cabin to reach the top. The view was more than worth the wait. Sunlight glinted off the placid, glassy blue surface of Elliott Bay. To the right, the Space Needle stood tall and proud against a clear, blue sky.

"Mount Rainier." He pointed at the snowcapped mountain looming majestically in the distance. "We picked a good day to come up here."

She dug into the depths of her bag for her phone, wanting more pictures. "It's beautiful."

"It is."

The space between her shoulder blades itched with awareness. She turned. He was staring at her, not the view, and his brown eyes were locked on her face, his lips tipped up at the corners.

"You ever miss San Francisco?" she asked, changing the subject. He wasn't implying *she* was beautiful. That would be ridiculous, not to mention utterly corny. People didn't say things like that in real life. Not to her, they didn't.

He shifted on the bench, his thigh pressing firmly alongside hers. "Sometimes. I miss In-N-Out, but Dick's isn't bad."

"*Dick's?*" What was that? A—she wasn't even going to let her brain fill in the blanks.

"Burger joint. Great fries. I've heard they make a decent milkshake." His smile went charmingly crooked. "Not that I'd know."

"I'll have to check it out. See for myself how it stacks up."

He nodded. "You picked the best time of year to visit. Nothing beats summer in Seattle. It's a running joke that if you want to convince someone to move here you should get them to visit May to September."

"Not October through April?"

He bobbed his head from side to side. "That's the rainy season. Not that it rains as much as people say it does. Miami gets almost double the rainfall annually as Seattle. It just drizzles a lot."

"I don't mind rain." A good thing, as London was known for being gray, almost as much as Seattle.

"It grows on you," he agreed. "How about you?"

"Do I miss San Francisco?"

He nodded.

She tucked her hair behind her ear and shrugged. "The last time I was in San Francisco was . . . four years ago? It's not really home anymore."

Not that anywhere felt like home these days.

"Four years?" He sounded surprised.

"My parents moved back to Greece after my dad retired."

His brows knit. "Wow. That's—far."

"I visit for Christmas. One year, I even managed to swing an extra week of vacation and I was able to spend my birthday over there."

"*One* year? What do you usually do for your birthday? It's on the nineteenth, right?"

"Facebook tell you that?" she teased.

He stared at her. "I don't need Facebook to remind me of your birthday, Annie. I've known you half my life."

Known was a bit of a stretch, but she knew what he meant.

"When Darcy was still in Philadelphia, we'd usually go out to celebrate at a restaurant of her choice, a fancy place she heard about on Food Network." Her eye roll was fond. "And if my birthday fell on a weekday, she'd have my favorite bakery deliver a dozen cupcakes to my office."

"Sounds like Darce." Brendon smiled.

Last year on Annie's birthday, she'd ordered an obscene amount of sushi and eaten it all by herself while bingeing her favorite French reality show. Darcy had still sent her cupcakes to the office, but it hadn't compared to spending her birthday with her best friend.

She could feel her smile slipping, wavering at the edges, melancholy threatening to overwhelm her, because next December Darcy would still be here in Seattle and Annie would be across the world and who knew if Darcy could even have cupcakes delivered from that far away? She clenched her back teeth together and grinned, reminding herself that Darcy was happy here and that was what mattered. "You must've been thrilled when Darcy moved to town. And then your mom?"

"Darcy, sure. Mom . . ." Brendon made a vague, frazzled gesture, his hand sweeping out in front of him before his fingers twitched and he ran them through his hair, leaving it sweetly disheveled. It was longer than she remembered it ever being. Not *long*, but nothing like the crop he'd had when he was a kid. His auburn hair was thick, lush, the kind of hair you could sink your fingers into. "I'm sure you know how my mom is."

She knew enough from Darcy. Gillian Lowell was, well— *mercurial* would be putting it kindly. Her highs were high and her lows *low*. She'd checked out following her divorce, leaving Darcy to care for Brendon until their grandmother stepped in.

Her heaping loads of undue responsibility on Annie's best friend would forever make Annie look at Gillian sideways.

"It seems like she's happy here," she said. "Darcy, I mean."

He cracked a smile. "All thanks to Elle."

She bumped his arm with hers. "All thanks to your matchmaking."

His shoulders rose, his shrug lazy as he sank back against the bench seat, slouching. The cocky smirk curling his lips should've been totally unappealing but instead it made her insides twist. The fuck? "There you have it. Proof that romance isn't dead."

Oh, Jesus. She laughed. "This again?"

He tsked softly. "Did you think I forgot?"

"Here I was hoping," she joked, crossing her legs.

She really should've peed. The pressure in her abdomen abated with the shift in position, the shouting of her bladder subsiding into something she could ignore . . . for now.

"Well, I didn't forget."

Of course he hadn't. Because that would be too easy and completely unlike Brendon. Pigheaded was right. "Look, I didn't say people couldn't fall in love. I just think true love is rare. The kind that goes the distance. Most people want easy. But every rule has an exception."

"Most people," he repeated, eyes locked on her face, studying her closely.

She dipped her chin.

"And this rule." He sat up straighter. "You'd say Elle was the exception for my sister?"

"I guess?"

"So it would stand to reason that maybe you haven't met your exception yet." He looked smug at his deductive reasoning, his twisting of her logic.

She wasn't going to hold her breath. Maybe every rule had an exception and maybe there was someone out there *perfect* for her, but while Brendon might've found the prospect of seven billion people promising, she found the odds bleak. Bleaker than bleak. "The exceptions *prove* the rule. The fact you can enumerate a finite list highlights the rarity of the exceptions."

"The exceptions prove the rule?" The arch of his brow screamed skepticism.

"It's a *thing*."

He threw his head back, laughter filling the glass-enclosed gondola. "Sure."

"Shut up." She pressed her hand to the cool glass. "Shouldn't we be moving?"

He shut his eyes, lips curling in a lazy little grin, his empty coffee cup resting against his flat stomach. "You're not scared of heights, are you?"

"I told you I love roller coasters. Heights don't bother me."

Her bladder, on the other hand, was hard to ignore.

Above their heads, crackling static came from a recessed speaker. A throat cleared. "Um, sorry for the interruption, folks. We're having some technical difficulties, which is why we've been stalled out for the last few minutes." *Few minutes?* They'd been up here for going on half an hour. "Good news is, our technician is taking a look as we speak. Sit tight and we should have the wheel up and running shortly."

Perfect. God only knew how long they'd be stuck in this cabin, dangling up in the air.

She crossed her legs tighter, and when that didn't relieve the pressure, she leaned forward, bracing her hands on the bench to either side of her, her fingers gripping the leather seat.

Brendon set his hand on her shoulder. "You okay?"

She opened her mouth, pausing when her bladder seized, cramping. Her lips twisted. "Yeah. I'm fine."

She was *not* fine. She felt like she was about to burst, to be honest. She released her grip on the bench and crossed her legs the opposite direction, squirming in her seat.

He frowned. "You sure?"

"I should've stopped by the restroom before getting on. I didn't think we'd get stuck up here," she admitted, warmth creeping up the back of her neck.

He winced. "Sorry."

"Because you're totally responsible for my bladder." She huffed out a laugh, scrunching her nose. On second thought, laughing was bad. "Distract me."

His eyes dipped, his gaze landing and lingering on her mouth, making her wonder for one bizarre moment what method of distraction he was considering.

She swallowed hard. Either Brendon freaking Lowell had miraculously gotten her wet with just that look, or she had peed a little. She *really* needed to up her Kegel game.

Whatever method of distraction he had in mind didn't matter when her phone rang, Rick Astley's "Never Gonna Give You Up" blaring from inside her bag.

He laughed. "Is that your ringtone?"

She fished around inside her purse, finding her phone buried deep beneath her wallet. "Just for Darcy."

Her thumb hovered over the screen, ultimately sending Darcy to voicemail. She was a smidge preoccupied at the moment, her bladder making it difficult to concentrate. That, and she was with Brendon. He deserved her—mostly—undivided attention.

She slipped her phone back inside her bag. She'd call Darcy later.

"Have you heard of the Astley paradox?" he asked.

She shook her head. "Is it like the Mandela effect? Where half the people remember something one way and half don't? Because I swear on all that's holy the Monopoly man once wore a monocle."

"Yes!" He slapped his thighs eagerly. "Or, *Rudolph the Red-Nosed Reindeer.* The Abominable Snowman—"

"Had a toothache!" Thank God she wasn't the only one who remembered that. "And the little dentist elf fixed it and then he—"

"Bumble," he said. "The Abominable Snowman's name was Bumble."

"Bumble." She nodded. "Then he wasn't abominable anymore."

He sighed grimly. "I don't get how people don't remember that."

"Right? Too weird." Her bladder gave another twinge. "So this Astley paradox?"

"Oh, right." He swiveled slightly, their knees knocking. "No, totally different. Okay, imagine you ask Rick Astley to borrow his copy of the movie *Up.*"

She nodded, going along with the hypothetical situation wherein she'd, first, *know* Rick Astley, and, second, need to borrow an animated movie. "All right."

Brendon laughed softly under his breath. "He can't give it to you because he promised he's never going to give you up."

Oh God. She shut her eyes. "Geez."

"*But*," he continued, "by not letting you borrow the movie, he's letting you down. Something else he promised to never do. A paradox."

"That's so hokey." She grinned. "I *do* love that movie, though."

"*Up?*"

She nodded. "Arguably my favorite Pixar film. Though, *WALL-E* is a close second."

His lips parted. "I think I'm in love."

She laughed and—bad idea. *Epically* bad idea. The pressure in her bladder grew harder to ignore. She breathed shallowly. "I'm guessing you like *Up*, too?"

"Don't tell Darcy, okay?" He reached for the bottom hem of his shirt and started to lift it, revealing his flat stomach with its *many* ridges. Chiseled. That was the word. Brendon's body was chiseled.

Heat crept up her jaw. "What are you doing?"

More like, why the hell was he taking his clothes off? Not that she was complaining, per se, but still . . .

He grinned, hiking his shirt up under his armpits. "Yeah, you could say *Up* is one of my favorites."

On his chest, over his left pectoral, was a bright splash of color. Hundreds of vividly colored balloons were inked into his skin in shades of pink and green and red and blue, just as bright and cheerful as the gum wall they'd visited. Beneath the balloons was a tiny house floating beneath his flat nipple.

She bit her lip, clenching her fingers into fists so she wouldn't do something silly like reach out and trace the pigmented lines. "That's adorable. Not to mention, really well done. I love it."

He beamed at her and dropped his shirt, covering himself back up. "Thanks."

"Why am I not supposed to tell Darcy?"

He shot her a look that screamed *duh*. "Darce *hates* tattoos. I mean, she's fine with them on other people, but me? I'd never hear the end of it."

She snickered. "You're kidding."

The look on his face said he wasn't.

"Okay, let me tell you a little about your sister," she said, grinning because this was juicy knowledge Darcy would *hate* his knowing, but harmless. Brendon would get a kick out of it. "The summer we moved to Philadelphia for college, Darcy and I— I'm glad you're sitting down—got matching tattoos."

His jaw dropped. "You're shitting me."

She shook her head. No, but she was worried she was going to pee herself. "Nope, matching *butterfly* tattoos."

She bit her lip, smiling around it. That had been a good night.

"Were you guys drunk?" he asked, agog.

"No. Well, I wasn't." She didn't need alcohol to make impulsive decisions. She made those just fine sober.

"Where? I've never seen—" His face scrunched in horror. "Forget I asked."

"Where does every eighteen-year-old girl born in the late eighties or early nineties get a butterfly tattoo when three sheets to the wind?" She grinned. "Your sister is one hundred percent in possession of a secret tramp stamp."

He grinned. "Oh, she's going to *hate* it when she finds out that I know."

"Which is why you aren't going to tell her I told you," she said sweetly, though her smile was a threat unto itself. "She'll *murder* me."

He dipped his chin. "Fair. I can keep a secret." He cocked his head to the side, eyes narrowing thoughtfully. "So, does this mean *you* also have a tattoo on your—"

Overhead, the speaker crackled to life once more. "Hi again. Sorry about the wait, folks. Nothing to worry about, but it does look like we've got a bit of an issue with our electrical system. The maintenance crew's working to get the backup generator up and running. They've estimated that it shouldn't take longer than fifteen minutes. We're sorry about the inconvenience, so we'll be refunding tickets once we get you all back down here safely."

Fifteen minutes. She whimpered.

She had no choice but to hold it, but she wasn't sure she could. She shifted, rocking forward, squirming in her seat, her feet tap-dancing against the glass floor.

Brendon popped the lid off his coffee. He held the cup out, offering it to her. "Okay. Enough is enough. *Urine* luck."

She stared at him. "I'm not peeing in a cup, Brendon."

"Look, I know it's not ideal—"

"No way."

It wasn't *not ideal*; it was not on the table. Not an option. She wasn't about to pee in a coffee cup in a glass-encased gondola hovering hundreds of feet in the air with Brendon beside her.

"Come on. Haven't you ever peed in front of Darcy?"

His point? "Yeah, *Darcy*. My best friend."

"How about people you've dated?"

Uh . . . "No?"

"Seriously?"

She stared at him. "Have you?"

"Well, no, but—"

She laughed, immediately regretting it when she was forced to clamp down hard on her pelvic floor muscles.

"Everyone pees, Annie."

"Not in front of people, they don't."

"You're telling me your parents never peed in front of each other?"

"That's different! They're married."

Not that anyone had, but under any circumstance where someone she'd dated would've witnessed her relieve herself, they'd have likely already seen her naked. Seeing as Brendon was neither her best friend, nor had he ever seen her naked, nor were they dating, she couldn't justify peeing in front of him.

He laughed. "Okay."

"I'm fine. I'll hold it."

Easier said than done. Breathing was beginning to hurt, her was stomach swollen, and squirming and crossing her legs were no longer providing any relief.

More static crackled over the speaker and she held her breath. "Our technicians are hard at work on getting our backup generator up and running, but we've hit a minor snag. We're now looking at about a thirty-minute delay."

Half an hour. She hugged her arms around her stomach and groaned.

He jiggled his coffee cup at her. "I promise I won't look."

She couldn't believe she was actually considering this. Peeing in a coffee cup in public. Not that anyone could see—save for Brendon—unless they had binoculars, but still.

Unfortunately, her bladder didn't care a whit about where she was. She sighed and snagged the cup from him, clutching it in her fist, staring down at the drops of coffee clinging to the wax-coated interior. Her bladder was stupid full; what if she peed too much? She had already had one disaster with a coffee cup over-flowing today, and that was one disaster too many. Overflowing this cup would be catastrophic.

Swallowing down her mortification, she pinned Brendon with a hard stare. "Turn around and . . . talk. Loudly."

Loudly enough to drown out her peeing, please.

Brendon spun around, throwing one leg over the seat, strad-dling the bench, giving her his broad back. "Am I going to have to do something to embarrass myself? Even the playing field to make you feel better?"

She slid forward on the bench and reached under her skirt, tugging her underwear down. Just like sitting on a toilet . . . hopefully there weren't cameras on this damn ride. "Are you of-fering to whip it out and pee in front of me?"

He laughed. "I mean . . . would that actually make you feel better?"

"Doubtful."

"Thought so."

"Hey. Brendon?"

"Mm-hmm?"

"You stopped talking."

"Oh, right. Uh . . . did Darcy ever tell you about the time we went down to the Underground for an escape room?"

"I think she mentioned something about it?"

"It was a lot of fun, actually. We wound up . . ."

She tuned out his words, instead focusing on the deep cadence of his voice, her face flaming as she prepared to pee in this stupid coffee cup. It took her bladder a moment to get the memo that it was okay to relax. At the first echoey splash, she nearly jumped out of her skin.

His words faltered for a split second before he raised his voice, nearly shouting. "So yeah, it was fun. Solved a bunch of puzzles, and you should've seen the look on Darcy's face when Elle . . ."

Her bladder breathed a sigh of relief, even as her head went dizzy with mortification. She'd actually done it. Peed in a coffee cup on top of a Ferris wheel. That was one item she could cross off her bucket list of unanticipated, humiliating acts she never wanted to repeat.

She wrinkled her nose at the cup and wiggled her underwear back up her thighs one-handed. "Brendon."

He stopped talking. "Yeah?"

Her face burned. "Can I have the lid?"

"Oh." He passed the flimsy plastic lid over his shoulder.

She snapped it on and then stared blandly at the cup in her hand. At least it was well insulated and opaque. No one would be the wiser as to its contents save for her and Brendon, which was bad enough.

"You can turn around now. I'm . . . done."

At first, she thought she was imagining things, the lightness

of her bladder throwing her off, making her feel like the gondola was moving. But no. Their cabin swayed, beginning a slow,
smooth descent back down to Earth.

She clutched the cup in her fist and groaned when Brendon
snorted, covering his laughter with a cough.

Thirty minutes, her ass.

Chapter Five

Brendon was 99 percent sure Annie's giant tote contained some sort of portal to another realm. How she crammed that much stuff inside one purse was a mystery, but she managed to withdraw a pair of earrings, several quarters, her passport, a tangled pair of earbuds, one of those ultra-flat flip-flops nail salons handed out, and a bottlecap, all before finally muttering a quick, "*Aha!*," Darcy's key jingling in her hand. "Let's pretend today never happened."

"Ah, come on. It wasn't—"

"Shh." She pressed a finger to her lips. "Let us never speak of this day again."

He chuckled. "It wasn't that bad. At least no worse than going to the hospital for emergency French fry removal after puking your guts up in front of the girl you have a crush on."

Annie shoved the key inside Darcy's door and paused, looking over her shoulder, her eyes wide.

"What?"

Her face flushed the prettiest shade of rose pink to match

her skirt. "I just—I wasn't expecting you to come right out and say it."

"Was it a secret?" He laughed. "Worst-kept secret ever, then. I wasn't exactly covert." There were probably prehistoric cave drawings, hieroglyphs detailing his feelings for her. That was how obvious he had been. "Darcy still gives me grief about it to this day."

"You were cute. I was flattered."

He ducked his chin and gripped the back of his neck. "Cute, what every teenage boy aspires to be." He lifted his eyes and stepped closer, leaning against the door frame. Close enough to breathe in the fruitiness of Annie's coconut body lotion. His tongue curled against the back of his teeth, his mouth watering. Sunscreen and watermelon Jolly Ranchers, coconut and sunshine—even in the dead of winter Annie had always smelled like summer. "I was delusional. You were so far out of my league."

The corners of Annie's mouth tightened when she swallowed, the smooth skin of her throat jerking, her lids fluttering as she stared up at him from beneath a fringe of dark lashes. "I don't know about that."

It was true. "You were beautiful and funny and my older sister's cool, popular best friend." All of which was still true. "And I could barely string a sentence together in front of you."

She scoffed, her blue-green eyes bright as she rolled them to the ceiling. "I was not—"

"You *were*." He dropped his hand, tucking both inside his front pockets so he wouldn't revert to bad habits and fidget.

He'd never known what to do with his hands around her. "And my idea of flirting was challenging you to a milkshake-drinking competition."

Annie's throaty chuckle made the hair on the back of his neck stand on end, his heart rate ratcheting up like he'd run a mile at breakneck speed. "You might've missed the mark on that one." Her tongue poked out between her lips as she lifted her hand, holding her fingers a smidge apart. "Just a little."

He clicked his tongue against the back of his teeth, shaking his head. "I knew I screwed up somewhere."

"I'm sure you know what you're doing now." She leaned her head back against the door, her blond waves cascading over her shoulders, the tips of her hair flirting with the swells of her breasts.

His mouth fell open as he stared at her.

"I mean . . ." Her eyes darted from side to side, pink creeping up the front of her throat. "You created a dating app, for Christ's sake." Her laugh was sharp, high-pitched. She scratched the side of her neck. "According to Darcy, you don't have any trouble meeting women."

Perhaps he didn't have trouble meeting women, and maybe he knew how to talk to them without flailing his hands like a fool—most of the time—but he had yet to meet the *right* woman. Someone he clicked with. Someone who made his heart race and his palms sweat with a single smile.

Someone like Annie.

He'd had more fun playing tourist in his own city with her than he'd had on the last ten dates he'd been on. She made him laugh, and if the way she had checked him out meant anything, he was positive the attraction was mutual.

His brows rose. "You and Darcy sure talk about me a lot."

"She cares about you." She shrugged and stared at his shoulder. "And I care about her."

What would it take to become someone Annie cared about? He wanted to find out everything there was to know about her, not just to prove her wrong about romance's being dead, but to satisfy his own burning curiosity.

What he'd told Margot this morning was no longer true. Not the whole truth, at least. This was no longer merely about a point of pride, the principle of the matter.

This *was* personal.

"I know you'd probably rather be spending time with Darcy, but I hope, in the meantime, I'm a suitable stand-in."

She smiled up at him. "More than suitable. I appreciate you showing me around. Today was fun." Her nose wrinkled. "Minus the mortification."

"Come on, we bonded, Annie."

"*Bonded?*" She laughed. "Okay."

"I told you I'd be happy to even the score. Humiliate myself somehow."

It was bound to happen at some point organically.

Her brows rose. "Promise?"

He held out his little finger. "*Pinky* promise."

"Ooh." She hooked her fingers around his and he held tight for a second longer than appropriate. "Serious stuff."

"Right up there with double-dog dares."

She snickered and dropped her hand, leaning her head against Darcy's door. The way she arched her back caused her cropped shirt to rise even higher, revealing a strip of smooth, golden skin. "I look forward to you following through."

She'd played into his hands perfectly.

"I always keep my promises. How's tomorrow work for you?"

Annie shot him a puzzled frown.

"Darcy's not back until Monday," he said.

"Right. I keep forgetting it's a holiday weekend. Tomorrow, then. As long as I'm not interfering with any plans you have."

He didn't have plans, but even if he had, Annie was only in town for two and a half weeks. The clock was ticking, the time to both prove his point and explore the sparks between them—to see if there was something more than simple attraction at play—limited.

He refused to waste a single moment.

☾

ANNIE (7:17 P.M.): You should've warned me your brother is even hotter in person.

Predictably, her phone rang two minutes later.

"You're disgusting," Darcy greeted her.

Annie threw herself down on Darcy's couch and laughed. "Hello to you, too. How's Vancouver?"

"Wonderful." She paused, muffled sounds filtering through the speaker. "Elle says hi. Now, don't change the subject."

"You're too easy. You realize that, right?" Darcy's mod, chrome-colored floor lamp cast shadows across the ceiling. Annie stretched her legs out, holding them up, tracing the shadows with her toes.

"Are you telling me you *don't* find my brother"—she gagged—"hotter in person?"

"No, no. I do. It's just, I bet if I'd have texted you, *Hey, what's up*, it would've taken you an hour to respond."

"We'll never know the answer to that now, will we?" Darcy sounded smug. "Besides, I called you earlier and you sent me to voicemail."

This was true. "I was a little preoccupied."

"It's fine. How was your first day in Seattle? See anything interesting?"

The way Brendon had looked at her had certainly been *interesting*, her own reactions even more so. But she wasn't about to confess that to Darcy. "As a matter of fact, I did. Your brother played tour guide."

A long pause followed. "He did, did he?"

"He did."

Darcy *hmm*ed quietly under her breath.

She rolled her eyes. "Don't *hmm* me. He took me to the Gum Wall and up on the Great Wheel. It was fun."

"Huh."

"What did I just say?"

"That was a *huh*, not a *hmm*. Phonetically worlds apart."

"Are you really going to condescend to me, of all people, about linguistic variants? Seriously?"

"I just think it's interesting. That's all."

That's all never meant that was *truly* all when it came from Darcy's mouth. It was the equivalent of a comma. Better yet, an ellipsis. A pregnant pause.

Predictably, Darcy took a breath before launching in. "You spent the day with my brother and then you text me that he's hotter in person."

"To get your attention."

"It worked." Darcy huffed. "He had a crush on you, you know."

"*Eight* years ago."

"I think you're underestimating Brendon's ability to hold on to things."

She laughed. "He's persistent, I'll give him that. But it was a *crush*. You're acting like he was in love with me." She rolled her eyes, finding this entire conversation ludicrous.

"You know how baby animals imprint? How attached they get?"

Annie palmed her face. "Your brother didn't *imprint* on me. I'm getting shades of *Twilight* here. I refuse to be the funky CGI baby in this equation."

Darcy snickered. "You were his first crush. He liked you for *years*."

"And it's been years since he last saw me. He doesn't know me. Not beyond the basics."

"You spent the day together."

"It wasn't that deep."

"Did you have fun?"

"Yeah?"

Darcy *hmm*ed.

"You *hmm* me one more time and I'm hanging up on you."

Darcy laughed. "Wouldn't it be an interesting twist if after all these years, you wound up with my brother?"

Annie lifted the phone away from her ear and stared at the screen. "Okay, my caller ID says this is Darcy Lowell, but I'm not convinced. Who the hell are you and what have you done with my best friend?"

"I'm not going to start spouting off about soul mates any time soon, but maybe Elle's rubbed off on me. A little."

"A little," she repeated, reeling.

"Come on, Annie. If you married my brother, we'd be sisters. You could move to Seattle."

Married? Sisters? Move to *Seattle*? The fuck? "Are you *drunk*?"

Darcy giggled. *Giggled.* "I am not entirely sober at the moment."

In the background, Elle laughed.

"Okay. I'm going to let you go. Enjoy your night."

"No, I'm not finished."

Yeah, well, Annie was.

Elle sang into the receiver, "*Dum, dum, da dum.*"

Darcy lost it, laughing harder.

Annie palmed her face, her lips twitching. She was losing the battle, trying and failing not to laugh. "*Stop.* I'm not interested in your brother. I'm definitely not marrying him. Absolutely not."

"'Absolutely not'? What's that supposed to mean? What's wrong with my brother?"

Damned if she did, damned if she didn't. "*Nothing* is wrong with your brother. I don't *know* your brother."

"What's there to know? He's successful. He owns his own company. He's—"

"—and you think he's hot," Elle added, oh so helpfully.

Darcy did a poor job of muffling her laughter. "Brendon's sweet—"

"—you think he's *gorgeous*. You want to *kiss* him. You want to *bone* him—"

Darcy choked on her laughter.

"I do not." Annie huffed. "No, I do *not* want to kiss him. I do *not* want to bone him. I do *not* like—"

"—him, Sam-I-Am." Elle dissolved into riotous giggles.

"I don't want to date anyone!" Annie blurted. "Okay? I have sworn off dating entirely."

Elle's laughter petered out. From the muffled whispers, Annie was pretty sure Darcy had covered the receiver. She bit her lip, tempted to shove her face in one of Darcy's decorative pillows.

On the other end of the line, a door shut quietly. Darcy cleared her throat. "Sorry. I didn't mean to—"

"You're fine. I really should let you get back to your vacation. Back to Elle."

"Elle's fine," Darcy said, brushing off Annie's concerns. "Are *you*?"

She scoffed out a laugh. "Of course."

"Annie."

Her shoulders slumped. "Contrary to how my little outburst might make it seem, I really am fine. Promise."

She was fine. Just fine.

Darcy sighed. "I know I've been . . . wrapped up in Elle—"

"As you should be."

"But you're my best friend. I should be better about reaching out."

Annie bit down on the inside of her lip.

It was fine.

It was the natural course of things. Darcy had moved to Seattle. Annie lived on the opposite side of the country. Darcy was now happily coupled up with Elle. Annie was no longer the first person she called, the first person she texted, the first person she turned to.

Darcy was still Annie's person, but Annie wasn't hers.

It wasn't bad. It was normal. Annie was happy for her. Darcy deserved to be happy, deserved to be with someone who loved her as much as Elle.

Yet, on a deeply irrational, shitty, never-would-she-in-a-million-years-admit-it-aloud level, it stung.

She didn't begrudge Darcy her relationship. She just wished it didn't feel like the whole world was moving on while she was stuck standing still. Ironic, seeing as she was the one in constant motion, bopping from city to city, bouncing from one destination to the next. All her friends were settling down or trying. And she used the word *friend* loosely. They were more like acquaintances at this point, because for most people it was out of sight, out of mind. Annie was out of sight more often than not these days, and her brunch invitations had suffered for it.

"You've sworn off dating?" Darcy asked.

Annie pinched the bridge of her nose. "It's not a *thing*. Just . . ." She shrugged even though Darcy couldn't see her. "Just a lot of little disappointments that added up."

Disappointments that made the thought of putting herself out there, baring her heart, completely unappealing.

"I'm burned out," she added. "It's not fun, you know? I'm pretty sure it's supposed to be fun and it's become the opposite."

First dates had become something she dreaded more than trips to the dentist. At best, they were unromantic, more akin to job interviews than anything. At worst, they made her hope. And hope was a dangerous thing.

How many more times was she supposed to go on first dates where the other person expected her to jump into bed with them, to put out just because they bought her a drink?

How many more times was she supposed to shrug and cut her losses when people didn't want to put up with long distance, her job making it hard to nail down plans?

How many times was she supposed to ease into a new relationship, only to stare at her phone, waiting, wondering if she'd ever get a text back?

She'd been ghosted, roached, benched—if there was a dating term for it, she'd experienced it firsthand.

The last guy she'd dated had been the straw that broke the camel's back. After two months of dating, she'd been certain things between them were going well. Ryker was nice, a little stiff, but he occasionally made her laugh. He wasn't allergic to texting her back and he could successfully get her off. All points in his favor. Then she'd gone out of town for a two-week business trip and, upon returning, discovered they were less exclusive than she'd assumed when he told her he couldn't do dinner because he had plans with someone else. A date with someone else. It was her fault for assuming, but he'd made her feel stupid about it. He'd *laughed* when she'd admitted she hadn't known he was seeing other people.

She was tired. She was *done*.

Sparks didn't mean shit. And butterflies? Buzzards circling overhead was far more apt.

The next person she dated, if and when she decided to put herself out there, would be a safe, reliable choice. She didn't need sparks; she wanted . . . stability. Steadiness. Someone with a mind like a Trapper Keeper. Maybe that sounded boring, but she was tired of investing herself in people who didn't invest in her, butterflies be damned.

Darcy cleared her throat. "You said you had fun with Brendon."

She had. "It wasn't a date, Darcy."

Yes, she'd had fun.

And it was true, Brendon was gorgeous in a way that had totally taken her by surprise.

But that was it.

A fun day with a funny, attractive guy.

It didn't change the fact that she wasn't looking for love. Not with anyone; certainly not with her best friend's baby brother who didn't know her. If he still liked her, it was only because he had some false idea of her inside his head, because he'd put her on a pedestal. If she gave him the chance, if she let him get to know her, he'd move on to greener pastures.

Everyone always did.

It didn't change the fact that in two weeks she'd be back

in Philadelphia, there for a short stint to finish packing up her apartment.

It didn't change the fact that soon she'd be in London, half a world away.

Whatever attraction there was?

It didn't change anything.

Pretending otherwise would be silly.

But she couldn't say that over the phone. Two more days and she could tell Darcy in person, but not now.

"Okay," Darcy said. "I just . . . I care about you. And I care about my brother."

Another reason why her attraction to Brendon didn't change a thing.

He was Darcy's brother. And Darcy meant too much to her to risk their friendship over the potential of something more transpiring between her and Brendon. Transpiring and, inevitably, fizzling.

"Brendon makes a very cute tour guide." A fine—*very* fine—distraction until Darcy returned from vacation. Good company so she wasn't stuck exploring on her own. "But that's it."

Chapter Six

BRENDON (12:19 P.M.): Hey! Are we still on for today?

*A*nnie sipped the Starbucks cinnamon dolce latte she'd purchased around the corner from Darcy's apartment and hovered her thumb over her keyboard, remembering what she'd told Darcy on the phone.

Brendon makes a very cute tour guide. But that's it.

Whatever Darcy thought was going on? She was wrong. Brendon was showing her around Seattle. He was being friendly. So what if he'd gone from adorable, gangly teenager to broad shouldered and gorgeous? So what if he was wicked funny and made her laugh? It didn't mean anything that his smiles—and dimples—made her tingle. Utterly irrelevant.

ANNIE (12:27 P.M.): Sure. What time?

BRENDON (12:31 P.M.): If I swing by at 5, does that work?

She tipped her cup back, draining the dregs of her latte. That was nearly five hours from now. Breakfast had consisted of left-over pastries. She'd have to track down some real food for lunch, because Darcy's refrigerator was empty save for a bottle of pinot grigio and a box of Go-Gurt she'd bet belonged to Elle.

ANNIE (12:34 P.M.): Works for me ☺
ANNIE (12:36 P.M.): Where are we going?
BRENDON (12:37 P.M.): 😣

A secret. *Interesting.*

BRENDON (12:38 P.M.): Bring a jacket. Temps are dropping into the low sixties tonight.

They'd be outside. Not much of a hint. It was summer, or as good as, and most landmarks were outdoors. He could be taking her anywhere. The Space Needle. The . . . okay, that was the only guess she had. There was the market and Microsoft and Mount Rainier, and according to Darcy, the city's culture was eclectic. Actually, the word she'd used was *weird*, but in the past couple of months *weird* had earned the addition of *wonderfully*, so Annie had read between the lines.

ANNIE (12:39 P.M.): Will do!

His determination to prove to her that romance wasn't dead lingered in the back of her mind. Yesterday he might've dropped a few comments about love and romance into their conversations, but nothing so overt that she felt as if he'd actually tried. She couldn't help but wonder what sort of ace he had up his sleeve.

> **ANNIE (12:40 P.M.):** Are you sure I can't get a teeny hint?
>
> **BRENDON (12:46 P.M.):** 😖

C

At 4:55, there was a knock at the door.

"Coming!"

She stole one last sip of wine from the glass she'd been nursing over the past half hour and opened the door.

She immediately zeroed in on the bouquet of pink roses clutched in Brendon's left hand. There were at least two dozen, their stems long and tied off with a grosgrain ribbon the same color as the blooms.

Her eyes darted between the bouquet and Brendon's crinkle-eyed grin.

"Hi." He dimpled, offering her the flowers. "These are for you."

His fingers brushed hers as she took the roses from him, pleased to note there weren't any thorns to contend with, though the bouquet was heavier than she'd expected. She choked up on the stems when the bouquet wobbled, teetering to the side.

She walked backward, waving him inside. Hopefully Darcy had a vase tucked away somewhere. "They're beautiful, Brendon. Thank you."

Truth be told, she found roses overrated—not to mention their aroma funky—but she wasn't about to tell him that because the gesture was sweet. She couldn't remember the last time anyone had bought her flowers.

He shut the door behind her, following her into the kitchen, where he went straight for the cabinet beside the sink and grabbed a crystal vase from the top shelf. He turned on the tap, filling it with several inches of water. "I wasn't sure whether you'd prefer pink or red."

"Pink's my favorite color."

Brendon beamed at her. "You ready to head out?"

"Still won't tell me where we're going?" She grabbed her jacket off the bar and slipped it over her arms, tying the belt around her waist. Beneath it, she had on a pair of black cigarette trousers and a striped boatneck tee, her flats sensible in case they had a far walk ahead of them.

Brendon was dressed in what she'd begun to think of as Pacific Northwestern attire. Jeans, a navy dress shirt unbuttoned over a tee that read *Beam Me Up, Scotty,* a pair of brown leather boots, and a black North Face rain jacket she'd seen on so many people she was pretty sure they handed them out when you moved to town. Her light pink trench stuck out like a sore thumb.

He pretended to lock his lips and throw away the key. She had to hand it to his commitment to keep her in the dark.

"Let's go," she said.

☾

Without any rain in the forecast, Brendon suggested they walk.

At the corner of Queen Anne Avenue North and Denny Way, Annie asked, "Still won't tell me where we're headed?"

He pointed across the street.

She frowned at the nondescript bar he was pointing at.

"You don't see the sign?" He led her across the street, one hand resting lightly on the small of her back. "*Look.*"

A sandwich-board sign set outside the bar read, *Hey, all you Whitney Wannabes and Halsey Hopefuls. Show off your singing skills at karaoke every Saturday and Sunday from six to close.*

"Got to love the alliteration," she joked, backing away slowly. The color drained from her face as she jerked her thumb over her shoulder. "Funny joke, Brendon. Want to tell me where we're actually going?"

"Not a joke."

"Karaoke? Getting up onstage and blustering my way through a song in front of a bunch of strangers?" She shuddered. "Hard pass. I don't sing."

"And I'm not asking you to. Do you remember the promise I made you yesterday? I think the exact words I used were *humiliate myself.*"

The hallmark of almost all his favorite romantic comedies was a musical number, and nine times out of ten, its purpose wasn't to impress. It was to *woo*.

Patrick running from the security guards while singing on the bleachers in *10 Things I Hate About You*.

Lloyd holding the boom box playing "In Your Eyes" by Peter Gabriel over his head in *Say Anything*.

Robbie strumming his guitar as he walked down the aisle of the airplane, serenading Julia in *The Wedding Singer*.

Annie wasn't the only one who couldn't sing. Public speaking was one thing. He could work a crowd. But carry a tune? Stay on pitch? He had no ear for music. He couldn't even hum on key. Hell, when he was in college, the RA had posted a sign on the bathroom door telling the whole dorm that, in addition to jacking off in the communal shower, singing there was strictly prohibited. He knew who that sign had been meant for, his proclivity for belting out the chorus to Adele's "Rolling in the Deep" during his early morning showers no secret.

Humiliate himself was right. But in the movies, no one cared if you sucked, because it wasn't about talent or technical skill. It was about effort, enthusiasm. About doing the unexpected.

Her eyes were bright and her smile broad. "I didn't think you were serious."

"I told you I always keep my promises." *All* his promises. "Ready to go watch me humiliate myself in front of a room full of strangers?"

Annie barked out a laugh. "Do you even have to ask?"

The inside of the bar was delightfully kitschy. The booths were decorated like huts. Palm trees in brightly colored ceramic planters, strings of neon lights, and tiki statues were scattered about on most surfaces. Hibiscus flowers, plumeria, and birds of paradise covered tables and swayed from the ceiling.

"Welcome to Hualani's," the hostess greeted them, reaching for the stack of menus. "Two?"

Annie's head swiveled, taking in the Polynesian tiki bar theme. "Could we get a table near the front?"

The waitress nodded and led them through a winding maze

of tables all the way to the front of the bar, smack-dab in front of the stage. "Your waitress will be with you shortly."

Annie slid her arms out of her jacket and tossed it over the back of her chair. Her shirt slipped, revealing the curve of her shoulder and the black strap of her bra. She adjusted the neck of her shirt, studying her menu, none the wiser that he suddenly felt like a thirteen-year-old again, getting his first glimpse of a woman's undergarments.

He tugged at his collar, eyes flitting between the laminated pages of his menu, the stage, and Annie.

A waitress appeared, pen and pad in hand. "Can I get you something to drink?"

He gestured for Annie to go first.

"Can I get a piña colada?"

The waitress nodded and scribbled the order on the pad. "And for you?"

Straight rum, maybe? Despite his blustering, he was going to need liquid courage to get through this. He skimmed the drink list, searching for something strong. "How big is the Late Night Buddha Call bowl?"

The waitress made a circle with her hands, her fingers nowhere close to touching. "Big."

Perfect. "Yeah, I'll have one of those."

"Do you know what you want to eat, or should I give you a minute?"

Annie folded her menu shut. "I'll have the Hula Burger."

His appetite had deserted him, his stomach a riot of nerves. "I'll have the same."

Once their waitress disappeared, Annie pointed to the edge of the stage, where a guy wearing a neon-orange floral-print shirt had a computer open and hooked up to the sound system. "I think that's where you put your name down."

He pushed his chair back and stood. "Be right back."

"Hey, man," the guy at the computer greeted him as he approached.

Brendon wiped his hands on his jeans and dipped his chin. "Is this where you sign up for karaoke?"

"Sure is. Got a song in mind?" The guy plopped a fat binder down in front of him. The vinyl cover was peeling, well-worn. "We've got this in case you need any inspo."

Brendon shoved his hands inside his pockets so they wouldn't shake. "You wouldn't happen to know any songs without high notes, would you?" He grimaced. "Low notes, either?"

"So, no notes?" The guy smirked.

Was that really too much to ask? Brendon sighed. "I'll, uh, peruse this. I guess."

He glanced over his shoulder. Annie was watching him from their table, a soft smile playing at the edges of her mouth. She lifted her piña colada into the air, saluting him.

He turned back around and flipped through the book, eyes widening. "Annie's Song" by John Denver.

He could take a crack at that.

He turned the binder around and jabbed his finger at the page. "This one."

The guy stared at him, one pierced brow rising slowly. "You sure about that?"

"Yeah?"

The guy chuckled and scratched his cheek. "Your funeral, dude." The guy spun his pencil between his fingers. "Name?"

"Brendon."

The guy set his clipboard aside and turned his attention to his computer screen. "All right, Brandon."

"Brendon."

The guy stared at him. "*Right.* I'll call you up when it's your turn. Got a few folks in front of you."

Brendon returned to the table, pep in his step.

Annie smiled around her straw and nodded at his fishbowl drink, which was served in a hollowed-out coconut. "Cheers?"

He hefted his in the air, knocking it gently against the rim of her far daintier glass, trying not to slosh any of his precious rum and mango juice. He took a sip through the decorative, bright green silly straw and coughed. *Holy shit.* He pulled a face, eyes scrunching shut at the shock of rum that hit the back of his throat, burning hot and sweet.

"I have one request and one request only. No recording," he warned, pointing at Annie's phone when he set his drink down, careful not to splash.

"Come on. Not even for . . ." She pinched her lips together. "Not even for posterity's sake?"

"You mean so you can forward the video to my sister."

She shut one eye and wrinkled her nose. "Guilty."

The waitress swung by, dropping off their food.

They reached for the ketchup at the same time, fingers brushing. He nudged the bottle closer to her and she smiled before covering her fries.

"I wanted to ask this the other day, but how did you even get into your line of work?"

"Human resources?" she asked, passing him the bottle.

He squirted his ketchup in a neat mound beside his fries. "Human resources, *international* human resources. How'd you go from wanting to be Carson Daly—"

She laughed. "A video jockey!"

"A video jockey," he said. "To HR. That's a . . . leap."

Annie chewed slowly on a fry, swallowing it down before speaking. "The whole VJ thing was a childhood dream. It wasn't serious. I like music and I spent way too much time watching MTV because my parents weren't around much. I was kind of a . . . latchkey kid, I guess? Raised on TV and microwave dinners." She laughed. "As for human resources . . ." She wrinkled her nose. "I don't know. In college, I majored in linguistics and cross-cultural communications and minored in French. I wasn't sure whether I wanted to teach or get a job in Greece to be closer to my parents since I knew their plan was to move back, so I went to the job fair for inspiration. As one does."

He lifted his burger and nodded for her to go on.

"Brockman and Brady had a booth, and the representatives from the company liked that I had a strong background in linguistics and could speak Greek and French, but suggested I spend the summer completing Temple's certificate program for corporate social responsibility if I was interested in applying for a job with them. So, I did. I thought working on international mergers and acquisitions would be a great opportunity to see the world."

"Sensing a *but* here."

"*But*"—she laughed wryly—"it's like I said the other night. It's not what I thought it would be. I hardly get to explore the cities I travel to and I hardly have anyone to explore them with. It gets a tad . . . lonely?" She frowned. "And my job barely has anything to do with any of the languages I know aside from the rare instance where I need to translate a comment here or there."

He couldn't help but feel like Annie didn't really like what she did. "So if you weren't working in HR or becoming the next Carson Daly"—that got her to crack a smile—"what would you be doing? Any job you could have. Not your childhood dream, but today's dream. Right here, right now."

She plucked another fry from her basket and shoved it into her mouth. "I don't think I'm cut out for teaching. I'm not patient enough." She grabbed her drink and took a slow sip. "But something to do with language. Translation, most likely. I just . . . I *love* the nuances of language and all their quirks. Like how certain words exist in foreign languages and have no direct English equivalent. *Meraki* in Greek means, basically, to do something with love, but there's no English word for it. The closest is 'labor of love,' but that sounds like you're being put-upon. *Meraki* means to do something with pleasure, to pour your whole heart into a task or craft. Like putting all your love into a meal or a gift." She ducked her chin and shrugged. "So, yeah. Translation would be my dream job. Puzzling out how to keep the text true even when it's not easy. There's a cultural component you can't ignore without"—her lips curved—"losing something in translation."

The way Annie's eyes lit up filled his chest with—he had no word for it. It was warm and light and also heavy at the same time, because she should be doing that. Something that lit her up inside. Something she was passionate about, her words coming quicker the longer she spoke. "That sounds like more of an art than a science."

Annie beamed at him. "It is. It's cool that you think so, too."

Staticky feedback filled the air, followed by a jarring tap against a microphone. The guy who'd given him grief over his choice of song stood on the stage, clipboard in hand. "All right, folks. Welcome to karaoke. First up, we've got Billy singing 'I Touch Myself' by the Divinyls. Come on up, Billy. Let's all give him a warm round of applause."

"I Touch Myself"? Seriously? And the dude was giving Brendon shit about a ballad?

"I wish I had a knack for languages," he confessed, returning to their conversation.

"Back in college, I wished *I* had a knack for numbers." She made a face, sticking out her tongue. "I hated calculus. I passed that class by the skin of my teeth, and because of your sister. She tutored me for *hours*. I'm talking she laminated my notes and stuck them on our shower wall. She was mortified when I got a B on the final."

Billy was currently getting into the song, one hand sliding down his belly as he crooned the lyrics. Brendon had to hand it to him. He was enthusiastic, that was for sure.

"I like numbers," he said. "Zeros and ones, mostly."

"That's a coding joke, right?"

He scratched his eyebrow, wincing. "A bad one."

Her lips twitched. "A binary one."

"See? You know what you're talking about."

"Barely." Her lips twitched and she popped two fries into her mouth at once. She chewed, then said, "The extent of my coding knowledge was how to personalize my Myspace theme."

He shuddered, having a violent flashback to 2005.

Onstage, Billy grabbed his crotch and gave a power thrust as the song ended.

Annie laughed. "That's going to be a tough act to follow."

His heart clawed its way up his throat, nerves ratcheting as the guy with the clipboard took the stage. Brendon sighed in relief when his name wasn't called.

She looked at his fries. "Are you going to finish those?"

He grinned and slid them toward her. "So, translation, huh? Not something to do with travel?"

She took a bite before answering. "I like traveling, I just wish I didn't have to do it so often. *Have to* being the operative words. Living out of a suitcase gets old after a while. Sometimes I wish I could get a . . . I don't know. A plant."

His brows rose. "A plant?"

"A plant." She nodded, wiping her fingers on her napkin. "I wish I could get a pet, but that's wishful thinking. One day I could see getting a fish or a cat, but I think maybe I'll start with something hard to kill, like a succulent, and work my way up to something finnicky, like"—she fingered the petals of the arrangement on the table—"an orchid, maybe. Your sister has a ficus. It seems . . . hardy."

He laughed. "Did Darcy tell you about the cilantro bush she gave Elle?"

Annie's face brightened. "You mean their love fern?"

He opened his mouth, the words dying in the back of his

throat when the guy with the clipboard tapped his microphone. "All right. Great job. Let's make some more noise for Anjani." He clapped his hands. "And up next we've got . . . Brandon."

Brendon sighed at the flub and stood.

It was time to face the music.

"Good luck?" Annie offered, a huge grin overtaking her face. She was enjoying this too much.

And that was fine. She had no idea he was about to totally blow her away with the best performance of his life.

Fingers crossed.

He took one final fortifying sip of his drink before standing and wiping his palms on his pants. He made his way up the stairs to the stage on shaky legs, reaching for and gripping the microphone stand, mostly for stability. He stared off into the audience. The lights up here were bright, too bright to see much of anything. Faces stared back at him, expressions washed out. Brendon blinked and found Annie in the crowd as the lights dimmed. She had her lips pressed together, her blue eyes shining across the restaurant as she beamed at him.

His chest loosened further. He could do this. He could totally do this.

He lifted the microphone to his lips and took a deep breath, eyes locked on the screen, waiting for the lyrics to scroll across. Ready to—

This wasn't "Annie's Song." He strangled the microphone, static filling his head as the countdown-style opening to "Annie Mae" by Warren G played over the sound system.

Fucking dude with the clipboard. Brendon shot a frantic glance at the bastard, frowning when the guy circled his hand in the air, telling Brendon to get on with it. Someone in the back of the bar booed.

He could walk offstage and return to the table with his tail tucked between his legs, or . . .

He could go for it. All in. Go big or go home.

Dizzy and sweating beneath the stage lights, Brendon opened his mouth and then—he was pretty sure he'd blacked out, because everyone in the bar was on their feet and they were— clapping? For him? On what planet?

He searched out Annie's face in the crowd. Tears streamed down her flushed cheeks, her shoulders shaking with laughter. She shoved her fingers in her mouth and wolf-whistled across the bar.

Chapter Seven

*B*rendon leaned against the wall as Annie fished around in the depths of her purse, fingers catching on a gum wrapper, a zipper, something fuzzy, a tube of her favorite bright pink lipstick she'd thought she'd lost last month, and *aha*! Darcy's key. She turned and smiled. His blush seemed permanent at this point, and there was something utterly charming about how he could go from opinionated and bold to bashful in the blink of an eye.

He ducked his chin and gripped the back of his neck, laughing softly beneath his breath. "Tonight was . . . not at all what I had planned."

She'd given up trying not to laugh early in the evening. Her stomach ached and her cheeks were sore from smiling more in one night than she had in weeks. "You mean it wasn't your plan all along to dedicate a nineties rap song to me?"

"It was supposed to be a John Denver song," he said for the umpteenth time before burying his face in his hands.

Poor Brendon. She reached up, setting a hand on his shoulder.

"It was definitely a first for me. No one's ever serenaded me before."

He cracked open his eyes, staring at her dubiously. "No one's ever serenaded you so poorly, you mean."

She shook her head. No one had ever dedicated a song to her or written her a poem—hell, no one had even recited one.

His teeth scraped against his bottom lip, drawing her eye to his mouth.

"I think you've been dating the wrong people." His tone was breezy, but his steady gaze screamed sincerity.

Her heartbeat faltered, then tripped over itself in its haste to climb into her throat.

Maybe it was true and he was right. Maybe she had been dating the wrong people, but that didn't mean she was interested in putting herself out there over and over again, praying to stumble across the right person.

And despite the fact Brendon was attractive and made her laugh and her pulse race, this wasn't a date. Even if she completely lost her mind and decided to throw caution to the wind, be reckless, risk her heart, there simply wasn't enough time.

It was pointless, hopeless. Asking for trouble.

She squared her shoulders. "I had fun tonight."

He bobbed his head, his smile adorably crooked. "So did I."

Her chest twinged at how unexpectedly difficult this was. There was a fuzzy disconnect between her brain and her body, between what was smart and what felt right. She needed to step back, but she couldn't bring herself to do it, to put the necessary distance between them and clear her head.

Brendon stepped forward, but not so close she felt boxed in.

Just close enough that she could smell the butterscotch candy she'd offered him after dinner each time he exhaled, the fresh laundry detergent scent clinging to his clothes. Just close enough that she wanted him closer. "Tell me you don't feel *something* here." The crests of his cheeks turned an endearing shade of pink. "Tell me you don't feel—feel *sparks*."

His tongue darted out, wetting his lips before his upper teeth sank into his bottom lip, and he watched her with raised brows.

"I—" Her voice cracked. She couldn't do it. She couldn't *lie*. Not when he was looking at her like he could see inside her head. Like he already knew. "If I do?"

She pressed her lips together, a hot flush creeping up her neck and around her jaw when he reached out, sliding his hand through the strands of her hair. His fingers felt slightly cool as he tucked her hair back, her skin undoubtedly red, her blush crawling up her temples and spreading across her cheeks.

Cradling her head in his hand, Brendon swept his thumb out, tracing the curve of her cheek, the skin beneath her eye. His other hand trembled when he rested his hand on the curve of her waist.

Her breath quickened, her chest rising and falling, unable to so much as blink. What the fuck was happening and why, *why* wasn't she stopping it?

He leaned down and closed the distance between their faces until the tip of his nose brushed hers, barely touching, even then, giving her an out.

An out she should've taken.

An out she didn't want to take.

She held so still she practically vibrated as Brendon's lips parted and he angled his head, sliding his nose against hers once, twice, drawing it out, pure torture. Her pulse pounded harder, so hard he could probably feel it against the side of his hand, her chest rising and falling against his as she arched into him further.

Brendon's mouth came crashing down against hers.

She'd watched enough movies, listened to enough of her friends moon over *magical* kisses. She'd rolled her eyes at descriptions of toes curling and breaths being snatched, of *drowning* in someone, that made it sound like a great time. Of hearts galloping like the hooves of a hundred wild horses and colors flashing prismatically behind closed lids. She'd laughed at how two people pressing their mouths together could *ever* be described with the sort of near-orgasmic passion that usually required she have her pants off.

She could say with certainty she'd had plenty of nice kisses in her life—a few god-awful ones, too—but nothing that lived up to the hype. Kisses, usually, were perfunctory. What you did before you got to the good stuff.

But kissing Brendon? This was a revelation. All those clichés? They didn't hold a candle to the way his lips turned her body into a living, breathing live wire of sensation.

His tongue snaked out, flirting with the tip of hers, and— *holy fuck*. She fisted his shirt, pulling him closer, before sliding her hand around the back of his neck and tangling her fingers in his short hair, tugging hard like a tiny part of her had wanted to do since their first dinner.

He hissed into her mouth and dragged his palm up her waist, dancing his fingers along the ladder of her ribs and over, skimming the thin skin of her inner elbow, her forearm. His fingers wrapped around her wrist, her pulse fluttering wildly inside her veins as he tangled their fingers together and pinned her hand against the door beside her head, a move that made her back bow.

He tore his mouth from hers and pressed his lips to the curve of her jaw. Her breath caught in the back of her throat when his teeth grazed a particularly sensitive spot on her neck, and she raked her nails over his scalp, hiking her thigh up his hip, her heel pressing into the back of his leg.

"*Annie.*" He panted against her throat, the gravel of his voice making her whimper.

Down the hall, a door slammed, the reverberation of wood on wood making her pulse leap.

Brendon chuckled quietly against her throat and pressed one last kiss to the hinge of her jaw. "Wow."

"Uh-huh," she said dumbly, having passed discombobulated at the first brush of their mouths. Air gusted from between her tender lips as she struggled to catch her breath.

She didn't do this, lose herself in kisses to the point where everything else faded away and she forgot where she was. *Who* she was. Who she was kissing.

She screwed her eyes shut. "This was a bad idea."

His breaths were almost as noisy as hers, the only sound that filled the hall before he cleared his throat. "Annie."

She cracked open her eyes.

"It sure felt like a fantastic idea to me." His smile was infuriatingly smug, like he was confident he could convince her this was a good idea. As if it were simple.

She wasn't sure whether she wanted to kiss the smile off his face or smack him.

"I'm not the person you want me to be. I—we're not looking for the same things."

His mouth turned down at the corners. "You're telling me you've never stumbled across something great? Maybe you weren't looking for it, but it turned out to be the best thing that ever happened to you? Don't you think that's possible? That sometimes we just get lucky?"

For some people, maybe.

But in her experience, if something seemed too good to be true, usually it was.

Everything he'd said sounded dreamy, but she'd been disappointed too many times to let her feelings get the better of her when she knew this wasn't smart. She knew better. "Even if any of that were true, I don't live here."

The most damning argument of all.

Brendon's throat jerked before he gave a quiet laugh. "What's three thousand miles?"

Everything?

His determination was as sweet as it was bound to be short-lived. No one she'd ever dated had been able to handle her traveling two weeks out of the month. And it wasn't just three thousand miles.

"Brendon." She lifted her hand to rest it against her breastbone, fingers splayed against the front of her throat. Her pulse pounded in her neck, her heart still hammering away. "It's a lot more than that."

His shoulders rose and fell, just jerky enough to show that he didn't feel as nonchalant about this as he was pretending to be. He bobbed his head. "I know your job—"

She shook her head. "You don't know." She hadn't wanted to do this, talk about this, but she had no choice. "I'm moving. To London. There was a promotion and I—I start in July."

He opened and shut his mouth, clearly at a loss for words.

Her stomach soured. "I really hope you find what you're looking for. But I'm not it." She reached back, her fingers curling around the doorknob. "Please don't tell Darcy. I want to tell her in person."

Then she slipped inside the apartment and shut the door, the crestfallen expression on his face more than she could stomach.

Chapter Eight

Monday, May 31

*T*he sudden scrape of the dead bolt caused Annie to jerk her head in the direction of the front door. For a split second, her whole body froze, save for the rapid pitter-patter of her heart. *Someone* was at the door. Then the time and place caught up with her.

Darcy was home.

Annie vaulted over the arm of the couch, stumbling on the slightly curled edge of the rug in her haste to make it to the front door. She righted herself against the wall, cringing when her bare toes bumped Darcy's entry table. *Ouch.*

The pain in her foot was all but forgotten when the door opened and a slightly windswept-looking Darcy wheeled her suitcase over the threshold.

"*Oof.*" Darcy froze with her arms at her sides when Annie launched herself at her. She laughed sharply and returned the hug, squeezing Annie back just as tight, so tight Annie ached.

But then the ugly, melancholic pressure in her chest let up, because Darcy was *here*.

She buried her face in Darcy's shoulder and inhaled the crisp, clean lavender and bergamot scent of Darcy's shampoo. "I missed you."

For a split second, she felt like a total loser, getting choked up after sniffing her best friend's hair, but when she drew back—Darcy's strong hold, while totally appreciated, made it hard for Annie's lungs to function—Darcy's eyes were glassy and her lips were pursed tight, like she was trying not to cry.

Darcy sniffed and tossed her head, flipping her long, coppery hair over her shoulder. "Thirteen months is entirely too long to go without seeing each other." She lifted her chin up in the air. "*Too long.* This is my official complaint on the matter. Visit me sooner, next time."

"I'm not the only one who can hop on a plane, you know."

Or call, or text, or FaceTime first.

Darcy's smile slipped, a line appearing between her expertly arched brows. "Annie—"

"I'm teasing," she blurted, pasting on a smile to soften the bite of her earlier words. "I know you've been busy."

Darcy had had a whirlwind of a year. Packing up her life in Philadelphia, starting over in Seattle. Working her way up the ranks at her new job. Meeting Elle.

Elle had changed Darcy's life for the better, so Annie wasn't about to begrudge her best friend's being busy. Her being happy.

Annie just wished she'd call sometimes instead of Annie's being the one to initiate nine times out of ten. That was all.

"Busy with *Elle*," she added, bumping Darcy's hip with hers.

A hint of color rose to the surface of Darcy's cheeks. Oh, she had it *bad*.

Darcy cleared her throat. "I—well." She dropped her head and laughed, pressing her palm to her forehead. "Yeah."

Annie's smiled widened. "Oh my God. You're *smitten*."

Darcy scoffed. "I hate that word." She lifted her eyes, one brow ticking higher. "That's *Brendon's* word."

Annie curled her toes in the plush carpet and shrugged. Brendon didn't own a word. So, maybe it had rubbed off on her. Big whoop. "It's fitting."

Darcy made a soft, curious *hmm*, her brown eyes flitting over Annie's face.

She fought against the squirmy urge to blurt out that she'd kissed Darcy's brother. Unnecessary information. Irrelevant. *Moving on.*

"How was Vancouver?" She wrapped her hand around Darcy's wrist and tugged her across the room, stopping when they reached the couch. She took a seat, tucking her legs under her. "Come on, spill."

Darcy joined her, leaning back and crossing her legs demurely at the ankle. "Beautiful. We had a lot of fun exploring. Elle wanted to go see the H. R. MacMillan Space Centre, which is an astronomy museum. They have an observatory and"—she chuckled—"the *Cosmic Courtyard*. They do live demonstrations and you can touch one of the only five touchable moon rocks on the planet. It's mostly for kids, field trips, that sort of thing, but you should've seen Elle's face."

Darcy should've seen her own face. When she talked about Elle, her eyes turned soft and her mouth curled fondly, her voice taking on this incredibly sweet tone Annie had never heard from her before.

She shoved Darcy lightly. "You're in *love*."

"Yeah, yeah." Darcy reached inside her pocket and withdrew her phone. She swiped at the screen and turned it toward Annie. "They had a photo op. Elle made me."

On the screen was a picture of Elle and Darcy with their faces poking through the helmets of two astronaut suits.

Annie chortled. "Looks like you had a good time."

Darcy tucked her phone away and nodded. "I think you'd like it, especially Gastown. Lots of cute boutiques and unique bars, plus there's a giant steam-powered clock smack-dab in the middle of the district."

"Sounds funky."

"Right up your alley," Darcy teased, eyes dipping and brows rising shortly after. "Nice muumuu, by the way."

"Excuse you, this is a caftan." Annie *loved* this caftan. She prioritized comfort when she lounged; sue her.

"I didn't mean anything by it. It's perfectly lovely." Darcy's lips twitched. "And I'm pretty sure my grandmother owned one just like it."

Annie rolled her eyes and hauled one of Darcy's decorative pillows onto her lap. "Enough about my caftan. Back to Elle and your first vacation together. This *was* your first vacation with Elle, right?"

"Mm-hmm."

"And you didn't want to kill each other by the end of it. Kudos."

Darcy's lips tipped up before pressing tightly together, her throat jerking hard, her gulp audible.

"You *didn't* want to kill each other by the end of it, right?"

Darcy gave a curt shake of her head and ran her fingers through her hair. "No. The opposite, actually." She took a deep breath. "I'm going to ask Elle to move in with me."

Annie's eyes widened. "Wow."

Moving in together.

Darcy was about to merge her stuff, her apartment, her world, with Elle's.

Then it would only be a matter of time before they'd get married, because deep down, Darcy was *all* about the proverbial white picket fence.

Before long, Annie would be in London and Darcy . . . Darcy wouldn't have room in her new life for a friend who lived halfway around the world.

"We've been together six months. Almost seven," Darcy said, a touch defensive.

Annie held up her hands. "I think it's great! I just wasn't expecting it. I'm really happy for you."

She refused to let the bittersweet ache in her chest put a damper on Darcy's mood, because if anyone deserved to be happy, it was Darcy.

"Thanks." Darcy sniffed and smiled. "But enough about me. How have you been?"

Her back teeth clenched together. "Great! I've been super."

Darcy blinked at her, looking startled. "Okay? I . . ." She

huffed out a quiet laugh. "Gosh, where were you last? Berlin? Paris?"

Annie pressed her lips together. "London, actually." No better time to tell Darcy the news than the present. She swallowed over the steadily growing lump in her throat and jumped up from the couch. Or she could wait. "But speaking of Germany . . ." She darted over to where her purse rested on the chair across the room. "I've got something for you. It's not much."

Darcy leaned forward, propping her elbows on her knees. "You didn't need to get me anything."

No, but she'd wanted to.

Annie wrapped her fingers around the package and carried it over to the couch. "I saw it in the window of this little shop in Nuremberg and I immediately thought of you."

Tearing delicately at the wrapping paper, Darcy gasped softly when the present was revealed. "It's beautiful."

"The object is to move the ball through the maze of gears and corridors. It's a puzzle, but it's pretty enough to be kept out."

Darcy smoothed her hand over the laser-cut wooden maze featuring intricate mechanics Annie knew would appeal to her analytical side. "I love it. It looks like a piece of art."

Annie smiled and silently patted herself on the back for a job well done. She prided herself on being stellar at gift giving and she was proud to say she'd outdone herself.

"Do you mind if we just order in?" Darcy asked. "I'm kind of beat and I want to hear more about what you've been up to."

"Sure, works for me." Minus the talking-about-herself bit.

Darcy cocked her head. "So."

Annie bit down on the tip of her tongue and smiled.

"You're acting weird." Darcy's eyes narrowed. "You're quiet. You're never quiet."

She scoffed. "I can be quiet. Maybe I'm tired."

Darcy's brows rose. "*Are* you tired?"

No, but that was beside the point. "I wouldn't mind a cup of coffee. Your espresso maker hates me."

"Annie." Darcy stared at her and she stared right back. Darcy caved first, rolling her eyes. "What did you do yesterday?"

Kissed your brother. Annie swallowed thickly and gave a noncommittal shrug. "I went for a long run. I saw the, um, sculpture park?"

Darcy nodded for her to go on.

Annie scratched the side of her neck, her skin suddenly itchy, tight. "Then Brendon swung by and we went to—well, it's a funny story."

Darcy's brows rose again. "Okay . . . I'm all ears."

Her stomach twisted in on itself, contorting into a pretzel. "We went to karaoke."

"Karaoke?" Darcy wrinkled her nose.

Annie shrugged. "It was fun. *Funny.* I had a lot of fun."

The most fun she could remember having in a long, *long* time. Too much fun.

Darcy's eyes narrowed. "What's with your face?"

"My face?" Annie's eyes widened. "There's nothing happening with my face."

"Hmm." Darcy cut her eyes at Annie. "No, there's definitely something going on with your face."

Annie's cheeks burned. "My face is just my face, Darcy. If you don't like it, don't look at it."

Darcy pursed her lips. "What aren't you telling me?"

"Nothing." Her voice came out as a squeak and she shut her eyes. "Fuck."

Darcy snickered. "You're a shitty liar."

Darcy didn't have to sound so damn happy about it.

Annie sighed and slumped back against the couch. "Okay, don't kill me."

"I'd never kill you. Depending on what you did, I might maim you a little, but I'd never kill you."

A shocked laugh burst from her. "*Darcy.*"

All Darcy did was stare, her lips twitching.

"Okay." She took a deep breath, steeling herself for Darcy's reaction. "I might've accidentally . . . kissed your brother."

One of Darcy's brows rose, a sign of impeccable forehead control Annie had never been able to master. Her own brows were strictly a two-for-one package. "How do you *accidentally* kiss someone? Did you trip?"

She huffed. "No."

Darcy's right brow rose, joining its twin. "Did he?"

"No. Smart-ass. Nobody tripped."

"Did someone require emergency resuscitation?"

Annie reached out and smacked Darcy's shoulder. "Shut up."

"Ooh." Darcy's eyes widened gleefully. "You're getting violent. I must've struck a nerve."

"You're such a bitch." Annie laughed. "I hate you."

"That's a rude thing to say to your future sister-in-law."

Annie buried her face in her hands and groaned. "Not gonna happen."

When she lifted her head, Darcy had schooled her expression. "I thought you said you weren't interested in my brother."

"I'm *not*."

"And yet your actions point to the contrary."

"For a minute, I forgot who he was and I forgot who I was and I forgot *where* I was and I just—" *Felt.* She had just let herself feel. "Got caught up in the moment." She shot Darcy a flimsy grin. "Your brother's really hot."

Darcy mimed a gag. "You already said that." She crossed her arms. "But I find it hard to believe you're so desperate you threw caution to the wind and kissed Brendon for the hell of it."

Annie shrugged. "You know, now that you mention it, it *has* been a while since I've gotten laid. So . . ."

"Ugh." Darcy shivered. "Stop trying to derail the conversation by yucking me out."

"Is it working?"

"No."

Annie laughed. "Let it go. We kissed. It's not a thing. It's not going to happen again. I only told you because I'm incapable of keeping secrets from you. End of story."

"*Not.*" Darcy swiveled, knees bumping Annie's. "It's not the end of the story. Not when you haven't *told* me the whole story. Spill."

Annie wrinkled her nose. "Spill what?" She laughed. "There's nothing *to* spill. Your brother is cute. He's funny. I had a good time. But I told you I'm not interested in dating anyone."

Darcy frowned. "That was before you went and kissed my brother."

"He kissed me." Annie tucked her hair behind her ears. "Or we kissed each other. That—that is beside the point."

Darcy's lips twisted to the side. "*Isn't* that the point? Or if not, what *is* the point? At the very least it's point adjacent."

Point adjacent. Jesus.

"It's not a thing."

Darcy stared.

"*Gah.*" Annie threw her hands up. "Brendon doesn't know me, so—"

"Would it be so bad? Letting him get to know you?"

Yes.

It wasn't just a bad idea.

It was the worst idea.

Because letting Brendon get to know her meant letting him in. It meant trusting him with a million little facts, all the haphazard pieces of herself, and hoping he'd remember them all.

You couldn't be disappointed when someone forgot your middle name if they didn't know your middle name. You couldn't be upset when someone forgot your favorite food or how you felt about your job if you never told them to begin with. You couldn't be disappointed when someone stopped caring if you never expected them to in the first place.

Rejections always stung, but nothing hurt quite as badly as sharing pieces of yourself, trusting someone with your heart, and then being cast aside when you cared more than they did.

"Jesus, Darce. Why are you pushing this so hard?"

"I'm not *pushing*. I'm asking." Darcy frowned. "Why are you getting so defensive?"

"I'm *not*. I'm—" Shit. She was. Annie shut her eyes. "Sorry."

Darcy made a soft sound in the back of her throat before waving off the apology. "It's fine. I just wish you'd talk to me. I know Brendon's my brother and I have a tendency to get a little protective—"

Annie snorted. Understatement of the century.

"Okay." Darcy rolled her eyes. "*A lot* protective. But you're my best friend and I care about you, too. I'm not trying to meddle, I swear. I'm trying to understand."

When Darcy put it like that, it was hard to remain defensive. Annie sighed. "Like I said, I got caught up in the moment. It was just a kiss. And it's not going to happen again."

Darcy didn't look convinced. "Why not?"

"Darcy . . ."

Darcy waited, hands clasped in her lap.

This was the moment Annie had come to town for, at least part of the impetus behind her decision to fly to Seattle. So she could tell Darcy this in person instead of over the phone.

She'd known this was coming and she'd already told Brendon, so why was it so hard to just *say* it? Maybe because telling Darcy made it real. That was the only thing she could come up with, the reason why she was stalling.

Annie squared her shoulders. "I got a promotion."

Darcy sucked in a breath. "You did?"

She nodded. "I did."

Darcy waited.

Here went nothing. "It's—it's a great opportunity. Higher salary, for one."

Darcy smiled tightly. "Long lead-in. I'm sensing a *but* here."

Annie dropped her eyes. "But it's in London."

A pause followed. "I'm assuming you accepted. You must've, if you're telling me."

"I did." Annie lifted her eyes. Darcy was staring behind her, glaring at the wall like it had personally offended her. "My flight is in exactly a month."

Darcy gave a curt nod. "That's—that's great. I'm happy for you."

Then how come she didn't sound like it? "Darcy."

She sniffed. "What?" She gave a wet laugh. "I'm trying really hard to work up some genuine enthusiasm. Give me a moment."

Annie waited, not bothering to hold her breath.

"*London?*" Darcy shook her head. "Why do you want to move to London? You—you don't even like tea. Christ, Annie, you *hate* tomatoes. They're constantly eating stewed tomatoes and baked beans and you—you're allergic to mushrooms. There's nothing about an English breakfast you'd eat."

"Toast," Annie said. "I like toast."

"Fuck toast," Darcy muttered. "It's dry bread. Completely overrated."

She was pretty sure they ate more than traditional breakfast foods in England. In fact, she *knew* they did. But now wasn't the time to point out the hilarity of Darcy's argument.

"Darcy."

"They have a monarchy. Who wants one of those? It's not all

fun royal weddings and hot duchesses. There is a grim history of colonialism and . . ." Darcy swiped angrily under her eyes. "Look, I understand I am being completely irrational, but you're going to have to give me a minute, okay? I see you for the first time in over a year and you tell me you're moving even further away?"

"I won't have to travel as often. I'm getting tired of constantly being on the go."

This job was offering her a chance to put down roots, a place to call home for longer than two weeks out of the month.

"And you can't, I don't know, pick a job that keeps you in one place and that place happens to be a little closer?" Darcy asked, voice small. "At least in the country?"

Annie fidgeted with the hem of her caftan. "It came out of nowhere. What was I supposed to say?"

The promotion was perfect on paper. Exactly what she'd been looking for as long as she kind of . . . squinted.

So what if working in HR wasn't her dream? Sometimes a job was just a job. She wasn't practical to the point of eschewing everything else, including her own happiness, but she couldn't turn her whole life upside down and, what? Change careers? No.

Darcy sniffled. "I know I'm the one who moved here to Seattle, but . . ." She pressed her fingers to the space between her brows. "Call it wishful thinking on my part, but I'd always hoped we'd wind up back in the same city. At least the same coast. Philadelphia's far enough as is, but London?"

"You never said," Annie murmured.

"I didn't think I needed to. I thought it went without saying. You're my best friend."

Annie said nothing, because honestly, she hadn't thought Darcy would care.

Darcy frowned. "I guess I was wrong. It didn't go without saying."

"I didn't mean to upset you," Annie said. "I don't want this to be a big black cloud hanging over us for the rest of my trip. Let's just . . ."

"Pretend you aren't moving halfway across the world?" Darcy's voice went dry.

"Darcy."

She held up her hands. "Fine. I'll drop it."

"Thank you."

"For now." Darcy's brows rose. "I'll drop it for now."

Chapter Nine

*B*rendon was no stranger to the sort of run-of-the-mill misfortune that everyone experienced from time to time. A bad haircut. Getting splashed by a car while standing on the curb. Sleeping through his alarm. Even getting stood up.

Hearing Annie tell him she was moving to London when he could still taste her on his lips? When he'd just discovered how perfectly she fit into his arms? He didn't have words for how badly that had blown.

Kissing her might not have been planned on his part, but the chemistry between them had been palpable. He'd had a great time and it was clear she had, too. Ending the night with a kiss had felt like the most natural thing in the world, the thought of her living on the opposite side of the country unimportant in light of the sparks he felt.

Philadelphia wasn't convenient, but London?

Traveling got lonely, Annie had said. Moving an ocean away would make her *less* lonely? What about how she'd said her job involved less translation than she'd hoped it would? Wouldn't it involve even *less* if she'd be traveling less frequently?

The longer he thought about it, the less sense it made.

"Brendon? Brendon?"

He jerked in his seat. Seven sets of eyes stared at him from around the conference table.

"Sorry." His face went hot at getting caught zoning out in the middle of a meeting. A meeting he was meant to lead. "It's been a long day. You were saying?"

Katie snickered. "Long day? Brendon, it isn't even noon."

"Someone had too much fun this weekend," Jenny, the senior director of marketing, teased.

"Hardly." Brendon laughed it off the best he could, pasting on a smile. "Now, this coming weekend? Whole other story."

Jian's face scrunched in mock confusion. "This weekend? Is something happening?"

"Probably something really boring." Katie beamed at him from across the table. "Not at all special."

A bittersweet ache gripped his heart.

Envy was too ugly a word for what he felt. He didn't begrudge anyone their happiness; the opposite, in fact. But he wanted the same, what Katie and Jian had. Darcy and Elle. The way they looked at each other was nothing short of magic, like everyone else faded away when their eyes met across the room.

"I couldn't be more excited for the both of you," he said,

choosing to focus on his friends and coworkers' happiness rather than stew in self-pity because he didn't have that. Yet.

Katie pinched her lips together, doing a poor job of smothering her smile. "We need to change the subject before Brendon gets too choked up to continue the meeting."

"The one he wasn't paying any attention to, you mean?" Jenny asked.

"Okay." He held up his hands. "Quit roasting me. Jian, you were saying?"

"Q two's numbers are in."

His eyes dropped to the manila folder sitting ominously atop the conference table in front of Jian. "Okay. Don't leave me in suspense."

"Our operating expenses rose, but we made some hefty changes. Investments."

Partnering with Oh My Stars had involved some heavy-duty shifts in their algorithms, not to mention their budgets.

"That being said"—Jian slid the folder across the table—"our numbers exceeded our projections. Revenue rose. More than we hoped."

Brendon flipped through the report, brows rising. These numbers were good. These numbers were *really* good. He set the report aside. "This is fantastic."

Jian winced. "I agree. *Those* numbers are certainly worth celebrating."

Brendon braced his elbows on the table, waiting for the other shoe to drop. That happened to him a lot lately. "But?"

"We had a bit of a slump in accounts."

"But we see that every year, people canceling their premium subscriptions post-cuffing season."

"Right." Jian tossed the stress ball between his hands. "Problem is, we've got a bit of an elephant in the room, and it's the fact that the whole market is seeing a slowdown in growth of new users."

"The whole market," Brendon stressed, looking to Katie for confirmation. "Not just us."

She offered him a smile and nodded.

Jian sighed. "I'm not trying to be a Donnie Downer or anything, but our model, what sets OTP apart, is that we promise to help users find their person so they can ditch the app and ride off into the sunset." He held up his hands. "I'm not harshing what we stand for. Just, from a business standpoint, if we want users to delete the app, we've got to replace them with others. If we've got a slowdown in growth—"

"We've got a problem," Brendon surmised.

Jian nodded. "Or we will. Right now, our revenue is exceeding expectations; great. User satisfaction?"

Katie shot him a thumbs-up. "Is at an all-time high."

"We don't need to panic, but we've got a problem on the horizon and it's one we're going to need to tackle sooner or later." Jian shrugged. "Personally, I'm in favor of sooner."

"Sooner sounds good," Brendon agreed, leaning back in his chair.

Jenny leaned forward. "If I'm understanding this correctly, our issue is attracting new users to the app? Refresh the pool of singles, so to speak?"

Jian nodded. "But don't ask me how. I'm the numbers guy."

Katie and Jenny exchanged a look before Katie gave a sharp nod. "We'll get right on it."

Jenny reached for her pen and began scribbling in her notebook. "Testimonials, maybe? Those usually work."

"If we want to see big growth, not just a trickle here and there like we get from users switching between apps, I think we've got to branch outside our usual demographic." Brendon turned to Katie. "Those thirty percent of dating app users who feel apps have made courtships devoid of romance."

Katie frowned sharply. "You want us to convince a bunch of skeptics?"

Jenny dropped her pen. "How are we supposed to do that?"

Therein lay the million-dollar question.

"*Challenge* is another word for *opportunity*," Katie said, shooting Jenny a glare. "We'll brainstorm."

"We've got time," Jian reminded them. "No rush."

Brendon wished he could say the same.

C

DARCY (3:16 P.M.): Could you please come over after work? I think Annie broke my espresso machine.

BRENDON (3:22 P.M.): Did you try turning it off and back on?

DARCY (3:25 P.M.): 😒

BRENDON (3:26 P.M.): Kidding! Yeah, I can drop by. What time?

DARCY (3:29 P.M.): I'll be home at 5:00.

BRENDON (3:32 P.M.): I'll swing by around 5:10. How's that sound?

DARCY (3:35 P.M.): That works. Thanks.

☾

Brendon rapped his knuckles against Darcy's door and waited.

And waited and waited and waited.

"Hey, Darce?" he called out. "It's Brendon. You told me to swing by after work?"

After a moment, a shadow appeared beneath the door before it opened. Arms crossed over her body, Annie stood blocking the threshold, her full bottom lip trapped between her teeth. "Hi."

His breath caught in the back of his throat, his lungs constricting. Fuck. She was gorgeous, her long hair swept up in a messy bun on the top of her head. Several tendrils had fallen, framing her heart-shaped face, which was free of makeup, making it possible to see the tiny spray of freckles dotting the bridge of her nose. She didn't have many—not like him; he was covered head to toe—which made the few she had all the more adorable. Precious in their scarcity.

"Hey." He pasted on a smile he prayed didn't give away the fact that just looking at her gave him palpitations. That his fingers itched with the urge to tuck one of those loose strands of hair behind her ear. That his mouth burned with the memory of how soft the skin beside her jaw had felt, how he'd been able to feel her pulse trip under his lips. He cracked his knuckles, not just because she made him nervous, but because the desire to reach out and touch her was too strong. "Is my sister home?"

When she tugged on the fabric, his eye was drawn to the expanse of golden skin left bare by Annie's skimpy shorts. It was obvious she hadn't been expecting company. "Darcy's still at work. She told me this morning she'd be late. She's, uh, playing catch-up, apparently. Since she took Friday off."

"She told you that this morning?"

Annie nodded.

That didn't make any sense. Darcy had texted him this afternoon. "She asked me to come over. Apparently, her espresso machine's busted."

She made a soft, embarrassed hum, a distant cousin of the throaty moan she'd made the other night, the one he'd felt vibrate against his lips. The space between his shoulder blades tingled, the hair on his arms standing on end, when she lifted her eyes, meeting his. "Whoops?"

"I'm sure it's not as bad as Darcy thinks," he fibbed.

She leaned against the door frame, reminding him of how he'd had her pressed up against the same place two nights ago. How she'd whimpered when he'd kissed her. How she had tasted like pineapple and coconut. *Fuck.* He sucked a shaky breath in through his mouth and shoved his hands inside his pockets.

"You're, um, welcome to come inside and wait," she offered, gesturing behind her. "Or take a look at it." She rolled her lips together, smile slightly wry. "I didn't realize I totally screwed it up that badly. Me and fancy appliances do not get along."

He laughed under his breath and followed her inside the kitchen, stopping in front of the espresso machine. It didn't *look* ruined.

"You think it's fixable?" she asked, leaning against Darcy's fridge. "Or did I kill it?"

"I'm hopeful," he said, reaching behind the machine to plug it into the outlet.

"Me too." Annie traced a grout line with the tip of her bare toe. Her nails were painted an electric shade of aqua that made her skin look tanner by contrast. "Otherwise, I owe Darcy a new coffeemaker."

He grabbed a mug and placed it beneath the spout before pressing the button for an eight-ounce Americano. The machine sputtered before dark coffee filled the cup.

That had been easy. *Too* easy. No fixing involved, just a press of a button and voilà, coffee. "Seems fine to me."

"Whew." Her lips turned up at the corners, her smile verging on shy as she pushed off the fridge and took a step toward him. "Brendon, about the other night. I don't want you to think I'm not—"

"Brendon? I saw your car out front."

The award for worst timing went to Darcy. Annie didn't want him to think she wasn't *what*?

He stared at Annie for a moment longer, willing his eyes to communicate what his mouth couldn't. *This isn't over.* He smiled at Darcy even though a huge part of him wanted to shove her back through the front door. "Your coffeemaker's fixed."

"Oh, good." Darcy set her purse down on the counter. "It wasn't too complicated, was it?"

"Complicated?" He laughed. "Try turning it on."

"How strange," she said, not quite meeting his eyes.

Something strange was certainly afoot. He just couldn't put his finger on *what*.

Darcy sighed and massaged the space between her brows, a quiet but not quite silent groan slipping out of her mouth.

Annie frowned. "Are you okay?"

"I'll be fine." Darcy waved her off with a strained smile. "Just exhausted. I opened up my email this morning and nearly had a heart attack. I take a few days off and I come back to the office in shambles. This week . . ." Her words trailed off, the lines forming around her lips filling in what she hadn't said. She offered Annie a contrite smile. "I'm just worried we're not going to have as much time together as I'd hoped. We'll have the weekend, obviously, but I've got my boss breathing down my neck about finalizing these reports for some of our high-priority accounts and . . . I'll probably be at the office late most days."

Annie gave an awkward laugh. "I picked a really bad time to visit, didn't I?"

"*No*," Darcy blurted. "You're here, which by default makes your timing excellent." She glanced between him and Annie. "Say, Brendon?"

He stole a sip of the test coffee he'd brewed. Not bad. "Hmm?"

Darcy's eyes narrowed, her head cocking. Oh, he knew that look, was quite familiar with it, if he was being honest. He'd given Darcy the same look a time or two. It was a look that said he, or in this instance Darcy, hadn't come to play. "What's your schedule look like this week?"

A seemingly innocuous question for an altogether not innocuous look. He frowned. Or was it *nocuous*? A nocuous look? Was that a word? If something could be innocuous, shouldn't *nocuous* be an option? Or was it like flammable versus inflammable? Wow, *tangent*. Thanks, brain. Brendon shook his head. "Not bad. Why?"

He had Jian and Katie's wedding, but that wasn't until Friday. With their all-team meeting out of the way, his days would mostly consist of fielding emails and racking his brain trying to figure out a solution to the problem Jian had rightfully posed this morning. Thursday, he had a big meeting with investors regarding their potential expansion out of North America, but the rest of his week was relatively malleable.

"I was thinking—"

"A danger to us all," he teased.

Darcy reached out, pinching the thin skin of his inner elbow, left bare from rolling up his shirtsleeves. Motherfucker, that hurt. "*Ow.*"

"As I was saying," she gritted out, her eyes wide like she was trying to silently communicate with him. "If you aren't too terribly busy, maybe you could show Annie around?" Darcy suggested, eyes twinkling in a way that had absolutely nothing to do with her fancy recessed lighting.

Another look he was familiar with. As the baby in the family, he'd perfected that look. All wide-eyed innocence, cunning lurking beneath the surface.

Brendon grinned and swallowed the urge to wipe away an imaginary tear. Clap, maybe. Darcy had played him, she'd played him *good*, and he couldn't even bring himself to be upset about it because—while he might not have been completely clear as to her motivations—it had worked out in his favor.

Annie, apparently none the wiser about his sister's machinations, shook her head. "Oh, no. That's—"

"Fine," he said, cutting Annie off. "I'd love to show you around."

Spending time with Annie was the opposite of an imposition.

Color rose in Annie's cheeks as their eyes met and their gazes held, his breath burning in his lungs until she dropped her eyes to the floor, breaking their magnetic eye contact.

It took a moment for his mouth to make words. "How's tomorrow afternoon sound? My last meeting's at three. Barring traffic, I could be here by a quarter after four."

Annie gnawed on her bottom lip before nodding slowly. "That . . . sounds like a plan."

"Perfect." Darcy beamed.

Still staring at the floor, Annie absently lifted a hand to her mouth, fingers tracing her lips in a way that made him immediately wonder whether she was thinking about their kiss.

"I'll text you when I'm on the way."

Annie startled slightly, lifting her head, the color in her cheeks deepening. She gave a sharp, decisive nod before smiling tightly. "Looking forward to it." She turned to Darcy. "I'm going to run through a shower. I ordered takeout since I wasn't sure when you'd be back."

"I'll answer the door." Darcy nodded.

With a fleeting smile aimed in his general direction, Annie scurried past, disappearing down the hall.

"Sorry to have you come all this way for nothing," Darcy said, walking him to the front door.

"Not a big deal. It was on my way."

And it gave him an opportunity to see Annie again. A win-win in his book.

"I'll walk you to the elevator," she offered, pulling the door shut behind her. As soon as they were halfway down the hall, she grabbed his arm, tugging him to a stop. Her lips pursed, dropping whatever act she'd done a surprisingly good job of putting on inside her kitchen. "Did she tell you?"

"Tell me what?"

She huffed. "Don't play dumb with me. *London*."

Right. *That.* He shoved his hands in his pockets and winced. "She made me promise not to tell you. She wanted to tell you herself."

"I hate it," Darcy muttered, beginning to pace slowly. "I told Elle when we were in Vancouver that I hoped to show Annie how great Seattle is. Her job in Philadelphia is—*was*—remote most of the time. She could've relocated. Or, she could've found another job. A job closer." She shut her eyes. "I *cried*, Brendon. I cried and made a big to-do over—over stewed tomatoes."

"Stewed tomatoes?"

Despite the glare she leveled at him, she looked on the verge of tears.

"Did you tell her you wished she wouldn't move?"

"What part of *cried over stewed tomatoes* did you not get?"

"Does she know you want her *here*? Did you tell her that? Did you tell her that before? When she was in Philadelphia?"

"I thought she knew." Darcy shifted her weight from one foot to the other. "I . . . assumed she did." Her eyes widened, growing even glossier. "Fuck. I messed up. My best friend is moving halfway across the world and—" She broke off, face splotching pink as she blinked hard. "I'm the worst."

"You're not. You've been busy."

"I've been wrapped up in myself, is what I've been." Darcy

took a deep breath, then paused, eyes flaring. "I can't believe I'm doing this."

"Doing what?"

"Meddling! That's your MO, not mine."

He scoffed. "I don't meddle. I nudge. I help."

"You meddle, Brendon. Not that I'm in any position to judge when I'm doing the same thing. At least I'm being honest about it."

"Honest. Right. Like when you asked me to come fix your broken coffeemaker."

"It got you over here, didn't it?" She tossed her hair over her shoulder. "Annie told me that you kissed."

"Does that bother you?"

"No. You're my brother. Annie's like a sister to me, you know that. I love you both." She shrugged. "Besides, I'm pretty sure Annie likes you, too."

His eyes darted down the hall, and even though the door was shut, he dropped his voice. "Did she tell you that?"

"Not in so many words. Which is why I'm asking you to do me a huge favor."

He raked a hand through his hair. "I'm listening."

"I need you to help me convince Annie to move here," she whispered. "You know the city better than I do."

"I already said I'd show her around."

"Yes, well, I need you to be all in. Give it your best. And maybe . . ." She trailed off, blushing. "Maybe show her what she'd be missing out on if she moves."

He frowned. "Isn't that the—" *Oh.* "Wow. Are you asking me to seduce your best friend?"

Darcy smacked his arm. "Gross. No." She paused. "Maybe? Ugh."

"I can't believe it." He tsked. "My own sister, pimping me out."

"I'm not asking you to do anything you weren't already. Just, I don't know, step it up. Consider the stakes a little higher now. That's all."

Never in a million years would he have imagined that Darcy would be giving him permission—no, *asking* him to woo her best friend. "Are you even planning on putting in long hours at the office or was that bullshit?"

Darcy had the decency to look chagrined. "Both? I *am* going to be busy this week and you and Annie seemed to hit it off so I thought . . . I'm willing to use whatever I can to my advantage." She frowned. "If you don't want to—"

"I never said that. I said I was in."

"Good." Darcy nodded decidedly. "This stays between us. Capiche?"

He rolled his eyes. "No, I'm going to run off and tell Annie as soon as I can."

"I'm serious, Brendon."

He met her eyes. "So am I."

Chapter Ten

Wednesday, June 2

At the red light, Brendon drummed his long fingers against the steering wheel.

Annie knew what those fingers felt like wrapped around her wrist, how easily he'd circled her arm and pinned her hand to the door when they'd kissed. His wide palm had gripped the back of her neck, and if she concentrated hard enough she could feel the phantom rasp of his calluses against the shell of her ear, the friction of skin on skin.

She shivered violently, hard enough that Brendon noticed.

"Cold? Want me to turn the air down?" he offered, reaching for the knob.

"I'm fine." Her words came out mortifyingly breathy, like she was auditioning for a job as a phone sex operator. She ground her back teeth together. *Get a grip.*

He nodded slowly and rested his hand back on the wheel, looking at her like she was behaving strangely. Because she *was.*

This had been a bad idea. Spending time with Brendon. Not that she'd had much of a choice, with Darcy and Brendon ganging up on her. Stubbornness clearly ran in their family.

Which was fine. Once she put her mind to something, she could be equally as stubborn as the Lowells. Annie was *not* going to let her attraction to Brendon get the better of her.

Remaining calm, cool, and collected was easier said than done when every time she looked at him her eyes were drawn to his mouth and all she could think about was that kiss. The kiss that put all others to shame. The kiss that made her wonder whether she could even call all the other kisses she'd had in her life kisses or if they needed a new name, something to denote them as lesser.

Maybe she'd stick to calling the kiss they'd shared a revelation. Fitting, because there'd be no repeat. No kissing Brendon. *Definitely* nothing more.

A change of subject was in order. Anything to get her mind off how impossibly hot his lips felt against hers. *Gah.* "Are we headed back to the market?"

Brendon shook his head, a secretive smile playing at the edges of his mouth. His very kissable-looking—

Jesus. Who was she kidding, underestimating the power— not to mention obstinacy—of her libido. The bitch clearly had a mind of her own.

She pivoted her body, staring out the window, her frowning face reflected in the glass. *Hangry* was a portmanteau of *hungry* and *angry*; was there a word for when you felt horny and were angry about it? *Horngry?* No, that sounded ridiculous, like she was hungry and horny, instead of angry at being aroused.

The giant wheel she'd been forced to relieve herself on zipped by as they cruised past the pier. "Space Needle?"

"Wrong direction."

She craned her neck, peering through the tiny back windshield. Right. They were heading *away* from Darcy's.

"How about—" She swallowed the rest of her guess when Brendon flipped his turn signal, making a smooth right at the . . . "Ferry terminal?"

Up ahead, a long line of cars moved steadily forward, stopping briefly at the attendant booth before boarding the ferry.

"We're heading out of the city?"

Brendon rolled down his window. "You'll see."

She let her head drop back against the headrest, barely biting back a groan of frustration.

She'd figured he'd show her around the city, the famous landmarks, all part of Darcy's plan to convince Annie Seattle was the greatest city on Earth. She'd assumed Brendon would take her to the Space Needle, maybe that funky cement bridge troll over in Fremont. A trip outside of the city was unexpected.

A fluttery feeling took up residence inside her stomach. The city provided a sort of . . . safety net. Restaurants and crowded tourist destinations, plenty of people. *Public.* She wasn't sure where Brendon was taking her, but it was outside the city, and that meant more time in his car, more time with him, no outside distractions or noise or—she swallowed hard—interruptions. No escape.

It wasn't Brendon she worried about; she didn't trust herself not to do something stupid and ill-advised like kiss him again. No, kissing Brendon would be bad because . . . oh, God. She drew a blank. Now was not the time to lose her head. There were reasons, good reasons, reasons she needed to routinely remind herself of if she was going to get through the day without doing a very bad thing that wouldn't be fair to either of them. Right. *Reasons.*

One, she was moving to London. *Huge* reason there. The mother of all reasons.

Two, she'd sworn off dating, tired of getting her hopes dashed.

If Brendon were just a cute, funny guy she'd met, maybe she could've given her libido the reins and let it run the show for a few days. A vacation fling, no strings, scratch this itch, get it out of her system before she got on a plane. Not her usual MO, but not something she was inherently opposed to, either. But Brendon wasn't just a random guy. He came with all sorts of strings attached. He was looking for the one. He was her best friend's brother. It didn't get much more complicated than that.

There was no way following through on her attraction to Brendon could end any way but badly.

After paying the fare, Brendon drove forward, following the signs for parking aboard the ferry. He pulled to a stop behind a large SUV and cut the engine. "Want to head up to the observation deck?"

She smiled and nodded, unlatching her seat belt. Exploring this attraction was out of the question, but that didn't mean she couldn't make the most of the day.

"Is it usually this crowded?" she asked, stumbling into Brendon when a group of kids raced past her.

"Unless it's raining." His chest brushed her back, heat from his body soaking into hers. God, he was a human furnace. For a brief second he rested his palm on the small of her back, warmth from his hand sinking into the sliver of skin left bare between her shorts and her shirt.

She needed to remember her reasons and treat them like a mantra. *Do not kiss Brendon. London. Dating equals disappointment. Lots of strings. Tangled, messy strings.*

Annie quickened her steps, making a beeline for the railing.

Despite its being a tad windy—Annie's hair was whipping in her face—it *was* nice out. The temperature was hovering in the midseventies and the sun had broken through the cloud cover.

Brendon joined her, resting his arms on the railing. He'd slipped on a pair of aviators, the lenses tinted black, making it impossible to see his eyes. For a moment, they stood in silence, staring out at the choppy water. When Brendon finally spoke, he threw her a curveball. "How'd your friends in Philadelphia take the news?"

She turned slightly, leaning her elbow against the railing as she faced him. "What do you mean?"

"You did tell them you're moving, didn't you?"

Oh. About *that*. "They're happy for me."

His dark bronze brows rose over his sunglasses. "Happy?"

Happy in the way people you saw once every other month at brunch could be. They'd gone through all the motions of *We'll miss you so much* and *We're absolutely going to stay in touch*. But Annie knew better. Proximity meant everything to most people, and if it was difficult enough to get close when she was living in Philadelphia and traveling for work, it would be impossible once she'd moved to London.

She nodded. "Mm-hmm."

He scratched his jaw. "I guess Zoom makes staying in touch a lot easier, huh?"

Her eyes flitted to his face before darting back to the dark water of Elliott Bay. "I'm not around very much as it is. I'm on a plane or I'm in a different time zone. Occasionally, I'm a whole day ahead. Zoom, Marco Polo, FaceTime—a million applications exist to make staying connected easier than ever. But even with all the right tools, no one can make people put in the effort if they don't want to." She offered him a pained smile. "I don't have very many—any, really—close friends in Philadelphia is what I'm saying. No one's going to miss me."

She traced a crack in the concrete deck with her toe and bit down hard on the side of her cheek.

Attraction wasn't the only risk Brendon posed. He was too damn easy to talk to, to confide in. Still, admitting that she had no close friends in Philadelphia? Embarrassing.

He stared at her gravely and her stomach pretzeled. Okay, make that *mortifying*.

"I find that hard to believe."

She looked at him sharply. "What's that supposed to mean?"

He gripped the back of his neck, posture relaxing as he slouched against the railing. "You said no one's really going to miss you. And I think . . ." His tongue sneaked out, wetting his lips. "I think you're underestimating the effect you have."

She looked at him askance. "The effect I have?"

He ducked his chin, a quiet chuckle rumbling from his chest. "You're easy to get along with. I'm having trouble wrapping my head around someone meeting you and getting to know you and not wanting to spend as much time with you as possible. You're like . . . Lay's potato chips. You can't eat just one."

A sunbeam of warmth flared inside her chest. "Did you just . . . compare me to a *potato chip?*"

He nodded, face twisted, looking pained. "I think I did?"

She laughed and reached out, wrapping her hand around his forearm to show him she wasn't mad. "That was—that was strangely sweet, Brendon. No one has ever compared me to a potato chip before."

A summer's day had nothing on her favorite junk food.

His flush deepened to the point where even his freckles were obscured, his whole face a shocking shade of neon. "I was trying to say . . . you know what? I'm going to quit while I'm—shit, not even ahead. I'm going to quit before I insert my *whole* foot in my mouth."

She swept her thumb against his skin, her fingers brushing the fine dusting of spun-copper hair along the side of his wrist. "I'm not mad."

Beneath her fingers, his tendons flexed. *Unf.* Not mad at all.

He was staring down at her, his sunglasses obscuring his eyes, but she could tell he was studying her, could *feel* it.

The mantra, remember the mantra. *Do not kiss Brendon. London. Dating equals disappointment. Lots of strings. Tangled, messy strings.*

She dropped his arm and stole several steps back, cringing when her hip knocked into the metal railing. That would leave a nice bruise. "I don't want to pretend like I'm not partially to blame. For not having close friends in town. I got tired of being the one always reaching out. *Usually* reaching out. Eventually, I stopped. Inevitably, get-togethers tapered off when I wasn't the one arranging them." She shrugged. "Friendships need more TLC than plants. Who'd have thought?"

He reached down, the fingers of his opposite hand absently brushing against the wrist she had previously circled. "For what it's worth, you'll always have Darcy. You know she's pretty upset, right?"

Seeing as she'd tried to use the fact England had a monarchy to sway Annie into staying, *yeah*. "She'll be fine. She has you and Elle and—it won't be any different than it was when I lived in Philly."

Brendon tugged off his glasses, squinting briefly at the brightness. "Can I ask you a question?"

She dipped her chin.

"Why London?"

"London's where the office is that I was offered—"

"No." He shook his head. "I mean, why'd you take the promotion?"

"Other than the fact that it's a *promotion*?" She laughed.

Brendon didn't. His lips didn't even twitch. "Feel free to tell me to fuck off if you want to, because I know it's not my place, but the way you sounded the other night . . . you don't seem to like your job."

That wasn't—okay, it was a little true. But so not the point.

"I'm tired of traveling, yes." Tired of traveling alone, mostly. "But as managing director of the London office, I won't have to travel as often. Once a quarter, maybe."

"But it's still HR, still not your dream job. You deserve to be doing something that makes you happy. Whether that's working in human resources or coming to steal Carson Daly's thunder or anything in between."

Annie gripped the railing until her knuckles turned white. "Sometimes a job is just a job, Brendon."

"True," he said quickly. "So if London isn't your dream city and this isn't your dream job, why not find another one? If a job is just a job, it should hardly be your whole reason for moving halfway across the world."

It was more complicated than that. Unless she was making it more complicated than it needed to be? She shut her eyes and let the subtle rocking of the ferry calm her.

"You're Darcy's best friend. She misses you, misses having you nearby. She's mentioned it. And if Philadelphia's far, London's even further." He cleared his throat. "Four thousand seven hundred eighty-one miles. I googled it."

She laughed. That sounded like something he'd do.

"You've got people here that care about you, Annie. People who would really like it if you were closer. Darcy." He took a step toward her and another, until she had to crane her neck to look up at him. He'd crowded her against the railing, not quite touching, but close enough that all it would take was one deep breath and their chests would brush.

Her breath hitched, escaping her lips in short, staccato pants as he lifted his hand and rested it on the side of her neck, cradling her jaw. It was all so reminiscent of their kiss that she ached, her bare toes clenching and curling inside her sandals.

Her knees felt loose, like marionette limbs linked with string, stiff until they weren't. Like she might collapse if not for the railing at her back. Her hands reached out, settling on his waist, clutching at his shirt.

His lids were low as his thumb swept against the curve of her cheek, tickling her skin with the rough whorls and ridges of his fingerprint. "Me."

For one dizzying moment, that sunbeam of warmth inside her chest returned and expanded, flaring hot and bright as Brendon stared at her, a soft smile playing at the edges of his mouth. A mouth she wanted so desperately to kiss.

Almost as desperately as she wished what he'd said was true. But how could it be?

Friday. Saturday. Sunday. Monday. Tuesday. Wednesday. Six days. Annie had been in town for less than a week. How could Brendon care about her if he barely knew her?

Dating equals disappointment. Lots of strings. Tangled, messy strings.

She dropped her hands from his solid torso and crossed her arms against a sudden chill. "I'll keep that in mind."

☾

The sun had just barely slipped below the horizon when Brendon's GPS told him to turn on the narrow road ahead.

Annie hunched forward in her seat, elbows resting on her knees. "Wheel-In Motor Movie. Wait. Is this a drive-in?"

His tires bounced along the gravel as he slowed to a crawl. "One of only four left in the state."

They were in Port Townsend, two hours northwest of Seattle.

His original plan had been to take Annie on a picnic near his apartment where they showed movies in the park during the summer months, a date reminiscent of *The Wedding Planner*, but the chance of rain in the forecast had caused the park association to cancel. Luckily, he had a backup plan, one he liked even better than the original.

Drive-ins were, by default, romantic. Plus, this plan allowed him to show Annie a little more of the state than if he had simply taken her to a park, managing to kill two birds with one stone.

"How does this even work?" she asked after he paid for their tickets at the booth located halfway up the gravel drive. "Don't we need speakers or something?"

"We just have to set the radio to the FM channel on the ticket." He parked in the center of the lot, a perfect distance from the dark screen. "Movie starts at dusk." He unhooked his seat belt. "Want something from concessions?"

Her answer was immediate and enthusiastic. "Popcorn, please."

They were relatively early, and the line outside the concession stand was short, moving fast.

Annie popped his door for him when he returned, arms laden with buckets of popcorn and an assortment of candy.

"I got extra," he said. "Just in case."

"What are we watching?" she asked, one hand already buried in her bucket of popcorn.

He grinned. "*Say Anything.*"

"Confession? I've never seen it."

That was unacceptable, a wrong he was glad to right immediately. "The boom box, Annie. John Cusack and the boom box playing 'In Your Eyes' by Peter Gabriel. Classic."

"Eh." She wrinkled her nose. "I know it's supposed to be all iconic and everything, but it always seemed . . . stalkerish to me."

"Stalker—no. *No.* It's romantic. He plays the song they listened to the night they first . . ." He wet his lips, brows rising suggestively. "You know."

She snorted. "Ah, *so* romantic. Here, let me stand outside your window playing the song we first banged to. You're right. Not stalkerish in the least."

When she put it like that, he winced. "All right. Maybe it hasn't aged well, but—"

"Chill." Annie smiled. "Plenty of my favorite movies haven't aged well. Maybe I just need to watch it before I pass judgment."

His shoulders dropped in relief that this night wasn't a bust before it had really begun. "It's set in Seattle, you know."

She swallowed her mouthful of popcorn. "Yeah?"

"Tons of the best movies are. *Sleepless in Seattle, 10 Things I Hate About You*—"

"*The Ring.*" Annie grinned when he grimaced. She set her bucket of popcorn on the floor between her feet and reached for the box of Sour Patch Kids. "I'm just teasing you. I enjoy a good rom-com as much as the next person." She paused. "Okay, maybe not as much as you."

A fair assumption. His love for romantic comedies was off the charts.

"I'm confused," he admitted.

Annie shook out a handful of candy before offering him the box. "About?"

"How can you possibly say romance is dead when these movies are proof that it isn't?"

Her laughter filled the car, sharp and sweet. It tapered off when she realized he wasn't laughing with her. Her eyes widened. "Are you serious? Oh my God, you are. They're movies. It's all fake. It would be like using *Jurassic Park* as proof that dinosaurs are real."

"Dinosaurs are real."

"Were real." She stared at him pointedly. "And now they're dead."

"The whole plot of *Jurassic Park* is that dinosaurs were revived using fossilized DNA."

She laughed. "Okay. Better example. It would be like using *Men in Black* as proof that aliens exist."

He refused to smile, refused to give himself away. "Aliens do exist. The Pentagon released footage of unidentified flying objects."

She clapped a hand over her mouth. "Oh my God."

"Area Fifty-One, Annie."

She dropped her hand and goggled at him. "Is an Air Force facility."

"Wow, I didn't realize believing in aliens was so controversial." He smiled, letting her know he was kidding . . . a little.

She shifted toward him, her knees bumping the center console. "Come here."

"What are you doing?" He slid over, dropping his head forward when she gestured for him to come closer to her height.

"Hold still." She laughed hard, her face turning red as she ran her fingers though his hair, messing it up. Her nails raked against his scalp, sending shivers skittering down his spine. "There. Now hold your hands up and say *aliens*."

Oh, Jesus. He patted his hair down. "I'm not nearly as fanatical as the dude from *Ancient Aliens*."

She pressed her lips together.

"Look, I'm not saying aliens had anything to do with Stonehenge, but I'm not not saying it."

Annie buried her face in her hands, shoulders shaking.

"Romance, dinosaurs, aliens." He tsked. "What's next? Are you going to tell me you don't believe in the Loch Ness Monster?"

Annie clutched her stomach, gasping with laughter. "*Brendon*."

Her eyes locked on his across the seat and for one heart-stopping moment he was trapped in her gaze like a fly in a web, his breath lodged in his throat. The hair on the back of his neck rose, his toes curling in his boots.

Outside, the stadium-style lights around the lot dimmed as the title card appeared on the giant screen. Annie broke their eye contact first, her gaze dropping to the bucket of popcorn between them. She shivered, and he'd have bet his last cent it wasn't because she was cold.

"I'll make a believer out of you, Annie," he whispered, earning himself a fleeting look he couldn't quite discern. "Just you wait."

Chapter Eleven

"What did you think? Exceed your expectations?"

Annie's head bobbed from side to side as he started the car and put it in reverse. "It was better than I thought it would be, I'll grant you that. I liked the ending."

"Why? Because it was over?"

She threw her head back and laughed. "No. I liked that he got on the plane with her. That part was sweet."

"I'm sensing a *but* here."

"*But*, after watching the whole movie, I can safely say my initial impression of the boom box scene stands. If I broke up with someone—regardless of why—and they stood outside my window playing the song we listened to after having sex, I'd be seriously creeped out. Even factoring in the teenage angst, no thanks." Annie shivered. "But before you get all bent out of shape about it, I feel that way about, like, ninety-nine percent of grand gestures in movies."

"And this is because . . . ?"

"Most of the time, they're performative and add pressure to something that should be private."

"You know, for someone who claimed romance is dead on her first day in town, you're sure a proponent of looking at love through a . . . practical lens."

Which he wasn't too proud to admit confused him greatly.

Her brows rose. "No, I simply don't view it through rose-colored glasses, and I never said anything about being happy that romance is dead. Only that I feel it is." She tucked her hair behind her ear. "I guess if you define romance as public proposals and kisses on Jumbotrons, crashing weddings and interrupting once-in-a-lifetime interviews so you can declare your love at the worst possible time, then sure, I seem practical by comparison." Annie shrugged. "All of that looks great on-screen, I guess. It's cinematic. Flashy. But at the expense of intimacy and . . . I don't know, I always wonder what happens after the screen goes black and the credits roll."

"What do you mean?"

"And they lived happily ever after." She snorted. "What does that even mean?"

"Is that a trick question?"

"No. I just mean, you never see what happens after the credits roll, because I guess no one wants to watch a movie about a couple filing their taxes or bickering about who was supposed to take out the trash or how to pay for their kids' dance lessons." Annie laughed. "That would be boring, granted. But I guess that's my point. Getting together is different than staying together. It's not all fireworks and sunshine and roses and splashy grand gestures. What happens after the kiss in the rain? The proposal at Fenway Park in front of the supposed love of your life and a thousand of your closest friends?" She rolled her eyes. "Am I really supposed to believe any of those couples have staying power? That those relationships have longevity?" She made a soft noise of disbelief. "You can bet your bottom dollar all that wooing comes to a screeching standstill as soon as the love interest is a sure thing."

"Okay, but the whole point of these movies is to show two characters falling in love and then, despite the odds, despite the fact that the circumstances conspiring to keep them apart are seemingly insurmountable, they surmount those obstacles. The storm they weather shows they can handle whatever else life will throw at them down the road. Taxes or trash or dance lessons, true love conquers all. And the right person? They wouldn't stop showing you how much they love you every day."

Annie scoffed softly, staring out the window. "I'm going to have to go with seeing is believing on that one."

He didn't know what to say to that; Annie's despondency was in direct opposition to his own optimistic outlook. Rather than potentially put his foot in his mouth, he turned up the radio, letting his acoustic playlist serve as background noise as they zipped down the highway. Ten minutes of near silence later, Brendon made a left, pulling into the lot for the ferry terminal. The booth was dim and the attendant was missing. He frowned, searching for an automated ticket dispenser.

"Um, Brendon?" Annie pointed at the Plexiglas partition above the booth's window, where the ferry's schedule and fares were posted.

He squinted. The last ferry to Seattle ran at ten thirty. Which was fine. It was only—

Ten forty.

His head thudded against the headrest.

Fuck.

C

"On the bright side, they have a TV?"

Brendon flipped the dead bolt and slumped against the door. That was the only bright side.

Between the missed ferry and the fifteen miles they'd had to drive out of their way to find a hotel that wasn't totally booked for the night, this trip had turned into a comedy of errors, heavy on the errors and light on the comedy. "True."

"And the place looks . . . clean."

Clean was generous. The industrial carpeting was the color of wine, probably chosen for its ability to disguise stains. The walls appeared to have once been white, but time and nicotine had stained them a dingy shade of cream.

"The bed looks . . . comfy. Oh, and look." Annie flourished her hand near the headboard. "Four pillows. Housekeeping was generous."

Bed. As in, just the one. The mustard-yellow duvet cover *appeared* free of mysterious stains, but he wouldn't have wanted to search the place with a black light.

He darted a glance at the stiff-looking armchair wedged into the corner of the room. Stuffing spilled out from one of the arms like beige cotton candy.

He let out his breath slowly, like air escaping from a dying balloon. "Comfy."

Annie pressed her lips together but the crinkling at the corners of her eyes gave her away. At least she wasn't upset by this wrench in their plans. In fact, it had been her idea to stop for the night and wait for the earliest ferry rather than drive the long way back to the city. "It could be worse?"

Against the wall, a rhythmic thumping started, joined by a chorus of grunts.

The back of his neck burned, a flush creeping up his chest, steadily bleeding up his jaw.

"Never mind." She blushed prettily. "This is pretty bad."

The lamp on the bedside table wobbled, the headboard from the room next door slamming into the wall. He winced. "I think I liked it better when you were being the unerringly optimistic one."

Her blond brows rose. "The place definitely has a certain . . . je ne sais quoi."

He palmed his face and groaned. "That's a polite way of saying this place sucks."

"Hey, *you're* the one who asked me to blow sunshine up your ass."

"I've always wondered about that phrase. How does one begin to blow sunshine, let alone up someone's ass? A very sturdy straw?"

Her laughter filled the room, sharp and sweet. "Gives new meaning to looking on the bright side."

"I guess it does, doesn't it?" His laughter tapered off, leaving his chest filled with pleasant warmth.

High-pitched, breathy moans joined the symphony of lewd sounds next door.

"TV?" he suggested, stripping off his jacket and tossing it atop the flimsy fiberboard dresser, suddenly so warm he could hardly stand it.

Annie circled the bed, plucking the remote off the nightstand. "Let's see what channels we have."

She collapsed on the bed, making a face when the mattress's springs squealed. She shifted atop the covers, getting comfortable. "It's not bad." She patted the space beside her.

He swallowed hard and jerked his chin at the chair. "I'm good."

"Oh, come on." She rolled her eyes. "Don't be stupid."

He hesitated. "Are you sure?"

Annie stared.

She was right. They could share this bed. No big deal. So what if he already knew how sweet she tasted and that he wanted her in the worst way? Annie was addictive, but no matter how fucking phenomenal kissing her had been, he didn't just want Annie, he wanted her to want him. Want him for longer than one night. Especially one night in a dingy motel that smelled faintly of cigarettes and stale sweat, with the soundtrack of some other couple sounding as if they were filming an amateur porno next door.

He sat gingerly on the edge of the bed and tugged off his shoes, leaving his socks on, because while the place appeared clean, looks could be deceiving. Annie smiled and turned the TV on as soon as he'd settled back against the headboard. Ear-splitting static immediately filled the room.

"Yikes." Annie flipped the channel, sighing in relief when the picture came through. "Okay, that's promising. It's golf, but it's . . . something." She navigated past C-SPAN, a cooking competition, easily a dozen channels. He was about to suggest they look for a channel guide when Annie gasped. "No way."

It took him a split second to realize the show she'd stopped on wasn't in English, instead in French.

"I can't believe this is on. Then again, we're kind of close to Canada, so I guess it makes sense that they might have a channel in French."

"What is this?"

"*L'amour est dans le pré.* It's a French dating show." A soft smile flirted at the edges of her mouth. "I bet you'd like it."

It sounded like Annie liked it, which was enough of an endorsement for him. "Sounds good."

Annie's smile broadened as she set the remote down between them. She leaned back against the pillows, her arm brushing his.

One episode and he was hooked. Granted, because it was entirely in French and un-subtitled, he couldn't understand a word anyone said. But laughter and love were universal; he didn't need to speak French to appreciate the magic of watching two people tentatively fall in love on-screen. Annie's sporadic translations did help.

"You never really answered my question," he said during a commercial.

"What question was that?"

"If you're not a fan of the grand gesture, what *do* you find romantic?"

She pressed her lips together and swallowed hard. "I feel like you want me to give you a list of activities or gestures and I don't know how to do that because I feel like it's sort of antithetical, in a way."

A list would certainly be convenient, but he held his tongue.

Annie drew her knees up to her chest. "In my mind, romance is just showing someone that you know them, you're thinking of them, you care about them, and you want them to know it. There's nothing wrong with chocolates and flowers and even grand gestures if that's what someone genuinely likes, if that's what makes them feel appreciated. Because *that's* romance. It depends on what your love language is."

He was familiar with the concept. "Words of affirmation, gifts, quality time, that sort of thing?"

Annie nodded. "Mm-hmm. It can be like speaking two different languages if you express love one way and someone else prefers to receive it differently."

"Lost in translation," he surmised. "Nice analogy."

"I was a linguistics major, what can I say?" She laughed. "I've already made my thoughts on flashy gestures clear. If someone proposed to me in public, I'm pretty sure I'd die of mortification." She shivered and cringed. "To me, the quiet gestures matter more. Someone remembering my coffee order or my favorite movie. Random *I'm thinking of you* texts. Believe it or not, this is pretty perfect." Her eyes widened. "Not that I'm saying this is a date. Because it's not. But if it were."

He filed away her exaggerated vehemence that this wasn't a date but bit his tongue against the urge to make a *doth protest too much* joke, positive it wouldn't fly. He spared a glance around the dingy hotel room, which smelled like body odor and cigarettes beneath several generous spritzes of Febreze. His brows rose. "This?"

Annie wrinkled her nose. "Okay, not exactly this. But low-key nights in? If we had a bottle of wine and Greek takeout, I'd be in heaven." Her smile went sheepish. "I know it probably seems totally at odds with my job, but I'm actually a homebody. Maybe it's because of my job, actually. I like downtime and I'd take sweatpants and slippers over heels and going out to clubs any day."

He grinned. "Same. The general idea, I mean. Not the heels. Can't speak to that experience."

The corners of her eyes crinkled. "I'm sure you could pull off a pair of pumps."

"With my arches?" he joked.

Her laugh made his stomach clench.

"What about you? When it comes to romance, you're the expert."

"Expert?" He scoffed. "I don't feel like much of an expert."

Between his foot-in-mouth blunders and the D-and-I report that had both him and his team puzzled over how to proceed if they wanted OTP to go the distance, he'd never felt so out of his depth.

"I find that hard to believe," Annie said. "You created a dating app. A successful one." That was up for debate. "Clearly, you must have opinions. Come on, hit me with it. What does Brendon Lowell find romantic? Public proposals? Kisses in the rain? Mad dashes to the airport, racing the clock?" Her smile went sly. "Serenading someone via karaoke?"

"That predictable, am I?" He chuckled awkwardly.

"I'm right?" Annie smacked her hands on the bedspread and twisted, facing him. "Is that what you were doing? Re-creating scenes from rom-coms to prove your point?"

That was how it had started, with wanting to prove a point. Then it had turned into something more, something that had nothing to do with winning a bet, unless the prize was more personal than mere bragging rights.

"And here I thought I was being stealthy." He paused, heart creeping into his throat. "Does that bother you?"

"Well, you didn't stick my face on a Jumbotron, so kudos for that. Until I put two and two together, which was, like, an hour ago, I was none the wiser. Then again, I'm not exactly a rom-com aficionado." She snickered, then sobered, her expression softening, her smile sweet. "I just felt like Annie, spending time with a guy who was going to great lengths to show me a good time in his favorite city."

His heart had yet to return to his chest, instead getting right at home in the hollow of his throat, his every word that much more vulnerable for it. "Can I ask you a question? Another one, I mean."

She nodded, albeit hesitantly. "You can ask."

He dug deep for courage, terrified of what her answer would be, but more afraid of not asking. Of looking back on this moment and regretting letting this chance pass him by. Even if it pained him, he needed to know. "If you weren't moving to London, would this be different? Would you give me a chance?"

With each increasingly fraught blink she made, her eyes growing glassier, his nerves ratcheted until his whole body had evolved into his final form, one raw, exposed nerve.

After a few seconds she pressed her lips into a sad little smile that made his heart twist.

"I don't know, Brendon. Maybe?" she whispered. "But I am moving to London, so it doesn't really matter, does it?"

Maybe.

It mattered to him.

He just needed to show her that it did.

☾

Thursday, June 3

Brendon cracked an eye open, blinking into pitch-blackness. The AC unit beneath the window whirred to life, ruffling the gauzy curtains covering the window, a sliver of golden sunlight illuminating a wedge of the hotel room.

The TV had shut off automatically due to inactivity, the black screen making the red lights from the clock below it appear brighter by contrast. Eight fifteen.

He stretched, then stilled when the heavy weight on his chest shifted. Annie had wrapped an arm around his stomach and buried her face against his chest. She hummed sweetly, sighed, and started to snore.

Not a quiet, snuffling snore, but a chain-saw roar that ruffled her hair, her lips quivering with each subsequent breath. The sort of snore that belonged to a man twice her size. A man twice her size who had a deviated septum and smoked a pack a day.

His chest rumbled with quiet laughter.

"Hey, Annie," he whispered, shaking her shoulder. "Annie."

Her brow furrowed and she shoved him roughly. "Whatisit. Shutup. 'M sleeping."

He laughed harder, causing her to rise and fall against his side. Still, she slept on. "Annie, it's morning."

She cuddled closer and continued to snore.

"Annie." He shook her shoulder with a little more gusto.

When she didn't respond, he sighed. Maybe he should just leave her be, let her sleep a little longer. He'd already emailed his assistant, Tyler, letting him know he'd be taking the day off. Technically, Annie could sleep until noon if she wanted. As long as they made it back before the last ferry of the day shipped out, they'd be fine.

He gave in to the urge he'd repressed all yesterday and brushed the soft wisps of baby-fine hair back from her forehead. His heart thudded hard when she smiled, burrowing closer into his chest. Her whole body went unnaturally still as her snoring stopped. A gasp flew from her mouth and she lifted her head.

Ambient light from the sun peeking in between the curtains bathed half her face in an amber glow, her blue eyes wide and alert. "Oh God. I fell asleep. When did I fall asleep?"

"We both did, at some point. I just woke up."

She scrubbed a hand over her face and yawned. "I must've been really out of it." She sniffed and wiped her eyes. "Normally I'm not a deep sleeper. I have trouble staying asleep more than a few hours." She smiled, sleepy and soft. "I must've been super comfortable."

His chest puffed up and he was glad his face was still in

shadow so that she couldn't see the completely involuntary smirk that curved his lips. "Maybe you should fall asleep on top of me more often."

A sliver of sunlight caught on her pale lashes when she blinked. She gave a sharp laugh, her eyes practically glowing. "Maybe I should. You make a damn good body pillow." Her tongue swept against her lips. "You're very solid."

He stared, enraptured by her mouth. How she was still half-way on top of him. "Solid."

She nodded, and the hand resting on his chest slipped lower, touching his stomach through his shirt. Her throat clicked and he held his breath. "Firm."

If she moved her hand any lower, she'd swiftly find out his chest wasn't the only thing that was hard.

His chuckle came out breathless. "Happy to have been of service."

She seemed regretful when she removed her hand from his body, her fingers lingering for a moment before she lifted them and scooted away, sitting and swinging her legs over the edge of the bed. She cleared her throat. "Let me, um, wash up and then whenever you're ready we can hit the road."

Annie grabbed her purse and scurried into the bathroom.

Chapter Twelve

Annie closed Darcy's front door and rested her weight against the wood. A whimper escaped her lips as she slid to the floor, landing in a pitiful heap atop the welcome mat. She shoved the heels of her hands into her eyes, her fingers trembling ever so slightly against her brows.

She was so entirely screwed.

"Ahem."

She jolted, knocking her arm into the door, groaning at the blow to her funny bone.

Darcy sat on the far end of her sofa, legs crossed neatly, her hair cascading over her shoulders in loose curls. She looked like a redheaded Veronica Lake, complete with a vintage-style dressing gown. Like some sort of film noir detective missing only a cigarette, Darcy drummed her fingers against the arm of the couch and scrutinized Annie through narrowed eyes.

"Have fun?" Her right brow arched.

Hands braced against the floor, Annie hauled herself to standing. Maybe Darcy would be kind enough to pretend she hadn't witnessed the beginning of Annie's meltdown. "Shouldn't you be at work? What happened to *I've got my boss breathing down my neck, important accounts, long nights,* et cetera?"

Darcy gestured to her open laptop atop her coffee table. "I decided to work from home when *someone* was out all night."

Annie rolled her eyes and slid off her flip-flops. She collapsed against the couch and kicked her feet up onto Darcy's lap. Darcy wrinkled her nose. "I texted you. We missed the last ferry. No big."

"No big?" Darcy's brows rose.

Life would've had to be too kind for Darcy to let Annie's sleepover and floor mini-meltdown go unmentioned.

No big.

Annie remembered how it had felt, waking up in Brendon's arms. How, for a moment, she'd forgotten all the reasons why getting close to Brendon, letting him in, was a bad idea. How it wasn't the first time she'd lost her head around Brendon. How it kept happening and how each time she struggled more and more to tear herself away.

Annie let out a desperate laugh. "I'm so confused," she muttered, staring up at the shadow shapes on Darcy's ceiling.

Darcy patted her hand gently. "Where's your head at?"

"*Pfff.*" Annie scoffed. "I don't know."

Darcy waited.

"Brendon's . . . he's sweet. He makes me laugh." Plus, she wanted to do dirty things to him she wasn't about to tell Darcy. "He seems like a great guy, but he's looking for . . ." Annie searched for the word. "*Magic.* He wants fireworks. He's got this picture in his head of what love's supposed to be like. It's all . . . feelings."

Darcy frowned. "Love *is* a feeling, Annie. A really great one."

"No. I mean, *yes.* Obviously. But it's also a choice. It's . . . it's a verb. Falling in love is one thing, but staying in love? Feelings fade, you know that."

Darcy nodded.

"It takes a . . . concerted effort to keep a relationship afloat."

An effort most people didn't want to expend. Not in her experience.

"And you don't think my brother can, what? Hack it?" Darcy asked, sounding offended on his behalf.

"I didn't say that. *You* are the one who told me he's constantly going on first dates looking for the *right girl.* The one. But"— she bit down hard on her cheek—"what happens when something better comes along?"

Not that she assumed he thought of her as that. The one. God, no. But he'd mentioned sparks. Said he wanted to get to know her.

Brendon seemed like a genuinely great guy, but for the most part, everyone she'd dated had seemed great at first. Just like she must've seemed—at the very least—pretty decent to those people, too. As much as she felt *something* for Brendon, he seemed in love with the idea of love. Infatuated with the chase. Maybe even a little infatuated with who he *thought* she was, perhaps some remnant of his teenage crush making her a little rosier to him than she'd have been had he not known her, once upon a time.

In a completely hypothetical situation where she wasn't

moving to London, where she lived here, what would happen if she let him in more than she already had? What if he didn't like her nearly as much as he thought he would? What if *she* liked him more than she already did after just a few short days? What if, as soon as she was a sure thing, she lost her shine?

"Brendon doesn't want to settle for anything less than someone who's perfect for him," Darcy said. "And there's nothing wrong with that."

Internally, she groaned. Talking about this with Darcy was a bad idea and she'd known it.

"Brendon deserves the best," Darcy plowed on. "But I'm biased. I'm also pretty sure there's not a person on this planet better than you, so . . ." Darcy cracked a smile. "Consider me biased on both fronts."

Her sinuses tingled, her eyes flooding. *Fuck.* "Warn me before you say something like that." Annie sniffed hard, blotting at the corners of her eyes. "Jesus."

She'd missed this. Missed *clicking* with someone the way she did with Darcy.

"I also think you aren't giving my brother the credit he's due," Darcy said. "I'm confident he'd be deeply committed. He just needs to find the right girl to commit to."

"Yeah, well." She shrugged. "That can't be me."

Even though, after the last week, and last night in particular, she'd started to wonder what it would be like if that girl were her. A what-if. Nothing more. She couldn't help what thoughts popped into her brain and wouldn't leave. She had zero control over that sort of thing.

Darcy pursed her lips and stood, wandering off toward her

kitchen. She opened the fridge and grabbed the bottle of wine inside the door. "Hmm."

Not this again. "Darcy. Cut it out."

She snagged two glasses and carried them into the living room, filling both and passing one to Annie. "I think you and my brother both want the same thing. Only, you have wildly different ways of reacting to not getting it."

Annie gripped the stem of her glass and stared. "Uh, yeah, that makes no sense."

"It makes *perfect* sense," Darcy said, sitting down. "You're clearly disenchanted with the people you've been dating because they haven't lived up to your expectations. You've been let down."

"I never said—"

"*A lot of little disappointments*," Darcy said, mimicking her, head teetering from side to side.

Annie bit her tongue.

"And Brendon's looking for someone who will live up to *his* expectations," Darcy said, swirling her wine. "Neither of you have found what you're looking for, but he's thrown himself into dating headfirst, searching high and low, upping the ante. You've pumped the brakes. He's got high hopes. You've lowered your expectations."

Annie scoffed. "Wow. Who needs therapy when you have a best friend who thinks they know everything? Runs in your family."

Darcy offered her a tiny smile. "Am I wrong?"

Annie said nothing.

"Look, you want to know why I wound up giving Elle a

chance? Giving my *feelings* a chance? It's because of what you told me. *Carpe diem.*" Darcy sipped her wine, studying Annie over the rim of her glass. "Maybe you should take your own advice."

They were good words, words to live by. Or they had been. Somewhere along the way, Annie had gotten tired of being the only one doing the seizing. The only one trying. The only one who cared.

"There will be no *seizing* when it comes to your brother," Annie said crisply. "In fact, I did some thinking on the drive back from Port Townsend."

Darcy cocked her head.

If Annie couldn't control her thoughts around Brendon, she'd simply have to see less of him. A lot less of him. "As much as I appreciate his offer to show me around, I think it would be in both our best interests if we . . . saw a little less of each other."

A *lot* less of each other.

"Sure." Darcy smirked. "You can start by seeing a lot less of each other tomorrow at game night."

Annie shut her eyes. *Damn it.*

"*Carpe diem,*" Darcy taunted.

Annie let loose the closest thing to a growl that had ever passed her lips, because this was *so* not going according to plan. "It is a moot point. I'm moving to London. I can't exactly give Brendon a chance from five thousand miles away."

"You're not five thousand miles away yet." Darcy reached out, covering Annie's hand. "You're here. He's here. And if my brother wants to try to give you a reason to stay? You'll have to excuse me if I'm not exactly keen on discouraging him."

Chapter Thirteen

Friday, June 4

What Board Game Are You Based on Your Zodiac Sign?

Aries—Battleship
Taurus—Life
Gemini—Trivial Pursuit
Cancer—Sorry
Leo—Clue
Virgo—Scrabble
Libra—Chutes and Ladders
Scorpio—Scruples
Sagittarius—Jenga
Capricorn—Monopoly
Aquarius—Cranium
Pisces—Candy Land

FROM: BrendonLowell@OTP.net
TO: JianZhao@OTP.net, KatieDrake@OTP.net,
JenniferSmith@OTP.net, . . . 6 others
SUBJECT: Meeting Invitation
WHEN: Friday, June 11, 2 p.m.–3 p.m.
WHERE: Microsoft Teams Meeting

Hey everyone,

I had an idea (💡!!!) re: the new user acquisition that we discussed during last week's meeting. I checked everyone's calendars before scheduling, but let me know if you have any conflicts and we can work a different date out. I blocked out an hour, but we might not need it.

I have a *great* feeling about this.

Best,
Brendon

P.S. It might be helpful to read up on the five love languages prior to our meeting. 👍

$\mathcal{W}$ith his last email of the day sent, Brendon powered down his monitor. He was reaching for his keys when his phone buzzed twice in quick succession, rattling loudly against the edge of his keyboard.

DARCY (6:03 P.M.): Where are you? Elle and Margot are getting restless. They're attempting to coerce me into having my aura photographed.
DARCY (6:03 P.M.): My *aura*, Brendon.

He checked the time and winced. He was only running a little late, but Darce was a stickler for punctuality. Even if it was only game night.

BRENDON (6:04 P.M.): On my way!

Elle and Margot's apartment was ten minutes from his office, fifteen if he caught every traffic light, which, mercifully, he did not. He made it across town in eight minutes, a new record, and glided to a stop beside the curb just as it started to drizzle.

Elle answered his knock, bouncing on her bare toes in the doorway. "Hey, Brendon. Come on in." She stepped back and shouted, "Darce, your brother's here!"

Like always, the place smelled faintly of patchouli, but beneath that was a sharper, more acrid smell. Cloyingly sweet and also . . . burned. Upon entering the kitchen, the culprit was clear. A plate of chocolate chip cookies—he was pretty sure those had been chocolate chips, perhaps raisins—sat on the counter, their edges charred black.

Elle reached inside a cabinet, withdrawing an assortment of cups, none of them matching. She placed his favorite, a cup resembling a mock Holy Grail, in front of him. "We've got the usual suspects. Wine, water, and . . ." She shut one eye, thinking. "Coffee."

"Water works, thanks."

"Oh! We might have hot chocolate but it's the kind without the marshmallows."

"No, you have the ones with marshmallows. They're behind your coffee filters, beside the box of apple cider packets that expired in 2014." Darcy stepped inside the kitchen, posting up against the counter. "Hey. You made it."

"When have I ever missed game night?" He smiled when Elle passed him his cup of water. "Thanks."

Elle paused in the doorway of the kitchen, a plastic souvenir cup of rosé in hand. "You guys coming?"

"In a second," Darcy said. "I need to talk to Brendon about something."

"Sure. We're still waiting on Annie, anyway."

Elle skipped from the kitchen, leaving him with Darcy.

"Annie didn't come with you?" He frowned.

Darcy crossed her arms, pinching the stem of her wineglass. It was probably the only real glass in this apartment. "No. She wasn't at my apartment when I came home from work. I texted her and she said something about wandering the market. I gave her Elle's address and she promised to meet us here." Darcy flipped her wrist over, checking the time. "If she's not here in fifteen minutes, I'll text her. Until then, I thought I'd take advantage of her not being here so you and I could have a little tête-à-tête."

He couldn't help but laugh. "Tête-à-tête?"

"Do you want to hear what Annie told me after you dropped her off yesterday or not?"

His stomach contorted, because of course he wanted to know what Annie had said, especially if it had to do with him. "Let me think . . . is water wet?"

Darcy rolled her eyes. "She thinks you're sweet. You make her laugh. She told me you have chemistry."

He nodded slowly. Sweet. Funny. Chemistry. His brows rose. Yeah, he could work with that. "Great."

"But—"

"Why does there always have to be a *but*?" he muttered.

Darcy frowned sympathetically. "I think she's afraid that you like the idea of her more than you like her."

Like the idea of her more than . . . "What gave her that idea? That's completely not true. That's—" He broke off with a groan. "Jesus. Does this have to do with my crush? Because come on. Last Friday was the first time I had seen Annie in eight years. I'm not carrying a torch for the girl I used to like when I was in high school. I like Annie *now*."

He'd had a great time getting to know who Annie was now. A fantastic time. She was hilarious, her sense of humor meshing perfectly with his. She could laugh at herself and she was—fuck, she was stunning. There were sparks. The sort of connection he'd been searching for, unable to find no matter how many dates he went on.

There was nothing wrong with any of the girls he'd dated, but they hadn't been right for him. The last few dates he'd gone on had been with women he'd met on OTP, and on paper, they'd had plenty in common. But in person? Nothing. He hadn't felt any of the sparks he was supposed to when they'd spoken, and his skin hadn't tingled when they touched. He hadn't even felt remotely warm.

Nothing held a candle to the way he burned when Annie touched him.

He didn't want to put the cart before the horse and call Annie *the one*, but there was too much potential between them for him to just throw in the towel. If anything, it sounded like he needed to step up his game.

"*I* know you do," Darcy stressed. "You're a romantic, but I never pegged you as certifiable. I'd have never asked you to spend time with my best friend if I thought you were just trying to live out some teenage fantasy."

"But that's what Annie thinks?"

"She didn't say that. She didn't mention your crush on her at all, actually." Darcy took a sip of wine and set her glass aside. "What I'm about to tell you is in confidence, okay?"

He was too engrossed in the conversation to make a quip about how all of this was in confidence. "Okay."

"Annie's dating history is . . . lackluster. She hasn't had the best experiences. I think she's afraid of being disappointed. Again." Darcy frowned. "She's a little . . . skittish. I think more so now that she's realized she really likes you. I just wanted you to know what you're up against."

He frowned, nodding slowly. He wouldn't call them confessions, but some of what Annie had said certainly aligned with what Darcy had said. How, when he'd said the point of his favorite movies was to show that love could conquer all, Annie had scoffed and said seeing was believing. How she believed romance was dead.

What Annie needed was someone to show her that disappointment wasn't an inevitability. Someone who knew how to listen. Someone who liked her, not the idea of her like she was worried about.

Not just anyone, but the right someone.

"I won't disappoint her."

Her expression softened. "I know you won't."

Darcy gave his arm a gentle squeeze on her way out of the kitchen.

Brendon eyed the plate of burned chocolate chip cookies and sad assortment of snacks on the counter before fishing inside his pocket for his phone.

☾

"Thank God. I was about to send out a search party," Darcy teased, waving Annie inside Elle's apartment.

Annie had spent the day exploring the parts of Pike Place Brendon hadn't gotten around to showing her last Saturday, namely the lower levels, which gave *eclectic* a whole new meaning. There was a magic shop, a luggage store, a store dedicated to all things purple—a real head scratcher—and more smoke shops than she could shake a stick at. The hours had flown by and she was still positive she hadn't explored every nook and cranny the market had to offer.

"Sorry I'm late. Completely lost track of time." She slipped off her sandals, leaving them beside a haphazard pile of shoes near the door. "I hope you guys weren't waiting for me to start."

A loud shriek came from further inside the apartment.

Darcy winced. "It's fine. They decided to play Egyptian Rat-screw to pass the time. I'm glad you're here because it's starting to get a little . . . violent." Her eyes dropped to the shopping bag Annie was holding. "What's that?"

Annie swung the bag behind her back. "It's nothing. Just something I saw at the market."

One of Darcy's brows rose. "Can I see?"

It was an impulse purchase. A dumb one she was already regretting.

Annie had spotted a colorful-looking store that, in addition to comics, sold movie memorabilia—everything from mugs to action figures to movie screenplays. The script of *When Harry Met Sally* had jumped out at her. Against her better judgment, she'd joined the checkout line with only one thought on her mind, and it was how she was dying to see the look on Brendon's face when she gave it to him.

It wasn't supposed to be a big deal. It was a screenplay. A reproduced screenplay. A million other copies existed. She bought her friends gifts all the time, little tokens and trinkets from her travels. *I'm thinking of you* gifts. Maybe that was why, standing in Elle's foyer with Darcy staring at her quizzically, it felt like a bigger deal than she'd bargained for.

In her hands was proof that even when he wasn't around, Annie was thinking of him, and on some level, she wanted him to know it.

"It's just something I saw in a comic book store," she said, downplaying it.

"*You* found something you liked in a comic book store." Darcy sounded skeptical.

"Excuse you, I *devoured* the *Archie* comics as a kid. My first crush was on Archie, for crying out loud."

Darcy's lips twitched. "Your first crush was on an accident-prone, well-meaning redheaded comic book character with a heart of gold?"

And her point was—

Her face went hot. Huh. The resemblance was uncanny, but she wasn't about to admit that. "Shut up."

Darcy held up her hands in supplication. "What's in the bag, Annie?"

Resistance was futile. "Fine. I saw a thing and it made me think of Brendon."

Darcy shot her a wicked smirk. "For Brendon, huh?"

Annie glared. "It's nothing."

"We'll see." Darcy turned. "Hey, Brendon. Annie brought you something."

"I hate you," she hissed, trying to keep from blushing through sheer force of will. "I hate you so much."

Brendon appeared around the corner, wearing a button-down shirt, the sleeves rolled up to his elbows, the top two buttons undone, revealing the all-too-lickable-looking hollow of his throat.

"Hey." His grin bordered on boyish, the crinkle of his eyes achingly earnest as he stared at her. "Glad you could make it."

Annie cleared her throat and wiped her palm against the side of her leg. Her hands had gone stupidly clammy. "Wasn't about to miss game night when I'd heard so much about it."

Brendon crossed his arms and leaned his shoulder against the wall. "Darcy told you things tend to get . . . intense?"

"I think the word she used was *vicious*. Not that I need a warning."

She'd witnessed enough flipped Monopoly boards to know how Brendon and Darcy could get when there were bragging rights at stake.

He gave another one of those easygoing smiles that brought out the dimples in his cheeks and made her knees weak. "Darcy said you brought me something?"

"Yeah, Annie. Why don't you show Brendon what you got him." Darcy smiled at her, all faux innocence. "I'm going to refresh my drink. Want me to grab you something?"

"Wine. Please. Or, on second thought, water. I haven't eaten anything."

Brendon reached inside his back pocket, withdrawing his phone. "I ordered a bunch of takeout. It should be here in about half an hour."

Darcy raised an eyebrow.

Annie caved. "Fine. Wine."

Darcy disappeared around the corner. Brendon looked at Annie expectantly.

Right. His present.

She cleared her throat and brought the plastic bag around to her front, fiddling with the straps. "It's just something I saw. And I—I thought of you."

His lips twitched as he stepped closer, close enough that he could reach inside the bag himself, if he wanted. Mostly close enough that she could smell his aftershave, even over the sharp smell of incense. "Don't leave me in suspense, Annie."

Her laugh came out breathless. "Says the guy who always refuses to tell me where he's taking me."

"Don't try to tell me you don't like surprises," he teased, stepping closer, resting his hand on top of hers. "Am I supposed to guess what's in the bag?"

"You can try." Her pulse pounded in her neck, her heart hammering away, some combination of nerves and proximity to Brendon making her dizzy.

"Hmm." Brendon's lips pulled to the side, eyes narrowing playfully. "Does it have something to do with somewhere we've been in the last few days?"

She mulled it over. "Yes and no."

He laughed. "Okay. I'm throwing in the towel." His thumb raked across the inside of her wrist as he loosened her grip on the bag. "Can I see?"

With a deep breath to brace herself, she let him take the bag. He delved inside, eyes staring up at the ceiling, stretching out the anticipation. Her eyes remained locked on his face as he finally lowered his gaze to the thick, bound script in his hands. His jaw dropped, his brown eyes doubling in size.

"Annie." The way he breathed her name put all the other times anyone had ever said her name to shame. It sounded different the way he uttered it, turning it into a form of praise that somehow rooted her to the spot and made her want to run, all at the same time. He lifted his eyes, and the intensity of them about bowled her over. "This is . . ."

She dropped her eyes to the scant space between them. "I just thought, you love romantic comedies and Nora Ephron and it was on the shelf, so—"

"I love it."

Her head snapped up. For a moment, she completely forgot how to suck air into her lungs when he looked at her, the weight of his stare a heavy, tangible thing ensnaring her. "This is the greatest present anyone's ever gotten me."

She batted at the air. "It's a reprint. It's nothing."

Had she the wherewithal to look up *meaningful glance* in the dictionary, there'd have been a picture of Brendon's whiskey-colored eyes gazing out at her from off the page. "It's not nothing."

No, she supposed it wasn't. This was something. *They* were something. What that something was, she didn't have the slightest clue, but continuing to call him her best friend's brother seemed woefully insufficient when she couldn't stop thinking about their kiss. A kiss she was pretty sure would haunt her for the rest of her life, with no other kiss capable of measuring up.

Darcy had asked her where her head was at, and if possible, she had even less of a clue today than she had yesterday. Liking Brendon wasn't smart, and wanting him to kiss her again definitely fell into the realm of bad ideas, but that hadn't stopped her from thinking about him as she wandered the market, wondering what he'd think of this little trinket or how he'd wrinkle his nose at the Starbucks cups littering the ground around the trash cans.

Utterly irrational, her own feelings were going to wind up giving her whiplash.

Annie wished . . . God, she didn't even know what she wanted at this point. Maybe to go back in time to before Brendon had turned her inside out, upside down. Back when she'd known exactly what she wanted, when it had made sense.

Take the job. Move to London. Buy a houseplant. Try to make some friends. Acquire a taste for tea. Familiarize herself with her vibrator.

Now she was all mixed up, what she wanted at war with what was smart, what was safe. This thing, whatever it was, couldn't go anywhere, but that didn't stop her from wishing it could.

"I don't know how to thank you for this," he murmured softly.

She had several ideas of where he could start.

He must've been thinking something along the same lines, because he reached out, cradling her jaw, his hand trembling softly, sweetly, against the side of her cheek as he brushed a wisp of hair out of her face. She held her breath, her bare toes curling against the linoleum floor, her whole body vibrating a little from holding still as he lowered his face to hers.

"Are you guys coming? If we keep playing this stupid fucking card game, I swear to God I'm going to wind up with a broken finger," a voice she didn't recognize shouted, shattering the moment.

A muscle in Brendon's jaw flexed as he stepped back with his eyes shut.

It was a blessing in disguise.

That's what she told herself as she stepped out of the foyer and into the living room, heart still racing.

On the floor in front of a well-loved sofa, Darcy sat with her legs crossed, a glass of rosé on the coffee table beside a stack of battered board games. Behind her on the couch, Elle was in the process of fashioning Darcy's long hair into an intricate braid.

Sprawled across the sole armchair, legs over one arm of the chair, head leaned back against the other, was a girl with a razor-sharp lob and cat-eye glasses that further accentuated her dark, almond-shaped eyes. Her checkered Vans bounced against the chair as she swung her legs.

Her lips spread in a smile and she sat up, curling her legs beneath her. "You're Annie."

"I am."

"I'm Margot." She reached for her glass and took a sip, appraising Annie over her drink. "So you're the girl who's got Brendon all in knots."

Brendon groaned and her stomach swooped. He'd talked about her. "*Margot.*"

"I'm sorry," Margot said, smiling, sounding the opposite of apologetic. "Was I not supposed to tell her that?"

He rubbed his eyebrow and sighed, his face turning a shade of pink she had no business finding adorable. And *yet.*

Elle nodded to the opposite end of the couch. "Have a seat. There's your drink."

Annie settled in on the center cushion, scooting over, trying to make room for Brendon and his long legs. It was a tight squeeze, their thighs pressed snug together, the rough denim of his jeans making her hyperaware of the fact that her shorts left her legs bare.

Margot smirked at her. "So, Annie. How are you liking Seattle so far?"

Annie reached for her glass of what appeared to be rosé and

took a quick sip. It was ultra-sweet, almost cloying, and more than likely a lot stronger than it seemed. "It's been great. I don't know, I guess I had this picture in my head of constant buckets of rain falling from the sky, and I'd heard rumors about the Seattle Freeze, but everyone I've met has been super friendly. And the food's been amazing. Darcy and I went out to . . . what was it?"

"The Pink Door," Darcy said, wincing when Elle accidentally tugged on her hair.

"Right. Best seafood of my life," Annie said.

"Great food, great beer, and we're super close to a bunch of wineries if your tastes are a little more refined than Elle's and mine." Margot smirked.

"Reliable public transportation if you don't want to drive," Elle chimed in.

Margot nodded. "Totally. We've got an awesome arts scene. Stellar music venues. Diverse communities. Super queer friendly."

"We've got mountains *and* water," Elle said. "And if you're willing to go for a drive, we've got a rain forest to the west and a desert to the east. All in one state. Plus, great day trips."

"Right? We've got Leavenworth, which is this quaint little Bavarian-style town that turns into Santa's village come winter. And Portland's only a couple of hours away."

"What more could you want?" Elle grinned.

Annie bit the inside of her cheek, trying not to laugh. "What more, indeed?"

"Washington has no state income tax," Darcy added, aiming for nonchalance and missing by a mile.

Annie shook her head, chuckling softly. "Why does this feel like an intervention?"

Darcy shrugged. "Not an intervention. Just facts. Do with them what you will."

Brendon cleared his throat. "As much as I'm sure Annie appreciates these selling points, maybe we should give her some time to, I don't know, digest them?" He shrugged. "Besides, it's game night."

Annie was both touched and overwhelmed by everyone's trying to sell her on their city. The logical part of her knew Darcy had put them up to it, but still. It was nice to feel wanted, something she hadn't felt in . . . too long.

But it was a lot to take in at once. Annie jostled Brendon lightly with her arm, staring up at him with a grateful smile. He squeezed her knee, his palm warm against the skin left bare by her shorts.

"Whose turn is it to pick?" Darcy asked.

"Pick?" Annie wondered aloud, still overly aware of Brendon's hand on her thigh. "Pick what?"

Elle worked a bright blue hair tie off her wrist, wrapping it around Darcy's new braid. "House rule. Winner of the last game night picks what game we play. *But* it can't be whatever game or games they won. Because that wouldn't be fair."

Brendon and Darcy shared a look, lips curving in twin smirks at the word *fair*.

"That would be me," Margot said, cracking her knuckles. "I won Jenga, remember?"

"How could I forget?" Darcy mumbled, shivering at the memory it must've evoked.

"True. *Or* we could let Annie choose," Elle suggested. "You know, since this is her first game night."

First and only, but Annie didn't correct her.

Margot deliberated for a minute, lips pursed and eyes narrowed behind her lenses. "All right. But choose wisely. I'll judge you if you pick something stupid like Candy Land."

"Hey! I love Candy Land," Elle argued. "Who here can say they *don't* have a little bit of a crush on Queen Frostine?"

Everyone stared at her.

"Fine, no Candy Land." Elle sank back into the couch, pouting.

Annie surveyed the boxes of board games stacked on the table. They had everything from Battleship to Cranium to Settlers of Catan, and even a game called Exploding Kittens. If this was a test, she wanted to pass, but she also didn't want to risk life and limb, knowing how competitive Darcy and Brendon could get. "How about Scruples?"

That sounded low risk.

Margot grinned. "I like you."

Darcy shook her head. "We should finish with Scruples. I need more wine before I play that game."

Elle laughed. "Charades first?"

"Fine." Darcy dropped her head back against Elle's thigh. "But we have to pick new teams."

"Normally Brendon and I partner up," Margot explained. "It's not safe to put those two"—she nodded at Darcy and Brendon—"on a team together. They're ruthless."

"I replaced your coffee table, didn't I?" Darcy arched a brow. "No harm, no foul."

"Brendon fell *through* the coffee table. It was scarring." Margot shivered. "I thought we were going to have to drive him to the emergency room."

Brendon turned to Annie and smiled. "Be my partner?"

"As long as I don't fall through a coffee table," she joked.

"Don't worry." He tried and failed to wink, an adorable quirk of his. Less adorable and far more arousing, his thumb rubbed a maddeningly little circle on the skin of her knee. "I'd catch you."

Logic told her it was time to move his hand away. That the longer she left it there without saying something, the more obvious it was she liked it when he touched her. That it would be harder to deny herself these little touches that didn't *feel* like nothing. Each brush of his skin against hers made her want another, made her want more. It was becoming harder and harder—nearly impossible—to remember why she wasn't supposed to be letting this happen.

She set her glass on the table and, in the process, shifted slightly forward, dislodging Brendon's hand from her knee.

Margot stood and stretched, her back popping. "I'll be with Elle and Darcy. Let me run and grab some paper."

She returned in a flash. In one hand she had a handful of scrap paper and in the other two plastic cups. "The rules are simple. Charades, at least according to our house rules, involves each player writing a ten-word-or-less phrase, song title, movie, or other pop culture reference on a slip of paper. You then fold your suggestion in half and slip it inside your designated cup. One player draws from the opposite team's cup, then has one minute to act out whatever is on the slip of paper. Sound good?"

Annie nodded. The next five minutes were spent in near silence, save for the occasional muffled whisper and snicker as they each individually filled out their slips.

Elle drew first, her smile immediate. "Okay. Everyone ready?"

Margot and Darcy nodded, both sitting up straighter. Brendon's thumb hovered over the timer on his phone.

"And . . . go!" he said, starting the clock.

Immediately, Elle pointed upward.

"Ceiling!"

"Roof!"

"Sky?" Margot guessed.

Elle bounced on her toes, grinning, gesturing for them to keep going.

"Sky . . . sky . . . stars?" Margot said.

Elle clapped her hands and nodded. She made a fist and punched at the air.

"Fight?"

She frowned and bobbed her head from side to side. With her thumb and forefinger, she made a gun, shooting at some invisible enemy.

"Shoot? Fire?" Darcy guessed.

As if holding a baseball bat, Elle swung, then stepped back, nearly tripping over the rug as she parried an imaginary blow.

"Battle! War! *Star Wars*!" Darcy screamed.

Elle shrieked and threw herself at Darcy. One point to the opposing team. Brendon stared at Annie with wide, serious eyes. "You want to act first or guess?"

She wiped her hands on her legs and stood, reaching inside the cup for a slip of paper. "You guess."

Her eyes skimmed the writing on the slip; she recognized Darcy's perfect, looping handwriting. Heat crept up Annie's jaw.

"Ready?" Darcy smiled.

No. No, she really wasn't.

Brendon had his forearms resting on his knees. He nodded. "And . . . go!"

Okay . . . she could figure out a way around this. She held up two fingers.

He frowned. "Two words?"

She nodded and held up one finger.

"First word."

She grimaced and got down on her hands and knees. Darcy snickered before clapping a hand over her face. Annie was *so* going to murder her in her sleep.

"Uh . . . ?" Brendon shook his head.

Here went nothing. Annie stuck out her tongue and started to pant.

Brendon stared, cocking his head to the side, doing a better job of looking like an adorably confused puppy dog than she was.

She couldn't believe she was about to do this. She started to shake her butt, still while on her hands and knees. Darcy covered her face with her hands, shaking so hard Annie was pretty sure Darcy was about to start crying.

"Um . . ." Brendon tugged on his hair. "Wiggle?"

Jesus. Annie swallowed down her mortification and hiked her leg in the air, pretending to pee on an imaginary hydrant.

Darcy fell over, and Elle and Margot lost it entirely, their laughter filling the apartment.

"Dog?" he guessed.

She waffled her head from side to side.

"Puppy?"

Gah. Annie made a frazzled gesture for him to keep guessing. "Dog . . . doggo . . . doggy!"

Annie collapsed to the floor with relief.

"Twenty seconds!" Margot shouted.

Annie held up two fingers.

"Second word," Brendon blurted, nodding quickly.

Annie stood and gestured to her blouse.

"Shirt? Clothes. Fashion."

Annie bounced up and down. So close.

Brendon's eyes widened before he pinched his lips shut and snorted. "Doggy style?"

Face on fire, Annie tossed Darcy a quick, gloating smile before Brendon wrapped his arms around her waist and hefted her in the air, spinning her in a dizzying circle that made her stomach swoop.

"Okay. This one's easy. I want to get it over with." Margot shoved the paper in her back pocket and took the floor. She stuck one arm out in front of her, then the next, before flipping her right arm palm side up, then the left.

Darcy laughed. "Oh! It's the—"

"Shh!" Elle snickered. "I'm confused. Keep going, Mar."

Margot rolled her eyes and cycled through the entire Macarena, Elle laughing the whole time. Lips curved in a grin, but her eyes locked on the timer, Darcy called out the guess when there were ten seconds left. Ever cautious.

"I hate you both," Margot said, collapsing back in her chair with a put-upon sigh.

"Oh please." Annie scoffed. "That was tame."

Darcy smirked. "So was *doggy style*."

Annie could feel the color drain from her face even as her eyes narrowed. What game were they playing?

Brendon was up next. He glanced at his slip of paper and immediately shook his head, a neon flush inching up his jaw. "Nope. Hard pass."

Margot smirked. "You could forfeit."

He clenched his jaw. "Fine. Start the clock."

"Go!"

He held up three fingers, then just one. She nodded. Brendon pointed at himself.

"I?"

He nodded. Two fingers went up before he wrapped his fingers around his opposite wrist.

"Grab? Hold? Grip?"

He grimaced, shooting Margot another *if looks could kill* glare, before changing tactics. He rested his hand on his chest and dragged it slowly down his body, stopping just before he reached indecent territory. He met Annie's eyes across the room, his brows rising and lips curling in a quick and dirty little smirk before he performed a quick hip thrust that made her flush to the roots of her hair.

"Um . . ." Her brain wasn't working.

"Twelve seconds."

Shit.

Brendon lifted three fingers then pointed at himself all over again.

"I?"

He shook his head.

"Me?"

He circled his hand for her to keep going.

"Um . . ." Oh. *Oh!* "I touch myself!"

Brendon collapsed on the floor and covered his face, groaning into his hands. "I hate you, Margot."

"Love you, too, babe. Darcy, you're up."

Last, but certainly not least, Darcy acted out *Pride and Prejudice*, resorting to pointing to herself in frustration. Down to the wire, Elle guessed correctly.

Darcy pulled a face, shuddering hard as she returned to her seat. "I can't be the only one who'd rather be playing Monopoly, right?"

Groans rose up around the living room.

"What?" Darcy crossed her arms.

"As if you don't know perfectly well," Annie said, shaking her head. "You once flipped the board when you lost."

"I was twelve." Darcy sniffed. "It's my favorite game. I get a little competitive. Sue me."

"A little?" Annie laughed. "Understatement of the year award goes to . . ."

Brendon gave a drumroll. "*Darcy.* Come on, admit it. You trounce everyone."

"You play without mercy, buying all the utilities and putting up hotels as soon as you can," Annie said.

Darcy turned to Elle, brows raised, clearly looking for help.

"Landlords suck," Elle muttered, avoiding Darcy's eyes.

"Wow." Darcy tutted. "That is the *point* of the game."

"All in favor of switching over to Monopoly?" Margot asked.

Predictably, one hand rose. Darcy's.

"All opposed?"

Everyone else raised a hand. Elle lifted both and blew Darcy a kiss.

"The nays have it," Margot said. "Someone pick another slip."

"Could we get new ones?" Brendon muttered. "I feel like this game is rigged."

It was true. She and Brendon were the only ones getting extremely innuendo-laden phrases.

"It's not our fault you didn't come to win," Darcy said, smirking.

Annie had a feeling there was something else afoot. She was getting some distinct matchmaking vibes, the none-too-subtle smirks exchanged by Darcy, Elle, and Margot impossible to ignore.

She reached for her phone and opened her texts, about to tell Darcy to cool it. She didn't need Darcy to play matchmaker for her and she *definitely* didn't need any help realizing she was crazy stupid attracted to Brendon. It was the rest she was fuzzy on, and no amount of miming lewd sex acts was going to bring her any clarity.

Her thumb hovered over the *send* button when someone pounded heavily against the front door.

"Food must be here," Brendon said, leaving the room, giving her an ample view of how snugly his jeans fit in all the right places.

Annie shut her eyes.

Maybe switching to Monopoly wasn't such a bad idea.

Annie's stomach hurt from laughing.

Elle and Darcy had ducked out for more wine, a bottle Darcy swore would go better with Greek food than Elle's boxed rosé. Margot had retreated to her bedroom to make a phone call, leaving Annie and Brendon alone.

"What did—" She clamped her lips together, about to lose her composure all over again. "What did you call it?"

Brendon wiped the tzatziki sauce off his chin. "*Zatzeekee* sauce." When she sputtered through tightly pressed lips, his cheeks began to color. "What? That's what it's called!"

She gasped through her laughter and held her stomach, praying she wouldn't slide off the counter and onto the floor. Oh God, her abs were starting to burn. "That's—that's not even remotely close to how you say it."

"It is!" His nose scrunched. "Isn't it?"

Nope. She shook her head.

"Ah, hell." He gripped the back of his neck, looking chagrined. "I thought it was like *tsar*. You know, but with a silent *t*."

"Tsah-see-key," she enunciated. "It's like saying pizza without the first syllable."

"I've been saying it wrong my whole life." He hung his head and groaned. "Every time I order, I ask for extra *zatzeekee* sauce. I'm impressed with everyone's ability to keep a straight face."

"Except for me," she teased.

Brendon grinned. "You are the exception."

She snickered into her Gyrito, a gyro/beer-battered burrito hybrid stuffed with gyro meat, tomatoes, and feta cheese. It was so delicious she was a smidge disappointed Brendon had ordered just one. On the other hand, he'd ordered Greek food, and she was 99 percent certain he'd done so because she'd mentioned how much she loved it the other night when they were stranded in that grimy motel. She was surprised he remembered, and even more surprised he'd actually ordered it when, according to Darcy, the group usually ordered from the Thai place right around the corner. "I'm sure plenty of people mispronounce it. Consonant clusters are a bitch. Try saying *strč prst skrz krk* five times fast."

"Was that—what *was* that?" He gaped.

He'd missed a spot of tzatziki at the corner of his mouth, making him look all the more adorable in his horror over his mispronunciation and her tongue-twister. Without thinking, she leaned forward and thumbed it away, gasping when his tongue darted out against her skin.

All Brendon did was smile, like licking her finger was no big deal.

Her pulse pounded in her head. "It's—it's a, um . . . a Czech tongue-twister. It means 'stick a finger through the throat.'"

He recoiled in horror and her head fell back against the cabinet, her stomach burning with laughter all over again. She did that a lot around him, laughing so hard she ached. Her stomach, her chest, her heart. All good aches, like stretching underused muscles.

"What it translates to doesn't really matter," she explained, wiping her fingers off on her napkin. "Each word has no vowels and a syllabic *r*, which—" She broke off, realizing he probably didn't care about the nuances of Slavic languages. "It's just a funny tongue-twister."

He cocked his head, looking genuinely curious. "Syllabic *r*?"

She smiled, more pleased than she'd admit. "Yeah. The *r* is a syllabic consonant sound unto itself, so you don't need vowels. Like the *m* in *rhythm*."

He hummed, sounding intrigued. "You never said you spoke Czech, too."

"I don't. In one of my linguistics courses in college that was an example of liquid consonants. Hard to forget."

He smiled crookedly. "Well, at least I know I'm saying *gyro* right."

She buried her smile in her napkin, because he *wasn't*. As with *tzatziki*, he'd butchered it, albeit not quite as horrifically. He was *close* by calling it a "euro."

His smile fell, replaced with a hangdog look of dismay. "No."

"Yep. It's *yee-roh*."

He hung his head. "I can never show my face in George's again."

"I'm sure they hear *way* worse all the time. At least you didn't call it a *jy-roh* or a *grrr-roh*."

He snickered. "At least."

She eyed his order of Greek-style poutine hungrily. Her Gyrito had been satisfying but not the most filling. She plucked a fry from the basket and cradled it with her other hand, careful not to drip grease all over the counter as she brought it to her mouth. Her taste buds exploded with that one perfectly balanced bite of feta cheese, tzatziki sauce, and Kalamata olives. She groaned and plucked another fry from the paper boat, scarfing it down before going back for one more.

"You fry thief." He laughed. "You're going to have to pay for that, you know."

She lowered her fry from her lips and frowned quizzically. "Hmm?"

A mischievous smile played at the edges of his mouth. "You eat my fries, you pay taxes."

"Taxes? What kind of taxes?"

Brendon stepped in front of her, one arm on either side of her hips, his palms resting on the counter. She swallowed hard, breath coming quicker as he leaned closer, boxing her in.

"Spend tomorrow with me."

She blinked twice.

Those were not the sort of taxes she had on the brain.

"What did you have in mind?"

"It's sort of . . . OTP adjacent."

"Is it, like, a company picnic or something?"

"Or something." Brendon smiled. "It's not every day our head of public relations ties the knot with our VP of analytics."

"A wedding? You're inviting me to a wedding?"

He took another step closer, firmly cradled between her thighs in a way that was unambiguously intimate. Friends didn't stand like this or touch each other like this, and they definitely, without a doubt, didn't stare at each other's mouths like Brendon was eyeing hers. "I was going to strongarm Margot into being my plus-one, but if you aren't doing anything"—he swallowed—"maybe you want to be my date?"

She held her breath.

The word rattled around inside her brain.

Date.

Date.

Date.

She leaned back against the cabinet, her head suddenly too heavy to hold upright. "I don't know, Brendon."

"It'll be fun, Annie," he promised. "We'll make it fun."

Having fun with Brendon wasn't her concern.

Weddings were . . . serious, this one bound to be more so seeing as Brendon worked with some percentage of the guest list. A *large* percentage, she'd wager. There would be questions. Who Annie was. Who she was to Brendon. Weddings had a funny way of making people comfortable asking prying questions that under any other circumstances would be deemed impolite.

How long have you been together? Is it serious? Think that'll be the two of you up there someday? You're not getting any younger. Why don't you try to catch the bouquet?

"The venue's on the water in Kirkland. You can see the whole city from there. Just think. Delicious food—"

"Rubbery chicken, you mean."

He chuckled. "I was thinking more along the lines of wedding cake. You like cake, don't you?"

Duh, but she couldn't help but tease, "Depends on the flavor."

Just like she'd imagined earlier, only better, Brendon's hands skimmed up her thighs, gripping her, thumbs making more of those maddening circles against her skin, leaving goose bumps in their wake. They inched higher, approaching the hem of her shorts, flirting with where denim met skin. "Dancing. You can't honestly tell me you don't want to watch me do the 'Cha Cha Slide'?"

It was difficult to string her thoughts together with Brendon touching her like this. "I—I don't know if I could h—handle the secondhand embarrassment."

Brendon's thumbs slipped just under the fabric of her shorts, his brows lifting high on his forehead. She shivered violently, making Brendon grin.

Oh, that was dirty pool. So utterly unfair.

His voice was rough-hewn and he sounded as breathless as she felt. "Please?"

Something about that one word completely undid her.

"Okay."

"Yeah?"

She nodded. "It's . . . it's a date."

One date. That was hardly promising anything. It wasn't like she'd agreed to move here and marry him or anything absurd like that. Just a date.

Brendon's tongue darted out, wetting his lips as he leaned in, arching over her. His fingers bit into the skin of her thighs, pleasant pressure that made her stomach clench in anticipation.

Yes. The moment she'd been dying for since their almost-kiss in the foyer. Before that, if she was being honest. Since their last kiss, their first kiss, what was supposed to have been their only kiss, because she had a mantra. A list of reasons that right now she couldn't have given less of a fuck about.

"We've got wine!"

Brendon swore quietly under his breath, tearing himself away quickly, regret shining in his dark eyes. Eyes that remained locked on hers as he reached down, adjusting himself in his jeans, not bothering to hide what he was doing.

She bit back a whimper.

Tearing herself from Brendon was becoming increasingly difficult, the ache between her thighs so intense she could hardly look Darcy in the eye when she stepped inside the kitchen, brown paper bag of wine in hand.

🌙

An hour later, after every last scrap of takeout had been devoured, game night had turned into less of a vicious competition and more of a lazy evening of chatting, music playing quietly in the background. Annie ducked out to use the restroom and when she stepped back into the hall, she nearly collided with Elle. "Whoops. Sorry."

Elle shook her head. "I was waiting for you."

Annie's brows rose. "Oh. Okay?"

"I was thinking, if you don't already have plans tomorrow, we could hang out? I have a few calls I have to make in the morning, but I'm free after noon if you want to grab lunch and maybe go shopping." Elle offered her a smile. "I know a great antique market, if that sounds like something you might be interested in."

Her lips twisted in a genuine apology, touched by the offer. "I'd love to, but I already promised Brendon I'd spent the afternoon with him."

"No worries. Next week, maybe?"

"I'm in."

Elle beamed at her before her eyes darted briefly to the living room. "This has been nice. All of us. I'm happy you're here."

"So am I. Aside from, you know, the total humiliation of having to act out *doggy style* in front of everyone, it was fun."

She was happier than she could remember being in a long,

long time. She didn't feel particularly compelled to do the math—any kind of math, but especially math this depressing—but it had been too long since she'd had friends who included her in any of their plans. Friends who bothered to remember when she was in town or where she was when she wasn't. True friends.

One night with Darcy, Elle, Margot, and Brendon and Annie already felt more welcome than she had the last five times she'd been out with her "friends" in Philadelphia. Even if Darcy had put them all up to their little *let's sell Annie on the virtues of Seattle spiel*, they'd obviously cared enough to go along with it.

These were people who wanted her around, and that was new. New and not something Annie was thrilled to leave behind.

She paused in the entryway of the hall, watching as Elle returned to her place on the couch behind Darcy. Brendon looked over his shoulder and smiled at Annie, gesturing to the space beside him.

Her chest grew tight.

In less than a week, she'd be on a plane to Philadelphia, a pitstop where she'd pack her apartment up and continue on to London.

Unless . . .

She pressed the heel of her hand to her chest, trying and failing to alleviate the pressure squeezing her, making her feel like the room was suddenly too small for five people plus all her tangled-up feelings.

Chapter Fourteen

Saturday, June 5

*E*arly showers had cooled the air considerably, the temperatures hovering in the midseventies. Rays of sunshine had broken through the cloud cover during the ceremony, right as Katie and Jian exchanged vows. Now the sun hovered at the horizon, streaking the blue sky with shades of sherbet orange and pink. Golden light reflected off the placid surface of Lake Washington, and a gentle breeze ruffled the crisp white tablecloths beneath the pavilion as Annie took a sip of champagne and admired the view.

Nothing she'd ever heard about Seattle had done the place justice. Not even pictures could capture the city in its glory. Blue skies streaked with white clouds served as a backdrop for the skyscrapers, mountains peeking out to the right. Everything was green—the trees, the grass—all thanks to the rain she didn't mind as much as she'd first thought she would. The whole city felt vibrant and alive in a way no place she'd ever lived before had.

Saying goodbye to Seattle might be the hardest thing she'd ever done. So hard, she was already dreading it, and she wasn't even gone yet.

"Is my tie crooked?" Brendon fidgeted with the hot-pink bow tie knotted at his throat. "It feels crooked."

She had to swallow fast before she spewed champagne across the table. "It's not crooked, it's completely lopsided. Come here."

He leaned forward, baring his throat, allowing her to adjust his bow tie, all the while staring down at her from beneath his coppery lashes. Fingers trembling ever so subtly, she smoothed the satin, then ran her hands along his broad shoulders, brushing away imaginary lint. A poor excuse to keep touching him.

Brendon was currently sporting the most dapper outfit she'd ever seen him in: a sharp-looking navy suit tailored to perfection—though he'd ditched the jacket after the ceremony—a white button-down, a pink tie, and polished brown loafers. His auburn hair was combed neatly back, save for one rogue strand that kept curling at his temple.

For some reason, probably because this was a wedding, Annie had a flashback to when she was five, maybe six, and had tagged along with Mom to the bakery to put in the order for Dad's birthday cake. In the center of the shop had been a display of the most gorgeous wedding cakes Annie had ever seen. Multitiered and covered in fondant and delicate sugar flowers, those cakes had captivated her. When no one was looking, Annie had swiped her finger through the frosting, dying for just one taste. Icing-laden finger poised an inch in front of her mouth, she'd frozen when the woman working behind the counter had wagged a finger, scolding her with a severe frown that had left Annie quaking.

Brendon was like one of those cakes. Delicious looking, tempting, completely off-limits if she knew what was good for her.

"There." She dropped her hands back to her lap, a safe distance away. "All better."

Brendon offered her a crooked smile and reached for his glass of water, draining half of it in one chug.

She curled her fingers around the taut muscles of his forearms, squeezing gently. Her hands had a mind of their own, apparently having missed the whole *no-touchy* memo. "Are you okay? You're looking a little . . . peaky."

During the ceremony, he'd shed a few happy tears, the vows even choking her up a little, but afterward, during cocktail hour, he'd grown pale faced and fidgety. For the life of her, she couldn't figure out why.

He set his water aside and grabbed his champagne, tipping it back and coughing. "Ah, bubbles." He pinched his nose, making her laugh. "I'm supposed to give a speech." He patted the breast pocket of his suit. "I jotted a few notes down but now I'm second-guessing myself."

"Just . . . speak from the heart? You're amazing at that."

A deep flush worked its way up his jaw, his skin matching his bow tie. She had the fiercest urge to press a kiss to the hinge of his strong jaw, feel his skin warm under her lips. "Thanks, Annie."

He squeezed her knee, his palm hot against the skin left bare by her dress. The familiarity of the gesture made her breath hitch, and a stupid part of her wanted to trap his hand between her thighs, to see what he'd do. If the flush would creep higher up his face, bleed into his hairline, or if he'd smirk and slide his hand even higher.

She hadn't brought any clothes to Seattle that were formal enough for a wedding, even an outdoor summer ceremony. Darcy had given her free rein in her closet, but the height difference made picking something out to borrow difficult. Darcy's short dresses fell at an unflattering spot on her calves, chopping her off just below the knees. Her maxis drowned Annie, fabric dragging on the ground. She'd chosen the one dress that didn't make her look like a little girl playing dress-up in her mom's closet, a number that was probably tea-length on Darcy but fell to Annie's ankles. The bodice was a little roomy, but because it was a halter, Annie hadn't had a problem adjusting it so there'd be no accidental slippage. There was a deep slit up the side, the blush silk fluttering around her legs.

His hand lingered on her thigh, an embarrassingly breathy sigh escaping her lips when his thumb caressed the crease of her knee.

"Shit," he swore under his breath, making her jump. This wasn't the time or the place to be thinking about what Brendon's face would look like if she grabbed his wrist and tugged it higher up her thigh beneath the privacy of the tablecloth.

Her sip of water did little to quench her thirst. "What's wrong?"

Brendon stared across the room, his smile verging on a grimace. "Jian's mother is gesturing for me."

Annie followed his eyes. An older woman wearing a beautiful sapphire gown winked at Brendon.

"I think that's your cue," Annie said.

He stood stiffly, looking almost as petrified as he had when he'd climbed the stage for karaoke. "Wish me luck."

Without thinking, she reached out, grabbing his hand. She squeezed his fingers, finding their clamminess adorable. "Good luck. I'll be here when it's over."

He squeezed back and marched off toward the front of the room, where the groom's mothers welcomed him with eager smiles.

"Your boyfriend seems nervous."

It took her a minute to realize the woman sitting at the next table over was speaking to her.

"Oh, he's not my—he's just . . ." Annie sighed and laughed. Here it was, the first of many times where she would be forced to explain her relationship to Brendon. "My friend."

A friend she was painfully attracted to, but a friend nonetheless.

The other woman smiled. "Friends. Ten years ago I was just friends with that guy over there"—she jerked her chin in the direction of a man standing and talking to the groom—"but then one thing led to another and we had three of those"—she pointed at the group of kids playing near the edge of the lake—"and now we're expecting another."

She rested her hand on her bump.

Annie laughed. "Congratulations?"

"Life comes at you fast." The woman beamed at her. "You don't look like 'just friends.'"

Was she really having this conversation? With a stranger? Of course she was. Awkward conversations with strangers were par for the course at weddings. "It's a long story."

"The best ones usually are." The woman laughed. "I'm just saying. I know that look. That *will we, won't we* look. Where he's looking at you when you aren't, and then you're looking at him when he isn't. When both of you are too scared to bite the bullet, so you dance around each other until finally . . ." She waggled her brows. "*Boom.*"

Annie dropped her elbow to the table and rested her chin on her hand. "*Boom*, huh? I guess I'm worried about the wrong sort of *boom*, if you catch my drift. The painful kind that implodes in your face."

She turned and Annie followed her gaze. Brendon stood at the front of the pavilion, watching Annie. He winked, both eyes shutting adorably.

"I doubt you have anything to worry about, because that guy?" The woman leaned in, whispering. "He looks at you like you hung the moon."

☾

Brendon had immediately been pulled into a conversation upon the conclusion of his speech, which had thankfully inspired as much laughter as it had tears. Problem was, as soon as he'd slipped away from *that* conversation, he'd been drawn into another and another, when all he wanted was to spend time with Annie.

"Hi." Speak of the devil. Only, Annie looked more like an angel in her pink dress, her blond hair creating a soft halo around her face as she wrapped her hand around his arm, tucking her fingers into the crook of his elbow. "I hope you don't mind if I steal my date."

The older woman he'd been speaking to, a great-aunt of Katie's, waved them off with a smile.

"Sorry it took me a minute to rescue you," Annie said as they crossed the room, circling the dance floor. "Cake came first."

"As it always should." He smiled down at her.

The sun had slinked beneath the horizon, leaving behind a fiery strip of crimson and burnished bronze that bled upward into navy and indigo. Around the same time the desserts had been brought out, someone had flipped on the looping strands of fairy lights strung up around the pavilion. Their golden glow brought out the flecks of darker blue in Annie's eyes. *Breathtaking* didn't do her beauty justice.

Throughout the ceremony, when he hadn't been focused on Katie and Jian, he'd stolen glances at Annie from the corner of his eye, scarcely believing that she was here. That she'd agreed to come with him. His date. No pretenses, no excuses; he'd asked her because he wanted her here. Not because Darcy needed his help convincing Annie to move to Seattle. Not because of their bet, his determination to prove to her romance wasn't dead. If he was lucky, witnessing two people vow to spend the rest of their lives together might help him do just that, but that wasn't why he'd asked Annie.

There wasn't a single person he'd have rather had with him.

"My speech wasn't a total cluster, was it?" he asked.

"I loved it," she said, sounding completely sincere.

"Yeah?" His brows rose.

She nodded. "It's been a year or so since I've been to a wedding, but after a while, all the speeches and vows start to blur together. Yours, I'd remember."

"Want to hear something wild?" Without asking, he led her over to the dance floor, just in time for the upbeat song to transition into something a little slower they could talk during while they swayed.

Annie rested her hands on his shoulders, their sizable height difference less disparate with her towering pumps. "Wild? Uh, *duh*. I'm not sure why you'd waste your breath asking."

He smiled and rested his hands on her hips. His fingers brushed the skin left bare by the low back of her dress. The way she shivered and stepped closer was intensely gratifying. "All right. This is the fifth wedding I've been to this year."

She jerked back, staring up at him with wide, horrified eyes. "*Fifth?*" She snickered. "Oh God, is this where you tell me you've been a groomsman twenty-seven times?"

He gripped her waist, not leading her in any particular set of steps as much as swaying softly to the music. They were near the edge of the dance floor, out of everyone's way. "Hardly. Besides, three of those weddings were for people who met on OTP and sent me an invitation."

She goggled at him. "People *do* that? Send strangers invitations? I mean, I know people invite, like, Taylor Swift to things, but . . ." She scrunched her nose. "You're not Taylor Swift. No offense."

"None taken."

"And you go?"

"Of course." He shrugged. "What's not to love about weddings?"

Her fingers gently twisted in the short strands at his nape. A pleasant shiver raced from his scalp down his spine. That was new. Someone playing with his hair. It was nice, something he could get used to.

"I can only speak to the weddings I've been to, but usually the food sucks, there's never an open bar, someone's aunt or uncle still manages to get sloppy drunk and make a pass at the wedding party, someone has a breakdown in the bathroom, the DJ thinks the chicken dance is still in vogue, and everyone makes *way* too big of a deal out of the bouquet toss." She stared up at him through long lashes made dark by the makeup around her eyes. "I guess weddings feel like a party for everyone *except* the bride and groom. It has nothing to do with their marriage."

"I've been to weddings like that," he conceded, stepping back before reaching for Annie's hand, spinning her in an unexpected twirl that made her laugh. The sound was music to his ears, better than whatever the DJ was playing, which had faded into the background, just noise. "Where everyone forgets what it's all supposed to be about."

"Which is?" Annie rested her hands on his chest, no doubt able to feel his heart thundering away beneath his breastbone.

"The party favors, obviously." He grinned. "Free stuff. What's not to love?"

She shoved him lightly, then let her hands drift back to his shoulders. She stepped closer than before, her stomach pressed intimately into his hips, a move that made him swallow hard. "I find it difficult to believe you come to all these weddings for cellophane-wrapped kettle corn and bottle openers engraved with someone else's initials."

"You got me there." He ran his hands down her back, stifling another smile when her breath caught, audible even over the music. "It's—don't laugh."

She mimed zipping her lips.

"There's just something about watching two people pledge their love to one another, celebrate their commitment surrounded by family and friends, and step into the next chapter of their lives. It more than makes up for the rubbery chicken." He traced absent circles along her back, staring down at her. Her blue eyes were serious as they flitted over his face, her lashes fluttering softly. "I've been thinking. The other night, in the hotel. You asked me what I think is romantic. And yeah, I am a fan of the grand gesture. Not every grand gesture, because I thought about it, and you're right. Plenty are flawed and creepy, poorly executed, or try to make up for shoddy communication skills. But emblematically? I do love it. That big, demonstrative moment where nothing else matters but making sure the person you care about knows it. That you're in. You're all in and you want everyone to know, no matter how wild or risky it is. Weddings are like that. The vows are, at least."

Something about the soft look in Annie's eyes, wistful almost, compelled him to keep going. To confess what he'd never told anyone before.

"I don't have a single memory of my mom and dad saying *I love you* to each other." Annie made a soft noise, but he soldiered on, wanting to get this out. "Maybe those movies aren't perfect, but for most of my life, they were the best proof I had that people could wind up happy together."

Their gentle swaying had come to a stop at the edge of the dance floor. Annie frowned sharply and her fingers tightened in his hair, forcing him to turn his face down. "Brendon."

"Sorry." He chuckled, eyes darting around the pavilion. Everyone else was in their own little world, paying the two of them no mind. "Didn't mean to go off on a tangent. Or be such a bummer."

She gave a quick, curt shake of her head. "No, no. That's . . . I always viewed the grand gesture as sort of selfish. *If I do this, I'll get this out of it.* I never thought of it the way you described it before."

An uneven exhale escaped from between his lips when Annie's thumb brushed the space beneath his ear. "And I never really thought about the little things, until you talked about it the other night. But I think you're right. With the right person, I don't think it matters what you do or where you are."

The smile she graced him with made his heart roll over like the engine of his junky first car. "Exactly."

The last strains of the slow song they'd swayed to ended, and the DJ switched over to something loud and poppy. Brendon stole a step back, bopping his head and shaking his hips from side to side in an exaggerated shimmy, trying to make Annie laugh.

His performance had the desired effect, causing Annie to grip her stomach as she giggled.

"Go on." She jerked her chin at him when he stopped. "I was enjoying myself."

Across the floor, someone wolf-whistled. He followed the sound to where Jian had his fingers in his mouth, Katie at his side, falling over herself laughing.

Brendon flushed. "Yeah, you and everyone else."

Annie smiled and reached for his hand, leading him off the dance floor.

Caught up in the feel of her much smaller fingers laced with his, he missed the fact she'd led them not in the direction of their table, but instead to a table covered in tiny vials of bubbles and other party favors.

Mixed in with the bubbles and miniature bottles of tequila were a dozen Fujifilm Instax cameras and a sign that read, *Please borrow a camera and help us capture our special day. Take a selfie or group picture and add it to our guestbook! Xoxo, Katie and Jian*

Brendon snagged a camera and snapped a candid of Annie. A startled laugh escaped her lips.

"Gimme." She snatched the camera right out of his hands. A bright flash filled his vision, making him jump even though he knew it was coming.

Annie lowered the camera and grabbed the photo that popped out from the top.

"Let me see," he said, reaching for the camera.

She shook her head, holding the camera out of reach. His arms were longer, so he could've grabbed it had he truly wanted, but he didn't. Not when Annie was beaming at him. Not when he'd do anything to keep her smiling. Smiling because of him. "Uh-uh. I bet that one turned out blurry."

She snapped another picture and another soon after that, capturing him midlaugh.

"Oh, come on. *Annie.*" He stepped forward. "Don't I get a turn?"

She backed away, leaving the cover of the pavilion, stepping out onto the strip of grass that led down to a set of concrete stairs that descended into the lake.

"Quit running away from me," he gasped out, laughing. He narrowly avoided the group of children playing and quickened his steps, practically running. Up ahead, Annie quickened her stride, her dress flapping around her ankles.

She stopped at the edge of the lake. His momentum too great, Brendon was forced to wrap his arms around her waist to keep from barreling into her. Annie caught herself with her hands splayed against his stomach.

He smiled down at her, and the blue-hued twilight played against the high crests of her cheeks, highlighting the sweep of her lashes and the curve of her upper lip.

"I think . . . I think I like having you chase me," she whispered.

Inhaling the brackish smell of lake water and the delicate scent of Annie's perfume, he held still as she slid her hands higher, resting them on his chest. Beneath her palms, his heart pounded, making it obvious how much he wanted her.

"I caught you," he rasped. "What do I get?"

Heat curled deep in his gut when the tip of her tongue slipped out from between her lips.

"I guess that would all depend on what you want," she whispered, eyes only leaving his for a split-second glance at his mouth.

Annie's hands drifted over his shoulders and wrapped around the back of his neck in a move that brought them closer, barely a sliver of space between their bodies. She twirled her fingers into the short strands at his nape and craned her neck, staring up at him from beneath low lids.

Somewhere not far behind them, a child's shriek pierced the air, reminding him they weren't alone. Even if he desperately wished they were, the things he wanted to do to her would be indecent for adult eyes, let alone children's.

He made to take a step back, putting some much needed distance between them. Only there wasn't room, one concrete stair the only thing separating him from the lake.

His contrite smile froze on his face as the ground disappeared from beneath him, the world tilting. Doing everything in his power to stay upright, he pinwheeled his arms at his sides as he careened backward, gasping as he plunged beneath the surface of the frigid water.

Chapter Fifteen

*I*t could've been worse."

Brendon flipped his blinker, turning onto Darcy's street. "How?"

She clamped her lips together, hiding her smile. "You could've pulled me in with you?"

He put the car in park and shook his head slowly, lips twitching. "Maybe I should've."

Had he, maybe they'd have had an excuse to leave the reception sooner. As it was, half the guests had rushed out of the pavilion at the sound of Brendon's splashing in the lake, fully dressed, and it had taken thirty minutes of his assuring everyone he was no worse for wear—only wet—before he was able to grab a change of clothes from the gym bag he had stored in the tiny trunk of his car. They'd made their exit shortly after.

Unfortunately, she didn't have his patience. Then again, he hadn't done anything to recapture the moment since they'd gotten in his car. He'd hopped directly on Highway 520 and driven to Darcy's without asking if she'd have rather gone to his place, so he didn't seem especially keen on rekindling the mood.

Which was fine. For the best, even. She'd gotten wrapped up in the moment, had too much fun, and let it go to her head. That was another problem with weddings, one she hadn't shared with Brendon. For all their rubbery chicken, line dances, and antiquated traditions like garter tosses, Brendon was right about one thing.

Annie would've needed a heart of stone not to feel *something* watching two people stand up in front of all their family and friends, vowing to spend the rest of their lives together no matter what obstacles life threw their way. She didn't have a heart of stone, not even close, and being here in Seattle, spending time with Brendon, was chipping away at the defenses she *had* erected around her heart. Making her want things she had no business wanting. Desires that scared her shitless.

Big things, forever things, the sort of things that with each failed relationship and bad date had felt a little further out of reach. Made her feel a little more hopeless, resigned to the idea that romance was dead and there was no one out there who could prove otherwise to her. No one who'd even bother to try.

And then came Brendon.

If the circumstances were different, maybe what she felt, what Brendon made her feel, would be a risk worth taking.

But they weren't.

So.

She reached for the door handle and gave Brendon a smile that felt fifty shades of flimsy, strained. *Pained.* "I had fun today, Brendon."

He ran a hand through his hair, wincing when his fingers snagged in the strands. It had dried since he'd fallen in the lake, but it stuck up oddly. *Adorably.* "Me too. Thanks for being my date."

Annie opened the door and reached down to the floorboard for her purse.

"Oh, hold on." He turned, fishing around in the backseat before swiveling and facing her. "Here."

He pressed a small cardboard box into her hands. *Breathe Right Nasal Strips.*

She frowned.

He scratched his jaw. "I noticed you snore the other night when we crashed at the hotel. And I didn't know if you knew, but I saw these."

"And you thought of me?"

"That's not weird, is it?" His eyes widened. "Ah shit, that's weird."

Without a doubt, it was the weirdest present anyone had ever given her.

But that didn't mean it wasn't welcome.

It was weird and wonderful and welcome because it meant he had been thinking of her. As far as gestures went, it was so strangely touching that saying thank you seemed woefully insufficient.

So she stretched across the console and kissed him instead.

For one heart-stopping moment, Brendon didn't move. His lips remained listless until she drew back, gut churning with disappointment and mortification that she'd read the moment so ridiculously wrong. Something about her lips leaving his must've brought him online, because his hand reached up and cradled her jaw, his fingers tickling the skin beneath her ear.

His tongue dragged against her bottom lip and she melted, distantly recognizing the moan that filled his tiny car as her own. Want overrode everything, making it impossible for her to churn up even an ounce of embarrassment when he captured her lip between his teeth and nipped.

Her fingers knotted in his collar. She pushed him back an inch and held him there. "Walk me up."

Without taking his eyes off her, Brendon reached down, releasing his seat belt. He searched blindly for the handle and as soon as the door was open, he climbed out, quickly circling the nonexistent nose of his car to help her up onto the curb. His thumb brushed the back of her knuckles and she shivered, mysteriously too hot and too cold at the same time. Her nipples pebbled against the silk bodice of her borrowed dress, and the AC inside the lobby of Darcy's apartment didn't lessen her predicament.

She was determined to get her mouth on Brendon as soon as they were in the elevator, but fate saw fit to throw a wrench in her plans. An older woman she recognized from Darcy's floor stuck her cane between the doors before they could touch, sending them rebounding open. She joined them, smiling, none the wiser to the fact that Annie wanted to press Brendon up against the glass paneling and have her wicked way with him ASAP, possible security cameras be damned.

"Nice weather we're having," the older woman, Mrs. . . . —shoot, Darcy had told Annie her name—said. "Lovely, lovely weather. I think I saw a rainbow earlier."

Brendon's fingers strangled her hand and his teeth sank into his bottom lip as he did an all-around shitty job of stifling his laughter. "Great weather, Mrs. Clarence. How's Princess?"

Annie scrunched her nose and mouthed, *"Princess?"*

His lips twitched. *"Cat."*

Mrs. Clarence prattled on about her Persian longhair, but most of it went in one ear and out the other. Brendon's thumb continued to swipe against the back of her hand, rhythmic as a metronome, and it drove her insane, making her breath come out in short, sharp gasps she struggled to soften.

His hands were maddening. She felt like some sort of Regency-era heroine, swooning over the way his fingers brushed hers, but it was like the ridges and furrows of his fingerprints were uniquely coded to make her brain fuzz out and her veins flood with heat. When his grip loosened and his thumb swept against the inside of her wrist, she clenched her thighs together. *Fuck.*

The elevator dinged and opened, spitting them out onto the ninth floor. Mrs. Clarence waved as she opened her door, the first off the hall, and disappeared inside. Annie's steps quickened as she dragged Brendon after her, on a mission.

Where was the key? Annie could've cried as she searched the depths of her purse, coming up empty until—there. She crowed her delight and shoved the key in the door, twisting the knob, stepping over the threshold.

The apartment was dark save for the lights above the bar. Annie peeked down the hall. No light beneath Darcy's door, either.

That didn't mean she wasn't home. She could've been sleeping or reading or simply lying in the dark.

They'd have to be quiet.

Something about that made Annie's breath hitch, then quicken. She liked a challenge.

Brendon shut the door and leaned against it, one hand buried in his pocket, the other raking through his hair.

"Do you want something to drink?" she asked, praying he'd say no, still feeling compelled to be polite. "Water? Coffee?"

His lips curved in a smirk and the words *panty dropping* flashed like a neon sign inside her head. "If I wanted coffee, could you even make it?"

She huffed. "Doubtful."

His smile grew and her knees trembled. "I don't want coffee, Annie."

He pressed off the door and stalked toward her. Her heart raced.

She backed in the direction of her room, encouraging him down the hall. "What *do* you want?"

"Short answer?" His long legs ate up the distance between them until he was so close she had to crane her neck to stare up at him as she tripped into the guest room she called home. "You."

He closed the door carefully and she took the chance to kick off her heels. They landed just shy of the closet and she could've wept with relief that they hadn't clattered against the louvered doors.

He turned the lock and her stomach somersaulted. The ache between her legs intensified, the heat in her veins growing hotter.

"Long answer?" she whispered.

Beneath his boyish grin and dimples, something daring flashed in his eyes. "I want you for longer than tonight."

Her heartbeat sped. She swallowed hard and laughed, breathless. "You haven't even had me once and you're already thinking about round two?"

He stared. "Annie."

She wet her lips, not knowing what to say in the face of his radical honesty. Honesty that could've sent her running for the hills. Honesty he had to have known could've brought this all to a total standstill, and yet he'd said it anyway. Her knees trembled and she locked them so she wouldn't visibly shake.

"But if you meant tonight, specifically," he said, "then what I want would depend on what you want."

The intensity of his gaze emboldened her, maybe not to quite the same level of vulnerability he'd displayed, but to tell the truth, nonetheless. "I'm pretty sure I'm going to die if you don't touch me."

He reached out, tucking her hair behind her ear. His hand lingered near her jaw, the friction of his fingers sweeping over her skin driving her wild, her thoughts spiraling to what his caress would feel like against the rest of her. "Touch you?"

She rested her hands on his stomach, clutching at the fabric of his shirt, bunching it in her hands as she yanked it free from his pants. "As a start."

He slid his hand around the back of her neck and buried his fingers in her hair, tugging gently, drawing her eyes back to his. "And then?"

Her lips curled. "That would depend on what you want."

His grip on her hair tightened, making her gasp, then whimper. Heat slithered down her body and settled between her thighs.

"I want to hear you make more of those sounds." His hands glided down her sides, over her dress to where the silk split. Brendon's fingertips made maddening little circles on the outside of her bare thigh. His tongue darted out, his throat bobbing as he swallowed hard. "I want to be the one who makes you make those sounds."

Her breath sped, growing shallow.

"You want to know what I want? More than anything?"

Yes. She slipped her hands under the bottom of his shirt and pressed her palms to the warm, bare skin of his stomach. He shuddered and his short, blunt nails scraped against the skin of her outer thigh. "Tell me."

He leaned closer, lips brushing the shell of her ear. "I want to bury my face between your thighs and make you *sing*, Annie. I want to taste you. I want to—"

He broke off with a low groan and she swayed into him, suddenly dizzy. All the blood in her body had rushed south, leaving little for her head.

He walked her backward, and when her knees hit the edge of the bed, they buckled, sending her sprawling atop the mattress.

He followed her down, boxing her in with an arm on either side of her head. He held himself up over her, his broad shoulders blocking out most of the light spilling from beneath the lampshade, leaving him backlit, shadowed. He dropped his head and pressed his forehead against hers, their noses bumping. "Can I? God, Annie. Please."

She wiggled beneath him, arching up, pressing her body against his. He gritted his teeth, a sharp exhale sliding out from between his lips. He was hard, his cock pressing against her hip through his pants, and she shuddered, her breath leaving her mouth in a broken pant.

"Yeah. *Yes.*"

He slipped backward off the bed and kneeled in front of the mattress. His hands circled her thighs, fingers pressing into her skin as he tugged, hauling her toward the edge of the bed, making her gasp. Her dress bunched around her hips, the slit splayed open, leaving her on display.

Bolder than before, he palmed the front of her thighs, his thumbs inching higher, closer, *closer*, almost grazing the crease where her legs met her body.

"Can I take this off?" he asked, tugging gently on her dress.

She nodded and arched up, helping him tug the fabric up and off her body. The dress sailed across the room, where it landed atop the lamp, knocking the shade askew and bathing the room in rose-colored shadows.

Brendon grinned. "Whoops?"

He sank back onto his haunches and lost his balance, toppling over onto his ass.

She snorted.

"Shh." He did a poor job of quieting his own laughter as he rose to his knees and crawled toward her. He hauled himself up the bed and leaned over her, pressing his fingers to her lips.

He looked at her then, eyes lingering, savoring, staring down at her with the most breath-snatching combination of covetousness and reverence. "Fuck. You're so beautiful."

She melted inside.

He looks at you like you hung the moon.

Annie didn't know what she'd done to deserve anyone, but especially Brendon, looking at her like she was something special. But she was going to revel in it, enjoy it for as long as she could. When the day inevitably came that he stopped looking at her like that, she'd at least have this memory.

Leaning over her, he pressed his lips to the corner of her mouth, trailing kisses down the curve of her jaw.

"Do you know how long I've been dying to taste you? How many times I've thought about it?" His voice rumbled against her throat, his kisses trailing lower, over the jut of her collarbone, soft brushes of his lips interspersed with nips of his teeth that made her gasp, never knowing which she was going to get. Soft or hard, sweet or rough.

Fitting, because the Brendon she'd gotten to know could be both cocky and bashful, serious and funny, pushy and sensitive. There was more to him than met the eye, and she liked him, all of him, more than she'd bargained for.

"If it's as many times as I've thought about it today alone, a lot."

He smiled against her skin. His mouth skimmed down the swell of her breast, his lips grazing her nipple, wrapping around it, worrying it gently between his teeth. Pleasure shot from her chest down to her core, making her throb, making her wish she could rub her thighs together and get a tiny bit of relief, friction, but she couldn't. Not with Brendon between her legs, keeping them spread wide.

He slid lower down the bed, lips brushing the bottom curve

of her breast, the ticklish skin over her ribs. He pressed an almost reverent kiss to the gnarly scar from her appendectomy, which she hated, and worked his way down to her belly button, his tongue dipping inside, making her squirm.

"Can I take these off?" Lightly, he snapped the lace band of her underwear against her hip.

She arched her back, struggling to lift her hips off the bed with her feet barely skimming the floor. A quiet huff of frustration passed her lips. "*Yes.*"

He reached under her, pulling the lace over her ass and down her legs, shifting between her thighs and settling back on his knees. Leaning up on her elbows, she watched as he bent forward and pressed a kiss to her mound, his hands sliding down her thighs. Her breath quickened and her face heated as Brendon stared at her, his eyes dark and low lidded. "You're so beautiful."

If kissing Brendon was a revelation, having his mouth on her was heaven. She whimpered and canted her hips, raising one hand to the back of his head, burying her fingers in his thick red hair as she rocked against his mouth. His eyes flashed up to her face, his pupils blown, the look in them almost enough to send her over the edge.

Her thighs shook and drew in. "*Brendon.*"

He pressed his right forearm against her stomach, pinning her to the bed, keeping her hips from dancing. The pressure between her thighs intensified, the thread holding her together fraying rapidly before he sent her flying, a gasp that verged on a sob spilling from her lips. Her neck arched and her abs burned as she crunched forward, one hand still fisted in his hair, until it became too much. Weakly, she shoved him away before flopping boneless against the bed, struggling to catch her breath, her lungs burning and her throat raw from sucking in air.

He pressed a kiss to the crease of her thigh before lowering it to the bed, then crawled across the covers, settling in beside her, and reached out, brushing strands of hair from her face, tucking them behind her ears. "Good?"

She gave a breathless laugh. "You're the Obi-Wan of oral."

As someone who prided herself on her own cunnilingus skills, she bowed down. Brendon gave her a run for her money.

The bed shook when he laughed. "A *Star Wars* reference? Be still my heart."

She rolled over and reached for the buttons on his shirt, hands trembling. She succeeded in freeing a grand total of two before he took mercy on her and helped. As soon as his shirt fell open, she trailed a finger down the center of his chest, zigzagging between his pecs, past his colorful tattoo, in a poor attempt at connecting his freckles. He had too many to count, and yet a silly part of her wanted to try to kiss them all.

When she reached his flank, he twitched, laughter bubbling between his lips before he pressed them tightly together and snagged her hand, holding it still.

"Ticklish?"

"No." His left eye twitched, then his lips. "Maybe."

She grinned. Something to explore some other time when being quiet wasn't paramount. She tugged on his shirttails. "You should be naked."

His brows rose and he grinned. "I should, should I?"

"You should." Like, yesterday.

He shed his shirt and stood, dropping his hands to the button on his pants. He was straining the zipper, visibly hard. The relief on his face was obvious when he tucked his fingers beneath the slackened waist of his pants and boxers, shedding both at once.

Her mouth went dry.

A flush had turned his chest pink, color wrapping around the front of his throat. Freckles dotted his chest, growing less concentrated the further south her eyes dipped. Her tongue slipped out, wetting her lips, wanting to trace the ridges of his stomach and kiss the deep cut of muscles that flared like an arrow, pointing to where his cock proudly jutted out from his body.

He took one step forward and froze, a line appearing between his brows. "Fuck."

That was kind of the point? "Yes?"

His head rolled back on his shoulders and he stared up at the ceiling. "I don't have a condom."

That would've been a problem had she not been 99 percent sure there was one inside her makeup bag. "Well, Darcy definitely won't have one lying around."

He shuddered and palmed his cock. "Please don't talk about my sister while I have an erection."

She stifled a laugh and pointed at her open suitcase. "Check the side pocket of the pink bag."

He found a condom quickly, holding it up, looking both pleased and relieved as he crossed the room toward the bed.

She sat up, watching Brendon's hands shake as he tore open the foil. His eyes flashed up, meeting hers, his lips twitching into a grin as he stroked his condom-covered shaft and set a knee on the bed.

She slid backward, higher up the bed, then changed her mind, rolling over onto her hands and knees.

Behind her, his breath hitched audibly and he groaned. "Fuck."

Even as her heart pounded and anticipation made her breath quicken, her lips curved. She craned her neck, looking over her shoulder. Brendon was watching her, lids heavy and color high on his cheeks, his hand gripping his cock.

"Is this okay?" she asked.

She wanted to feel him surrounding her, wanted him to touch as much of her as possible, to feel his heart pound, his chest pressed against her back.

The bed dipped, sinking beneath their combined weight, as he crawled closer on his knees. His throat jerked when he swallowed and nodded.

Just like she'd wanted, he molded himself to her back, pressing an openmouthed kiss to the ball of her shoulder. She turned her head and he was right there, close enough to kiss, so she did.

His mouth still covering hers, he guided himself to her entrance, the head of his cock sliding through her folds, making her quake with anticipation verging on impatience. He drew back an inch and asked, "You sure?"

She'd have rolled her eyes had she not been stupidly smitten with how *sweet* he was.

She nodded, then gasped against his lips, her fingers twisting in the sheets, as he sank inside her, stretching her, stopping only when his hips were flush with hers. Her head fell forward, breaking the kiss, as she panted softly.

He exhaled sharply, his hands settling on her hips, fingers

pressing into her skin as he drew back. His first thrust was slow but still managed to knock the wind from her lungs as she hung her head and closed her eyes.

"Fuck." He set a slow place, too slow, the friction of his cock inside her making her desperate.

It was good, *so good*, but not enough. "Harder."

His hips snapped, making her mewl and clench the sheet in her fists, the force of his thrusts almost driving her up the bed.

"Like this?" He panted, his breaths hot and ragged against her skin, as he delivered on exactly what she'd asked for.

She nodded and he swore, his teeth nipping her earlobe gently. She gasped at the subtle sting that shot straight to her core. His tongue swept the shell of her ear, making her shiver.

One of his arms banded around her waist, yanking her back onto his lap as he kneeled. Wordless gasps spilled from her mouth, desperate little sounds she couldn't have swallowed had she tried.

This was a million times better than she'd imagined.

His other hand wrapped around her chin, turning her head so he could kiss her, swallow her cries as he rocked into her.

The look in his eyes was unbelievably intense. So intense she could barely breathe. Her chest burned, her heart squeezing. She wanted to look away but she couldn't, completely trapped in his gaze, spiraling, coming apart at the seams in a way that had nothing to do with what he was doing to her body.

Needing something to hold on to, something to steady herself, she lifted a shaking arm and hooked it around the back of his neck.

Eyes hazy, she licked her dry lips, wishing she could press her mouth to his skin, taste his sweat. She was close, achingly close, her heart pounding against her sternum, her blood thrumming in her head, her ears ringing like she was underwater. She just needed a little more, a little something to send her over the edge, make her come. "Please."

He reached up, running his callused thumb along her bottom lip, groaning when her tongue darted out, tasting, curling around it, trying to suck it between her lips. He let her, pressing his thumb against her tongue, his eyes darkening as she sucked, teeth scraping the pad of his finger.

Her head fell back against his shoulder, releasing his thumb, and he dropped his hand between her thighs, circling her clit. She shattered, biting down hard on her lip so she wouldn't make too much noise as Brendon drove her over the edge, her brain blanking out as she clenched, pleasure washing over her.

His teeth closed around her shoulder, the sound of his groan rumbling through her, his heart beating erratically against her back as he followed her over the edge with one final hard thrust.

His lips skimmed up her throat and over her jaw; when he finally kissed her it was slow, gentle, so different from a moment before, when everything had been fast and hard and so intense she couldn't breathe. She was still having trouble catching her breath, panting into Brendon's mouth, sharing air.

After a moment, he drew back, resting his forehead against her temple.

Her arm fell to her side and her lids fluttered open; she blinked into the dim, pink-tinged light of the room.

Brendon was smiling at her, a look so achingly intimate her heart pounded faster again, beating against her sternum.

"I'll be right back," she whispered, sliding past him and off the bed. She padded across the room and fled into the adjoining bathroom, shutting the door behind her.

She peed fast and washed her hands, unable to keep from staring at her reflection. At the back of her head, her hair was a knotted mess, her chignon more of a bird's nest thanks to her thrashing against the covers when Brendon had gone down on her. Beneath her eyes, her liner was smudged, and the skin around her mouth was pink from his stubble.

She shut off the faucet and dried her hands, reaching for her makeup remover wipes, too lazy to wash her face.

When she stepped back into the bedroom, Brendon was sitting on the edge of the bed, his pants in his lap, but not on. He lifted his head and smiled at her crookedly. "Hey."

Her toes curled in the carpet, pleasant warmth filling her veins, replacing the heat from earlier. "Hi." She nodded at his pants. "You're not . . . leaving, are you?"

Saying it put an unexpected lump in her throat.

"Oh." His fingers closed around his clothes. "I didn't know if you wanted me to stay."

What she wanted was a topic for a different time, the morning maybe. She needed to do some serious . . . *soul searching*, but not now.

Right now, what she wanted was to wiggle beneath the sheets and sleep, preferably with Brendon spooned behind her. She wanted the weight of his arm around her waist, his chin hooked over the top of her head. She wanted to press her slightly chilly feet back against the furnace of his body and discover what he'd do. If he'd yelp or chuckle or lean closer. She wanted to lie in bed with him talking until midnight, and she wanted to wake up beside him in the morning and watch the sun peek through the slats in the blinds, dawn turning his auburn hair into burnished bronze.

Her chest ached and her fingertips tingled and the lump in her throat tripled in size.

She'd caught capital-F *Feelings* for Brendon. Feelings that had nothing—okay, a little something—to do with orgasms. Feelings that had everything to do with liking the sound of his laugh and how he could just look at her and turn her bones into butter. Feelings that had to do with his earnest efforts to bring joy to everyone he knew, even the people he didn't. It was his corny jokes and how he put his whole heart into everything he did, from rapping in front of a room full of strangers to giving a heartfelt speech at a coworker's wedding.

Brendon cared.

And so did she.

"I do," she said, casting a glance around the room. He'd moved her dress off the lamp in the corner, so the cream-colored walls were no longer pink. His shirt still lay in a heap on the floor along with her underwear, but that wasn't why she blushed. Nor was it because she was naked and so was he. "I'd like it if you stayed." Her smile was a touch hesitant, not shy but . . . hopeful. "I mean, if you're willing to risk running into your sister in the morning."

Brendon tossed his pants aside and reached for the duvet. He stripped it back, the top sheet, too, and fluffed the pillows.

"Left or right?" he asked, grinning at her.

"No preference," she said, stepping closer.

He stood, letting her slide in first. "I'll take the left."

She crawled in and he made to slide in beside her, but she said, "The lamp?"

He nodded, crossing the room. His footsteps faltered when he reached the foot of the bed and he doubled back, bending down and grabbing her purse.

She frowned.

"You forgot your Breathe Right strip."

Her bones liquefied and her heart swelled. "Grab them for me?"

He reached inside her purse, plucking out the box and ripping it open. He grabbed a single-use strip and returned to the bed, peeling off the plastic backing. "Come here."

She scooted to the edge of the bed and he pressed the strip beneath the bridge of her nose. "Is this lavender scented?"

His cheeks colored. "You mentioned liking the lavender fields in Provence, so I . . . yeah."

Her heart climbed into her throat, her breath quickening. Surely he could feel each exhale against his wrist as he adjusted the strip. She could feel her nostrils flare subtly open when he finished.

"How do I look?" she asked. "Super sexy, I'm sure."

"So sexy." He chuckled and brushed his thumb against the curve of her cheek. "I'm having trouble keeping my hands to myself."

She turned her face into his hand and pressed a kiss to the inside of his wrist, loving how his breath stuttered loudly.

Good thing he didn't have to.

Chapter Sixteen

Sunday, June 6

Sprawled across Brendon like a starfish, Annie had left a small puddle of drool on his chest. It was a sure sign he was completely and utterly gone, a lost cause if there ever was one, if he found drool adorable. Drool. He was such a sucker for her he found her *spit* cute.

Last night, something had shifted. He wasn't so oblivious as to have missed the subtle signs before, but had he, last night would've been in his face, unmistakable.

He wasn't entirely sure *what* had changed for Annie or *why* it had changed, but he wasn't one to look a gift horse in the mouth. She wanted him and he wanted her, and the rest? The rest was just noise.

Ever so carefully, he extracted himself out from under Annie, rolling to the side and setting her arm gently down on the mattress between them. She snuffled softly but didn't snore—score one for the nasal strips—and grabbed for her pillow in place of his body, cuddling it tight, tucking it beneath her chin.

He rested his head on his hand and watched her snuggle her pillow until his need to relieve his bladder outweighed his desire to watch her sleep.

Tiptoeing quietly out of the bathroom, he paused in the middle of the room, weighing out whether to wake her or not. He didn't know the time—his phone had joined him for his impromptu swim and was fried—only that it was light out, sun streaming in through the slatted blinds, blanketing the room in a dusty golden glow.

Slipping on his boxers, he padded his way out into the hall. Coffee would have to come before pants and *absolutely* before he even entertained the idea of putting on socks and shoes.

Softly humming "Walking on Sunshine," he choked on his spit when his sister greeted him.

"Morning." Darcy stared over the rim of her mug. One of her brows arched severely.

Uh. He crossed his arms over his chest, shoulders hunching high up by his ears. "Morning?"

She sniffed and gestured toward the kitchen with a wide wave of her cup. "Help yourself." She paused. "You honestly couldn't put clothes on? Seriously?"

He sighed and sank down on her sofa. "I wasn't exactly expecting to run into you."

"In *my* apartment? At seven fifteen on a Sunday morning?"

"When you put it like that . . ."

She flung a throw blanket at him. "Cover yourself, please.

That's too much thigh for me." Her eyes widened. "And since when do you have a *tattoo*?"

He wrapped the blanket around his shoulders, clutching it in front of his throat. "Don't start. I know all about your butterfly."

She flushed neon and said nothing.

"You're up early," he added.

She set her coffee on the table. "I could say the same to you."

He scratched his eyebrow. "This is awkward."

He tucked the blanket tighter around his shoulders, praying the flap of his boxers hadn't parted before he could cover himself.

Darcy cocked her head. "Annie still asleep?"

His ears burned. "Yup."

"Are you *blushing*?"

"Likely."

Her shoulders shook as she laughed at him, taking too much pleasure in his embarrassment.

"Can you . . . I don't know, spare me the teasing? Please. I haven't had any coffee yet. I'm at an automatic disadvantage."

"In your dreams." She stood and crossed over to her kitchen. "I won't spare you the teasing but I will make you coffee."

"Bless you."

Her coffeemaker whirred to life, the crunch of beans filling the air. As appealing as coffee was, and as much as he loved his sister, he was sorely tempted to sneak down the hall and crawl back in bed beside Annie for a few blissful hours of respite.

Darcy returned, mug in hand. "Here." Her lips twitched. "Do I need to check Annie for fangs? You have a hickey the size of Texas on your throat. You're not in high school, for crying out loud."

No, but sometimes Annie made him feel like he was. Like he was a kid discovering everything for the first time, things he'd never felt before. He liked it. He *loved* it, loved that everything with Annie felt shiny and new, like the sunlight streaming in through the window. Golden.

He brought the mug to his lips. The hot coffee was a touch over-extracted for his taste, Darcy's beans a little too finely ground, resulting in a bitter brew. But he wasn't about to complain, certainly not when the coffee was a nice buffer from the embarrassment. "Shut up."

"So, what happened last night?"

He coughed, spraying coffee spittle against the back of his hand.

"Not *that*." Darcy wrinkled her nose. "I can add two and two together perfectly well, *thanks*. When I asked Annie about you inviting her to a wedding, all I heard was a lot of protesting about how she was *just your plus-one*."

"I guess . . . something changed between us."

Somewhere between the ceremony, their dance, his confession, and their almost-kiss by the water, it seemed that Annie had finally joined him on the same page.

Darcy's face sobered as she stared at him. "I know I put you up to this—"

"You did no such thing," he argued. "I've been spending time with Annie because I want to. All you did was ask me to show her around Seattle and I'd have done that anyway, okay?"

"I only want for you to be careful, okay? Careful and realistic."

"Look at that, my two middle names."

She drummed her fingers against the side of her mug. "Be serious, Brendon."

He didn't want to be serious. Or he did, but he didn't think that being serious required taking a sharp turn for the melancholic. "I am serious. I feel *very* serious about Annie, okay? But everything's going to work itself out."

Darcy pursed her lips. "Look. Mom said—"

"Since when do *you* quote Mom?" His stomach sank to his knees. "Since when do you *listen* to Mom?"

"I take everything she says with a heaping tablespoon of salt." Her lips twisted to the side in a wry smile. "It was back in December."

Ah. When Mom had dumped her own fears about love all over Darcy, made her second-guess her feelings, her relationship with Elle. "What wisdom did she impart this time?"

Darcy's tongue poked against the side of her cheek. "She was trying to make a point about how she and I are similar. That we don't get over things as quickly as . . ."

"As?" he prompted, not liking where this was going.

Darcy's eyes closed briefly. "As you do."

He frowned. What did that even mean?

"She said your heart is like a rubber band," Darcy added, and yeah, that sounded like something Mom would say, something strange and hippie-ish, something she probably thought sounded way deeper and more meaningful than it was. Half the things she said were probably regurgitated advice off a kombucha bottle or the inside of a Dove chocolate wrapper. "That you snap back was her point." The corners of her mouth pinched, her lips pressed together. "But I think Mom's wrong."

"Yeah, well, I love Mom, but I think we can both agree she's wrong about a lot of things."

Darcy's throat jerked. "*My* point is that Mom thinks your heart is elastic but I think the real truth is that your heart is as breakable as everyone else's, only you've never had it broken before." She reached across the couch and squeezed his hand, the one not preserving his modesty. "The last thing I want is for you to get hurt."

He squeezed her fingers back and smiled. "Please don't worry about me."

She shook her head, her grip around his fingers tightening. "You're my brother, it's my job to worry about you."

Brendon's chest squeezed. "I wish you wouldn't."

He knew better than to tell her not to again, tell her there was nothing to worry about. Worrying was something Darcy came by naturally.

"Every time I try to slip London into the conversation, Annie changes the subject. She's not talking about it." She blinked fast, lashes fluttering against her cheeks. "What if, no matter how hard we try, Annie still moves away?"

Darcy's concerns were legitimate, definitely not unfounded. But he didn't want to worry. "There's still time, Darce."

Time to show her that Seattle was amazing. That she could make this city her home. That she had people here who cared about her.

Time to show her that he was a good choice. That if she jumped, he'd be there to catch her. He wouldn't let her down like she'd been let down before.

He could be her exception if she only gave him—*them*—a chance.

She looked at him, dark eyes glassy. "I just don't want you to get your hopes up."

Too late.

A throat cleared, followed by a stifled giggle.

Standing just off the hall, wearing nothing but his button-down, was Annie. Her hair resembled a nest, her face was bright pink, and she still had her Breathe Right strip molded to her nose.

Brendon had never seen anyone more beautiful.

"Good morning." Annie padded over to the couch, tugging at the hem of her borrowed shirt. She studiously avoided look-ing at Darcy as she sat on the arm of the sofa beside him. Her lips twitched as she eyed his ensemble. "Nice blanket."

He let his eyes drag down her body and back up to her face. "Nice shirt."

"Ew," Darcy muttered.

Annie stole his cup and took a sip. Her nose wrinkled and his heart rolled over like a golden retriever wanting its belly scratched. "Needs sugar."

☾

BRENDON (7:19 P.M.): Got a new phone, FYI. ☺

ANNIE (7:21 P.M.): Old one couldn't be salvaged?

BRENDON (7:23 P.M.): Waterlogged beyond repair. Guy at the Verizon store found my story about falling in the lake hilarious, though.

ANNIE (7:25 P.M.): It *was* hilarious 😂

BRENDON (7:26 P.M.): 😔

ANNIE (7:27 P.M.): I'd say your night was far from ruined 😊

BRENDON (7:39 P.M.): I've drafted and deleted a dozen different texts and I can't seem to find a smooth way of saying I had an amazing time last night without sounding like my mind's in the gutter.

Heat settled in a distinctly different part of her body than she'd been expecting when she'd sent her last text. Not between her thighs, but in her chest. A pleasant squeezing warmth, because what Brendon had said sounded the opposite of guttery. Sweet, *so* sweet, but she could do with its being a little more sinfully so.

ANNIE (7:39 P.M.): Or . . .
BRENDON (7:39 P.M.): Or?
ANNIE (7:39 P.M.): You could come to the dark side and join me down here in the gutter.
BRENDON (7:40 P.M.): Dark side, huh? Do you, uh, have cookies?

She stifled a laugh.

ANNIE (7:41 P.M.): Cookies, sure. If that's what you want to call it.

As seconds turned to minutes and Brendon didn't respond, she read back through her messages and worried she'd crossed the line from flirty to thirsty. *Desperately* thirsty.

BRENDON (7:44 P.M.): Then I guess you won't judge me too harshly if I tell you I can't stop thinking about that little gasp you made when I slid inside you.

BRENDON (7:45 P.M.): Or the way I could feel your pulse flutter against my tongue when you clenched around my fingers.

Her breath quickened and the warmth that had settled in her chest slithered lower.

BRENDON (7:46 P.M.): And that, if I'd had my way, I would have spent the morning with my head between your thighs making you come so hard you forgot your name.

She lifted a hand, pressing her fingers against the notch at the base of her throat. Jesus Christ.

BRENDON (7:47 P.M.): That the thought of getting you in my bed, where you can be as loud as you want, has me so hard I can't think straight. That I'm supposed to be prepping for a meeting tomorrow and instead I have my hand wrapped around my dick thinking about how you taste.

She whimpered. It was like a switch had been flipped, Brendon going from adorable to filthy in under five minutes. She liked it, she *really* liked it.

ANNIE (7:48 P.M.): Jfc, Brendon.
BRENDON (7:49 P.M.): That, uh, guttery enough for you?
ANNIE (7:50 P.M.): I'd say that earns you a cookie, yeah. If only I could reward you in person.
BRENDON (7:51 P.M.): Tomorrow.

BRENDON (7:52 P.M.): Come over.

BRENDON (7:52 P.M.): So I can make you come.

Her teeth scraped her bottom lip.

She didn't regret sleeping with him, not in the slightest. She'd be remiss to say it had been solely due to the heat of the moment, but that had been a big part of it. This tension between them had been simmering and last night it had boiled over.

Planning ahead felt different. Deliberate. Like it meant more than just . . . scratching an itch. Like if she agreed, she'd be acknowledging she wanted him, not just for one night, but longer. Like she wanted to keep doing this. Keep *him*.

BRENDON (7:54 P.M.): And we can watch more of that show. With the French farmers?

Her chest clenched. She was so screwed.

ANNIE (7:55 P.M.): Don't you have to work tomorrow?

BRENDON (7:56 P.M.): Tomorrow evening, then. We can go out to eat first.

BRENDON (7:57 P.M.): Then we can go back to my place and I can eat you out.

She wet her lips, breathing heavily.

ANNIE (7:59 P.M.): Yes.

Chapter Seventeen

Monday, June 7

Through the window of the car, Brendon gestured to Annie that he was going to duck inside the gas station. He'd just filled his tank, but the machine was out of receipt paper.

"*Need anything?*" he mouthed.

She shook her head and smiled before returning to her phone.

Inside, he quickly retrieved his receipt. Beside the register sat a Lucite tray of potted plants. Miniature succulents in palm-sized terra-cotta planters. He laughed under his breath and selected one with chunky, pale blue-green leaves that curled into a tight rosette atop the small mound of dirt. He set it beside the register and passed the cashier his credit card.

"We've got a five-dollar minimum," the guy said.

Brendon grabbed a Snickers and waved off a plastic bag.

Annie looked up when he slid inside the car and graced him with a smile. "All set?"

He nodded and opened his hand, revealing the plant. "I got you a present."

A furrow appeared between her brows for a split second before her eyes widened with glee. "Is that—"

"A succulent." He nodded, letting her take it from him. "You said you wanted a houseplant, so . . ."

He'd buy her a million tiny succulents if they made her smile like she was now.

"Brendon," she simpered, and held the plant aloft between them. "You bought me a *love fern*."

He palmed his face and laughed. "Try not to kill it?"

She stroked the buttery-soft leaves with a finger and murmured nonsense to it under her breath, in turn making him chuckle. "I'll do my best."

He started the car. "Can you, uh, take plants on a plane?"

From the corner of his eye, Annie frowned, still stroking the succulent with her fingers. "I don't know. I guess I'll have to check."

He hummed and pulled out of the parking lot.

Five days. That's how long it was until she boarded a plane back to Philadelphia.

At least, that was her plan. She hadn't said anything to the contrary, but he hadn't asked, too nervous to hear her answer. To hear her say nothing had changed. That not *enough* had changed. That she was still planning on moving to London.

By the time they reached his apartment, he'd psyched himself up. He could do this. Broach this conversation. Tell her how he felt. Tell her he wanted her to stay.

Annie set the succulent on his bar, then leaned back against the counter, smiling. "I had fun tonight. Hands down, that was the best sandwich of my life. I'm going to have very, *very* fond dreams of that sandwich."

He reached out, cupping her jaw, smoothing his thumb against her cheek. She leaned into his palm and pressed a kiss to the inside of his wrist. He'd never considered it to be an erogenous zone before, but the feel of her warm lips against his skin had his heart beating faster and his breath quickening. "I'm glad you enjoyed yourself."

He'd taken her to Beth's Café, a local greasy spoon. It had been featured on the Food Network and was a favorite of his, for both the food and the quintessential Seattle atmosphere. In the mornings, you could easily find people in business attire ordering coffee and pastries at the counter, whereas in the evenings, theater kids belted show tunes while couples cozied up in the booths near the back of the restaurant.

He smiled and stepped closer, boxing her in against the counter. She sucked in a quick gasp that made him bite the inside of his cheek. "I, on the other hand, am going to have very, *very* fond dreams of your Meg Ryan impression."

As a joke, Annie had insisted on ordering a turkey sandwich with all the fixings on the side à la Sally in the infamous diner scene in *When Harry Met Sally*. Much to his delight, she'd even gone so far as to—*quietly*—reenact the *I'll have what's she having* fake-orgasm scene. It was as hilarious as it was arousing, a novel combination.

She craned her neck back, staring at him from beneath her lashes. "Was it an Oscar-worthy performance?"

He had a feeling she wouldn't be winning an award for her acting any time soon. "I feel like that's a trick question, so I'm going to stick with saying I prefer the real thing."

Annie snickered. "You don't want me to fake it?"

Fuck no. He lifted a hand, running his thumb along the curve of her cheek. "I'd rather it be real."

All of it. He wanted everything about them to be real. Not a vacation romance, a layover on her way to London, but something that could have an actual shot at longevity if Annie would just give him a chance.

Annie's hands drifted down his chest, lingering on the button of his jeans. "Faking it's overrated."

She undid the button and his breath caught in the back of his throat. Fuck.

Her fingers nimbly lowered the zipper and the waist of his jeans slackened around his hips. All his thoughts left his head as she reached her hand inside his boxers and wrapped her fingers around his dick.

This was not at all what he'd meant, but talking could wait.

It would have to because he couldn't form words, let alone coherent ones.

An embarrassing groan was the most he could manage.

Annie chuckled against his shoulder and gripped him tighter, making his eyes roll back in his head. "You want to take this to the bedroom?"

He swallowed and wrapped his fingers around her wrist, stilling her hand, causing her to frown. He shook his head and dropped his hands to the button of her shorts, fumbling to work it free. "Too far."

As soon as her shorts hit the hardwood, she stepped out of them. She gasped quietly when he wrapped his hands around her thighs and lifted her onto the counter. She threw her head back, narrowly avoiding the cabinet behind her, and laughed, sharp and bright.

"Cold," she said, wiggling atop the granite.

He smiled crookedly and stepped between her thighs. "Sorry?"

She reached down, whipping her shirt up over her head.

Barely-there cream lace did a poor job of covering her breasts, but it did a *stellar* job of making it hard for him to speak, words dying on his tongue.

Most words.

"Fuck." He bent down and wrapped his lips around her nipple, laving it through the lace.

Annie keened and the sound made his cock swell. Her hands flew to the back of his head, burying in his hair, tugging, holding him to her chest. "Shit, that feels nice."

Nice? He could do better than nice.

He lifted his head, sealing his mouth over hers, swallowing the soft, needy sounds she made as he let his hands drift down her sides, her skin like silk under his fingertips. When he encountered lace, her tugged the crotch of her underwear to the side and drew his mouth from hers, eyes darting down. He groaned quietly at the sight she made. Cream lace framed golden skin and pretty pink flesh atop the dark marble beneath her.

He ran his fingers up her slit, parting her folds, gathering wetness, dragging it up to her clit. She moaned and clutched his shoulders, drawing his mouth back down to hers as her nails dug into the skin at the back of his neck.

He'd learned she liked it best when he made short, quick circles around her clit. Her breath hitched, then sped, her thighs quivering and drawing in around his hips as she got close.

Dragging his mouth along the curve of her cheek and down her jawline, he nipped at her skin and soothed each gentle bite with a kiss. When he reached her ear, he sucked the lobe between his lips and scraped it with the edge of his teeth. Her nails bit harder into his skin, making him hiss and speed up his ministrations between her thighs.

He nudged the shell of her ear with the tip of his nose and murmured softly, "Does this feel *nice*?"

Her hips bucked against his hand and she gave a sharp, breathless laugh. "*Shut up.*"

He laughed and replaced his fingers with his thumb, sliding two fingers inside her, crooking them upward.

Her breasts shoved against his chest as her back bowed, a soft whine filling the kitchen as she shook and came apart under his fingers.

"Fuck," she murmured, and dropped her head to his chest, clutching at his arms. She continued to flutter around his fingers, her body twitching with the occasional aftershock he drew out, pumping his fingers inside of her slowly, curling them occasionally, making her whimper sweetly, sounds that went straight to his cock. A louder moan tore itself from her throat as she rocked against his hand harder. "You're going to make me come again."

He pressed a kiss to her forehead and curled his fingers harder. "That was the plan."

He'd see her *nice* and raise her *earth-shattering*. He might not have been the expert on all things love related like he'd once thought, but he was positive that—in addition to making her laugh and showering her with affection in the form of thought-ful little gestures—spending as much time with his head and his hands between her thighs as she'd allow put him on the right track.

Beneath his lips, sweat broke out along her forehead, mak-ing her skin damp and dewy, and the baby-fine hair around her temples clung to it. His heart beat faster, in time with the desperate noises falling off her lips.

Annie buried her face in his shoulder, stifling a shriek he'd have rather heard. But the way her hot breaths tickled his neck and sent shivers down his spine made up for it.

Her breathing had come close to approaching normal when she shoved his shoulders back and slipped off the counter. The suddenness made him frown. "Annie—"

The question died on his tongue when she sank down to her knees in front of him and curled her fingers around his cock.

"Jesus." He gripped the edge of the counter when she wrapped her lips around him, drawing him into the exquisite heat of her mouth.

All his plans to wring another orgasm from her with his cock flew out the window. He made a mental note to make it up to her later.

His eyes fluttered shut and he lost himself in the perfect feel of Annie—her hands, one on his thigh and the other wrapped around the base of his cock, the ever-quickening glide of her mouth up his length, the way she flicked her tongue against the vein on the underside of his shaft. The silk of her hair when he gently threaded his fingers through it.

He was close. A soft hum around his cock made his eyes fly open, and the sight of Annie on her knees, staring up at him with wide blue eyes and hollowed cheeks, was enough to make his knees weaken. He gripped the counter harder, his knuckles turning white.

"'M close," he warned, cupping her face and stroking her cheek with his thumb.

She doubled her efforts and hummed softly, his undoing. His eyes snapped shut and behind his clenched lids, bright stars flashed.

"Holy shit," were the first words out of his mouth as soon as he regained the ability to speak.

Annie laughed, and with her hands wrapped around the bottom of his shirt, she dragged him down to the floor. The tile was hard and unforgiving, but he followed because he'd have been a fool to put up a fight. If she asked him to go to the moon for her, he'd figure out a way to get there. Try his damnedest at the very least.

He'd do anything, if he had even an inkling it would bring a smile to her face.

Sometime later—how long he didn't know because the clock was out of sight and he was too lazy to check—after he'd regained enough feeling in his limbs to successfully bunch his pants behind his head, unable to move any further in search of an actual pillow, he swallowed hard. "Hey, Annie?"

More than ever before, his chest burned with the need to

speak his truth. To make his feelings known and hope they were on the same page.

She traced shapes into his stomach that made him shiver pleasantly, her fingers raking through the coarse hair beneath his belly button. "Mm-hmm?"

Caring about Annie made him feel like he was reaching for the sun; how close would she let him get? Would he wind up burning like Icarus if he flew too close, pressed too hard, wanted too much?

It was now or never. "Just—let me get this out, okay? Don't say anything, or . . . don't feel like you *have* to say anything. Not until—"

"Brendon." She rested her chin on the notch at the bottom of his sternum, and it was a wonder her head didn't bounce with the way his heart pounded against the wall of his chest. Her lips twitched upward, her expression verging on bemused. "Breathe."

Breathing would help. Passing out would *not*. He let his hand drift down to the small of her back and up again, breathing in time with the leisurely drag of his palm against her smooth skin.

"I don't want you to move to London."

Her expression shuttered, her eyes falling to his chin.

Words fell from his lips in a dizzying rush because he had to get this out. "I don't want you to move to London and I know that's selfish of me, but it's also not? Because I want you to be happy and I don't think you'll be as happy there as you could be here."

"Brendon—"

"Please. Let me finish."

She nodded, eyes darting warily over his face.

"I want more time with you. This past week has been the greatest and somehow, also the worst of my life because—"

"What does that mean?" Annie scrunched her face up. "Sorry. Go on."

He laughed and ran his hand up her back, smiling when she shivered and pressed closer. "Because it's been everything I wanted, and the thought of you getting on a plane and this all going away? Of you going away?" He shook his head. "That's the last thing I want."

She resumed her lip nibbling.

"A week and a half hasn't been enough." He debated the next part, not wanting to scare her, but . . . if he was being honest, he might as well go for broke. "I don't think any amount of time would be enough."

She lifted her eyes, her lip popping out from between her teeth when her jaw dropped.

"I want more mornings waking up next to you. I want to show you the rest of my favorite places around town. I want to take you out to Sequim to show you the lavender fields and I want lazy nights spent with you, watching French television shows I can't understand."

She cracked a smile.

"Everything I learn about you makes me want to know more."

Her eyes went glassy, her lashes fluttering against her cheeks.

"I want to know how you prefer yours eggs and whether you like the Beatles or the Rolling Stones better, or if you hate them both. If you've been bungee jumping. Whether you've ever stayed up until four in the morning reading. Your opinion on oatmeal cookies. Your favorite way to spend Sunday afternoons."

Annie gave a watery laugh. "Soft boiled, the Rolling Stones, no but I want to, yes, I don't discriminate against cookies, and"—she swallowed hard—"if you asked me two weeks ago, I'd have told you the best Sundays are when I don't get out of my pajamas, but now? Right now I'd say my favorite way to spend any afternoon is with you."

His heart flung itself at her through the wall of his chest. "I can't believe you like oatmeal cookies. You heathen."

She smiled at him, and his awareness of his heartbeat increased threefold. "I even like them with raisins."

"*Gah.*" He laughed, even though his sinuses burned. "Well, that's that. Time for you to go."

Annie laughed and nothing sounded sweeter.

"I've never felt this way about anyone before," he whispered. "And I don't really know what I'm doing. But I want the chance to figure it out, Annie. I want the chance to figure it out with you."

Annie raised her chin, shifting almost to sitting. She folded her arms on top of his chest and leaned over him.

"I don't know what I'm doing, either," she admitted, her voice a whisper he had to strain to hear. "I never planned for any of this to happen. I never thought . . ."

She shut her eyes and pressed her lips together, and his chest ached with the desire to make it better. Whatever she was feeling, whatever was tearing her up inside, leaving her conflicted, he wanted to take care of it, shoulder the weight for her, or at least share in it. He continued to rub her back, because if that was the only thing he could do for her, the only thing to make her feel marginally better at the moment? He'd do it well.

"I knew I wasn't happy in Philadelphia, but I tried not to think about it. No one wants to *think* about how unhappy they are," she admitted. "I think . . . I think I've been settling for less than happy for so long that I'd forgotten what being happy *really* felt like." The smile she gave him started slow, almost shy, before brightening into something steady and sure. "Until I came here. You've been a huge part of that, Brendon."

Laughter built in his chest, bursting from between his lips, incandescent and joyful. Unstoppable. The insides of his eyes stung.

"I don't know what I'm doing," she repeated, but this time it didn't make his chest ache as intensely. It sounded more like a confession than an apology, and that gave him hope. Annie rested her hand against his cheek, her fingers brushing the thin skin beneath his eye. "But I promise . . . I promise you'll be the first to know."

Chapter Eighteen

Wednesday, June 9

"Do you like these?" Elle held up a pair of earrings shaped like sparkly, pale pink sugar cubes. "Or these better?" She held up another pair shaped like swirling bunches of cotton candy.

Annie tore herself from the curio cabinet full of antique estate jewelry and took in the options Elle held. Both were kitschy but so perfectly Elle that it made it hard for Annie to choose. "That's a dilemma. Both?"

Elle flipped over the cardboard cards they were affixed to. "On sale." She beamed. "Both it is. Thanks."

Texting and even the occasional FaceTime chat with Elle hadn't done her spunky, whimsical, occasionally harebrained personality justice. She was a hyperactive ray of sunshine with a penchant for looking on the bright side and tossing out random resonant pieces of wisdom.

Annie held up a pair of leather ankle boots. "What do you think?"

"Cute." Elle smiled but shook her head. "But you're not supposed to buy shoes secondhand."

"Right." Annie set them back on the rack with a wistful sigh. "Throws off your gait."

Elle gave her a startled frown. "No. I mean, yeah, I guess. But it's bad luck."

Annie stared at her.

"You know. If you buy secondhand shoes you'll wind up walking someone else's path."

Annie snickered. "Guess that completely rules out purchasing vintage lingerie."

"No." Elle smiled. "I think that's fine as long as you have it laundered first. But not underwear." She frowned. "That's just gross."

Shopping with Elle was an unparalleled experience. *Antiquing* was next-level. The shop they were currently browsing was divided roughly by decade, with the oldest wares in the back and the newest near the front, with the exception of the fine jewelry, which was kept beneath glass close to the register. Elle bounced from aisle to aisle, her enthusiasm contagious.

"Pink cups!" Elle hurried down the aisle, stopping in front of a collection of brightly colored Depression glass in almost every color of the rainbow, from avocado green and dusty pink to milky blue and canary yellow. "Margot and I *should* probably invest in matching dishes. It's past time."

Little did Elle know Darcy planned to ask her to move in. Annie bit back a smirk. On second thought . . . "You should *definitely* buy the whole set. But make it rainbow. Green plates and pink wineglasses."

Elle laughed. "To match my rosé."

"And blue water glasses."

"Yellow bowls."

"You *need* an ultramarine cookie jar."

Elle threw her head back. "I think I do."

Darcy was going to have kittens when the time came to merge their belongings. Annie could picture Elle's Depression glassware beside Darcy's pristine porcelain plates and stainless flatware. Hell, if Elle didn't buy it, Annie would, and she'd gift it to her. A nice housewarming present.

Elle took off for the front of the store and returned a moment later with a shopping basket, which she quickly and carefully filled with Depression glass and her new earrings.

While Elle weighed the merits of aquamarine versus delphite cups, Annie meandered down the aisle, pausing in front of a metal carousel of old postcards. The cardstock was buttery soft and slightly yellowed with age, the picturesque fronts faded in places from fingerprints, but otherwise they were preserved, the ink only slightly grayed. Annie selected a beautiful black and white postcard that looked like something straight out of a French fairy tale. It reminded her of a town she'd visited in Provence. In the bottom left corner was the location— Palais des Papes, Avignon. She bounced on her toes. It *was* in Provence.

She flipped the postcard over. The handwriting was beautiful, all slanted cursive. French, too. Upon closer inspection, it wasn't merely a postcard but a love letter, if the salutation, "*Ma chère femme*," was anything to go off. A love letter from 1935. Her jaw dropped.

"Find something?" Elle chirped.

Annie spun quickly, clasping the postcard delicately to her chest. "Just a postcard."

She flipped it over, showing Elle the writing.

Elle cocked her head. "French?"

Annie nodded. "A love letter. It's . . ." She scanned the words, some of the swooping letters tricky to decipher. Her heart warmed. "It's really sweet actually. It's from a man to his wife. He talks about missing her and how they've been married"—she squinted to make out the number—"forty-five years. He seems . . . smitten."

Elle smiled. "You should buy it."

Maybe she would. Only, she didn't think she'd keep it. As much as she loved it, it felt like something Brendon would treasure. She glanced at the postcard and smiled. Oh yeah, he'd love it, even if she had to translate it for him.

"Hey, Elle?" she asked after they'd turned the corner.

"Mm-hmm?"

"Can I ask you a question?"

"That is a question." Elle winked. "But sure."

"Your job is . . ."

"Weird?" Elle grinned knowingly.

Annie laughed. "I was going to say *unique*, but sure. That."

If Elle was bothered, she certainly didn't seem it. She gave a nonchalant shrug and leaned against a shelf, first checking to make sure it was sturdy enough to hold her weight. "It is a little offbeat. I'm under no delusions about it."

"But it makes you really happy," Annie said. "What you do. Being an astrologer."

"It does. I wouldn't trade it for the chance to do anything." She pursed her lips. "Maybe go to space."

"But it wasn't what you originally planned on being, right?"

Elle shook her head. "No. I dropped out of my PhD program in astronomy."

Annie's pulse quickened at the idea of veering so far off one's path. Especially a path so heavily invested in. "Did you just . . . wake up one morning and decide to pull the trigger?"

"Kind of?" Elle wrinkled her nose, then laughed. "I'd been laying the groundwork to make the leap for a while and I'd been thinking about it, disenchanted with what I was doing for longer. It wasn't some spur-of-the-moment, *I'm dropping out* kind of crisis. I'd thought about it, but I *did* wake up one morning completely fed up with the idea of getting out of bed and teaching a bunch of undergrads about astronomy knowing most of them were only there because Rocks for Jocks had already filled up. I decided enough was enough. I wanted to feel . . . excited again. I wanted to love what I do." She shrugged and smiled impishly. "So I did it."

"Didn't it . . . scare you shitless?" Annie asked, laughing lightly. "Talk about a leap of faith."

Elle nodded. "I'd be remiss if I didn't acknowledge I was extremely privileged to be in the position to shift course like I did. I had my family to fall back on—not that they liked my decision or even supported it, but they'd never have let me suffer because of it. And I had Margot, which made it easier since I wasn't alone in shifting to Oh My Stars full-time. But yeah, of course it scared me. But I was more afraid of waking up one day and wondering how my life had become something so far from what I'd originally wanted for myself. I never wanted to wake up and wonder whether I'd be happier if I'd followed my heart. If I had taken that risk. Life's too short for should-haves."

"Carpe diem," Annie said with a wry smile.

Elle smiled brightly. "Exactly! I knew there was a reason I liked you."

"Likewise."

Elle jerked her head in the direction of a wall of vintage hats; simply looking at them made Annie's skin crawl.

"Life's too short to waste on what-ifs and regrets. Life should be lived to the fullest. Quit school. Take a weird job. Pursue your passion. Ask the girl out." She looked at Annie askance. "Or guy."

Her lips curved upward. "*Or* girl."

Elle's smile brightened and she held out a hand. "Bi five."

Annie laughed and gave Elle a high five. It had been a long time since she'd had friends, close friends, whom she felt she could be herself around. Friends around whom she could let her hair down, be dorky without feeling judged for it. Friends who weren't afraid to be unabashedly themselves and preferred funky antiquing outings to drinking bottomless mimosas at brunch. Not that Annie had anything against bottomless mimosas *or* brunch, but she liked to mix it up.

With an eager gasp, Elle plucked a cloche hat with a giant blue butterfly affixed to it off the wall and shoved it on her head. Annie struggled not to full-body cringe, but she held her tongue. Clothes were one thing, shoes even, but *hats*? Hard pass.

"So." Elle modeled her selection in the vertical mirror. "Is this about not liking your job or is it about liking Brendon?"

Annie stared, because *wow*, she hadn't expected Elle to come out and just *say* it.

Elle winced, one eye shutting. "Shoot. Was that too blunt?"

Annie laughed, recovering from her shock. "Blunt? Yes. Too blunt? No. I like that you say what's on your mind. It's . . . refreshing."

Elle cackled. "That's one way to put it. My lack of a brain-to-mouth filter drives Darcy up the wall."

"No way. She *loves* it."

Elle worried her bottom lip. "Did she tell you that?"

"She didn't have to," Annie said. "I know Darcy."

Most days, she was convinced she knew Darcy better than she knew herself. And vice versa.

Elle continued to look skeptical.

"Look, did Darcy ever tell you how we became best friends?"

"She told me you moved in down the street."

That didn't even skim the surface of their story. "I did. My family didn't move to the United States until I was seven. And even then, first we moved to Chicago, where my mom was originally from, and we were living in an apartment building and there were no kids close to my age. When we moved to San Francisco and I saw Darcy, I was *so* excited. I'd played with cousins, but they were either older than me or younger, so having someone my age around was completely new. I was a little . . . overzealous?" She laughed, memories flooding back. "I asked Darcy if she wanted to be my friend and she told me she already had a brother and *he* was her best friend. She slammed her front door in my face."

"Oh my God." Elle laughed.

"Yeah." Annie slouched against the wall beside the mirror and remembered the acute sense of disappointment that came with someone rejecting her for the first time. A laugh burst from between her lips, because Darcy's hesitance had been no match for Annie's dogged determination. "So, Darcy successfully kept me at arm's length until October, when we had sex ed."

Elle's dark blue eyes widened comically.

"We had a unit on sexually transmitted infections and, look, I *know* there's nothing funny about syphilis, but it's like there's some sort of short inside my head that makes me laugh at the most inopportune times. I kept giggling, and Darcy was in the desk next to me, and for some reason our teacher sent both of us to the principal's office."

Elle's jaw dropped. "No."

"Right?" Darcy had fumed. "The principal asked us what was so funny about venereal disease and I just—I lost it. Round two. I couldn't stop laughing no matter how hard I tried. All of a sudden, Darcy started snickering, and we were both . . . we were a mess. Crying, shaking, falling against each other, laughing so hard we couldn't speak. It was contagious and terrible and amazing, and our principal finally threw her hands up and called our parents. We were both sent home and assigned two-page essays on the importance of taking sexual health seriously."

Elle's eyes were bright and glassy from laughing. "And the rest is history?"

"Well, the rest is that Darcy ignored me for three days because I ruined her perfect record—and honestly, what kind of middle schooler is concerned about their record?"

"Darcy." Elle's smile softened.

"Darcy." She nodded. "Well, then she knocked on my front door and asked if I'd written my essay, only to berate me for slacking off and not turning it in early like she had. She harangued me into writing it and lectured me about the importance of condom usage, which, in retrospect? Hilarious."

Elle posed in front of the mirror, tugging on the brim of her hat. She laughed and ripped it off, hanging it back on its hook. "And *then* the rest is history?"

"Which is my long-winded way of telling you she appreciates your lack of brain-to-mouth filter. Because she's put up with mine for about twenty years."

"Okay, I'm convinced. I firmly retract my apology for being blunt." Elle grinned. "Tell me about Brendon."

Her face warmed. "I don't want to be the type of person to make big life decisions all because of someone I'm seeing."

"But is that really what this is?" Elle asked. "Or is it a little more complicated than that?"

"*Complicated* is certainly a word for what I'm feeling."

"Welcome to Gemini season," Elle said, which meant exactly nothing to Annie.

"Ah."

Elle laughed. "Gemini is a mutable sign, so it's a good time to approach the possibility of change with an open mind and heart, meet a new lover, and reconnect with old friends. Being an air sign, it's *also* all about rationality. So I can see why you're struggling. You're a Sagittarius, right?"

Annie nodded.

Elle wrinkled her nose, eyes darting up and to the left, the gears in her head visibly whirring. "I'd need your whole chart, but Gemini is your opposite sign, so the season tends to affect you strongly. I'd say now is a pertinent time to consider ridding yourself of the baggage that doesn't belong to you so you can make room for who you're meant to be."

Everything Elle had said resonated, but Annie was pretty sure that had nothing to do with its being Gemini season and everything to do with her own mixed-up feelings.

"Astrology aside"—Elle shot her a conciliatory smile—"you're struggling with what you want and what you *think* you should want, right?"

Annie pressed a palm to her forehead and sighed. "I don't know? Yes?"

"Do you love him?" Elle asked, completely out of the blue.

Sweat broke out along her hairline. It had been *two weeks.* "Not yet. But I think I could. Is that crazy? Oh my God, please don't answer that."

Elle laughed. "If you want my opinion, it doesn't sound like you want to move to London. What part of the equation is tripping you up here?"

The timing? The magnitude of the decision awaiting her? The idea of rearranging her whole life?

She was at a crossroads. Not having a job in Philadelphia meant there was nothing there for her. She could go through with the plan and move to London, start over there, or, technically, she could move anywhere she wanted, assuming she could find a job.

She liked everything Seattle had to offer: her best friend lived here; there were people here she liked and wanted to know better, people she could see letting herself get close to. The city was beautiful.

And then there was Brendon.

He wasn't her sole reason for considering the wildest decision of her life, but he was certainly a piece of the puzzle. She liked him, more than a little. She already cared about him, which was scary all on its own.

She shrugged. "I don't feel particularly invested in moving to London or the job there. It all sounds great on paper. Good pay. A chance to put down roots. But I don't . . . *care* about it."

"But there are things you care about here? People you care about?"

Annie nodded.

"Isn't that a good thing?" Elle frowned.

She shrugged.

"Caring about people isn't a weakness, you know," Elle said.

Annie gave a sharp laugh, then winced. "No, no it's not. As long as you don't care too much."

"There's no such thing as caring too much."

What an utterly sweet, guileless sentiment. "It's when you start hoping that others will care that you wind up in hot water."

"You think Brendon doesn't care about you?"

I've never felt this way about anyone before.

Annie swallowed hard. "No, I believe he does. But it's been thirteen days. I think he cares now, but . . ." She shook her head. "Brendon's never been in a relationship before. Not one that lasted longer than a few weeks. I believe he wants me now, but what happens if he changes his mind? Right now, everything is new and exciting, but what happens when it's not new? What happens if I pack up and move across the country and he decides I'm not what he wants anymore?"

If she didn't live up to the fantasy expectations he had in his head of what a relationship was supposed to be?

Elle offered her a tiny smile and reached out, resting her hand on Annie's arm. "You're worried it's going to go wrong, but what if it goes right? What if Brendon turns out to be the best thing that ever happened to you?"

Chapter Nineteen

"You think they're ever going to give us a gay season of *The Bachelor*?"

Darcy dug her chopsticks into her carton of pad thai. "What's that spin-off show? The one where they sequester the rejects on an island?"

Annie tried in vain to fluff one of Darcy's decorative pillows, but it still felt like lying on a shiny satin brick. "*Bachelor in Paradise*?"

"I guess? Wasn't someone bi?"

"Yeah, but I mean a whole season dedicated to a queer lead. MTV did it back in 2007 with *Shot at Love with Tila Tequila*. Over ten years later and we're still thirsting for a full-fledged season of *The Bachelorette* where two dozen women in slinky ballgowns and bespoke pantsuits compete for the affection of one woman." Annie snagged her phone off the coffee table and set it face down on her stomach. "I'm telling you, *L'amour est dans le pré* is infinitely superior to—"

Darcy snorted.

Annie cut her eyes at her. "What?"

"The French version of *Farmer Wants a Wife*?" Her brown eyes widened gleefully. "Annie, I've had an epiphany."

She waited, staring at Darcy askance.

"The reason you've never had any success with dating apps is because you were using the wrong ones."

Annie laughed. "Your brother already espoused the values of OTP—"

"Not OTP." Darcy snickered. "Farmers Only."

"Ugh." Annie kicked Darcy's leg. "I forgot how mean you can be. I don't think *L'amour est dans le pré* would resonate the same over here anyway."

She liked watching *The Bachelor* as much as the next person, but it wasn't *real*. *L'amour est dans le pré* appealed to both her romantic and pragmatic sensibilities. And they'd featured several gay farmers, something *The Bachelor* had yet to do. Feature gay contestants, *not* farmers.

"Probably not," Darcy agreed. "Cheese and wine and olives are sexier than soybeans."

A stranger sentence had never been spoken, not that Annie disagreed.

"And"—Darcy scrutinized her chopsticks, studiously avoiding Annie's eyes—"maybe if you lived closer, you wouldn't forget integral parts of my personality."

Another sly yet less-than-subtle hint. Darcy had been dropping them regularly and with increasing frequency over the past forty-eight hours.

"Being a bitch is an integral part of your personality?" Annie laughed. "Way to embrace your bad self."

"If the shoe fits," Darcy said, droll.

Annie's stomach vibrated. She checked her phone, swiping hard and huffing when her swipes wouldn't register. The crack had spread across her screen, rendering her device practically worthless.

ELLE (9:41 P.M.): 🍷🥂

Annie zoomed in, laughing out loud at the box of rosé posed beside Elle's new pink Depression glassware.

Darcy lifted her head, a curious furrow forming between her eyes. "Brendon?" She wrinkled her nose. "You're not sending *more* inappropriate texts while you sit on my couch, are you?"

She rolled her eyes. "Do you often laugh when you sext?" When Darcy turned an unhealthy shade of pink, she added, "On second thought, forget I asked."

"Forgotten," Darcy murmured.

"Relax, I'm texting Elle."

Darcy's expression went melty. "Oh."

"You know what? You're not a bitch, you're a marshmallow."

Darcy balked. "I am not a *marshmallow*."

"You are. You're an ooey, gooey ball of sugary, cavity-inducing fluff. You make me sick and I love every second of it."

"Take it back." Darcy set her dinner aside.

"Nope. You're exactly like one of those Lucky Charms marshmallows I watched you feed Elle in her kitchen the other night when you thought no one was watching."

Crunchy on the outside, but melt-in-your-mouth sweet.

Darcy buried her flushed face in her hands.

Annie sat up and threw her arms around Darcy's neck, rocking them both from side to side. "I'm happy you're happy."

"Me too." Darcy drew back, the serious look in her eyes un-
dermining her smile. "You know my guest room always has
your name on it, right? Even if Elle moves in—"

"When. *When* Elle moves in."

"When," Darcy said with a nod. "My apartment is large
enough for three people if you want to stay for two weeks or two
months or two years or—"

"Whoa." Annie held up her hands, nipping that idea in the
bud. "I'm not crashing your love nest, Darce."

"You wouldn't." With a vehement shake of her head, Darcy
set her jaw. She looked fierce, bound and determined to reassure
Annie.

Annie wrinkled her nose. "Pretty sure I *did* crash. Showing
up unexpectedly—"

"Well, now I'm inviting you. I'm *asking*," Darcy said. She
drew her lip between her teeth and blinked several times in
quick succession, dispelling the glassy sheen that had formed in
her eyes. "This place is big enough for three people and you're
my best friend and you and Elle get along like a house on fire."

This was all true, but . . . "What happens when you want to
cook naked or—"

"That's just asking to wind up with third-degree burns somewhere embarrassing," Darcy blurted.

"Oh my God. I'm not cockblocking my best friend in her own
apartment. The last thing you and Elle need is a roommate."

Darcy frowned sharply. "The last thing I need is my best
friend moving halfway around the world."

It was the first time Darcy had so bluntly expressed her displeasure over Annie's potential move since their original conversation.

Annie drew her lip between her teeth and nodded. "I know you aren't thrilled—"

"Thrilled?" Darcy scoffed. "I'm not *thrilled* about Elle bringing a bunch of multicolored glassware into my—*our* kitchen. I'm not *thrilled* when I have to work late on Fridays. I'm not *thrilled* when I forget to pack a lunch. But this?" Her bottom lip trembled. "I'm devastated, Annie."

Annie winced and turned away. "I know—"

"You don't." Darcy rested her fingers on the back of Annie's hand. "You don't know. Because I'm—I'm upset about you moving, but what kills me is that I messed up."

Annie's head snapped to the side. "What?"

"Let me finish," Darcy demanded, expression stern despite the red rimming her eyes. "I took you and I took our friendship for granted."

"You did *no*—"

Darcy squeezed her hand and frowned. "I *said* let me finish."

She rolled her eyes but pressed her lips together, holding her tongue.

"We've been friends since middle school. We moved across the country together for school. We shared a dorm and an apartment and—you've always been there. After everything happened with Natasha—"

Annie sneered at the mention of Darcy's terrible ex.

"I needed a fresh start," Darcy continued. "I needed distance. But not from you. Never from you."

A lump formed in Annie's throat, making it hard to swallow. It was a good thing she wasn't allowed to speak.

"I should've been better about texting and calling and *being* there even if I was here and you were there. If that makes sense?"

"It—can I talk?"

Darcy gave a tight nod.

"It makes sense, but I'm not upset. You needed a fresh start and I couldn't be happier for you. You moved on and you met Elle and you have a whole life here. That's how it's supposed to be. That's what I wanted for you when you decided to move to Seattle."

"Yes, but—let me be selfish, okay?" Darcy gave a wet laugh and wiped under her eyes, her mascara smudging. "I want *you* to be a part of my life here, too. I want to have my cake and eat it, too, Annie."

Fuck. She pressed the heels of her hands to her eyes and sucked in a deep breath. "I don't know what I'm doing."

Darcy sniffled and shifted closer until they were pressed together, hip to hip, thigh to thigh. She rested her hand on Annie's back and rubbed soothing circles between her shoulder blades.

"Is this about my brother?" she asked quietly.

Annie lifted her head and blew her hair out of her face with a sharp sigh. "I don't know."

Without question, Brendon contributed to her confusion. She'd be remiss if she didn't acknowledge him as the driving force behind her reevaluation of her choices, of what she thought she wanted. Beyond that, he inspired feelings in her she'd sworn off and elevated her expectations, and it was terrifying and exciting and all happening so *fast*.

"I came to Seattle to tell you I was moving. A bon voyage. I've been here less than two weeks and I'm questioning everything." She groaned and let her head drop back on her shoulders. "I'm seriously considering changing all my plans after *days*, Darcy. I have a job lined up in London and it's what I thought I wanted and now . . . I don't know if that's what I want anymore."

"If London isn't what you want, what's your alternative?"

Annie covered her face with a hand. "I could turn down the promotion and stay on with Brockman and Brady in the Philadelphia office. Problem with that is, I already have a sublet lined up. I would need to find a new apartment. Stat."

"*Or*"—Darcy took a deep breath—"you could pack up all of your things and move here."

Until two weeks ago, moving to London had been *the plan*, the only one she'd had. But that wasn't true anymore. She had options. Options that terrified her but thrilled her, too. Options that felt *right* in a way that moving to London didn't.

She let herself think about it. Not just a peripheral glimpse at what the future might hold before she tore her eyes away, too afraid of staring it down. This time, she forced herself to confront it, head-on. What it would be like, living in Seattle, making a life here. Calling this city home.

There'd be no need to cross days off on a calendar. Sure, she'd have to fly back to Philadelphia and take care of things, tie up loose ends, put her plans in motion, figure out the finer details, but she could be back in the blink of an eye, and all of this? Darcy, not just a phone call away, but within driving distance. Game nights and spectacularly strange shopping trips with Elle. Nights with Brendon on his couch, laughing until she cried and her stomach ached. Exploring the city and discovering Brendon, letting him discover her.

Annie stared up at the ceiling. "I could."

"Wait." Darcy shoved Annie's shoulder. *Hard.* "Are you serious?"

Annie laughed. "I said I could. Not that I was going to."

"So it's a maybe?"

Annie nodded slowly.

"What do you need to turn that *maybe* into a *yes*?"

"A crystal ball?" Annie joked, pressing her fingertips to her right temple. Her head was beginning to hurt. "A glimpse into the future would help."

Darcy frowned. "Look, I don't believe in astrology, but if you need me to ask Elle—"

"I was kidding. What I need is far harder to come by. A plan. A job."

She had enough money in savings to swing a few months in limbo, but that was it.

Darcy waved her hand like it was no big deal. "We can find you a job. Easy. You have references, experience." She pursed her lips. "I bet I could get you an interview at Devereaux and Horton. I think our HR department might be hiring."

That was nice and all but . . . "I don't know if I want to work in HR anymore."

If—and it was a big, up-in-the-air *if*—she was starting over, she might as well look for a job she actually liked.

"Okay." Darcy nodded, taking Annie's confession in stride. "If not HR, what?"

"I'm not sure," she admitted. "Maybe something that actually puts my degree in linguistics to use? Translation?"

"All right. We can do some research. I can put feelers out."

Time was of the essence and all, but this was moving at a rapid pace. A cart-before-the-horse rapid pace. "I never said I was sure, Darcy. It's a possibility. I still have to think about it."

"What's there to think about? You don't want to work in human resources. You don't know anyone in London. You've already subleased your apartment in Philadelphia. You like it here, don't you?"

Annie nodded. There was nothing about Seattle she didn't like. The city was vibrant, the geography stunning. Based on what she'd seen, she had a feeling she'd never be bored, not with everything the city had to offer.

"You have friends here, Annie."

True. Everything Darcy had said was true. And yet . . .

This was a huge decision. A life-altering one. Not one to make lightly or quickly.

Darcy rested her hands on her knees. "You want to make a list? Pros and cons? A cost-benefit analysis?"

"You're biased. You'd have to, like, recuse yourself from evaluating my risk."

"Recuse myself? Annie, I'm an actuary, not an attorney, and we're discussing your inevitable move to Seattle, not an insurance claim. It just *feels* like a life-or-death situation; it isn't one."

Annie's chin wobbled, her smile shaking. "God, I really missed you. You're such a smart-ass."

"Pro"—Darcy reached for her phone, opening up her notes

app—"you move to Seattle and you get twenty-four/seven access to me in all my smart-ass glory."

"Twenty-four/seven? Really? I could call you at two in the morning and expect a pithy quip?"

"You *could*. But let's go with sixteen/seven," she said. "I don't perform well on fewer than eight hours of sleep."

Warmth spread through Annie's chest, along with an overwhelming sense of rightness. *Certainty.* This was what she wanted.

Chapter Twenty

What Controversy Are You Based on Your Zodiac Sign?

Aries—Ross and Rachel: were they on a break?
Taurus—Reclining your seat on an airplane: acceptable or infuriating?
Gemini—Pineapple on a pizza: delicious or disgusting?
Cancer—Team Edward vs. Team Jacob
Leo—Pet names for significant others: cute or gag-worthy?
Virgo—Toilet paper: over or under?
Libra—*Pride & Prejudice* (2005 movie) vs. *Pride and Prejudice* (1995 miniseries)
Scorpio—Martinis: gin or vodka?
Sagittarius—Centaur penis placement: human or horse?
Capricorn—The left lane is for passing only: yay or nay?
Aquarius—-Aliens-
Pisces—Peeing in the shower: gross or acceptable?

Friday, June 11

*B*rendon exited out of Twitter and set his phone aside when someone knocked on his office door.

"Come in." He leaned back in his chair, swiveling gently from side to side, steepling his fingers in front of him.

The door opened and Margot entered, shutting the door behind her. One of her brows quirked high on her forehead as her dark eyes swept over his seated form. "Wasn't aware I stepped inside the office of Hugo Drax."

He frowned. "Hugo *who*?"

"Drax." At his blank stare, she huffed. "Hugo Drax, Bond villain." She mimicked him, tenting her fingers in front of her body. "You look very dastardly. Like you're about to fire a laser at the moon unless someone sends you one million dollars."

He dropped his hands and slumped back in his chair. "It's a sign of impassioned intelligence according to the leading experts in body language psychology."

"Did you research that?" Margot threw her messenger bag on the floor and collapsed into one of his chairs. She kicked her feet up on his desk, sending his stress ball rolling. "Who am I kidding? Of course you did."

He leaned down and snagged it off the floor, tossing it at Margot. She snatched it out of the air and gave it a hard clench.

"Did you come here to give me shit or was there some other reason for your visit?"

She rifled around inside her bag before tossing what he was

pretty sure was an aluminum foil brick on his desk. "Chipotle. Enjoy."

Ah, *food*. He'd spent most of the morning going over his notes for this afternoon's all-team meeting and had completely lost track of time. By the time he'd checked the clock, it was too late to dash out for a quick bite. He tore the foil open, revealing a steamy burrito nearly the size of his head. "Thanks."

Margot already had her mouth wrapped around hers, tearing into her meal with gusto.

"Hey, Mar?"

She nodded and continued to chew.

"Is centaur penis placement seriously up for debate?"

She coughed, catching a handful of half-chewed burrito. "Jesus, Brendon."

"I mean, it's obviously back by the horse half, right?" He frowned. "Or no? Then again, centaurs have two rib cages, which suggests the possibility of *two* hearts, so—"

"*Okay*. Warn a girl before you start talking about penises, *please*." Margot snagged a napkin off his desk.

"We're hardly in public and you have the foulest mouth of anyone I've ever met. Don't act scandalized."

She lifted a hand to her chest and sniffed. "Fuck, that might be the nicest thing you've ever said to me. I am touched. Touched, I tell you."

He balled up his napkin and tossed it at her head. She batted it aside and cackled.

"For the record, I'm the one who made this particular meme." Margot preened. "I'm especially proud."

He cracked a smile. "It's a good one."

She studied him over her burrito. "How's Annie?"

"Annie's great."

She stared at him blankly. "She's great?"

He laughed. "Yeah, Mar. Great. As in that state of being that denotes goodness. Positivity. Ring any bells?"

"Normally I can't get you to shut up about the girls you go out with. Now you're being all tight-lipped?"

Margot wasn't wrong. Usually he was eager to share when he'd had a great date. For some reason, this felt different.

This thing between him and Annie was already so precious to him that he felt . . . protective. Like he was holding something fragile in the palms of his hands. Holding too tight might crush it; not tight enough and it might drift away. And talking about it?

"I don't want to jinx this." He slumped back in his chair and kicked away from his desk, spinning in a slow circle as he stared up at the ceiling. "Does that sound weird?"

"Weird." Margot smirked. "Right up your alley."

"Funny."

"I wasn't finished. Right up your alley *and* we love you for it."

"We? Who is this *we* you speak of?"

"I was using the royal *we*, you douche, but I take it back."

He sniffled. "That is the nicest thing *you* have ever said to me."

"Calling you a douche? Whatever floats your boat, I guess."

He checked to make sure his office door was shut, then flipped her off. "I really like her, Margot."

Margot's expression softened. "I can tell. Hell, you've got a pretty serious case of heart eyes going on. Someone says *Annie* and your face does this melty thing and it's so gross it makes me want to hurl, but like, in a happy way."

"Happy hurling," he repeated. "And you called me weird."

She threw a packet of hot sauce at him. "Giving you grief is how I show affection."

He glanced at his notebook. "Ah, yes, shit-giving. The lesser-known sixth love language."

Her brows rose over the top of her glasses.

"Nothing." He waved her off. "Thinking about the meeting I've got in"—he checked the time—"ten minutes. We're trying to reach a new demographic."

Margot snagged another packet of sauce and tore it open with her teeth. "Which would be . . . ?"

"The thirty percent of dating app users who believe apps have rendered courtships impersonal and devoid of romance."

A flicker of recognition passed over her face, her brows ticking higher. "Damn. Well, you like a challenge. Example: Annie. Only you would fall hard and fast for a girl who doesn't live here."

He shot her a wry smile. "Since when is love supposed to be convenient?"

Margot squeezed her burrito so hard the filling squashed out the bottom, splattering against the foil on her lap. "Whoa, *whoa.* Did you just imply that you *love* her?"

He set his burrito down carefully. Had he?

When Annie stepped into a room, everything else fell away. Touching Annie, kissing her, her laugh alone, made his heart skip several beats like he'd downed a red-eye coffee. Under that was an overwhelming sense of rightness. When his heartbeat returned to normal, she was still the only person he wanted, and he'd have given anything to be that person for her.

Perhaps it wasn't love, but it was headed in that direction. Or, it could.

"She's leaving tomorrow night."

With an aggrieved huff, she set her deconstructed burrito aside. "That was not the answer to my question."

"But a valid point, nonetheless."

She pinned him with a no-nonsense stare. "Those dimples, while adorable, don't work on me."

Obfuscation was getting him nowhere. "Look, even I'm willing to admit this has all happened at breakneck speed, okay? Excuse me if I don't want to cheapen my feelings by sticking a label on them too soon."

Her brows rose over the top of her glasses. "Holy shit. You're *really* serious about her."

"I am, but—" His voice broke off abruptly and he forced down a swallow before coughing to clear his throat. "Again, she's leaving tomorrow."

And she had yet to say if she was moving to London or staying in Philadelphia or maybe, just maybe, thinking of relocating here.

Margot frowned, picking at the outer fold of the tortilla. "How goes *the plan?*"

"Plan?"

"You know, *the plan*. The one I inadvertently inspired? What you've been doing this entire time? Proving to Annie that romance isn't dead by wooing, taking cues from all your favorite sappy movies? It must've worked better than I thought if it got you this far."

"Do my ears deceive me or did you just admit you were wrong about something?"

Margot rolled her eyes. "Shouldn't you be, I don't know, hiring a skywriter or getting her face tattooed on your stomach or something?"

"If that's what you think passes for romance, I pity the person you fall in love with." He smiled, softening the barb.

"Good thing I'm not looking to fall in love with anyone."

"One of these days—"

"Finish that sentence." She narrowed her eyes. "I dare you."

He held his tongue, knowing better than to press the issue. But *God*, he was going to love to say *I told you so* to her one day. "The movie scene recreations worked as far as giving us the opportunity to get to know one another while also showing Annie around town. I *think* she appreciates the effort I put into our dates"—even he had to admit his execution, at times, was a bit of a fail, what with the Great Wheel malfunctioning, the wrong song playing at karaoke, getting stranded by the ferry, falling in the water at the wedding—"but grand gestures aren't her love language."

Margot shrugged. "Okay, then speak her language."

He slumped back in his chair and pressed the heels of his hands into his eye sockets. "What do you think I've been trying to do?"

Show Annie he cared via thoughtful gifts and quality time, all without overwhelming her.

She winced. "Maybe grab a megaphone and speak her language louder?"

Maybe Margot was right. Tomorrow, Annie would be on a plane. Now wasn't the time to play it safe.

He checked his phone. Five minutes until his meeting. He balled up his foil burrito wrapper and tossed it in the trash. "Speaking of time, I've got to head over to the conference room. You're welcome to hang around in here if you want."

"Nah, I've got places to be." Margot kicked her feet off his desk and stood, following him out of his office. She paused in the hall, just before the bank of elevators. "Good luck with your meeting."

He rocked back on his heels. Nerves were settling in, his hopes for this meeting high. "Thanks."

"And, Brendon?" She reached out, patting him on the shoulder. "Good luck with Annie. Just remember, there's only so much anyone can do. You, Darcy, Elle—we all think it would be great if Annie stayed, but at the end of the day? Whether she stays or goes is her choice."

Brendon sank down into the couch and snagged Annie around the waist, dragging her into his lap. His fingers dug into her sides and she squirmed, howling.

"Oh my God, Brendon! Stop! That tickles!"

He cut it out, chuckling softly.

She shifted, getting comfy, her head pillowed atop his thighs. "You're in a good mood."

His nose scrunched. "Aren't I usually?"

"Yes, but you're, like, extra cheerful right now." She snagged his hand and laced their fingers together atop her stomach. "Your enthusiasm's beginning to rub off on me."

He waggled his brows, making her snort-laugh. "*Brendon.*"

"Sorry." He didn't sound it. "I had a great day."

"Yeah? Tell me about it."

"You remember how I mentioned the intimacy-and-dating survey?"

Her lips twitched. How could she have possibly forgotten *that* conversation? "Vaguely."

Brendon pinched her hip lightly, making her squeal. "You're hilarious."

She flourished her free hand in the air. "Thank you, thank you. I'll be here all night."

"*Well*, I've been doing some thinking—"

She gasped. "No way."

"Quit!" Brendon snickered, fingers once again digging into her sides, making her shriek with laughter.

"*Uncle!*" She sniffed, face on fire and eyes damp. "I'm sorry. I'm listening. I promise."

She really did want to hear what he had to say. It was just difficult to focus when his hands were on her. When he was wearing next to nothing, only his boxer shorts, and she was in her underwear and a shirt of his she'd *borrowed*. She had zero intention of giving it back.

"As I was saying." He narrowed his eyes playfully. "We've all been doing some brainstorming about how to draw in new users to the app because, right now? Growth is stagnating. Not an issue at the moment, but down the road . . ."

"Got it. Easier to prevent a fire from starting than be forced to put one out." She nodded, showing she was following along.

"Exactly." Brendon stroked his thumb across her wrist. "I already told you about how, at OTP, we emphasize compatibility and communication—we've even got helpful icebreakers to inspire users to keep a dialogue running so conversations don't drag—but at the end of the day, it's all meant to help users *find* their one true pairing, their person." His teeth scraped against his lip. "We're good at what we do, the finding part, but what comes next is out of our hands."

"That's true for any dating app."

"Right, but then something you said got me thinking."

"What did I say that was so poignant?"

"Try, everything?"

Her face warmed and so did the rest of her. "Brendon."

"I thought about our conversation, what you find romantic, what romance means to you. About how we all have our own love language that dictates how we show affection and how we recognize affection. That two people can have the best intentions and still struggle if they're speaking two different languages and don't even know it." He smiled down at her. "At today's meeting, I proposed that we make a few small tweaks. Not to the matching algorithm, but in the account setup. Maybe we should have users take a quick 'What Love Language Do You Speak?' quiz, and the results can appear on their profile along with a link to what each language means."

She smiled up at him. The warm, amber glow of the lamp beside his couch played against the chiseled edge of his jaw, his cheeks, highlighting the sharp strength of his features.

"That's not a bad idea," she admitted. "It's a great idea, actually."

"I have you to thank for planting the seed in my head." He beamed down at her. "And I know—how'd you put it? Even with all the right tools, you can't make someone put in the effort? What users choose to do with the additional knowledge will be up to them, but *maybe* those thirty percent of skeptical dating app users will at least know we've heard them and we're trying. Maybe they need to try, too."

"As far as dating apps go?" She sat forward and twisted around, settling into his lap with a smile, her knees bracketing his thighs. "What you guys do at OTP seems really . . . thoughtful."

Everything Brendon did was thoughtful. He tried at everything he did, tried harder than anyone she'd ever met.

"Thoughtful, huh?" he whispered, staring at her mouth. "I'll take it."

With his hand on the back of her head, he angled her just so, allowing his mouth to cover hers. His lips pillowed her bottom lip briefly before nipping it gently, the pleasant sting making her gasp and grind her hips downward.

He grunted into her mouth. "Fuck, Annie."

Brendon's cursing should've been outlawed, not because she didn't like it, but because she liked it *too* much. He seldom ever swore except during sex. Hearing the word *fuck* fall from his tongue was a promise and prelude all in one, and it never failed to make her heart stutter, a heady sense of anticipation threatening to overwhelm her.

She ran her hands down his chest, splaying her fingers against the dips and valleys of his abs through his thin T-shirt. When she dug her nails in, he tore his mouth away, pressing their foreheads together and panting softly.

"Why'd you stop?"

He grasped her chin and tilted it back, staring down at her, lids low. "I want to take my time." He pressed a kiss to the corner of her mouth and another and another in a meandering line across her jaw that led down to the hollow beneath her ear. "Besides"—his tongue curled around her lobe and his teeth grazed her skin, causing her back to bow—"aren't you the slightest bit curious whether I managed to figure out your love language?"

"As long as you keep kissing me," she murmured, tilting her head to the side, "I'm all ears."

"Lucky for you, I'm a pro at multitasking." His lips skimmed her throat in a gentle kiss. "Quality time."

Her brain went fuzzy when he sucked at the skin over her pounding pulse. "Huh?"

"Love languages, Annie." He chuckled against her neck. "Yours is quality time. Spending time just being together."

Her eyes drifted shut, relishing the feeling of his lips against her skin. Brendon wasn't wrong.

He tugged at the neck of her borrowed shirt, his kisses trailing lower. "According to my research, we tend to show affection the way we prefer to receive it." His teeth scraped the thin skin over her collarbone, making her shiver. "Yours is also receiving gifts. Not because it's material, but because of the thought and effort that goes into it. Your actions speak louder than words."

She swallowed hard, her throat suddenly narrow. "What about physical touch? That's a love language, isn't it?"

Brendon lifted his head, staring up at her. The glow of the lamp caught on his copper lashes and brought out the tawny flecks in his warm brown eyes. He dimpled at her. "You *are* multilingual, so . . ."

Letting Brendon in, letting him this close, had never been her intention. Somehow, without meaning to, he'd slipped past her defenses, scaled her walls, and now he knew her better than people she'd dated for *months*.

If quality time and gifts were her love languages, words of affirmation was Brendon's.

She leaned forward and captured his lips in an unhurried kiss, mostly to stifle the smile threatening to split her face in two. Against his mouth, she whispered, "Remember how you told me you've never felt this way about anyone before?" She swallowed hard and confessed, "No one's ever made me feel this way before, either."

She was pretty sure there were butterflies in her stomach; either that or her food wasn't agreeing with her, because she felt like she was going to hurl but also like she wanted to laugh? Both? And maybe kiss Brendon? It was an extremely confusing feeling that would've been off-putting if not for the fact that he was looking at her now and the crinkles at the corners of his eyes and the dimples in his cheeks, the crooked curve of his mouth, made her think that maybe this feeling wasn't so scary. Not if she wasn't the only one who felt like this, the only one who cared. If they were in this together.

He swept the hair off her face, fingers tracing the shell of her ear after tucking her hair behind it. "Say you'll move here. Say you'll move to Seattle." The expression on his face was achingly tender. "Say you want to be with me."

She *did*. She wanted Brendon to be hers and she wanted to be his. Wanted it with a sudden ferocity that stole her breath and made her heart race. It battered against the wall of her chest, fluttering viciously inside her veins.

Annie swallowed hard and threw herself over the edge of the cliff. "I want that."

Brendon's smile put the sun and moon and all the stars in the sky to shame. He whispered her name, his thumb grazing her cheek as he rested his forehead against hers. For a moment, they simply breathed each other's air.

Something buzzed against her thigh.

A line appeared between Brendon's brows as he drew back, feeling around atop the couch for what must've been his phone. Hers was buried somewhere in the bottom of her purse.

"Everything okay?" she asked, reaching up and tracing the chiseled line of his jaw with her fingertips. God, he was handsome. And she was lucky.

"Hmm?" He glanced up from his phone and smiled. "Yeah, yeah. Unknown caller. Lost a bunch of my contacts when I fell in the lake with my phone. This could be about today's meeting—"

"It's fine." She smiled and let her hand fall to his shoulder. "Take it."

He swiped and lifted the phone to his ear. "Hello? Yeah, this is Brendon." His eyes doubled in size. "Oh, hey." His gaze flickered to her face and he offered her a brief, tight smile. "Listen, I'm sorry, Danielle, but I'm going to have to bow out. I'm actually seeing someone."

Without meaning to, she stiffened. He offered her another smile, this one a little broader, but it did nothing to alleviate her confusion.

"Thanks. You, too." He ended the call and set his phone aside.

Nosy was the last thing she wanted to be, but she was pretty sure her curiosity was warranted seeing as his call had had something to do with her. "Who was that?"

His lips pressed together and he reached for her hand, playing with her too-stiff fingers. "Ah, that was . . ." He laughed. "It's kind of a funny story?"

She was all ears.

"The day you came into town and Darcy called, asking me to drop off her key, I actually"—he gave another awkward chuckle and scratched the side of his neck—"I was supposed to go out for a drink."

She connected the dots. "You had a date."

He winced. "Yeah. I canceled, obviously. Then we said we'd play it by ear because she had a family vacation scheduled and I completely forgot about it, to be honest." His thumb brushed the back of her knuckles. "I've been a little preoccupied."

His smile went crooked and her heart squeezed, even as her stomach made a slow descent, sinking. She reached for the hem of her—his—shirt and tugged it down her thighs before sliding off his lap and tucking her knees beneath her.

"Hey." His smile fell and the furrow between his brows reappeared, and it made her chest twist, because what she was feeling was nonsensical and she knew it. She didn't need him to know it, too. "You're not . . . upset, are you?"

She waved off his concern. "No. No. Of course not. Why would I be upset?"

Even to her own ears that sounded a bit *doth protest too much* to be entirely genuine. Her grimace was sharp and instantaneous. Fuck.

Brendon saw straight through her bullshit and slid closer, leaning his head down, forcing her to look up at him. His face was a picture of concern, his forehead wrinkled and his brown eyes flitting over her face. He reached out, tucking that same errant strand of hair behind her ear, the wily one with a mind of its own. "We matched on the app. I never even went out with her. It was going to be a first date, drinks. And I told her—"

She cut him off with a sharp jerk of her chin, her face burning. "You really don't have to explain. I get it, I promise."

It didn't bother her that he'd had plans with someone before her. Everyone had a past. What bothered her was that she'd been in town for such a short stint of time that his rain check coincided with her visit. That his past was so recent it butted up against their present, practically overlapping.

He hadn't done anything wrong. She didn't feel betrayed or hurt or like he'd played her. She'd had no claim over him, hadn't wanted him to be hers until a few days ago.

This was a not-so-gentle reminder that all of this—not just her relationship with Brendon, but her job, Seattle, *everything*—was moving awfully fast.

Perhaps too fast.

She found it hard to swallow, but she soldiered on, taking it one step further and pasting on a smile, choking out what she prayed sounded like a breezy laugh. She needed Brendon to understand she wasn't upset with him. "I'm not mad. Promise."

Two minutes ago she'd been so achingly certain that this was right, and now? Now she wasn't so sure she was making a smart decision.

She'd always had a tendency to leap before she looked. To speak before she thought. What made this any different?

What she'd told him was true. She wanted him, wanted to be with him, but it terrified her how fast she'd fallen for him in such a short period of time. How fast she'd deviated from her plan, the one that up until two weeks ago might've been her only plan, but a sound one.

She believed Brendon when he said he'd never felt this way before either, but what was stopping him from changing his mind? From feeling differently in two weeks or a month if someone else caught his eye and made him feel sparks, a stronger connection than he had with her? What was stopping her from becoming the girl on the phone he was canceling plans with?

She had no idea.

And that terrified her.

Chapter Twenty-One

Saturday, June 12

*A*fter picking up a truly obscene order of sweet and savory piroshkis from the Russian bakery across from the market, Brendon headed straight to Darcy's, parking out front and dashing inside, rain beginning to fall in a light sprinkle from the heavy clouds hanging overhead.

Annie answered the door, her smile strained and her eyes drawn. "Hey."

She stepped aside, letting him through into the apartment.

"I know your flight isn't until this evening, but I thought I'd swing by a little early. See if you were hungry. Figured you'd be head-down with the packing and not thinking about food." He set the box of pastries on the kitchen counter, a folder full of research he'd done for Annie perched atop it. "Where's Darce?"

"She's grabbing lunch with Elle and borrowing her car so she can drive me to the airport later."

"I could've driven you."

Her brows rose, humor dancing in her eyes. "In your car? No offense, but I don't think I could fit my carry-on in your backseat, let alone my suitcase."

She had a point. "Fair."

Annie rose up on her tiptoes, lips brushing his throat. "Thanks for the offer. And the food."

Every inch of her—from the wisps of hair that floated free of her bun to the polish on her pinky toes—had the power to bring him to his knees, but her lips against his skin were especially dangerous. Her mouth made him lose his mind, made it impossible for him to think straight.

Her fingers trailed down his front, freezing, splayed against his stomach when it rumbled. Her eyes widened with mirth.

"Hungry?" she asked, dropping her hand.

He smiled sheepishly. "Starving."

She hefted herself up onto the counter, legs swinging, her bare feet knocking gently against the cabinet beneath her while he dug into the bag. She took the spinach piroshki he offered her and smiled.

"Thank you," she said, stretching her leg out and tapping him with her toes.

He leaned back against the counter. From across the room he spotted the tiny succulent he'd purchased her sitting neatly on Darcy's coffee table atop a coaster.

"Did you ever find out if you can bring plants on a plane?"

"Plants on a—" She followed his gaze, her eyes widening as understanding dawned on her. "Oh. Right. No, I didn't. I guess I should check the TSA's website?"

"You could do that." He licked at his suddenly dry lips. "Or I could"—he gave a chuckle that sounded as desperate and confused as he felt—"hold on to it for you."

Until you get back.

The way Annie's face fell freaked him out. She lifted a hand, resting her fingers at the hollow of her throat. "I'm not sure when that's going to be."

He picked at his thumbnail and shrugged, as nonchalantly as he could manage when it felt like he'd swallowed a brick and it was trapped in his chest. "Annie."

Her brows rose but she didn't lift her eyes, staring resolutely off into space over his shoulder.

He pressed off the counter and stepped toward her. "Look at me."

His request went unmet for one breath, two, before she lifted her eyes, gaze steady but guarded.

He tried not to let the frustration he was feeling leach out into his voice. "You're getting on a plane in twelve hours."

"Thanks, I'd almost forgotten," she sniped. As soon as the words were out of her mouth, she shut her eyes, lips flattening inward in obvious contrition. "I'm sorry. It's just . . . I *know* I'm leaving and I know there's plenty we need to talk about but . . . I don't know what to say."

"If you're open to suggestions, I have a few," he joked. "*I've decided not to move to London* is a good one. Or, *I'm moving to Seattle.*"

She frowned. "It's not that simple."

Wasn't it? He shoved his hands in his pockets and rocked

back on his heels. "Last night you told me this is what you want. I think you're making this more difficult than it needs to be."

Her eyes lifted and widened, goggling at him. "You think this is easy? This is my whole life we're talking about. What I want is only one piece of the puzzle. There are logistics to consider if I . . . *if.*" She shook her head. "Figuring out what to do for work—"

"Here." He reached for the folder, Annie's name scribbled across the front in thick black Sharpie. "A dozen career ideas involving linguistics and foreign languages." He tapped the folder. "Freelance ideas and even a few places that are hiring here in Seattle."

Annie took the folder from him and traced the swooping *A* of her name with one trembling finger. "This . . . you didn't have to do this for me, Brendon."

This was small, but it was something for him to do, and he'd needed to do *something* so he didn't feel like he was sitting around and *waiting.* There was nothing he hated more than feeling powerless, unable to help, spinning his wheels and getting nowhere. "I know I didn't have to. I wanted to."

"Thank you. This is wonderful and—really helpful." Her throat jerked as she lifted her eyes. "There's still packing and hiring a moving company and—and looking for an apartment because I refuse to overstay my welcome at Darcy's—"

"You're welcome to stay at my place."

For some reason, she blanched. "Brendon."

She'd spent the night at his place more often than not since the night of the wedding. "I'm not asking you to move in with me. Not that I'd complain."

She was welcome to stay with him as long as she wanted and she'd hear not a single peep out of him. He'd gotten used to waking up next to her, her body curved into his, her hair in his mouth. Or the cold press of her feet against his when they crawled beneath the covers.

"That's—that's . . ." She trailed off with a hard shake of her head as if to dismiss the suggestion entirely. "I'm going to pretend you didn't seriously say that."

What was the big deal with his offering her a solution? "I'm not proposing, Annie."

What little color remained in her face drained, leaving her pale as a sheet. His grimace was immediate and instinctive, and he tried to quash it. When that didn't work, he hid it with his hand instead, covering his mouth with his palm. He *wasn't* proposing, but her horrified reaction stung.

"I'm not—I *can't* be the type of girl who moves across the country on a whim," she whispered, setting the folder he'd given her aside.

A whim. This didn't feel like a whim, not to him. His whole life, he'd been waiting for something that felt this right. And now she wanted to walk away.

"I don't know if I've given this enough thought. I need time to think. And I can't—I can't do that around you." She lifted her head and stared up at him, her eyes bloodshot and glossy. "Because when I'm around you, I lose my head."

"The feeling's mutual. I told you, I've never felt this way about anyone before."

When he was with Annie, she became the only thing he could think about. The only thing that mattered in those moments when it was just the two of them. Only, he didn't feel like that was wrong.

"And two weeks from now? Am I going to be the girl you're canceling plans with for someone else you've *never felt this way about*?"

Her insinuation—no, *accusation*—knocked the wind out of him.

He didn't know how to make her understand that this was different.

It felt like he was fighting a losing battle, showing her he cared without overwhelming her, without moving too fast. With every step he took forward, she took one back. Soon enough, there'd be an entire ocean between them.

"I don't know how to prove to you I'm serious. I—" He swallowed hard, words clogging in his throat as realization sank in. "If this is about that phone call—"

"It's not about the phone call." Her denial came too quickly and was too emphatic to be sincere. She must've known it, too, because she shut her eyes and pressed her hand to her forehead, looking chagrined at her outburst. "It's *not*. It's about the fact that I remembered I've been here two weeks. *Two* weeks. Long enough that your rain check hadn't even come to fruition."

He clenched his jaw. "So it is about the phone call."

A call he had no control over.

"I don't care about your date—"

"I canceled it," he reiterated, raking his fingers through his hair and fisting the strands. "Because I haven't thought about a single person but you since you came to town, Annie."

Every waking moment, he thought about her. She existed at the forefront of his brain. What she was doing, what was she thinking, if she was thinking about him. With every kiss he fell a little harder, and he wondered if it was the same for her.

It looked like he had his answer.

"Which was two weeks ago." She hopped off the counter and began to pace across the kitchen, wringing her hands together. "*Two weeks.*"

"Fifteen days," he muttered.

She stopped pacing and scoffed. "Jesus Christ, you are *such* a smart-ass."

"You like it," he said, taking a step toward her and another and another until she was close enough for him to reach out and touch. His hand skimmed her waist, but before he could hold her, she stepped back, slipping through his fingers.

She wasn't even two feet from him but she might as well have been a million miles away already. He could see her, he was looking right at her, but it felt like he'd already lost her. If she had even been his to begin with.

"I do." Her bottom lip wobbled and his chest ached. "I like everything about you, Brendon. But . . ." She pressed her fingers to her lips, staring at the sliver of space between them. "I think we're moving a little fast. I think *all* of this is moving a little fast." Tears pooled in her eyes, moisture clumping her lower lashes together. "A *lot* fast."

One tear slipped down her cheek when she blinked. Another followed, sluicing the same path, picking up speed. At her jaw, it curved, sliding down her chin. He clenched his hands into fists at his sides, the temptation to erase the evidence of her unhappiness too great.

He wanted to *fix* this, but at every turn, his hands were tied.

"Why do I feel like when you get on that plane, I'm not going to see you for eight more years?"

"No. *No.* That's not going to happen. I just need—God, this sounds so cliché." She sniffled hard and gulped in a deeper breath. Her eyes fluttered open, her lashes sticking together, and what *he* needed was for her to finish that sentence. Anything she needed, he'd give it to her. "Time."

Why couldn't it have been something simple? A place to stay? He'd make her a million promises, but he couldn't speed up time and he couldn't make up her mind for her.

No matter how badly he wished he could fix this, he couldn't.

The word *hope* flashed through his mind. Hope that all she needed was a little time and space. Hope that with enough of both, she'd realize what she wanted was here. Hope that she'd choose him, choose what made her happy. Hope. If he thought it enough times, the word ceased to lose meaning.

He bit the inside of his cheek. "I just really want you to be happy."

Her lashes fluttered and she sniffed, staring at him, studying him, eyes flitting over his face, growing gradually wider. "You really mean that, don't you?"

"Of course I do," he said.

All the way down to the marrow of his bones.

With his eyes, he begged her to understand. For those two words to mean enough to her. That maybe she would want to stay.

When she dropped her eyes to the floor and curled her arms tighter around herself, he knew his hopes had been in vain.

Call it selfish, but he couldn't stomach the thought of letting her leave without getting the chance to hold her in his arms one more time. He stepped forward, hands trembling as he reached for her, praying she'd let him. He held his breath and let one hand fall against the curve of her waist, the other cupping the side of her face. Beneath his fingers, her skin was feverishly hot, her cheeks flushed and damp from crying.

"I hope you figure out what it is you want." His tongue darted out, wetting his lips. "Until then, I'll be here. Waiting."

"Brendon." His name burst from her lips as a weak sob. Briefly, she turned into his hand, mouth brushing the inside of his wrist, making his pulse go haywire. Her breath ghosted against his skin like a brand and his whole body burned, his throat, the back of his eyelids, his chest worst of all. "What if it takes me longer than a week to make up my mind?"

She craned her head back, staring up at him with wide, round eyes, bluer than he'd ever seen them due to how bloodshot they were.

That fist squeezing his heart gripped it harder, turning it to pulp.

His jaw slid forward and back, his composure close to cracking. *Fuck.* The inside of his nose burned, sinuses tingling.

"Then it takes you longer than a week." He bit down hard on the side of his tongue and forced himself to smile through the pain. "The way I see it, you can't rush something you want to last forever."

She buried her face in his chest and fisted her fingers in his shirt, knotting the fabric in her hands. He closed his eyes and let his hand drift, fingers threading through her silky-soft hair, holding her, memorizing the feel of her and hating that when he thought about what it felt like to hold her, the memory would be tainted by the dampness of her tears soaking into his shirt and the way her body trembled against him, racked with near-silent sobs.

If his heart was elastic, it had snapped in two.

The lights mounted above the cabinets blurred as he leaned in, pressing his lips to her forehead. She smelled like summer, like the cool night air after a hot, rainy day, electric and a little wild. Under that, she smelled like his shampoo. He breathed deep, drawing her into his lungs, and let his lips linger against her skin.

Her breath evened out and her fingers released his shirt and—he swallowed hard, stealing a second longer. Just a second. Two seconds. Three. *Fuck.* No amount of time would be sufficient because he couldn't get enough of her.

He closed his eyes and forced himself to let her go.

"Text me?" he asked, voice raspy from all the words he'd swallowed. "When you land?"

She gave a jerky nod and dragged the heel of her hand under each eye, mopping up what remained of her tears. "I will," she murmured.

"Have a safe flight."

She offered him a wan, watery smile in return that waned quickly.

If he didn't leave now, didn't drag himself out of Darcy's apartment, he feared desperation might drive him to do something drastic. Get down on his knees and beg Annie to stay. Plead a little too hard and push her even further away.

Forcing his feet to move, he turned and walked out of the kitchen, grabbing his keys off the entry table and letting himself out the front door. Leaving what felt like a piece of his heart behind.

Chapter Twenty-Two

Which Star-Crossed Lovers Are You Based on Your Zodiac Sign? (Check Your Venus, Too!)

Aries—Romeo and Juliet
Taurus—Cecilia and Robbie from *Atonement*
Gemini—William and Viola from *Shakespeare in Love*
Cancer—Jack and Ennis from *Brokeback Mountain*
Leo—Satine and Christian from *Moulin Rouge!*
Virgo—Hero and Leander
Libra—Marianne and Héloïse from *Portrait of a Lady on Fire*
Scorpio—Catherine and Heathcliff from *Wuthering Heights*
Sagittarius—Jack and Rose from *Titanic*
Capricorn—Liang Shanbo and Zhu Yingtai from *The Butterfly Lovers*
Aquarius—Neo and Trinity from *The Matrix*
Pisces—Landon and Jamie from *A Walk to Remember*

*Y*ou have everything?" Darcy stepped to the side when a harried-looking mother dragging two small children muttered *Excuse me* and bolted around her, heading toward security.

Even if Annie had forgotten something, it was too late to go back for it. She had a flight to catch. "I think so."

Darcy frowned at Annie's carry-on. "You have your phone? Charger?"

Check and double check. "Got 'em. If I forgot anything—"

"I can mail it to you." Darcy crossed her arms, still staring at Annie's bag. Darcy hadn't looked at her straight-on since Annie had briefly filled her in on what had happened between her and Brendon while she was gone. "Or I can always hold on to it for safekeeping."

Annie's smile went strained.

Over the airport intercom a voice proclaimed it was now a quarter to ten P.M. Her flight was at 12:01, and from the looks of the crowd heading through the central terminal toward the S gates, getting through security would take a while.

This was it.

She turned back to Darcy, her traitorous eyes sparing a quick glance over Darcy's shoulder in the direction of the glass doors. Her heart climbed into her throat as she thought for a split second maybe that was—*no*, it was a different guy, not tall enough, hair too dark, not bronze enough, not Brendon.

It was stupid, but she couldn't make herself stop looking for him in the crowd, searching for his face in a sea of strangers, a tiny part of her hoping she'd turn around and he'd be there. That he'd rush through the terminal, leap over a luggage cart or something equally ridiculous, and stop in front of her, panting, smiling, eyes pleading. That at the eleventh hour he'd show up and—what? Ask her to stay?

He'd done that already, and she'd told him she needed time to think. Which was true, she *did*, but that didn't stop a tiny, irrational part of her from hoping he'd show up and kiss her one last time.

Irrational was right. Brendon wasn't here and he wasn't coming because she wasn't living in the last ten minutes of one of those movies he loved.

"I should probably—" She jerked her thumb behind her, gesturing toward the security line.

"Speaking as someone with experience, it feels like you're running away," Darcy said, not bothering to beat around the bush, instead lunging straight for Annie's throat.

Annie winced and tucked her hair behind her ear, accidentally tugging strands loose from the sloppy fishtail braid she'd thrown her hair into in the car on the way to the airport. "Running away would've been booking an earlier flight, cutting my trip short. I had this booked, Darce. Round-trip. Besides, how do you run away to the place you already live?"

"When it's not home. When you're leaving for the wrong reasons." Darcy frowned sharply. "When you're leaving not because it's smart but because you're scared."

"Oof." Annie huffed. Darcy's words had hit their mark. "You had those at the ready."

"I'm a fount of knowledge and rotten firsthand experience with running scared," Darcy said, wry.

"That's not true. You moved to Seattle because you needed space. Distance."

"I'm not talking about that. I'm talking about when I pushed Elle away because I was scared to tell her how I felt. Because I was scared of how much I felt."

Darcy's eyes narrowed shrewdly and Annie looked away, unsure of what Darcy could see on her face but sure it was more than Annie wanted. She felt like her feelings were stamped on her forehead, like she was completely transparent. In that moment, she both loved and hated how well Darcy knew her. How well Darcy could read her.

"I'm not running away," she reiterated. "I'm heading back to Philadelphia to think. I need time. You can't honestly begrudge me that, can you?"

Of all people, Darcy, with her pros and cons and checklists and risk analyses, had to understand where Annie was coming from. That little more than two weeks wasn't enough time to shift the entire course of her life. Annie didn't know how much time was enough, but it had to be more than fifteen days.

Lips pinched tight and eyes wide, Darcy sniffed hard and threw her arms around Annie, enveloping her in a hug. Annie buried her nose against Darcy's shoulder and squeezed her tight.

"I get it," Darcy whispered. "I don't like it, but I understand."

Annie willed herself not to cry. "I'm going to miss you."

Darcy squeezed her tighter, so tight it was difficult to breathe, but Annie couldn't find it in her to complain. "Don't say that."

Annie coughed out a laugh. "You're supposed to say you'll miss me, too."

"That makes it sound like you've already made your decision and you're not coming back and I'm not going to see you for another year and a half." Hands squeezing Annie's shoulders,

Darcy stepped back, holding her in place. The sheen of tears in her eyes did nothing to soften the glare Darcy leveled at her. "You're my best friend, Annie. You're irreplaceable. Of course I'd miss you. I just don't want a reason to *have* to miss you."

"Sound logic," Annie joked. "Leave it to you to be rational about missing me."

Darcy pursed her lips. The tip of her nose was red, as was the delicate skin beneath her eyes. "Quit using humor to defuse the situation."

Annie dropped her eyes, cowed. "Sometimes I think you know me a little *too* well."

"No, you don't. You're just saying that because it would be easier for you to hide how you're feeling from anyone else. But I see through your bullshit."

"Precisely why I said what I said," Annie muttered.

Darcy shoved her arm. Hard. "I am going to miss you, Annie." She ducked her head, forcing Annie to meet her eyes. "And so is Brendon."

Hearing his name made her eyes burn. She felt a pang in her chest and she swallowed over the lump that had yet to disappear since he had left Darcy's kitchen. "Maybe."

That was the wrong thing to say. Darcy stepped back and crossed her arms, expression turning frosty, the glare in her eyes downright glacial. "You know what's going to happen if you don't come back, right?"

Annie drew her bottom lip between her teeth.

"Perhaps he'll mope for a month, maybe longer. Who knows? He'll move on, meet some other girl and take her to . . . I don't know, karaoke."

Annie clenched her back teeth, eyes burning, her vision beginning to swim.

Darcy cocked her head, lips pursed in contemplation. "She'll be his date to weddings and he'll bring her along to game night. They'll wind up having all sorts of stupid inside jokes about television shows they both love."

"Stop it," Annie gritted out.

Darcy's brows rose and Annie wanted to smack the smug, mean little smirk off her face. "He might even buy her Breathe Right strips, because he'll definitely find out whether she snores."

"Shut up," she whispered. "Please just shut up."

"He might buy her a houseplant and help her take care of it and one day—"

"I *said* shut up." Annie swiped beneath her eyes angrily, pissed that Darcy had driven her to tears when she'd cried enough for one day. "Jesus, that wasn't an invitation to be cruel."

Darcy reached out and rubbed Annie's arm. "I'm not being cruel. I was just making a point."

"Well, congratulations." Annie took a stuttered breath in. "You made it."

And then some.

"You asked for a crystal ball, Annie," Darcy reminded her. "I'm just giving you a glimpse into the inevitable future if you don't come back. Some variation of what I just described? That's what's going to happen." She paused. "But it doesn't have to happen like that and you know it."

Annie's moving to Seattle wouldn't necessarily prevent everything Darcy had described from playing out. It just meant she would have turned her life upside down, moved across the country, fallen a little deeper for Brendon. If she took that risk and Brendon moved on, just like everyone she'd ever dated had, the resulting disappointment wouldn't just sting, it would crush her. If she were in Seattle, she'd have a front-row seat to the show when Brendon moved on and would get to watch it play out in painful detail. Her life would become entangled with his, Darcy forever tethering them together.

Annie curled her arms around herself tighter, hugging herself, trying and failing to hold it together. "I *don't* know." Her shoulders rose and fell in a halfhearted shrug. "That's why I need some time. To figure out where my head is at. You know how I am." She laughed sharply. "I leap before I look. I speak before I think. I—"

"And you'd jump in front of a bus for the people you care about," Darcy said. "Between you and me, I think you should be less concerned with where your head's at and more focused on your heart." As soon as she'd said it, she held up her hands. "I know. Who am I and what have I done with Darcy?"

Annie laughed. "Took the words right out of my mouth."

"Yeah, yeah." Darcy rolled her eyes. "Let *me* be your voice of reason, okay? If *I'm* telling you I think taking a chance is a good idea, perhaps you should listen."

The security line had grown.

"I have to go," she murmured.

Darcy's lips flattened and she nodded. "Please think about what I said."

How could she not? She had a feeling it would be the only thing she thought about. What Darcy had said. What Brendon had said. What she felt. What it meant.

The first thing she was going to do once she got through TSA was pop two ibuprofens; her head was beginning to throb dully. Recycled air and barometric pressure changes wouldn't help.

"I will," she promised. "I'll think about it."

Without warning, Darcy threw herself at Annie, wrapping her up in a hug so tight she was nearly sure something in her chest cracked. It was hard to tell when she ached enough as it was.

"Text me when you land, okay?"

She nodded. If she opened her mouth, she'd start to cry, for real this time, and once she started, once the floodgates were open, there'd be no closing them. She'd be a sniveling, splotchy-faced mess for the rest of the night.

Darcy sniffed and shoved Annie away, blinking hard and fast before schooling her features into a stoic mask. "I'm going to text you every day you're gone. And call you, too. All hours. Elle will, too. You're going to be so sick of us that you'll have no choice but to fly back and make us stop in person."

A tear slipped from the corner of her eye when she laughed. "Darcy."

"I mean it." Darcy's eyes darted toward the long stretch of hall that led to security. "Now get out of here."

Annie waved weakly and turned, heading toward the terminal. When it was time to veer left, she turned around again, but Darcy was already gone.

No final wave, no smile, no stretching it out. Darcy had always been the worst at goodbyes, but maybe it was better this way. A clean break.

Trudging through the terminal, she joined the line for security. It took twenty minutes to move through the winding queue to the body scanners because *some people* thought they were the exception to the rules, leaving keys in their pockets, full bottles of water in their purses, thinking they didn't need to remove their shoes.

Even then, she still made it to her gate with time to spare before boarding began. Taking a seat near the window overlooking the tarmac, she watched blandly as children chased each other down the airside and men in suits hurried toward their gates with phones pressed to their ears. A sullen-looking teen with her earphones on followed a few steps behind her family, feet dragging, a travel pillow dangling from her fingers.

She was a pro at people watching, looking in from the outside.

When they called her boarding class, she stood and joined the line, going through the motions on autopilot. She stepped off the jet bridge and onto the plane and searched for her seat, 23A, the aisle.

Both seats beside her remained empty until eventually an older woman with kind eyes pointed at the window seat. The rest of the plane filled up and still no one had taken the middle seat, not even when the flight attendants began to stroll down the aisle, checking to make sure everyone had stored their bags properly.

Her pulse started to pound.

She could picture it. Brendon rushing onto the plane, saying something as dorky as it was charming. *Is this seat taken?* He'd make a speech and the flight attendants would try to interrupt but someone, maybe the sweet-looking old lady in the window seat, would hush them. *Let the boy talk.* Brendon would beg

Annie to stay and then he'd kiss her to the applause of everyone around them. Even the pilot would clap as Brendon dragged her off the plane.

"Cabin crew, prepare for takeoff."

She glared at the headrest in front of her, her face reflected in the screen attached to the seat back, and scolded herself for being silly. She wasn't one for splashy gestures and she'd told Brendon she needed space. She'd meant it. The fact that he was respecting her wishes should have made her happy, but instead, she just felt hollow. Disappointed even though she had no right to be.

Chapter Twenty-Three

Sunday, June 13

> **ANNIE (9:57 A.M.):** Hey. I wanted to let you know I just landed.
> **BRENDON (10:00 A.M.):** I'm glad you made it safely.
> **ANNIE (10:02 A.M.):** Thanks, Brendon.
> **BRENDON (10:03 A.M.):** ☺

Friday, June 18

*B*rendon stabbed at his salmon salad, huffing when he sent a stupid cherry tomato rolling across the table. He didn't trust a fruit that disguised itself as a vegetable, and cherry tomatoes were, by and large, the worst. It wasn't so much the taste but the texture of tomato guts spraying against the roof of his mouth. Disgusting. He'd asked for them to be left off, but here they were.

"Brendon . . . did you hear what I said?"

Without lifting his head, he scooped the tomatoes off his

salad one by one and deposited them on Darcy's plate beside her so-rare-it-was-mooing prime rib. The tomatoes rolled into a puddle of pink-tinged au jus. "Sorry, what?"

She waited to speak until he looked at her, and when she did, her voice was a touch too soft, setting his teeth on edge. "I asked how you were doing."

He nodded briskly. "Good, good. Katie, Jenny, and I had a great brainstorming session about our new marketing campaign. We looped the engineering department in for the profile tweaks we've got planned, and our expansion is going ahead—I mentioned that to you already, yeah?" He continued to ferry tomatoes from his plate to Darcy's. "We're starting with the Canadian expansion later this year, beginning in—well, Q one, technically. And then we'll move on to Mexico before expanding to Europe. Our investors are jazzed, I'm jazzed, we're all—"

"Jazzed?" Darcy quirked a brow. "Brendon."

He reached for Darcy's coffee and stole a sip. One taste was more than enough to remind him why he didn't order coffee at this restaurant. "Hm?"

"How are you, *really*?"

He chewed on his lip. "Fine?"

"Fine."

He pasted on a smile. "Are you going to repeat everything I say?"

With a hard swallow that made the column of her throat jerk, Darcy set her fork and knife on her plate, the silverware quietly clanking against the porcelain. She lifted her napkin to her lips, dabbing carefully at the corners of her mouth, careful not to mess up her lipstick. Only once she'd replaced the napkin in her lap, smoothing the linen over her legs, did she look at him.

He wished she hadn't. The sheer amount of pity in her gaze about bowled him over.

"It's okay if you're not, you know. Fine."

He shoved his salad to the side and ran a hand over the back of his head. "What do you want me to say, Darce? You want me to tell you I'm *not* fine?"

Her tongue poked against the inside of her cheek and he could practically hear her counting to five before she spoke. "You don't have to put on an act around me. It's pointless. I can see through it. I wish you didn't feel like it was necessary to lie to me—"

"I'm not lying. I don't really see the point in hashing it out."

Talking wouldn't bring Annie back to Seattle any sooner. *Talking* wouldn't bring her back at all.

Darcy's teeth sank into her bottom lip before she must've remembered her lipstick. She released it, pursing her mouth instead. "Bottling up your emotions and pasting on a happy-go-lucky façade isn't the way to handle this. I am speaking from experience when I tell you that you will wind up the emotional equivalent of Pop Rocks in a bottle of soda. You'll bubble over and you'll burst, and it would be better if you let it out rather than let it fester and explode."

He scratched his eyebrow. "Are you auditioning for the role of my therapist now?"

Her eyes narrowed. "Don't be a prick, Brendon. I'm your sister, and I *got* that advice from my therapist."

Her expression dared him to laugh, something he wouldn't have dreamed of doing.

"Sorry," he muttered, feeling every inch the prick she'd called him. "I didn't know. That's—that's great, Darce. I'm . . . happy you're talking to someone?"

She rolled her eyes. "You give great advice, don't get me wrong, but I figured I needed an impartial third party to talk to about . . . things."

"Things," he echoed, not wanting to pry, but curious nonetheless.

She circled the rim of her cup with her finger. "*Things*. Mom and Dad things. Grandma things. Natasha things. Elle things." She lifted her eyes, her gaze unguarded. "I love Elle. *A lot.* And I don't want whatever baggage I'm carrying around that I don't even know about to jeopardize our relationship. So yes, I decided it would be wise for me to see someone."

He pressed his tongue against the back of his teeth and reached out, covering Darcy's hand with his. "I'm proud of you."

She tossed her hair over her shoulder and rolled her eyes. "Whatever, Brendon. It's not a *thing*." The way she flipped her hand over and squeezed his fingers said otherwise. "I asked Elle to move in with me."

His lips curved in a genuine smile, the first of the day. "Yeah? When do you need me to help with the boxes?"

"As if your tiny car could *hold* any boxes," Darcy teased, eyes sparkling. "And shouldn't you be asking me if she said yes?"

"Psh." He waved her off. "Of course she said yes."

Darcy smiled softly. "She said yes."

He gave her fingers a gentle squeeze. "I'm really happy for you."

Her smile went watery and she ducked her chin, sniffing

hard. "Me too." She cleared her throat and lifted her head, pinning him with a stare. "It's okay if you're upset."

His back teeth clacked together and for a second he was tempted to brush her off with another breezy smile. Her honesty compelled him to be truthful in return.

"If I don't talk about—about Annie, it's easier for me to tell myself she's coming back. That *this* is temporary. Talking about it, saying it out loud, makes it real. It's—it's hard to keep acting like everything's going to be okay when I put it out there." He dragged his thumb along his lower lip and shrugged. "Annie's been gone a week. And as much as I want to pretend like everything is okay, I know that's wishful thinking. I just . . ."

Darcy frowned and waited while he gathered his thoughts, preparing himself to ask the question that had been on his mind for the past six days.

He swallowed over the ever-growing lump in his throat, the one he had no hope of getting rid of any time soon. "I keep wondering if there's something else I could've done, something I could've said, something I *should've* said that might've made a difference and—"

"Brendon." Darcy squeezed his fingers and gave a quick jerk of her head. "Don't do this to yourself. Don't play that game. *What if.* There's nothing you could've done differently that would've swayed Annie's decision. She has to make her own choices."

He ducked his chin, a sardonic laugh bubbling up that he couldn't stop. "Why is that such a hard pill to swallow?"

Her fingers rubbed the back of his knuckles soothingly, nearly hypnotic in their rhythm. Like a metronome. "Because you want to solve everything for everybody. Make everyone happy. You like to fix things, but some things aren't yours to fix."

He shut his eyes against the wave of emotion that crashed over him. *Everything* had a solution. Nothing was unfixable, beyond repair. It was never too late if you cared about someone. You just had to want to fix it badly enough, try harder, and—he coughed, lifting his head and looking up at Darcy, his brow furrowed. "Margot told me I have a hero complex."

Darcy smiled sadly. "You do. You created an entire dating app because you're desperate to bring people joy. You have been ever since Mom and Dad split. You tried to bake her snickerdoodles when Dad moved out. You forgot to pull the pans out when you preheated the oven and you used cloves instead of cinnamon because we didn't have any. They were barely edible. Remember?"

He pressed his knuckles against the seam of his lips. "Vaguely."

Mostly, he just remembered feeling confused, because to him, they'd appeared perfectly happy until they weren't. He remembered staring out his bedroom window and wishing Dad would move back home. That Mom would leave her room, because she hadn't in days. He remembered the sickening sense of dread, his stomach dropping out his ass, when he'd first heard the word *divorce* whispered. He remembered feeling helpless and then relieved once they moved in with Grandma. And then *guilty* over his relief.

He didn't really remember the cookies, though he was sure Darcy wasn't wrong. It sounded like something he'd have done at twelve. Think that cookies could—maybe not *heal* a broken heart, but help. Want to fix a situation that wasn't his to repair with a little sugar and a lot of hope.

"You should probably talk to someone about it. A professional," Darcy said, matter-of-fact.

He laughed. "Probably."

"Have you talked to Annie since she left?"

"A few texts." He hedged, not wanting to admit that for every text he'd sent her, another three had languished in his drafts, unsent. He hadn't wanted to overwhelm her with every tiny, insignificant moment that made him think of her and therefore felt significant to him.

"That's good. Make sure she knows you're still thinking about her, that she's still on your mind even though she isn't here."

Even though she might not come back.

Knowing that didn't change how he felt. Even if Annie wasn't his, wouldn't ever be his, even if she moved halfway across the world, he'd still care about her. And he wanted her to know that, because caring for her came without strings.

He had to wet his lips before he could force the words up his throat. "Annie's not coming back, is she?"

She dropped her eyes, staring down at the starched tablecloth. "She hasn't said—"

"Don't do that," he rasped.

She frowned sharply. "Don't do *what*?"

"That *thing*." He tugged his hand out from her grasp and pulled hard at his hair in frustration. "You're asking me to be honest and you're sitting there lying to protect my feelings."

Her mouth opened and shut several times before she finally managed to get out, "I'm not lying, Brendon. I'm—"

"Covering up the truth, then. Brushing it under the rug. Bandaging it up in a neat bow so I won't worry. Whatever you want to call it, you've been doing it for as long as I can remember. Hell, Darce, you realize it's not exactly normal that you pretended to be Santa Claus just so I'd keep believing in him after Mom and Dad dropped the ball, right?"

Her lips parted, her jaw falling open. "You weren't supposed to know about that."

She had been protecting him from the harshness of reality for most of his life, but she couldn't protect him from feeling *this*. This crushing sense of disappointment that came from wanting Annie so badly and doing everything in his power to show her he cared and still not measuring up. From the fact that after everything, she'd still questioned the veracity of his feelings. That she hadn't felt secure enough with him to let herself want him, maybe.

"I know," he said.

He could only imagine everything Darcy had done for him that he hadn't witnessed. A fresh ache settled in his chest and he tapped her shin lightly with his foot beneath the table.

Darcy's chin quivered. "I honestly don't know if Annie's coming back."

Darcy's inhale sounded more like a gasp. Her face had gone red, her eyes, too. A renegade tear slipped down her cheek and she swiped at it angrily.

He clutched the armrests tighter. "I didn't mean to make you cry."

Her eyes lifted and her lips parted, a disbelieving huff leaving her mouth. "*You're* crying, Brendon. I'm crying because you are."

He lifted a hand to his face and—fuck. His fingers were wet

because he was crying in the middle of a restaurant in the middle of his lunch hour. He scrambled for his napkin and wiped his burning face with the stiff, overly starched cloth. As soon as he staunched his tears, he stood, reaching inside his back pocket for his wallet. He ignored Darcy's look of dismay and threw down enough cash to cover their meal.

"Brendon—"

"I need some space," he blurted, a hysterical laugh following on the heels of his explanation as soon as his choice of words sank in.

Her fingers snared his wrist, stopping him from making a quick escape. "Are you going to be okay?"

I'll be fine hovered on the tip of his tongue, but something in her stare drove him to be honest. "Ask me in another week, okay?"

He didn't know what he was right now, only that everything hurt.

She nodded, looking on the verge of tears.

"Hey." He tapped her on the shoulder. "I really am happy for you and Elle."

She blotted her eyes and offered him a small smile. "Thanks, Brendon."

When it came to matchmaking, bringing people together, helping them find their happily-ever-after, he got it right more often than he didn't.

He only wished he wasn't the exception.

Chapter Twenty-Four

Sunday, June 20

*A*nnie stared at the pros-and-cons list she'd scribbled on a napkin during her flight. Aside from a few added scribbles, it hadn't changed in the week since she'd been back in Philadelphia.

Seattle

+*Friends*
+*Darcy*
+*Brendon*
+*Great food*
+*Nice weather (even the rain isn't bad)*
+*Funky shops*
+*No state income tax*
+*Brendon*
-*No job?! (addendum, no job yet)*

London

+Job security
-A job I don't love
+Nice accents?!

It took her a few days to realize she'd added Brendon's name twice.

A month ago, on paper, moving to London had seemed like *the decision*. Not simply the only one, but the right one. The smart one. Now, looking at this list, seeing it all laid out on paper, it was obvious Seattle had more going for it than London did. The sheer number of pros was irrefutable.

But job security was important.

So was being happy.

But what if she moved to Seattle and things with Brendon didn't work out? She'd have Darcy, but Brendon was Darcy's brother and that would inevitably be *messy*.

Maybe she was overcomplicating matters. But what if she wasn't? What if—

Annie shut her eyes.

Her heart was in Seattle and her head . . . she didn't know where her head was.

Time wasn't an inexhaustible resource. Her flight to London was leaving in ten days and regardless of whether she was on it, her subletter was moving in on the fifth of July.

No matter what, she had no choice but to pack.

Perched atop a stack of books on her nightstand, Annie's phone buzzed. She stretched across her bed to grab it and her lips curved into an involuntary smile, warmth blooming wild in her chest.

Brendon.

He'd texted almost daily. Not often enough to overwhelm her, but the little reminders that he was thinking about her made her feel . . . cherished? Whatever the opposite of neglected was.

BRENDON (11:19 P.M.): What does "petite a petite le wasoh fay son need" mean?

She squinted at the screen. Gibberish was what that was.

ANNIE (11:27 P.M.): Um, what language is that supposed to be?

She mouthed the words he'd sent and snickered softly. *Not* gibberish, just French typed out phonetically. *Poorly.*

ANNIE (11:29 P.M.): Oh. Do you mean "petit a petit, l'oiseau fait son nid"?

BRENDON (11:31 P.M.): I guess? 😬

BRENDON (11:32 P.M.): I'm watching L'amour est dans le pré and there are no subtitles.

BRENDON (11:32 P.M.): I lost my favorite translator and I'm dying here.

A vicious ache rippled through her chest as she slipped back beneath the covers. He was still watching even though she wasn't there to explain what was happening.

If she could've blinked her eyes and been sitting on his couch beside him, she'd have done it in a heartbeat.

ANNIE (11:34 P.M.): It means "little by little, the bird makes its nest." It's a French proverb about persevering and having patience. Like, Rome wasn't built in a day.
BRENDON (11:36 P.M.): Ah, okay. That makes sense. Thank you ☺

Her fingers faltered on her keypad, second-guessing what she'd typed out.

Thank you for being patient with me. I miss you, by the way. More than is fair, but I do.

She scrunched her eyes shut and hit delete, playing it safe.

ANNIE (11:37 P.M.): Anytime.

Monday, June 21

Annie flipped through the folder Brendon had given her on job opportunities for linguistics majors.

- Lexicography
- Speech and language therapy
- Teaching
- Freelance translation
- Copyediting
- Technical writing

Half the options made her wrinkle her nose. Others had promise. Lexicography had a certain appeal; the idea of compiling and editing dictionaries, especially dictionaries for bilingual speakers, was intriguing.

Freelance translation caught her eye. That was totally up her alley.

She reached for her phone and navigated to her web browser. She had some research to do.

C

Tuesday, June 22

BRENDON (10:56 P.M.): I'm in need of translation again.

She smiled. God, was that the first time she'd smiled all day? She hadn't had much to smile about lately.

ANNIE (10:59 P.M.): Hit me with it.

BRENDON (11:02 P.M.): C'est a tes coat que je view construir ma vee

It took a minute to translate what he'd typed into actual French. The words materialized inside her mind and she dropped her head, staring at her toes against the bare laminate flooring of her living room.

ANNIE (11:04 P.M.): C'est à tes côtés que je veux construire ma vie.

Her vision swam and a knot formed in her throat. *God*, she missed him.

ANNIE (11:04 P.M.): It means "I'd like to build my life with you by my side."

She stared at her phone, watching the time tick by, seconds turning into minutes. Her heart leaped into her throat when another message appeared.

BRENDON (11:07 P.M.): Ah.
BRENDON (11:08 P.M.): Thank you.

She set her phone down and buried her face in her hands.

☾

Thursday, June 24

Her passport was *somewhere* in the black hole of her purse. The exact location was yet to be seen, but it wasn't where it was supposed to be, neatly tucked away in the side zipped pocket where she kept her important documents for travel.

She dumped her bag upside down on her bedroom floor, a mountain of miscellaneous items forming atop the carpet. Lipstick. Another lipstick. Sunscreen. Wallet. She wrinkled her nose. Junk. Panic gripped her chest. Where the *hell* was her passport?

Sorting through the pile with clammy fingers, she sucked in a deep breath, trying to calm her racing heart.

Maybe this wasn't a bad thing.

Maybe if she lost her passport, it was the universe's way of telling her not to move to London, not to take the job, financial security be damned. Fate had taken the wheel and was deciding her path for—

Buried at the bottom of the pile, beneath her tin of cinnamon Altoids, was her passport. Her shoulders slumped. There went that theory. Her destiny was still hers to control. She plucked her passport from the pile and something tucked inside fluttered to the floor.

Her hand stilled, hovering over the photo. It was one of the pictures Brendon had taken of her at the wedding, her face fuzzy as she reached for the camera. As she reached for Brendon.

She lifted the photo up, studying her slash of a smile, tracing it with her fingertips. Even blurry, she radiated happiness. She lifted a hand to her face and traced the poor facsimile curving her mouth.

The photo was nice, but it couldn't compare to the real thing. Being there. Laughing with Brendon. Her fingertips pulsing as she'd rested them against his chest. *His dimples.* Her heart leaping into her throat when he'd fallen backward into the water. Her stomach aching from holding in her laughter when he'd broken the surface, sputtering.

Blindly, Annie patted the carpet behind her, searching for her phone so she could take a picture of the photo and send it to Brendon. A small gesture, maybe, but she wanted him to know she was thinking about him. That she appreciated his patience, his putting up with her indecision. That he'd given her the space to make up her mind and do it on her terms.

Her phone was somewhere. She grimaced. Fingers crossed she hadn't accidentally packed it in one of her boxes. Hunting it down would be a *real* treat seeing as it was on silent.

She found it beneath her roll of packing tape and breathed a sigh of relief that she hadn't totally fucked up; it would have rendered her packing useless if she had to reopen all her boxes and dig through her belongings just to find her phone. She set the volume on full blast just in case she misplaced it again. *When* she misplaced it again.

Before she could open her camera, she noticed a notification and swiped to open it.

Elle had tagged her in a photo on Instagram.

She frowned because she wasn't in the photo. Elle had snapped a picture selfie-style of her, Margot, Darcy, and Brendon seated around the coffee table, where Monopoly was spread out. Annie tapped the photo and pressed her lips together, her eyes watering viciously. Elle had tagged her on the empty cushion beside Brendon.

His arms were resting casually on his knees and his smile was the brightest thing in the photo. She could hear his throaty chuckle when she shut her eyes, knew exactly how his lips felt curving against her mouth in that same grin.

The caption read, *The gang's all here minus @anniekyriakos. We miss you!* 😊 🫂

She couldn't stop herself from clicking on his profile, getting her fix any way she could.

She shouldn't have.

Her breath escaped her in a punched-out exhale, her chest threatening to cave in on itself. She ground her teeth together to keep her chin from trembling, vision blurring and face burning as she stared at Brendon's latest post.

He looked gorgeous, like he always did. So did the girl practically draped over him as they both smiled for the camera.

The way I see it, you can't rush something you want to last forever.

That had lasted, what? Little more than a week?

Her breath hitched, her lungs constricting. She hiccupped and hugged her knees to her chest.

She wasn't sure who she was angrier with, herself or Brendon.

There was moving on and then there was—*this*. She hadn't even been gone two weeks when he'd posted this picture. This felt like rubbing her face in the fact that he'd found someone new. That Annie had only been a blip on his radar, completely replaceable.

Her lips flattened. She hadn't asked him to wait for her. She had no right to be upset. This wasn't—she swallowed hard—a long-distance relationship. They weren't even on a break. He wasn't hers. *Clearly.*

Darcy had warned her this would happen, that Brendon would move on. She just hadn't expected it to happen this soon. Or for it to feel like someone had carved into her chest with a dull knife, ripping her open from her throat to her belly button. Gutting her.

She jammed the heel of her hand into her breastbone and sucked in a stuttered breath. She'd done this to herself, first by getting involved with Brendon and then by pushing him away. She had no one to blame but herself, because she'd known better than to play with fire.

She always cared more. *Always.* Why had she thought this would be any different? Because she *felt* more than she ever had? Jesus. She scoffed into the silence of her bedroom and buried her face in her hands. How stupidly naïve, believing this would be different. That this would be the exception when all it did was prove that she was right.

She'd never hated being right this much in her life.

"Never Gonna Give You Up" by Rick Astley blared, making her jump, her head knocking into the boxes stacked precariously behind her. She blinked up, watching the tower sway ominously over her head, and wondered if they'd all come crashing down. If they'd split open at the seams, if everything she owned would spread out around her in a pile as messy and turbulent as the feelings hastening through her veins. If she'd be able to tape them back together or if it would be as impossible as using packing tape to Humpty Dumpty her heart back together again.

She pressed her hand to her mouth and choked down a sob as Darcy's ringtone continued to blast, Rick Astley promising that he'd never give her up. Never let her down.

For a chunk of cheap plastic, her phone felt a lot like a brick in her hand as she lifted it, thumb hovering over the screen to send Darcy to voicemail.

But *persistent* might as well have been Darcy's middle name. She'd call again and again until Annie answered, if the last few days were anything to go off.

Annie prayed her voice wouldn't wobble. "Hello?"

"Just checking in," Darcy said. "Elle says hi."

She sucked in a breath, needing to breathe, but wires crossed and her eyes watered, her nose, too. Her next inhale was noisy and ragged, and she pinched her lips together, face burning, her whole body sizzling with shame at how *obvious* she was in her sadness. That she couldn't be a neater crier, keep her emotions contained for a few fucking minutes to put Darcy off her trail. She just *had* to choose this minute to be a wreck and fall apart while talking to the worst possible person. The person who, without fail, saw through her bullshit, her best defenses. Annie wasn't even playing at 50 percent.

"Annie?" Darcy sounded worried. Typical. Go fucking figure. "Are you okay?"

"Mm-hmm," she lied, grinding her molars together because it was better than the alternative: Bursting into tears and having to explain herself. Hearing Darcy say *I told you so*. Or worse, offer platitudes of condolence. Even though Annie was the one who'd gotten herself into this mess and Darcy *had* warned her. Annie just hadn't listened. "Just dandy."

"Want to try that again?"

Annie laughed through her tears, which had started to flow with a vengeance. They dripped down her face and ran down her neck, settling in the hollows above her collarbone. She swiped at them furiously, unable to staunch the flow. "It's— allergies." She sniffed hard, sinuses burning. "All this fucking pollen is killing me."

"Bullshit," Darcy said.

Annie scoffed and dropped her head back, watching the boxes wobble to and fro like a tree in gale-force winds. "You were right."

"I usually am." Darcy paused, clearing her throat delicately. "Care to tell me what I was right about this time?"

Her laugh was watery and weak. "Not really."

"Let's try again."

Annie rolled her eyes. "Just—can we *not*? Can you drop it? Please, Darce."

"If you don't tell me what's wrong, I'm booking the next flight I can find to Philadelphia."

There wasn't a doubt in her mind Darcy meant it.

She pinched her lips together and tried to regulate her heart rate. It was too fast, pounding too hard against her sternum, each beat like a punch against the wall of her chest. Her throat felt raw, gritty, and sore when she swallowed. "Darcy."

"Expedia is telling me I can book a seat on a flight out tonight."

Annie sniffed. "For how much? A thousand dollars?"

"Helping you is priceless, Annie."

She scrunched her eyes, hot tears spilling down her cheeks. "Please don't."

"Talk to me," Darcy pleaded. "Or else I'll drop an ungodly amount of cash flying to Philadelphia."

It was no empty threat. Darcy would do it in a heartbeat. Annie knew it because she'd do it for Darcy, too.

"You were right. About Brendon moving on. He did. And I'm—"

"*What?*" Darcy had the audacity to laugh. Annie was sitting on her bedroom floor, tears dripping off her chin, and Darcy was laughing at her. "Annie."

"Don't *Annie* me. I saw what I saw."

"What *exactly* do you think you saw?" Darcy demanded, and

Annie wasn't sure if the anger in Darcy's voice was directed at her or at Brendon.

Annie rolled her eyes. "Instagram. Elle tagged me and I—I went to his profile and . . . she's really pretty and he looks—"

Happy.

Like Annie's being gone hadn't affected him at all. He definitely didn't look broken up over it. Every day, Annie missed him, and every day she grew a little surer that she wasn't supposed to move to London. Seattle called her name. She woke up and thought about Brendon. She fell asleep thinking about him. She read his texts and *ached*.

And in the short span of twelve days he'd moved on, his texts to her a total sham, throwing her off the fact that he'd found someone new.

Darcy growled. "What the fuck are you talking about?"

"*Instagram,*" she repeated, pounding her free hand against the carpet, wishing for more than a dull thud to punctuate her frustration.

"I don't *have* Instagram." Darcy huffed. "Just give me a second."

Through the line, Annie could hear Darcy typing, her nails clicking quickly against her keyboard. There was a brief pause before Darcy started to laugh.

"I'm hanging up," Annie threatened.

"*Annie.*" Darcy sniffled. "Oh my God. Please calm down."

"You calm down," she fired back, lacking a better rebuttal.

"That's Jenny."

Whoop-dee-freaking-do.

"She works in the marketing department at OTP." Darcy spoke in a slow, soothing way that verged on condescending, but Annie couldn't bring herself to complain because it was working magic on her nervous system. "They work together, Annie. They're friends."

She went dizzy with shame. "Oh."

"*Oh*," Darcy teased.

"Shut up," she groused. "There are, like, a million and one HR violations in that picture. Their faces are touching."

Darcy cackled. "You're jealous."

"I'm *not*, I'm—"

"Annie, it's okay."

It really wasn't okay. When did she become the type of person to hop on Instagram and jump to wild conclusions?

"I hate this." She palmed her face and groaned. "This is so humiliating."

"Remember who you're talking to," Darcy reminded her. "Remember my thirteenth birthday when you slept over and you—"

"We pinky-swore *never* to talk about that. It didn't happen."

"Point being," Darcy continued, "you've done far more humiliating things."

"You *really* know how to make a girl feel better."

"Annie."

She swallowed hard. "I am jealous. And it's stupid. *I'm* stupid."

"Shut up. That's my best friend you're talking about."

Annie laughed. "Your best friend is stupid. Deal with it."

"My best friend is stupid about my brother. I'll accept that."

"Yeah." Annie nodded even though Darcy couldn't see her. Her voice dropped to a pathetic whisper. "I really am."

"He's been moping, you know? He really misses you."

Her eyelids burned. "I miss him, too. A lot."

A *lot*, a lot.

What was she doing? Sitting here, packing her apartment, torturing herself looking at photos and *thinking* about Brendon when she could have the real thing? She'd *had* the real thing and she *wanted* the real thing.

She didn't want another stamp in her passport. She wanted Brendon.

"Are you ready to come home?" Darcy asked gently, as if afraid of spooking her, like she was some startled horse.

Home.

It was a risk, but wasn't having everything she wanted worth it when the alternative was never having it at all? Was sitting here, alone, miserable because of her own choices?

Her eyes stung as she made a slow sweep around her room, most of her belongings packed, the rest strewn haphazardly across the carpet awaiting boxes or a suitcase. There were no pictures on the walls. Her bookshelves were empty. In a little over a week, someone else would inhabit this apartment. Hopefully they would do more living here than she had.

She sucked a breath in and listened to the relentless pounding of her heart. "Yeah. I think I am."

Darcy gave a sharp cry, breathless and shocked. "Thank *fuck*."

Annie pressed her trembling fingers to her lips and blubbered out a laugh. "Eloquent."

"Shut up." Darcy sniffled. "Are you serious?"

Since when is love supposed to be convenient?

She'd known it all along, but she'd been afraid. Scared shit-less. Scared that Brendon would be like everyone else she'd ever dated. But the truth was, he was unlike anyone she'd ever known. And he'd never given her reason to doubt him or his affections. At every turn, he'd shown her he cared. Even now, when he had no reason to believe she'd be back, he'd texted her more frequently than any of her so-called friends here in Phila-delphia. She was the one who'd compared him to the people from her past, misjudging him. That was a wrong she wanted— *needed*—desperately to right.

"Yes." She nodded. "I am. I'm—" Her ears popped when she slid her jaw forward, trying to fend off another wave of tears. "Am I too late?"

"Too late?" Darcy scoffed loudly into the line. "For Brendon? Are you kidding me? Are we talking about the same person? My brother, who told me when I finally pulled my head out of my ass that it's never too late if you love someone? *That* Brendon? A walking, talking Hallmark greeting card with red hair and a heart of gold? Six-foot-four—"

"*Darcy.*"

"Brendon's not going to begrudge you a couple weeks to make a life-altering decision. He understands. He'll be relieved when he—"

"You can't say anything," she blurted.

"I can't?" Darcy sounded suspicious.

"No. You can't." She sat up a little straighter, easing her weight off the boxes at her back. "I want to tell him."

And she wanted to do it in person. See the look on his face

when he realized she was in Seattle. For good. That she was *all in*.

"I won't say anything." She couldn't see Darcy's eye roll, but she could practically hear it.

"And you can't mention this," she urged, rolling to her knees. "You can't tell him about the picture or me freaking out. He'll think—"

"That you're human and sometimes we have messy reactions that aren't always grounded in rationality? I won't tell him."

"Thank you. Not for the condescension, but the rest."

"You're welcome. Now, tell me when I can pick you up from the airport."

Chapter Twenty-Five

Saturday, June 26

ANNIE (8:15 A.M.): Look what I found.

$\mathcal{B}$rendon grinned at the blurry photo of Annie he'd snapped the night of Katie and Jian's wedding. She was bathed in blue light, the sun slinking below the horizon behind her. Her smile was fuzzy but blinding, making his entire chest throb.

He reached for his towel, wiping the chalk dust off his hands from his morning climb, before he typed his response.

BRENDON (8:22 A.M.): You look beautiful.
ANNIE (8:26 A.M.): I was looking at you.

Tuesday, June 29

ANNIE (4:23 P.M.): I miss you.

His fingers hovered over his keypad.

You don't have to miss me. Come back. Please.

BRENDON (4:25 P.M.): Me too.

ANNIE (4:31 P.M.): ❤

Thursday, July 1

BRENDON (11:11 A.M.): Thinking about you.

"Brendon. *Brendon.*"

He tore his eyes from his phone. No unread messages. He offered Mom a tight smile from across the table of the bistro she'd chosen for their lunch. "Sorry. You were saying?"

"I said we should grab dinner together on Saturday. There's this new restaurant that opened up on Main Street I've been dying to try. Maybe you could even drag your sister along if you can pry her away from her girlfriend for long enough."

He pinched the bridge of his nose. Mom and Darcy's relationship had been contentious for nearly as long as he could remember, but the subtle pokes and prods from Mom that put him in the middle wore on him.

"Sure." He nodded absently, glancing at his phone when it vibrated.

It was a call, and from a wrong number, no less.

"It's rude to keep checking your phone at the table."

He gritted his teeth. "Sorry. You're right. I'm just . . . waiting on a text."

"From someone . . . *special*?" Mom drew out the word.

She had no idea.

"I've been seeing someone, actually." He braced himself. "It's Annie."

Mom pursed her lips. "Annie? Your sister's Annie?"

The one and only Annie he knew, yes. "That Annie."

"Huh." She laughed. "You used to have the biggest crush on her."

He fiddled with his silverware. "Mm-hmm. I did."

"I didn't know Annie lived in Seattle."

He winced. "She doesn't actually. She's still in Philadelphia, but she's thinking about moving. I'm . . . I'm hoping she does."

His phone vibrated atop the table.

ANNIE (12:01 P.M.): Sorry! I was up in the air. Thinking about you, too.

Up in the air . . . he sucked in a rasping breath.

Mom cooed. "You're such an optimist, Brendon. I love how nothing gets you down. You just bounce right back. I admire that, you know?"

Brendon clenched his jaw. He didn't feel like much of an optimist.

☾

Friday, July 2

BRENDON (11:14 A.M.): Hey. Hope you're settling in.

He stared at his screen, praying an explanation would materialize. At the very least a message that she'd made it to London safely.

ANNIE (11:22 A.M.): ☺

He closed his eyes and threw his phone across the room, where it bounced against his bed.

☾

Saturday, July 4

Brendon rested his arms on the railing of the *Argosy* and stared out at the dark, choppy water of Lake Union. The sun had sunk beneath the horizon forty-five minutes ago, the sky now an indigo canvas dotted with bright twinkling stars. The moon, almost full, reflected off the turbulent water, turning the surface into liquid chrome.

Bracing himself against the breeze, he tucked his arms in tighter, trying to keep the wind from cutting through him on the upper deck of the boat, where Elle had dragged him. None of this had been his idea, celebrating the Fourth of July, going out on the lake, standing on the top observation deck.

July Fourth. Three weeks had passed since Annie had left Seattle. Three days since her scheduled flight to London. It was time—*past* time—for him to accept the fact she wasn't coming back.

Darcy could've let him stew in peace, but oh no. She, Elle,

and Margot had dragged him out onto a boat to watch the fireworks with a hundred strangers. He'd been perfectly content to stay at home and catch the fireworks from his balcony overlooking the park like he did every year, the only part of this holiday he'd ever enjoyed. This year he was struggling to muster the enthusiasm for even that.

Elle bumped him with her hip and smiled. "Excited for the show?"

"Sure." He smiled briefly before turning and facing the water and the city beyond.

Pretending to be okay when he felt anything but was exhausting.

A loud whistle filled the air, followed by a sharp crackle as the first firework burst overhead. Bright white light lit up the air in a quick strobe of flickers and flashes that signaled the start of the show. A dozen pops followed in quick succession as cascading stars filled the sky, their tails long and glittering as palm frond–shaped sparkles rained down, golden in color.

Flashes of red and blue illuminated the night, reflecting off the lake, making it bright as midday. Beside him, Elle oohed softly. He tore his eyes from the light show and watched as she sank back against Darcy, who stood behind her. Darcy's arm was braced on the railing, bracketing Elle in. She whispered something in Elle's ear that made Elle beam and turn, pressing a quick kiss to Darcy's cheek, before looking back at the sky. On his left, Margot narrated the show on Instagram Live, calling each firework by its proper name. *Brocade. Chrysanthemum. Pistil. Palm. Spinner. Fish.*

One glowing comet rocketed high into the air, a tight ball of bright white light. It burst and sparkles rained down, reigniting and sending off another cascade of stars that dissolved as they floated toward the earth.

His eyes burned as he stared unblinkingly at the sky. When he was finally forced to break his stare, a reverse image wound up imprinted on his retinas, a zigzag of black against bright white on the backs of his eyelids. He swallowed hard, over the sudden sour knot that had taken up residence in the back of his throat.

Had he not been standing on the observation deck of a boat in the middle of the lake, the breeze ruffling his hair and pushing it off his forehead, he'd have thought he needed air. He didn't know what he needed, but it wasn't here. He had a feeling it was five thousand miles away. Unreachable. Untouchable. Not his.

He stepped away from the railing, needing—needing a minute. Just a minute. A minute to . . . he didn't actually know what he needed to do. Standing here, watching the fireworks and feeling painfully alone despite being surrounded by a crowd of people, his friends, his family, was too fucking much for him.

Fingers circled his wrist, stopping him from going far.

"Where are you going?" Darcy asked, frowning. "You're going to miss the show."

He sank his teeth into the flesh of his cheeks, needing the brief flicker of pain to ground himself, and shrugged, still feeling disjointed. "Okay."

Her frown deepened, the line between her delicate brows turning into a trench. "You love fireworks, Brendon."

He used to, yeah, back when he'd had something to celebrate. Something to rejoice over. "I'm not in the mood, Darce."

When he was a kid, he'd wished on those fireworks as if they were real shooting stars. Now he wasn't so naïve. When the show was over and the boat returned to the harbor, the sky would return to a black slate. He would climb inside his car and drive back to his empty apartment, and Annie . . . Annie would still be in London. No amount of wishing would bring her back. Watching fireworks explode was a poor substitute for the way he'd felt when Annie had touched him, when they'd kissed, when she'd *breathed* in his vicinity.

He tugged his hand free as gently as he could. "I'll be back."

After all, it was hard to go far on a boat.

Ignoring the almost crushing weight of Darcy's gaze, he turned.

And froze.

Several yards away, in the center of the observation deck beside the stairs, stood Annie.

Color from the fireworks reflected off her face, off her white halter dress. Her blond hair turned shades of vivid pink and purple, illuminated like fiber-optic strands. A loud crash filled the air, but it had nothing on the thunder of his heartbeat inside his head.

Someone nudged him hard and he stumbled forward, stopping several feet from Annie, giving her a wide berth because— he had to be seeing things. Dreaming.

Her lips curved a tentative smile that verged on shy. "You're missing the fireworks."

Another loud boom sounded behind him and his heart crashed against his sternum.

"No." He swallowed hard and shook his head. "I'm not."

Annie threw her head back and blinked hard up at the sky, her lashes beating against her cheek. She sniffed hard and laughed. "You're not supposed to say things like that."

The lump in his throat swelled to epic proportions, making it hard for him to breathe. "I'm not?"

She gave a quick, curt shake of her head. She was *here*. On this boat, standing in front of him, more beautiful and breathtaking than any firework show he had ever witnessed.

She lifted her chin and the fireworks overhead exploded in a bright spray of strobing sparkles. Blues and reds and greens and purples all reflected in Annie's eyes. A rainbow captured on the plains of her face for his eyes only. His heart beat harder, a violent clatter of cymbals and thunderous booms joining the symphony of pyrotechnic pops and whistles and crackles overhead.

She blinked and her eyes shined brighter than all the fireworks. Brighter than the stars and the moon and the city lights across the lake. His heart stuttered when she swallowed, her throat jerking visibly.

"No." She shook her head, lashes continuing to flutter with each fast blink.

He stepped toward her, gaining confidence as he slowly closed the distance between them. "No?"

She stood a little straighter, chin lifting. "This is *my* grand gesture. I came here to sweep all six feet four inches of you off your feet and you saying something like *that* is—it's not fair. Stealing my thunder when I tried so hard to—"

He cupped her face in his hands and leaned in, swallowing her words, smiling when she melted against him, her whole body sinking into his. He wasn't sure when he'd crossed the remainder of the distance between them, only that he had, his feet carrying him across the deck, something in his chest tugging hard with a need to be near her. To touch her. He clutched her close, determined to never let her go again.

She laughed against his lips and he'd never tasted anything sweeter than her joy. He grinned, and he could hardly call what they were doing kissing, their mouths merely mashed together as they laughed.

Annie shoved weakly at his chest with one hand, not so much stepping back as curving her spine and craning her neck, staring up at him with soft, fond eyes that made him weak. It almost brought him to his knees, dragging her to the deck with him. Fireworks continued to rain down behind him; he knew only because Annie's face remained washed in color.

"Sorry?" He shrugged, circling her waist with his hands, resting his fingers against the small of her back.

"No, you're not," she said, still smiling.

"No, I'm really not." He shook his head, scarcely able to believe she was here. That she was here and she was smiling up at him and he was touching her. He huffed out a quiet, disbelieving laugh. "Pinch me?"

"Is that an invitation?" she asked, her smile cheeky. Her hands dipped lower, tucking beneath the waistband of his jeans, inching into indecent territory.

He grinned. "You have permission to feel me up whenever you want."

Someone gave him a sharp pinch on the ass. "Hey!"

Over his shoulder, Margot shot him a saucy wink, no longer

filming the fireworks. Instead, her phone was trained on him and Annie. He rolled his eyes and turned back to the only thing at the moment that mattered.

"You're really here."

Annie nodded.

"What are you doing here?" he whispered, almost too afraid to ask, but unable to help himself. Unable to shove down the insatiable curiosity gnawing at him, dying to know if she was here for good or if this was just a visit. A layover. A dream.

Too good to be true.

With one hand, Annie reached up, curling her fingers around the back of his neck, playing with his hair. She continued to smile up at him, and something in his chest crackled when fireworks burst in her eyes. "Don't you know? I live here now."

He choked out a laugh and his eyes prickled at the corners. "Yeah?"

"Mm-hmm." Her smile brightened, the white of her teeth reflecting raspberry blue as the fireworks behind them burst. "I do."

"When I said I hoped you were settling in . . ."

Annie leaned forward, nose nudging his. "I was. Settling in. Here."

"Are you living with Darce?"

She shook her head, waves of her hair swishing against her bare shoulders, her skin golden. "I now live with Margot in Elle's old room."

He craned his neck, laughing because Margot was still recording, her tongue stuck out. She mouthed *yuck* and blew him a kiss.

Annie lived with Margot. Annie now lived in Capitol Hill. Annie lived in Seattle. Annie lived *here*.

His eyes stung. "Really?"

Her head bobbed. "I know I told you you'd be the first to know, but I wanted to surprise you so—"

"I can settle for second. Or third." He tried to wink and failed miserably, but Annie laughed anyway.

"Fourth?" Her eyes darted behind him. "It was a group effort getting you to agree to come here. But I know—" She pressed her lips together, eyes flooding, making his sting, too. "I know how you feel about fireworks."

A confetti cannon exploded inside his chest. "Fireworks are nice. What I wanted was you."

The wait was worth it. Worth this. Annie was worth it. She'd have been worth waiting weeks, months, for. This feeling, this rightness in his gut, in his soul, had no expiration date. He'd meant what he said; forever couldn't be rushed.

A tear slipped down her cheek, fast and furious, dripping off her chin. One of his hands lifted and his thumb swept against the thin skin beneath her eye.

She clutched his shoulder and sniffed hard, eyes filling, tears spilling over.

His stomach somersaulted. "Hey. What's wrong?"

She blubbered out a laugh. "*Nothing*, I'm just . . . verklempt."

His whole body shook with laughter. "You're *verklempt*?"

"Shut up." She batted his hands away and swiped at her eyes.

He threaded his fingers through her hair and cupped the back of her head. "I'm not making fun of you." When she leveled a glare at him, he laughed. "Okay, I am. A little. But mostly

I feel the need to tell you that if you say the word *verklempt* again, and with a straight face, I'm absolutely going to fall in love with you."

He rubbed the lobe of her ear between his fingers and she leaned into his touch, letting him cradle her face in his hand.

"Fair warning?" she whispered.

He smiled and drew her in with the hand cradling the back of her head. Her lips were warm against his and yet he shivered all the same.

"Fair warning," he murmured against her mouth.

"Verklempt," she whispered, lips curling.

His heart soared. "Is that a dare?"

She beamed up at him. "A double-dog dare."

"I'll do you one better," he muttered. "How about I promise?"

Annie's smiled softened when he dropped his forehead down to hers. "Brendon?"

"Yeah?"

"Shut up and kiss me."

Epilogue

Sunday, December 19

*B*rendon, you know I love riding Space Mountain almost as much as I love you, but isn't five times in a row a little excessive?"

He paused, tugging at the double neckline of his shirts, and beamed at Annie. No matter how many times she said those words—*I love you*—they'd never get old. His heart, already lodged in the back of his throat, swelled.

"One more time," he begged, tangling their fingers together and dragging her to the winding line rapidly growing longer.

Annie adjusted the Minnie Mouse ears perched atop her head, the matching set to his Mickey ears. She then tugged on the hem of her denim romper. Over the course of the last three days in sunny California, her skin had turned the same shade of gold it had over the summer. Even in December, the temps were sweltering, the sun oppressive.

"All I'm saying is, maybe we could change it up a little and come back later. Ride something else in between. Like, Pirates of the Caribbean. Or the Haunted Mansion ride." Her smile turned sly and she leaned into him, stretching up onto her toes. He bent down so she could whisper in his ear. "I'll even let you feel me up when the lights go out."

His brows rocketed to his rapidly dampening hairline, his scalp sweating. All of him was sweating. "Kinky," he said, winking as well as he could, which wasn't at all.

She beamed up at him. "Is that a yes?"

As tempting as her offer was, he had a plan. A plan he'd failed to enact four times in a row. A plan he'd be damned if he didn't get right. Not right, perfect.

He shook his head and tugged harder on his neckline. Wearing two shirts in the middle of the Anaheim heat was a bad idea, but it was part and parcel of his plan. He had no intention of wearing both shirts all day, only until he did what he'd come here to do.

"No?" Annie pouted. "Brendon, are you serious?"

"One last time," he promised, as much to her as to himself.

He was giving himself one last shot to do this. He refused to chicken out again.

She rolled her eyes, smiling up at him fondly. "One more time. And then we get to go on whatever rides I want for the next hour, okay?" She bumped his hip with hers. "Or did you forget it's my birthday?"

Of course he hadn't.

Today was Annie's birthday, and it was almost seven months since her fateful trip to Seattle. Two hundred and three days since their first kiss. He'd counted. Almost six months since she'd moved to Seattle permanently. Five months since he'd blurted out that he loved her and she'd shyly returned the sentiment. Also five months since she'd gotten her business up and running, working as a freelance translator specializing in business contracts while occasionally taking on passion projects outside her field of specialization. Four months since she'd given up living with Margot and moved in with him because she spent most of her time at his place anyway. It was the practical choice.

He was 99.99 percent sure she'd say yes, but it was the .01 percent that had him sweating.

Well, that and the fact he was wearing two shirts.

He leaned down, brushing his lips against her forehead. "Of course not." How could he have when he'd booked this trip as a surprise specifically for her birthday, whisking her out of Washington for an impromptu vacation? Hopefully, the first of a lifetime of vacations for them. Vacations to places much more exciting than California. But he had a goal and it required Space Mountain. "You can pick the next ride. And I promise to feel you up on it."

She threw her head back and laughed, making him grin. "How magnanimous of you."

The line moved forward. Inside his left pocket, his cell buzzed. He surreptitiously checked it.

MARGOT (12:32 P.M.): Did you do it yet? Did you? I'm fucking dying over here.

He bit back a chuckle.

BRENDON (12:35 P.M.): Not yet. You that eager to be my Best Woman?

MARGOT (12:36 P.M.): As long as I get to wear a killer tux, I'm all in. Now, pony the fuck up and do it already!!!! 🐻

He tucked his phone away, nerves diminishing, but only for a moment. The closer they got to the front, snaking their way through the winding queue, the more difficult he found it to stand still. He rocked forward on his toes and back on his heels, bouncing worse than the group of small children several paces ahead. He raked his fingers through his damp hair and tugged at his neckline again, sweat dripping down his scalp and the back of his neck, soaking through both his layers. He was rocking armpit sweat stains, for crying out loud, but he couldn't back down. Not when he'd come this far, this close.

As soon as this was over, he'd need about a gallon of water to rehydrate. Hell, something with electrolytes, too. All this stress was probably wreaking havoc on his B vitamins.

"Hey." Annie tugged on his sleeve, brow pinched in concern. "Take one of these off. I swear, you don't need two shirts when it's over eighty out."

"I'm fine," he lied, adjusting the collar of his chambray button-down. "I'm going for a certain aesthetic, Annie."

She looked at him like he'd lost it but smiled affably. "You're so weird."

"You love me anyway."

She beamed up at him. "I must be just as weird, because I do."

I do.

He rolled his shoulders back and stepped forward when the

line moved. He could do this. Five more minutes of risking heat-stroke and—fuck, he'd think about the rest when it came time.

Maybe it was the feel of Annie's fingers laced through his, her thumb stroking soothing circles against the back of his hand, but time flew until the attendant waved them forward, gesturing for them to take the first two seats on the cart. He let Annie slide in first and then crawled in after, pulling down the safety bar over his shoulders.

This was the point where he'd chickened out the last four times they'd ridden this ride. All he had to do was unbutton his shirt, revealing the tee beneath. Which had a very important question printed on it, just for this occasion.

While Annie was preoccupied strapping herself in, he reached for the topmost button of his shirt, fingers trembling. He stole a deep breath in and parted his shirt the rest of the way, careful to keep the message beneath hidden until they took off, rocketing into the darkness.

The ride began to move and Annie reached out, gripping his hand. He squeezed back and, with his right hand, adjusted his shirt until the words beneath could be seen. Not by Annie, but by the hidden camera, wherever it was located, the one that snapped a picture of passengers on the ride.

As the roller coaster crept up the tracks and plummeted down into the dark abyss, he prayed his face didn't look too nauseated. Annie was right; five times was pushing it. As much as he adored roller coasters, loved *this* roller coaster, riding it five times back-to-back was rougher on his system now than it had been when he was a kid. His nerves weren't helping his queasiness, either.

At the first drop, their cart zipping along the track, her grip on his hand intensified, strangling his fingers. He squeezed back and clenched his eyes shut, smiling despite the anxious churning of his stomach. There was no going back now. Not that he'd want to. He never wanted to go back. Not when he could go forward with Annie.

In what felt like no time at all, the ride slowed to a stop and docked where they'd first climbed on. Exiting to the left instead of the right, he buttoned his shirt up haphazardly, mismatching his buttons, not giving a fuck because in a few minutes he could hopefully shed the thing altogether and stuff it inside the locker they'd rented with the rest of their belongings.

At the gift shop, Annie made a hard right toward the outside exit. He wrapped his fingers around her wrist, keeping her from leaving. She shot him a quizzical frown.

"Don't you want to see our picture?" His tongue darted out, wetting his suddenly parched lips.

She wrinkled her nose. "Souvenir photos? Brendon, those cost a fortune and no one ever looks halfway decent. They're embarrassing and blurry and I'd rather not see my screaming face immortalized on overpriced photo paper."

No, no. She had to look at the photos. It was crucial. He shot a quick glance over his shoulder at the screens. *Loading, please be patient* flashed across the monitors. He swallowed hard and turned back to face her. "Let's at least take a look. We don't have to buy anything if we don't want."

With a good-natured eye roll, Annie nodded and followed him over to the counter where the digital photos were processing. It was a good thing she'd let go of his hand in order to post up against the counter, because his palms were starting to sweat all over again, worse than before. In as nonchalant a move as possible, he shoved his hands inside the pockets of his cargo shorts and quadruple-checked that the velvet box he'd tucked inside this morning was still there. That, despite the button closure, it hadn't flown out on the ride, lost forever, or until one of the ride techs could recover it for him.

It was there. He rubbed his thumb over the smooth velvet and tried to regulate his breathing as the photos began to appear in their respective boxes across the screen.

"Where are we?" She leaned closer, eyes flitting from one screen to the next. "I don't see us anywhere."

He scanned and—there they were. Smack-dab in the center; Annie simply hadn't noticed yet. While she was preoccupied, he withdrew the box from his pocket, hand trembling, holding it at the ready.

Her blue eyes widened and she bounced on her toes. "I see us! Oh my God, my hair is all over the—" She froze, save for the flaring of her eyes and drop of her jaw.

There, on the screen, clear as day, in black on white, his shirt read, *Will you marry me?*

He sank down on one knee, wobbling, briefly losing his balance and winding up on both knees.

This was it.

He stole a deep breath that rattled in his throat. "Annie Kyriakos—"

"Yes," she blurted, quickly clapping a hand over her mouth.

Laughter built inside his chest. "*Annie.* I—I had a speech."

Her eyes doubled in size and behind her palm, she snorted. "I'm sorry? Keep going."

He nodded and—blanked. He completely spaced out on what he wanted to say, his mind just poof, empty. She'd said yes and all his carefully rehearsed words had flown out of his head. He'd practiced in front of the mirror for weeks, in the shower— any time she wasn't nearby, he'd gone over what he wanted to say. Hell, he'd roped Margot into listening, and now . . . nothing. His brain had gone kaput at the worst possible time.

He ducked his chin, laughing at the irony of it. How he, someone who made a hobby of watching viral proposals on You- Tube, could just completely forget everything he'd painstak- ingly planned on saying about how she made him laugh, how she made him want to be better, how she made him feel like he could conquer the world, except much, much more eloquently than all of that. Her vehement yes had done that to him, and he couldn't churn up one single ounce of indignation because holy fuck. She'd said yes.

"I forgot what I wanted to say," he confessed, the tips of his ears burning even though his face hurt from smiling.

Annie threw her head back and laughed. "Stand up and give me my damn ring, Brendon."

Legs still trembling, he stood and pried open the box, re- vealing a 1930s-era marquise diamond ring Elle and Darcy had helped him pick out from one of Annie's favorite antique stores.

"Holy fuck," she blurted. Annie wiggled her finger eagerly and sputtered out another laugh when he slipped the ring over her knuckle.

Rather than let go of her hand and allow her to admire her new jewelry, he held fast, staring into her eyes. He couldn't remember everything he'd planned on saying, but he remembered this.

"Annie, I promise to always have a cup ready for you to pee in on a Ferris wheel." He grinned when Annie snorted and turned red, ducking her chin. "I promise to always keep you stocked in Breathe Right strips and to never overwater our succulents." He rested his free hand on her face, cupping her jaw. "I promise—"

"Those are vows." Annie beamed at him, eyes going glassy and squinting at the corners, and not because of the bright midday sun. "You're supposed to save those for our wedding."

Wedding. Holy fuck was right. He was getting married to Annie Kyriakos, the girl who far surpassed his wildest dreams.

"Whoops?" He chuckled and brushed his thumb along the curve of her cheek, aching with how much he loved her. "Annie, knowing you and loving you, being loved by you, has made me a better man in more ways than I can count, and you've made me the luckiest person on the planet—no, in the universe. Vows or not, I promise to always love you. I promise to always try. I promise to never stop giving it my all even when you put the toilet paper on the holder the wrong way—"

"It goes over, you monster!"

His smile softened, as did hers. "And I promise we'll travel somewhere much better for our honeymoon than Disneyland."

She wrinkled her nose, then grinned. "What do you think about Disneyland Paris?"

He'd fly her to the moon if it made her happy.

Acknowledgments

I feel so fortunate that I have an abundance of amazing people to thank for helping this book come to fruition.

To my amazing agent, Sarah Younger, thank you, thank you, *thank you* for everything you do. I am beyond lucky to have you in my corner. Thank you to my fabulous editor, Nicole Fischer, for helping me polish this book. You have no idea how much I appreciate your patience, guidance, and value your feedback.

Thank you to the entire team at Avon/HarperCollins for making my dreams come true. And a very special thank you to the Harper Library Lovefest team for being such vocal and steadfast supporters of *Written in the Stars*. It was a pleasure meeting you all at PLA!

Writing is often said to be a solitary endeavor and in 2020 this could've proven especially true. Lucky for me, I have the greatest group of friends to lean on. Rompire, your unwavering support means the world to me. Anna, Amy, Em, Julia, Lana, Lisa, and Megan, we might be scattered across the country, but you all have been my bright spot this year. Thank you for being my cheerleaders, therapists, and always being there when I need to brainstorm. I'm crossing my fingers that one day soon we'll all be able to get together and have a writing retreat in person.

To the 2020 Debuts, thank you for your kindness, support, and commiseration. Debuting in 2020 was a unique experience, to say the least, but I'm grateful to be in a debut class with such talented authors. I am so happy for all of you and I can't wait to see what's in store for all of us next!

Mom, thank you for being my rock and always, without fail, having my back. You've been my biggest fan and greatest supporter since day one and there's no way that words can do justice to how much I love and appreciate you. You're the best person I know.

I'd be remiss if I didn't mention my fur baby, Samantha. Thank you for being an endless source of joy and laughter in my life and for only destroying *half* of my notebooks. I wasn't planning on using them anyway.

Last, but certainly not least, I want to thank my readers. There are so many wonderful books in the world, and the fact that you've taken the time to read mine means everything to me. My sincerest wish is that my words provide an escape, a warm hug, and hope to whoever needs it.

Keep an eye out for Margot's story . . .

COUNT YOUR LUCKY STARS

Coming in early 2022!

About the Author

Alexandria Bellefleur is an author of swoony contemporary romance often featuring lovable grumps and the sunshine characters who bring them to their knees. A Pacific Northwesterner at heart, Alexandria has a weakness for good coffee, Pike IPA, and Voodoo Doughnuts. Her special skills include finding the best pad thai in every city she visits, remembering faces but not names, falling asleep in movie theaters, and keeping cool while reading smutty books in public. She was a 2018 Romance Writers of America Golden Heart finalist. You can find her at alexandriabellefleur.com or on Twitter @ambellefleur.

"Everything I want from a rom-com: fun, whimsical, sexy."
—TALIA HIBBERT, USA TODAY BESTSELLING AUTHOR OF
GET A LIFE, CHLOE BROWN

ALEXANDRIA BELLEFLEUR

Written in the Stars

IS THIS RELATIONSHIP FAKE OR
IS IT TRUE LOVE . . .

"I was hooked from the very first page!"
—CHRISTINA LAUREN, NEW YORK TIMES
BESTSELLING AUTHOR

WRITTEN IN THE STARS

"This book is a delight." – *New York Times Book Review*

Named one of the Best Romances of 2020 by *Washington Post*, *Bustle*, and *Buzzfeed*!

With nods to *Bridget Jones* and *Pride & Prejudice*, this debut is a delightful #ownvoices queer rom-com about a free-spirited social media astrologer who agrees to fake a relationship with an uptight actuary until New Year's Eve—with results not even the stars could predict!

After a disastrous blind date, Darcy Lowell is desperate to stop her well-meaning brother from playing matchmaker ever again. Love—and the inevitable heartbreak—is the last thing she wants. So she fibs and says her latest set up was a success. Darcy doesn't expect her lie to bite her in the ass.

Elle Jones, one of the astrologers behind the popular Twitter account Oh My Stars, dreams of finding her soul mate. But she knows it is most assuredly not Darcy... a no-nonsense stick-in-the-mud, who is way too analytical, punctual, and skeptical for someone as free-spirited as Elle. When Darcy's brother—and Elle's new business partner—expresses how happy he is that they hit it off, Elle is baffled. Was Darcy on the same date? Because... awkward.

Darcy begs Elle to play along and she agrees to pretend they're dating. But with a few conditions: Darcy must help Elle navigate her own overbearing family during the holidays and their arrangement expires on New Year's Eve. The last thing they expect is to develop real feelings during a faux relationship. But maybe opposites can attract when true love is written in the stars?

DISCOVER GREAT AUTHORS, EXCLUSIVE OFFERS, AND MORE AT HC.COM.